James D[...] down th[...] wrap of [...] to the fir[...]

"I like the heat," she said, even as she loosened the velvet around her waist, letting the fabric slide ever so slightly down her shoulders.

Then let me show you more. The words sprang to his mind but would not leave his mouth. "Don't you think you should return to the dance?"

"I've had enough of dancing," she said, lowering her glass. "Haven't you?"

"Elizabeth . . . your reputation . . ."

"Is safe. I doubt anyone saw us leave. And speaking of reputations, aren't you supposed to be a notorious libertine?" Still seated on the floor, she wriggled closer to where he sat on the fainting couch. "I've never been kissed by a libertine."

He reached down and grasped the fabric gathered about her elbows, pulling it—and her—closer toward him. "You have much to learn."

"I know that." She smiled impishly up at him. "Why else would I be here?"

"Then let the lessons begin," he whispered, burying his regrets within the sweet recesses of her mouth.

Don't miss

The Souvenir Countess
—also by Joanna Novins

SOUVENIR
of LOVE

JOANNA NOVINS

BERKLEY SENSATION, NEW YORK

SOUVENIR OF LOVE

A Berkley Sensation Book / published by arrangement with the author

PRINTING HISTORY
Berkley Sensation edition / February 2004

For information address: The Berkley Publishing Group, a division of Penguin Group (USA) Inc., 375 Hudson Street, New York, New York 10014.

ISBN: 0-425-19456-6

BERKLEY SENSATION™
Berkley Sensation Books are published by The Berkley Publishing Group, a division of Penguin Group (USA) Inc., 375 Hudson Street, New York, New York 10014. BERKLEY SENSATION and the "B" design are trademarks belonging to Penguin Group (USA) Inc.

PRINTED IN THE UNITED STATES OF AMERICA

10 9 8 7 6 5 4 3 2 1

My mother always said you should dress nicely for a plane flight—you never know who you might meet.

This book is dedicated to my mother with thanks for a lifetime of sage advice and to my husband, the truly amazing man who was standing in front of me on the customs line on that August day in 1988.

Chapter 1

*Elizabeth Harcrest stood on the threshold of the ball-*room and scanned Lady Anne Dinsmore's elegant assembly. The ambience of the room was intoxicating: civet and musk mingled with the scents of pomander and wine. Music like birdsong rose above the forest of voices. Candlelight shimmered across satins and silks and danced across the gems that bedecked the hands, the hair, and the bosoms of the ladies and the gentlemen; including the one she most hoped would be present.

Anne Dinsmore glided forward, slim hands outstretched, and blocked the view.

"Lord Moreham, Lady Moreham, Lady Elizabeth, I am delighted you could attend our little soiree."

"You know we would not have missed it for the world." Elizabeth's brother Rafe, the Earl of Moreham, leaned forward and kissed Anne's cheek. His wife Alix inclined her head politely. "You look lovely, Anne."

Elizabeth thought the gown—a cream-colored satin, trimmed with scarlet ribbons—made the pale, ash-blond

Anne look as if she were struggling to recover from a lingering illness. "Indeed, Anne, you should wear those colors more often." She mustered a smile for the woman, who, when they were children, would pinch her and then complain to Rafe that "Elizabeth is a crybaby."

"And you have grown into quite the elegant young lady." Anne waved a jeweled forefinger. "I hope you've been behaving yourself. A first season is so critical to one's future."

"I shall look to your experience," Elizabeth replied, resisting the urge to say, *And you should know, having been out for so long.*

Anne turned her attention back towards Rafe. "Lord and Lady Davenport were announced a few moments ago. I believe Cole mentioned an interest in the hazard tables, and, of course, Lady Moreham, your mother, Madame la Comtesse, is here. Such an astonishing sense of style! Each time I see her, I am overcome with regret I was never able to attend court at Versailles. But now with the horrid doings of those wicked men in Paris . . ."

"Ah, yes, intolerable how revolution disrupts one's travel plans," interrupted Cole Ashbourne, slapping Rafe on the back. "Though in truth, Anne, I had no idea your interests exceeded the bounds of Mayfair."

"You see, Lord Moreham," Anne said with measured politeness, "I told you Lord Davenport had arrived."

"Moreham, a pleasure to see you," Cole said, the single dimple indenting his cheek deepening as he turned his smile to Alix. "*Lady* Moreham, an even *greater* pleasure. My wife has been awaiting your appearance with great impatience."

"Tell me Davenport, is there anything Phoebe does *with* patience?" asked Rafe.

"Walk with me, Moreham, and I'll think on it."

Rafe turned back towards Anne. "If you'll excuse us . . . ?"

"Anne doesn't mind." Cole grinned at her. "This crowd will be a crush by midnight. Only imagine the reputations she will have flayed by then."

"You know Cole." Anne lifted her chin. "If I didn't cherish the memory of our families' friendship, I might be wounded by your unkindness."

"Confess, Anne, family friendship has little to do with the matter." He winked at her. "It's my title you cherish."

Her smile stretched tight. "There are occasions, my lord, when it is the most appealing aspect of your nature."

He chuckled and offered his arm to Elizabeth. "Come little one, it's dangerous for small fish like you to linger in the depths among the sharks."

"You are terrible, you know," Elizabeth whispered, as she slid her hand around Cole's claret-colored silk-clad arm, and their group moved out of earshot.

"She is right," Alix agreed. "One of these days you will push Anne Dinsmore too far. And her wrath, I suspect, will be sharper than that of Madame la Guillotine."

Rafe sighed, "You said very much the same thing about Anne this past December, when we married; yet she has never said an unkind word, though she fully expected I would offer for *her* hand . . ."

"And you would have, if Alix hadn't rescued you," Cole interrupted. "I vow, the very thought of Phoebe and Anne sharing a table every Christmas Eve gives me the shudders as if I had caught the ague."

Rafe glanced down at the mahogany tresses of his wife. "One might debate who rescued whom."

Alix pinched him through his green velvet sleeve.

"Though, suffice it to say, I'm quite happy with the outcome." He smiled. "Nevertheless, Anne Dinsmore is perfectly respectable. She has behaved with the graciousness I would expect from a duke's daughter."

"A mad duke's daughter," Cole muttered

"Just because His Lordship prefers to pursue his study of Hannibal's crossing of the Alps in seclusion—"

"Rafe, His Grace believes he *is* Hannibal. If Anne and

James hadn't locked him away, he'd have squandered what little remains of the family fortune on imaginary herds of elephants."

Rafe purposefully ignored his friend. "As I have said, she's been the very definition of graciousness. Never an unkind word."

"Not so long as one is facing her," Elizabeth teased. She cast a questioning look up at Cole. "Is it true, His Grace believes he *is* the Carthaginian general?"

Cole lowered his dark head conspiratorially. "I've seen his toga."

"Carthaginians didn't wear togas," Rafe interjected.

"Are you certain?"

"Alix, *ma petite*!" A tiny woman dressed elegantly in a gown of dark purple velvet interrupted their debate. A matching velvet puff fastened with a large diamond pin perched at a jaunty angle atop her dark curls. "I have been waiting *ages* for you and Rafe to arrive."

"Good evening, *Maman*." Alix kissed her mother's cheeks.

"Madeleine, you look beautiful," Rafe said, as he kissed her cheeks in turn.

"Lady Dinsmore's eyebrows simply vanished into her hairline when I made my entrance," Madeleine, la Comtesse de La Brou, confessed. Then she shook her head. "That woman, did you see the ghastly robe she has on?"

"Ordinarily she dresses in pastels, as if she were just emerged from the schoolroom." Alix laughed.

"I suspect that is her purpose. To convince some unwitting suitor that she has . . ."

"The man would have to be an exile not to know she has been out for *ages*," Cole interjected

"Or nearly blind, like Sir Edmund Bogglesworth," Elizabeth added giggling.

Madeleine held up a small white hand. "I fear we go too far in mocking our hostess. Sir Edmund may be dull, but I believe he would not be an unkind husband, and, *vraiment*, he has a fortune that would make Lady Anne most comfortable. You must bear in mind, Elizabeth, not every woman has the fortune, face, and figure to make the choices you shall have."

An uncomfortable silence settled over the company; Madeleine had been married against her will and at an early age to Alix's father.

"Choices she shall have," Rafe broke in lightly, "*if* she behaves respectably and chooses her companions wisely." His eyes darkened as they drifted across the ballroom and settled on the figure of James Dinsmore, leaning nonchalantly against the wall. Candlelight from a nearby sconce gleamed on the waves of his loosely braided blond queue and spilled across the broad shoulders of his midnight blue velvet coat.

"How can I do otherwise, brother dear, when you select them for me?" Elizabeth resisted the urge to follow the direction of Rafe's gaze. She already knew where James was standing. It was the first thing she did when she entered any assembly.

"Your sister has a point, Moreham."

"My sister, Davenport, has an unfortunate fascination for charming rakes."

"Perhaps because I have grown up surrounded by them?" she asked with a smile.

James Dinsmore nodded absently at some crude comment tossed off by Arthur Lounsbury, his blue eyes fixed on the Earl of Moreham's sister. Elizabeth looked charming tonight, dressed in a soft gold color that reminded him of a fragrant chardonnay. Her chestnut hair was swept back, and thick curls tumbled down over the amber velvet of her mantelet. She was guarded, as usual, by her brother and by Davenport. But if he knew Lady Elizabeth Harcrest, and by now he was fairly certain that he did, she would eventually escape their watch and make her way to him.

A slight smile of expectation curved his sensuous lips.

She really was quite amusing, brash and bright, with none of the false timorousness of the other debutantes this season. He suspected she sought him out to annoy Moreham, and he always encouraged her. *Moreham that self-righteous prig. He'd treated Anne shabbily, dashing off to France when everyone expected him to make an offer of marriage. And then, entangling himself with Alix de La Brou! Of course, there was something in the earl's eyes whenever he looked at Alix, something that had never been there when he'd looked at Anne. . . . Still, Anne had been so certain the émigré would be nothing more than a brief affair. And then Moreham had married her!* God, he hated to remember how devastating that was . . .

Elizabeth had linked arms with Davenport and she was laughing.

He might be jealous if it weren't a well-known fact that Davenport was absurdly devoted to his wife. *Ridiculous, the notion that I could be jealous over another man's attention to Elizabeth. . . .* He was bored; he desired the amusements of her quick wit that was all.

But her fall from grace would be a loss to the ton.

The lines to a poem he'd once committed to memory slipped unbidden from his lips, "What! Were ye born to be an hour or half's delight/And so to bid good night?/'Twas pity Nature brought you forth/Merely to show your worth/And lose you quite."

"What's that, Dinsmore?" Arthur Lounsbury frowned in exasperation. "Damn me, if you've not heard a word I've been saying."

"Lounsbury," James reassured his companion, wondering idly how long it would be before the brandy Arthur consumed in such quantities turned his boyish features to florid fat, "I have been listening with *unbridled* fascination. The bay mare Harding sold you last Tuesday has been wheezing suspiciously, and you're wondering if you've been cozened. Having warned you repeatedly that the man is a scoundrel, I'd wager my fortune the answer is yes."

"*If* you had a fortune Dinsmore . . ."

"You wound me, Lounsbury. I find it most insensitive that you should make light of my impoverished state, particularly as you stand in my family hall drinking my father's vintage brandy. Indeed, I have no money. Nor have I the dukedom, since my sire persists in surviving into ripe old age while the majority of his fellows have done the decent thing and passed into the great hereafter. Alas, I am forced to live by my wits." He paused, smiling, at Lounsbury. "Thank heaven I have them."

"Wounded my arse." As a footman passed with a tray of brimming brandy snifters, Lounsbury tossed back his remaining liquor and swapped his empty glass for a full one.

Sir Richard Ashton, a man whose nose loomed large over his receding chin, chimed in with an amused chuckle. "Sensitivities? You've sensitivities Dinsmore? I'd wager *my* fortune that even the most skilled surgeon would be hard-pressed to find your heart."

James pressed a hand to his chest. "I am a most sensitive man. Why I anguished over whether to purchase this sapphire blue silk waistcoat. The beauty of the silver embroidery nearly made me weep. It shall break my heart to tell the tradesman that I haven't the funds to pay him for his exquisite work."

"Good to make 'em wait," Lounsbury snorted between sips. "Incentive for the rascals to work harder." Ashton chuckled again.

James's smile did not reach his eyes; not paying tradesman did indeed give them an incentive to work harder—harder at hounding the Dinsmores. As for his heart, he supposed it would take a talented surgeon to find it; he'd buried it deep. Otherwise, the pain of seeing Anne stitching together the satins and laces of old gowns so that no one would guess she couldn't afford fashionable new ones might be intolerable. More painful still, he reflected sipping his brandy, the prospect of her settling for some moneyed dolt like Ashton or Lounsbury, or that half-witted idiot who'd been following her about lately, Edmund Bogglesworth.

Damn Moreham, he could have made such a difference in their lives.

"Why is it, do you suppose," Lounsbury asked, waving his half-filled snifter at a cluster of young women, "that every pretty girl has to be accompanied by at least two ugly friends? I mean, regard me that threesome over there."

James eyed his drinking companions over his snifter.

"You've got Annabella Fenwinkle, who looks like a pug in ruffles, and her unmarried sister, Arabella Norcroft, who isn't much better."

"A pug in ruffles," Ashton actually giggled.

Better than boors in britches, James mused.

"And then you have the delectable Elizabeth Harcrest."

James made a quick visual sweep of the ballroom. Moreham, Davenport, and their wives were standing to the far right, near the doorway to the card room. Elizabeth had made her way to the center of the room, where she stood chatting with her friends the Norcroft sisters.

"Most delectable," Ashton agreed, "perhaps I should ask her to dance later this evening . . ."

"Moreham would have your arm if you attempted to lead her out," James shot back without thinking.

"Dinsmore, Dinsmore," Lounsbury tsked. "Certainly His Lordship is most protective where Lady Elizabeth is concerned, but simply because he spurned *your* sister doesn't mean he'd scorn a man with the breeding *and* the fortune of Ashton."

"I shall ask her," Ashton said firmly.

"Move swiftly, my friend, the chit's dance card is likely to fill up quickly. She's a title, a fortune, and, from what I hear from the clubs, quite the reputation as a frisky young filly."

"Plays it fast and loose, eh?" Ashton said with a brandied leer.

James took a deep swallow, drowning a sudden urge to defend Elizabeth's honor. The vintage liquor burned as it made its descent. He had little doubt such rumors bloomed from the seeds of his sister's careful sowing.

He was Anne's only brother.

What choice had he but to help her reap her bitter harvest of revenge?

Chapter 2

"I wish I might be certain. He is such a fine figure of a man, and I . . ." Arabella's small hand fluttered dismissively about her rose-patterned gown. "If not for flounces and fichus, I fear I should have no bosom at all."

Elizabeth leaned conspiratorially towards her friend. "I hear tell the fashion is shifting away from padding and petticoats, towards a straighter line. Then you shall be all the rage and my poor rounded bosoms shall be desperately outmoded."

"You outmoded? Never!" Annabella, Arabella's sister laughed. "Your style shall always be uniquely your own."

Elizabeth cast a discrete glance over her shoulder as she pretended to adjust her mantelet. There James was, standing about with those tiresome boors, Lounsbury and Ashton. He looked bored, lounging against the wall like a dustman on his break. Her lips twitched at this far-fetched comparison; James was far too elegant, far too handsome to ever pass for a dustman. She turned her attention back to Arabella Norcroft's unyielding speculation as to whether Thomas Stirling would ask her to dance. Arabella might not be considered a classic beauty by the ton, Elizabeth thought, but she had beautiful brown eyes and a delightful smile, like a brownie up to mischief.

". . . and when my mother and I passed him earlier, he smiled and nodded at me. I think he *would* have approached us, if he had not been engaged in conversation with another young gentleman."

"You must dance with someone else. It will distract your mind while reminding Mr. Stirling that if he persists in shilly-shallying about he risks losing your heart and hand to another." Elizabeth offered her arm. "Come, let us survey the room for a man with a stout heart and a sound wit."

Arabella's eyes danced above the edge of her fan, "If it's not too much trouble, might he be somewhat handsome as well?" Anabella smiled, and Elizabeth cast another quick glance across the ballroom at James Dinsmore: *Handsome might be too much trouble, indeed.*

Anne Dinsmore watched Elizabeth Harcrest drift across the ballroom arm-in-arm with that drab brown wren, Arabella Norcroft. A wren, she reflected disdainfully, a fledgling fresh from the nest. Her ballroom floor was littered with similar young things, chirping and flapping about. And the men, well, they were as pleased with the display as barnyard cats eyeing an easy banquet. She resisted the urge to frown; it would only encourage wrinkles. She had no desire to appear even a day older than her twenty-five years.

She willed her expression into a smile. These were her guests, unwitting players in a drama she had been scripting for months and would now direct to a final, dramatic conclusion. Moreham had publicly scorned her. He would learn there was a price to pay for toying with a woman's expectations, for forcing a woman to once again trawl the pool of men she knew were either too short or too fat, too venal, or too stupid to make a suitable husband. Anne's smile eased into a more natural curve as Arabella joined the dancing, and Elizabeth Harcrest drifted towards James like a leaf drawn into a whirlpool.

She purposefully flicked open her scarlet and gold fan. The sharp snap of the ivory ribs attracted the attention of the women gathered around her; the aging but influential Lady Morton and Mrs. Henderson, the daughter of a wool merchant who'd married above her station and used gossip as an entrance ticket to the inner circles of the ton. "It is amusing, is it not," she said with an idle wave of her fan, "how the Earl of Moreham's sister throws herself at my brother James."

"He is most handsome," Jane Henderson said responsively.

Anne smiled fondly in the direction of her brother. "And so tenderhearted. He has tried, in so many subtle, and yet clearly unmistakable ways, to let Lady Elizabeth know he has no interest in her. And yet . . ." She allowed her words to trail off in a regretful sigh.

"She is a brash young thing." Lady Morton arched the sparse remainders of her over-plucked eyebrows disapprovingly. Her hat gave the appearance that an exotic bird had taken roost upon her head.

"Youth will be headstrong," Anne said gently.

"In my day," Lady Morton sniffed, "young girls knew better. They didn't roam about the dance floor unattended. They stayed close to their mamas."

"Well, we all know how . . . distracted . . . Elizabeth's mother can be."

"Is Louisa even here tonight?" Lady Morton demanded.

Anne shook her head slightly, so as not to dislodge her carefully arranged ash-blond hair. "Louisa is more comfortable among her flowers. Elizabeth is under her brother's watchful eye this evening."

"Moreham's eye, indeed," Lady Morton sniffed more

loudly this time. "The man only has eyes for his new French wife. What is her name? Armoire?"

"Alix," Jane Henderson supplied helpfully.

"Don't know why those people can't give their children decent English names. But then, what can you expect from people who persist in speaking such an incomprehensible language?" Lady Morton shook her head, the plumes in her hat now feathered flags signaling her disdain. "Don't know why they can't stay in their own country."

"There are troubles with the new government," Jane offered.

"How can you possibly refer to that common rabble as a government?" Lady Morton raised a hand laden with rings and patted the stiff curls of her outmoded coiffure. "Those *troubles*, as you call them, would never have occurred if the French had stood their ground like proper Englishmen." She turned suddenly towards Anne. "And speaking of standing one's ground, I must say I have the greatest respect for how you've handled Moreham's decision to marry that girl."

Anne resisted the urge to smack Lady Morton with her fan.

Her fingers tightened around the ivory handle. "Moreham and I are old *friends*. I wish him nothing but happiness." Anne's smile was as sweet as icing on a cake. "And I cannot help but think how fortunate I am to have discovered his affections were engaged elsewhere *before* we plighted our troth."

Jane Henderson shot a quick glance at Lady Morton. It was well-known amongst the ton that Lord Morton was more devoted to his mistress of twenty-eight years than to his wife of the past twenty-six. The plumes abruptly stilled. "Indeed," Lady Morton said quietly.

"One must be so *careful* about entrusting one's hand and one's heart to a man." Anne's smile widened. "That is why I have taken my time in choosing a husband. Better to end my days as a spinster than an unhappy wife," she said, turning her attention to the dance floor. Elizabeth Harcrest, she noted with satisfaction, was engaged in conversation with James and his friends. Snapping her fan shut, she pointed it significantly in Elizabeth's direction.

"Or worse still, a foolish girl with a desperate reputation."

"Does your brother permit you to drink champagne?" James inquired as Elizabeth lifted a glass from the tray of a passing footman.

"He said I should avoid strong drink. But I must say," she lifted her glass so that light from the chandelier flooded it, turning the trails of bubbles into a tiny galaxy of stars. "I cannot imagine how such a frothy drink could be considered strong." Her tongue darted out, capturing a drop that quivered on the edge of the flute. James knew he was not the only one watching the slim column of her throat as she swallowed.

"I'll drink to that," said Lounsbury.

Moreham should be keeping better watch on his little sister. *Moreham's* sister, he reminded himself. Not his. He tossed back the last bit of his brandy and put the empty glass on the footman's tray.

Ashton, who'd been watching Elizabeth like a border collie eying a ewe, edged closer. "I'd be most honored if you'd dance with me, Lady Elizabeth."

"The lady has promised this dance to me." James plucked Elizabeth's glass from her fingers and handed it to Ashton.

"Amazing," she sputtered as he led her onto the floor. "How I could promise a dance to a man who never even asked me."

"Would you have preferred to dance with Ashton?"

She glanced back over her shoulder; Ashton bobbed and smiled at her. "Is he a better dancer?" she asked her voice speculative, her eyes brimming with laughter.

"Not even close."

"You're very sure of yourself James Dinsmore."

"Nearly as sure as you are reckless, Elizabeth Harcrest."

"You're beginning to sound like my brother."

"He's beginning to have my sympathies."

"A rake with sympathies," she smiled up at him as they took their places for the dance. "Isn't that a dangerous thing?"

"You have naïve ideas about men, Elizabeth."

"Of course I have naïve ideas. I've been imprisoned in the countryside for the past eighteen years." She paused to observe the patterns danced by the first couple in the line. "In case you haven't noticed, I am endeavoring to become educated."

"Ashton and Lounsbury certainly noticed."

She cocked her head at him. "Did you?"

He thought of her lips, soft and wet against the glass. "No."

"I don't believe you." She turned back to watch the dancers.

"Now who seems overly sure of herself?" he murmured.

She smiled.

The first couple finished dancing and made their way to the end of the line.

With this one, James thought uncomfortably, *my usual words of seduction seem somehow wrong . . . like cheating at checkers with a child.* Anne had asked him to flirt with Elizabeth, lead her on. And he'd agreed. Ton affairs were tedious, overflowing with poor conversation and worse liquor. *Without flirtation and the occasional sexual escapade, a man might go mad from boredom. . . .*

James and Elizabeth moved forward and the second couple began the forms.

And Lord knew, there was already far too much madness in the Dinsmore line. James cast his eyes to the ceiling, painted with a scene from a long-forgotten battle in which his ancestors had fought. Two floors above, his father, dressed in bedsheets and wearing a silver flower bowl upon his head, paced and planned the progress of his imaginary troops.

Out of the corner of his eye, he caught the crimsón and cream of his sister's gown. She'd made it from the silk of an old court gown of their mother's and trimmed it with ribbons cut from a doublet she'd found in a trunk. She'd spent the mornings, when most fashionable ladies were still abed, sewing by the light of the upstairs parlor window. She didn't like to waste time, she said, but he knew it was candles she did not want to waste.

"What are you thinking James?"

Elizabeth's voice intruded upon his thoughts, and he glanced back at her, at the lush velvet mantelet that crossed over her full round breasts, wrapped around her slender waist and tucked behind. She might be young and innocent, but Elizabeth Harcrest certainly wasn't a child.

"I was thinking that amber velvet sets off the haunting colors of your eyes."

She wrinkled her nose. "And that was why you were frowning?"

"No," he replied smoothly. "I was frowning because this line is appallingly long and I fear this dance will never end."

"And you wish to be rid of me?"

"No, I have no wish to be rid of you." He gestured toward the line. "But I would like to be shed of them."

Her eyes danced with far more life than the couple moving ponderously around each other at the front of the line. "You could offer to show me the famed Dinsmore portrait gallery."

"I could, but I would never resort to such an obvious cliché."

"You might offer to fetch me some more champagne."

"Lady Elizabeth, I am not a dog. I do not fetch."

"Dear Lord Dinsmore, my throat is as parched as the

Gobi desert. I fear if I do not find refreshment I shall fall into a swoon."

"We cannot have that, Lady Elizabeth." He turned a smile upon her that had encouraged numerous ladies to unlace their corsets. "Just think of how it would further slow the progress of the dance. Good gracious, we might be forced to provide breakfast for all these people."

"You're incorrigible." She laughed.

"Indeed, I am," he said as he reached for her hand, "a man without heart, without scruples, and unlikely to change." *So don't trust me for a moment.*

"I don't believe that for a moment," she said, slipping her slender fingers into his.

"You should," he said softly.

She shook her head.

"Would you believe, then, that I have a chilled bottle of champagne, tucked among the tomes of the library?"

"I would." Embers of mischief glowed in her eyes. "Though I might wonder if it had been placed there solely for *my* pleasure."

"It might have been . . ." He tucked her arm in his and drew her away from the dance.

"There you see," she said triumphantly, "if you were completely heartless, you would have said, 'Yes, of course, my darling Elizabeth, that wine is meant for your rosy lips, and yours alone.'"

Her lips, James observed, did resemble the curved petals of a rose. "I would never be so trite."

"And you should say that the sparkle of the wine is surpassed only by the sparkle of my eyes . . ."

"Good Lord Elizabeth, you've either been reading far too much romantic poetry, or listening to far too many young men with limited imaginations."

"The latter," she said firmly, looking at him with eyes that did, indeed, surpass the sparkle of the finest wine.

He led her through the double doors of the ballroom into

a crowded corridor. "Though many still consider *you* a young man, James Dinsmore, even at the ripe old age of twenty-seven."

"It is not how many years you have, my dear," he said as he guided her past the clusters of guests, "but how you choose to spend them."

As they continued down the hall, the crowds thinned, until there were only a few clusters here and there engaged in conversation. James led Elizabeth down another hall, lit by a few flickering sconces. He paused at a paneled door of rich mahogany, his hand on the brass knob.

"Elizabeth?" He turned the knob and swung the door open. She entered, her skirts rustling against him. He stood for a moment, watching her as she explored the room, her fingers trailing against the spines of the shelved books.

And then he slid a ribbon from the bottom of his braided queue, draped it over the outside knob, and quietly closed the door.

Chapter 3

Blue velvet curtains trimmed in gold braid were drawn across the long windows, and in the soft light of the candelabras on the mantel, the library seemed like a flowery cave. There was, indeed, a bottle of champagne perspiring in a silver bucket, and twin goblets on the floor next to the rose-colored fainting couch. Elizabeth was gazing at the books that filled the floor-to-ceiling shelves.

"Magnificent," she breathed.

Magnificent, he knew he should respond, and then begin the seduction Anne demanded. *Magnificent*, the word he needed came easily to mind. "You enjoy reading," he asked instead.

"Does that surprise you?" She turned to him with a beguiling smile. "That there is more in my head than the latest fashions and the current dance steps?"

"I suspect that even if I should know you for a hundred years, Elizabeth Harcrest, I would still discover things about you that surprised me."

"Very good," she said, returning her attention to the

shelves. "Most men seem to think women are simple creatures and believe they understand everything there is to
know about us."

"Like your brother?"

"Like my brother," she chuckled, "until he fell in love
with Alix. Now he knows better."

Alix, Al-ix. The sharp syllables of the name seemed to
echo the ticking of the ebony and gilt clock on the mantel-
piece. Alix, the reason he was here in the room with Elizabeth, the reason he must move quickly.

"I am well aware that women are complex creatures." He
walked over to the fainting couch and drew the champagne
out of its bed of ice. "And that is why they fascinate me."
The cork popped and bubbles escaped in a foamy hiss down
the side of the bottle.

"Oh, no." Elizabeth reached quickly for the glasses on the
floor. "Let me help you." Kneeling, she held the flutes up for
him to fill.

He was beyond help, he reflected, pouring the sparkling
wine. He glanced at the pearly face of the clock: twenty before one; in twenty minutes he'd be beyond redemption.

He clinked his glass with hers.

"I don't see Elizabeth." Rafe Moreham cast another glance
over the Dinsmore's ballroom and frowned. "Has anyone
any idea where she's gone?"

"Good Lord Moreham,"—Cole waved his hand towards
the dance floor—"she's probably caught up in the crush."
He shook his head, murmuring audibly enough for his friend
to hear, "Next thing you know the fellow will want to post
guards in the retiring rooms."

"In the case of my half sister, not an entirely bad idea. I
knew I should have convinced Louisa to accompany us."

"Rafe," Alix shook her head, "you know how Louisa ab-
hors crowds and noise. She'd have gotten a megrim simply
walking through the door."

"The Dinsmores do have that effect on a number of people," Cole added.

"Baiting Moreham like a bear when he's worrying over Elizabeth will only get you swiped," Phoebe advised slipping her arm through her husband's.

"Not to worry love, I can best him with swords. Of course," he added lightly, "if he insists on pistols, that's another thing entirely."

Rafe tugged at the watch fob hanging beneath his green and gold embroidered waistcoat. "Quarter of one. I leave her unattended for less than a half hour and she disappears." *Blast the girl, why can't she ever stay put?* "You and Phoebe take the left side of the ballroom," he directed tersely, "Alix and I shall search the right. If you don't find her, look outside and see if she's out on the veranda." *Then I'll check the portrait gallery,* he thought grimly.

"Most likely she's stepped out for some air," Alix said gently. "It's beastly hot in here and no doubt she's perishing in that velvet wrap you insisted she wear."

"That gown was cut too low! It didn't look a bit like the drawings the modiste showed me. . . . It revealed too much. . . ." His words trailed off and he gestured vaguely in the region of his chest.

"Bosom," Cole offered. "She's of marriageable age, Moreham. That's why you brought her out. As for her breasts . . ."

"That's my little sister you're talking about," Rafe growled warningly.

"Try to think of them like teeth on a horse, men like to get a glimpse of 'em before they decide whether to buy."

"I'll be certain to remind you of that Davenport, when you finally father a girl."

"After four boys, I suppose it's a possibility . . ."

"I think it's time we split up and searched for Elizabeth," Phoebe suggested, a shade too brightly.

• • •

James Dinsmore's eyes followed the dip of her collarbone down the smooth slope of her breasts into the concealing wrap of her mantelet. "You must be warm, sitting so close to the fire."

Flames from the hearth behind them reflected gold in her eyes, mingling with the natural copper and green. "I like the heat," she said, even as she loosened the velvet around her waist, letting the fabric slide, ever so slightly down her shoulders.

Then let me show you more. The words sprang with practiced ease into his mind, but would not leave his mouth. "Don't you think you should return to the dance?"

"I've had enough of dancing," she said, lowering her glass. "Haven't you?"

"Elizabeth . . . your reputation . . ."

"Is safe. In a crush like this, I doubt anyone saw us leave."

"In a crush like this, where people cannot move, they have little to do besides stand and watch . . .".

"And speaking of reputations, aren't you supposed to be a notorious libertine?" Still seated on the floor, she wriggled closer to where he sat on the fainting couch. "I've never been kissed by a libertine."

"And have you been kissed by a great many men?" he smoothed a stray chestnut curl from her forehead.

"A dancing master, a French tutor, and a footman." She tilted her head thoughtfully. "But I was *very* young when I kissed the footman."

"You are still very young." His hand drifted to her cheek, soft as the velvet wrap that had slipped down off her shoulders.

The clock chimed a quarter to the hour.

He reached down and grasped the fabric gathered about her elbows, pulling it—and her—closer towards him. "You have much to learn."

"I know that." She smiled impishly up at him. "Why else would I be here?"

"Then let the lessons begin," he whispered, burying his regrets within the sweet recesses of her mouth.

"Moreham." Anne Dinsmore affected an air of concern, one she'd practiced for nearly an hour in front of her mirror that afternoon. "You look worried. Is something wrong? Have you lost something?" She glanced about the floor. "A button? An earbob?" As she straightened, she noticed Rafe cast a questioning glance at his wife, saw Alix give an almost imperceptible, negative shake of her head.

"In a crowd such as this," she continued with a gesture that set the scarlet ribbons at her elbow fluttering, "delicate things can so easily be caught underfoot and crushed. I had a diamond hairpin once, belonged to the third Duchess of Dinsmore. It slipped unnoticed from my hair and by the time I'd found it, it was ruined beyond repair. Shall I call a footman to help?"

"It is nothing," Rafe replied, "nothing you need trouble your staff over, Lady Anne. We were just discussing . . ." he paused.

"Louisa," Alix said quickly, "she's caught a bit of a chest cold I'm afraid."

"And we were wondering whether we should leave early to make sure her condition has not worsened," Rafe concluded.

"If my dear mother were still alive,"—Anne clasped a hand to the flat of her chest—"I know I should feel the same. If you need make your farewells early, I assure you, I shall not take the slightest offense. As a matter of fact, I shall have your coach brought round to the front of the line right now. It will be waiting at the ready."

"That is most kind of you, Anne,"

"It is nothing," she waved dismissively. Then, abruptly,

she glanced about. "Where is Lady Elizabeth? Surely you must let her know if you are planning to leave. . . ."

"I believe she is dancing with Thomas Stirling," Rafe said smoothly.

"A charming gentleman." Anne nodded approvingly. "Well then, if there is nothing I can do here, I will be off to the library. My father has had some improvements made, and when I described them to Lady Morton and some of the others, well, nothing would satisfy them, but to see the room for themselves. Would you care to join us? You both have such impeccable taste, I should be delighted to hear your impressions. . . ."

Rafe shook his head.

"Ah, well," she sighed, "I do hope you change your mind and decide to stay at least a tiny bit longer. I have arranged a number of entertainments for this evening that I've no doubt you will all find most diverting."

Champagne and sugar cakes, James thought, as he tasted Elizabeth's lips. An odd combination of sophistication and sweetness, much like the womanly girl he held in his arms. *Soft lips.* He traced them with his tongue and she parted them. He entered, not with ferocity, but with tender, ticklish exploration. Each dip of his tongue a little deeper until at last she drew him in, demanding more.

He was sitting on the couch, Elizabeth between his knees.

He pulled her up against him, hands sliding up the arms that tangled around his neck. And down. He caressed the draped curve of her arms.

"That tickles James," she giggled, breaking their kiss.

He looked down at her rosy face and smiled, his blue eyes burning like the deepest part of a fire. "But does this?"

His hands moved lower following the downward curve of her breasts, then trailed his thumbs under and up, towards the tips straining against silk. As his thumbs brushed against her nipples, he heard her sudden intake of her breath. "I didn't think so," he whispered. His thumbs swept round them, like the relentless hands on the clock; James glanced briefly at the mantel—ten minutes before one.

"Shall I stop?" he whispered, his teeth nipping at the silken lobe of her ear, knowing that he should.

"Don't," she whispered. "Not yet." And leaned into his hands.

The heat of her, the scent of her, the taste, drove all thoughts from his head. But he could feel. And he wanted to feel her beneath him. Needed her there. His hands slid down her back, sweeping aside folds of velvet, crushing layers of padding and petticoat, until he felt the firm backs of her thighs. Still kissing her, he lifted her up, her body pressed hard against him, nearly as hard as the length of him. *Dear God, to be rid of the layers of satin and silk, muslin and cambric that separated them!* He laid her back against the couch, settling between her legs, mouth and hands desperately seeking naked flesh. He kissed her eyes, her nose, brushed a farewell to her lips, as his mouth discovered her neck. She surrendered this smooth white property to him, bending her head back so he could more fully explore its curves and hollows. Like a thief craving riches, he plundered and moved on, towards the ripe promise of her breasts. He slid his hands to her shoulders, pushing her gown down, down, while she arched up, freeing her aching flesh as he longed to free his . . . *Would there be time?*

"Oh please, God, yes!" Unwittingly Elizabeth gave shuddering voice to his own silent prayers.

And please, God, no. His mouth shaped the word no, his lips rounded just enough to suck a nipple in, and savor it with his tongue. Round and round his tongue swirled, again like the hands of clock, only this time maddeningly fast, time sped up and crazed. Elizabeth arched against him, filling his mouth with the fullness of her breast. He turned his attention to the other, licking, kissing, suckling. Her nipples were wet, slick with his attentions.

Between her legs he knew she must be wetter still. If only he could find his way through the tangled labyrinth of fabric that lay between them. *If he could pull her skirts up. . . .* He lifted his hips from hers; it was torture. He tugged. She helped him; it was madness. His fingers grazed the ribbons of her garters, felt the smoothness of her thigh, touched her damp curls.

"James?"

Beneath his hand, he felt her hips stiffen, uncertain whether to pull back or continue. *Too late*, he thought. "Elizabeth," he said, as reassuringly as he could. And let his fingers advance.

"Enough, James." Her voice wavered.

He stroked a moist fold. Closed his eyes, imaging himself, not simply his finger sliding inside her. "Elizabeth," he whispered, his voice nearly as unsteady as hers.

"James?" the voice was sure. Strong. Shocked.

"Anne?" he drew up.

"Anne!" Elizabeth clutched the front of her gown.

"*Elizabeth!*" Anne's tone was scandalized, but she stepped forward into the room so the women behind her in the doorway could share her view. "LADY ELIZABETH HARCREST!" she repeated loudly enough to make certain they all would know exactly who lay on the couch, half clad beneath her brother.

Chapter 4

Anne stood in silence as the crowd behind her stared. The moment seemed frozen. Then she turned abruptly, and began quickly herding scandalized guests back towards the hallway. "This does not appear to be an appropriate time to discuss the décor of the library," she said to the gaping faces of her invited guests. "If you will excuse me, I will rejoin you all in just a moment."

And then she closed the library door.

"Well," she said dryly, "this *is* a pretty tableau."

Elizabeth, struggling to rewrap her mantelet, refused to look in Anne's direction. She had a fair idea of what she'd see: shock and disapproval. This was all so embarrassing, humiliating, horrifying . . . and a tempest in a teapot compared to how her brother would react. *Rafe, oh God, Rafe, how could she explain? Would he forgive her? Would he even listen?* She pulled her mantelet tight around her waist, as if the velvet might protect her. Or at least fortify her spine. She'd have to turn and face Anne.

Worse yet, she'd have to face the people in the hallway.

The people who had seen . . . had seen her . . . exposed.

An enormous wave of shame flooded her. She, who'd kissed James, who'd wrapped her arms around him, allowed him to slide her bodice down and her skirts up, hardly dared look at him now. Out of the corner of her eye, she saw him straightening his stock, his eyes fixed on his sister. He smoothed his hair. He was missing a ribbon from the bottom of his braided queue, she noticed distractedly. She glanced about the floor for it, as if finding the ribbon might somehow tidy the mess into which they'd gotten themselves.

She heard Anne moving towards them, the rustle of her skirts, the rasp of her slippers on the nap of the carpet. Turning to look, she saw a length of blue velvet dangling from Anne's outstretched hand.

"James," Anne said. "You'll be needing this if you plan to return to the assembly."

"Keep it." His voice was oddly flat. "I won't be returning."

"But the night is young. There is still so much *entertainment* to be had."

It was the oddest conversation, as if nothing out of the ordinary had occurred, as if nothing more had come undone than James's ribbon.

"I've had enough entertainment."

Disgust was in his voice, and Elizabeth shivered; was his disgust meant for her? She straightened, staring openly at him, but his gaze remained fixed on his sister.

"As you wish." The ribbon slid through Anne's fingers and fluttered to the floor. "You've done more than enough this evening. I'll see to the rest."

The rest. Was she the rest? Elizabeth turned towards Anne, completely missing the expression in James's eyes as he turned at last to look at her. It was the expression of a man watching something inconceivably precious slip from his grasp. His fingers flexed, his arm tensed as if to reach for her.

"If you wish to leave unnoticed James," Anne said sharply, "use the door to the music room. I'll take Elizabeth down the back stairs, through the kitchen to the mews. Her brother's coach is waiting."

Rafe's coach . . . but how?

"I spoke with your brother and his wife earlier this evening, Elizabeth. They seemed most concerned about your mother. An inflammation of the lungs I believe they said. They were worried about leaving her home alone, worried things might suddenly take a turn for the worse. As a precaution, I ordered his coach brought round to the front of the line. Most fortunate as it turns out, don't you think?"

Elizabeth couldn't think, she didn't understand. Louisa seemed fine when they'd left. But she hadn't paid a great deal of attention to her—another of her sins, she knew, not paying enough attention to what people said and did and warned. She'd been so excited at the promise of the party, the prospect of adventure . . .

Relief rippled briefly over her.

Thank God Louisa hadn't been here, a witness! Her mother would never rail at her the way Rafe most certainly would, but there would be deep, silent disappointment in her eyes. And that would be harder to bear; her mother trusted her. Elizabeth hated to let her down. Again.

"Can I leave?" she struggled to keep her voice composed. "Now?"

"Of course my dear." Anne smiled gently. "Follow me."

Elizabeth glanced back at James. He stood stiffly, his face expressionless.

"Come along Elizabeth," Anne prompted, "people are waiting."

As the backstairs door to the Dinsmore's library clicked closed behind the two women, James sank to his knees beside the couch, hands pressed against the fading warmth where Elizabeth had been.

Why, he wondered, did people imagine hell was hot? Hell, he felt certain, was deathly cold.

How strange, Elizabeth thought, to have entered a party with your head held high, your stomach fluttering with excitement, only to leave this way; creeping down the back stairs. Head bowed, she followed a mercifully silent Anne Dinsmore, their skirts brushing the walls of the narrow, poorly lit passage.

They entered the kitchen, steamy and close, rank with the aromas of exhausted servants and roasting meats. A chaos of noise faded abruptly as the footmen and serving girls, cooks and scullery maids stared as Anne and Elizabeth made their way past long tables piled high with half-eaten food and empty glasses.

Stepping out into the cool darkness of the mews, Elizabeth felt as if she'd been expelled from hell. She pulled her mantelet close, her eyes adjusting to the abrupt shift from the fiery brightness of the kitchen. The outline of her brother's coach emerged from the shadows. The matched blacks lifted their hooves, impatient to be home. A footman in Dinsmore livery stepped forward, released the steps to the coach and held the door open.

Elizabeth took a step forward, then turned, more from habit than thought.

She must thank her hostess.

She opened her mouth, but the usual platitudes seemed impossibly absurd. She *wasn't* grateful she'd been invited, she *wasn't* glad she'd come. The evening had turned out far from lovely. But she was the daughter of an earl, the sister of an earl, schooled in proper manners. Like carefully crafted clockworks she responded, "Thank you Lady Anne."

Anne smiled, a genuine smile that reached her pale blue eyes and filled them with delight. "My pleasure Lady Elizabeth."

"How *could* you, Elizabeth?" Rafe demanded, a moment

after the door to the carriage closed and the horses started forward.

"How do you know?" The question tumbled from her lips.

"How do we *know*? The same way that everyone in that ballroom knows! Anne's friends couldn't wait to tell their friends what they'd seen. Elizabeth Harcrest seduced by James Dinsmore. *What were you thinking?*" He held up his hand as if to halt any explanation she might attempt. "No, let me amend that . . . you *weren't* thinking. You never think Elizabeth, at least not ahead. I tried to warn you, but you wouldn't listen . . ."

Unwilling to face Rafe or his wife, sitting silently beside him, Elizabeth stared out the window, eyes fixed on the receding lights of the Dinsmore's estate as her brother's voice droned on in her ear. As the carriage rolled out of the drive, the house was framed under the arch of a wrought-iron gate emblazoned with the scarlet and white family crest. Unfurled along the bottom in bold gold lettering was the family motto. Mindlessly, Elizabeth translated the Latin: *Honor our shield, vengeance our sword.*

"And now," she tuned back in to Rafe's voice, "I haven't the *slightest* idea how we shall repair your reputation."

Alix reached over and took his hand in hers. "We'll think of something, in the morning, when our heads are clearer. Things always look worse at night."

"Perhaps, Alix." His hand clenched in a fist. "But in this case, things will look far *worse* by morning. The Dinsmore's guests have the remainder of the ball to gossip and speculate. . . . By the time James Dinsmore has finished gloating about how he seduced the Earl of Moreham's sister . . ."

"He wouldn't do that," Elizabeth broke in.

"He wouldn't?" Skepticism dripped from Rafe's voice.

"I know James."

"Ah, yes, and after this evening, the rest of the ton will know precisely *how* well."

"Rafe, enough," Alix hissed sharply. "I know you are distressed, but there is no reason to be cruel."

"You'd rather I be kind? Understanding? That I listen to her watery declarations that she'll mend her ways if I just forgive her one more time?" He released a long sigh. When he spoke again, his voice was tired. "I'd like to forgive her, to forget this sordid mess ever happened. But society will not. There will be no invitations to Almack's after this, the best parties, the most exclusive circles will be closed to her. As to who shall marry her now . . ."

"She's still sister to the Earl of Moreham and an heiress," Alix protested.

"Indeed. And after tonight's events it will be so much easier to sort out the fortune hunters amongst her suitors," he added sourly.

"In the morning," Alix said firmly, "we will have a family meeting. We'll discuss what has happened with Louisa and Madeleine."

"Louisa? I doubt she'll have much advice to offer on the subject of Elizabeth's disgrace."

"You think not, Rafe Moreham? And why do you think she spends so much time in the garden?"

"Because she likes flowers."

"As usual, my beloved husband, you underestimate the strength of women. Haven't you noticed that when talk turns to your father and his parties and his women, Louisa suddenly realizes she's forgotten some critical item? Or how her talk turns to grafting and fertilizers? She's not nearly so absentminded, nor so absorbed in her flowers as she'd have you believe. She's simply decided that the sharpest thorns in the garden are more comforting than the kindest words of the ton."

"Fascinating. So you're suggesting we abandon all hope of marrying Elizabeth off, and set her up as an apprentice gardener? Although I suppose," he said dryly, "it would be better than whatever flamboyant plan *your* mother might concoct. Let me guess: dress her in red, accessorize her with plumes, encourage the broadsheets to herald the praises of the 'Scarlet Dove'?"

"I am suggesting that together we might come up with a plan to help Elizabeth through this mess," Alix said calmly, pointedly ignoring the sarcastic reference to how her mother arranged for her to wear gray gowns when she first arrived in London, and how the papers then labeled her the "Silver Siren."

"That is *my* responsibility," he replied, tersely.

"And that, my love, is what concerns me. Promise me, you'll do nothing rash, nothing without telling me first."

"I promise I'll do what's best for Elizabeth."

Elizabeth winced. They were discussing her as if she weren't even there. A part of her felt as if she were not. The rest of her was nearly overcome by the desire to fling open the carriage door, leap out, and run screaming through the streets of London. That would be briefly satisfying, but eventually, she'd find herself nowhere . . . rather where she found herself now. She closed her eyes.

She'd done a reckless thing, a scandalous thing. *Very well*, she admitted, *a stupid thing*. There'd be gossip, snickers at her expense, some of the older, stuffier sort might cut her directly, but completely disgraced? It couldn't happen. She was still Rafe's sister, still sister to, and daughter of, the Earl of Moreham, heiress to a comfortable fortune. *After tonight's events it will be so much easier to sort out the fortune hunters amongst her suitors. . . .* That fragment of Rafe's conversation floated back to her. He always predicted the worst. She clapped a mental hand over the voice inside her head suggesting this time he might be right; this time she might have bent the rules so far back they'd finally broken. *Nonsense*, she told the voice. And anyway, this might be a *good* thing, a test of sorts, weed out the men drawn to her simply for her lineage, her place in society. Make it simpler to find the man who'd liked her, perhaps even loved her, for herself.

A smile, the first since she'd kissed James Dinsmore, crossed her face.

"She's smiling." Rafe nudged Alix. "She hasn't the slightest notion of what she's done."

"Rafe, leave her be." Alix slipped into French.

Elizabeth never understood why her sister-in-law did that; her own French was nearly as fluent as Rafe's—he'd seen to that just as he'd seen to every other detail of her education.

"The night has been horrible enough for her."

"This isn't," Rafe replied, also in French, "like being discovered kissing a dance master, Alix."

It wasn't. And not simply for the reasons Rafe and Alix were concerned with. Her other kisses had been experiments, no sentimentality involved—though most certainly the subjects had been attractive. Another smile flickered across her face as she recalled the freckles sprinkling the nose of the footman she'd kissed when she was fourteen.

"There Alix, she's doing it again, smiling. Do you think that devil Dinsmore got her drunk?"

Drunk, it was how she'd felt when James had touched her. But while the champagne had given her the courage to kiss him, it hadn't been the liquor that had led her to do more. It had felt so right, so good. Elizabeth shifted in her seat at the restless memory of precisely how good. Even now, with all that had happened, her body wanted more.

"I'll wager he did get her drunk. Lecherous bastard probably made certain her glass was never empty."

"As you did the first time you kissed me?"

"If I might correct your memory, my love, I wasn't filling your glass that night; you were. And I wasn't trying to seduce you. I was trying to help you to see reason. To understand why you should marry me."

"Is that what it was?" Alix's tone was amused.

"Don't try and change the subject, Alix. This isn't like Elizabeth's previous escapades. I can't simply send her to another school, or find her another tutor."

She didn't want to go anywhere, Elizabeth suddenly realized. She didn't need any more lessons. In James, she found the master.

"What are we going to do, Rafe?"

Elizabeth had a fairly good idea of what *she* was going to do. She was going to see James again. She was going to kiss him again, and see if he created the same havoc of emotions and sensations. She'd need to do it in the bright light of day, she mused, without the benefit of champagne. Not that she believed candlelight and champagne had anything to do with her reaction to him, but simply to make certain. Her mind bumped up against the question: *certain of what?* Certain of . . . she paused struck by the dimensions of what she was thinking; certain that James Dinsmore was the man for her. She had the strongest notion that he was . . .

He'd be resistant, of course; James wasn't exactly the marrying kind. But he'd ruined her, she thought confidently. After the events of this evening, Rafe and Anne would bring him up to scratch. *That* she knew with sudden surety.

The smile that had blossomed on her lips bloomed.

"My God," she heard her brother swear. "She's radiant Alix, just look at her. No question about it, my sister's gone utterly mad."

Chapter 5

His valet removed his satin evening clothes, drew a cambric nightshirt over his head, and waited as James Dinsmore poured himself a brandy and finally sat at his dressing table.

"Is something wrong, sir?" The valet began brushing the waves out of James's unbraided queue. Master Dinsmore usually retired closer to dawn and never poured his own drink.

"Quite all right." James waved the question away with a moisturized hand. Actually, he felt unsettled, unclean even. "But I believe that will be enough brushing."

"Very good, sir. Shall I draw the curtains?"

James nodded as he rose from his dressing table, picked up his brandy and headed towards the bed, draped in a half-canopy of champagne-colored silk. He put the almost empty glass down on a marble-topped nightstand and climbed under the threadbare sheets. A tad damp, but not nearly as cold as they had been when he and Anne first arrived in September.

"Shall I put out the candles, sir?"

"All but this one by my bed Simmons."

The pale gold room faded into darkness, until all that could be seen lay within the shivery domain of the single candlestick on the nightstand. A book of poetry, a glass of water, three copper coins. The circle shifted briefly as Simmons opened the bedroom door and a draft from James's study swept the room. He paused, looking back at the golden figure in the bed. "Will there be anything else, sir?"

James shook his head. "Good night, Simmons."

"Good night, sir."

The door swung quietly closed.

James put his glass down, drew his knees up and rested his chin on them. He closed his eyes. Occasional bursts of laughter drifted up from the first floor ballroom. Outside his window he could hear voices, words of farewell, promises of future meetings, and the clatter of carriage wheels on cobblestones.

For a moment he felt like the child he'd once been in this London town house—fascinated by the glittering world of his parents' parties, frustrated that he wasn't allowed to attend, and ultimately reassured by the sound of the coaches outside that, when all was said and done, his parents would remain behind with him.

Sometimes during those parties, Anne would sneak into his room, and, standing on tiptoe, they'd peer out the windows, watching the guests. Anne liked to imagine which sort of gowns and jewels she'd wear. James liked to compare the men's short ceremonial swords. "When I'm married, to a rich handsome fellow like that," Anne would say, pointing with a child's chubby finger, "I'll buy you one for *every* day of the week!"

But then their mother died and the parties stopped.

As their father became increasingly obsessed with the possibility of a Roman invasion, his solicitors became increasingly concerned about the decline of the Dinsmore fortune. They wanted to have the duke declared insane and have his title and responsibilities transferred to James.

Anne protested. Vehemently. Their father was grieving, she insisted, it was natural. Who knew but that his wits might return any day?

And the scandal! The ton might overlook idiosyncrasies in a peer. They might sympathize with a downturn in fortunes. But insanity would dash any hopes they might have of making truly suitable matches. James allowed himself to be persuaded by his sister's arguments. If it made her happy to pretend their father was a reclusive scholar engrossed in the antiquities, fine by him. He'd just as soon avoid the responsibilities of heading up the family and overseeing the estates.

He didn't really care about inheriting the title.

And he wasn't particularly interested in marriage.

He wasn't particularly interested in anything, he thought with the weariness of a man of seventy, rather than twenty-seven. A trim figure with a head full of chestnut curls and hazel eyes that bespoke trouble, blazed into his head. "Not even you," he sighed.

Just another body then? His inner voice mocked him. *Just another set of lips that fitted yours as if they'd been made to meet? Just another pair of warm, smooth breasts seemingly designed to fill your hands. And the heat . . .*

"It was the champagne," he murmured.

You weren't drinking champagne.

"The brandy then." He was, he realized wryly, talking out loud to himself.

Does that explain why even now you're as hard as a . . .

"Bloody Hell!" he flopped back on his pillows, disgusted. Even his *thoughts* were indecent. "It's true," he said to the shadows. "I've no sense of decency, no sense of honor, no sense of responsibility. Everyone knows it. Ask Lounsbury, ask Ashton. Christ, just ask Elizabeth's *brother.*"

What about your sister?

Anne?

What about all the things you've given up for her?

He frowned. He hadn't given up all that much. Anne was his sister, he did what needed to be done to make her happy. Lord knew she had little enough of that . . . God, what was it he was feeling? Was it *guilt*? He put his hands over his eyes and groaned, *Why didn't you say no, Elizabeth?*

Other people might believe James Dinsmore was a conscienceless cad, but Elizabeth had faith in him. She sat up in bed. He would come for her this morning, she felt sure of it.

It was an intuition based on a vague but never quite forgotten memory.

A slim blond boy holding his fragile sister, reassuring her that the other children really did like her, that they teased her because they were jealous of her wit, her creativity, and her elfin beauty. *Elfin beauty*, Elizabeth recalled those words most vividly. They hadn't only sounded magical; Anne had cheered up, and Elizabeth had found herself suddenly, ragingly jealous. She wanted to be told she was wondrous, too— and not, as Rafe seemed overly fond of saying, a disaster waiting to be unleashed.

At the thought of disaster, Elizabeth threw off her covers. She needed to get up, and get ready. She needed to figure out what to wear. She yanked the embroidered bellpull hanging near her canopied bed. Then yanked again for good measure. Her maid, Molly, rushed nearly breathless into the room, a cup of chocolate and a roll teetering precariously on a tray.

"What is it, my lady? You're up so early, what do you need? I brought you something to eat, in case you were hungry."

"Molly, you're a marvel, I *am* famished."

Elizabeth tore a corner off the roll and began chewing thoughtfully, eyes surveying the contents of her armoire, like a general studying a battle plan.

"Are you expecting someone special to pay a call today, my lady?" Molly settled the tray on a table near the hearth, carefully arranging the silverware. "It's been very quiet downstairs. Hardly anyone's come round to leave a card."

"The white muslin with the roses," Elizabeth said firmly. She pulled a length of gauzy rose fabric from a drawer. "And could you see that this fichu is pressed for me?"

"I'll take it downstairs this moment. And then I'll return and help you dress."

"Good morning all." Elizabeth glided into the breakfast room an hour later, a vision in rose and ribbons. She picked up a plate from the sideboard and began peering under the lids of the silver chafing dishes. "Smells delicious." She inhaled the fragrant steam rising from a dish of sausages. Piling her plate high, she turned. "Did everyone sleep well?"

Rafe, Alix, Louisa, and Madeleine were staring at her, as if she were wearing garters on her head.

"I don't know about the rest of you, but I awaken after these late nights feeling as if I might devour the contents of the kitchen."

"It's the shock," Rafe said dourly, "the shock of the scandal has sent her completely round the bend. She's mad. Mad as Ophelia. Next thing you know, she'll come skipping in with a bouquet of weeds."

"There's rosemary for remembrance?" Elizabeth shook her head. "Not to worry, I know that rosemary is meant for chicken." She set her plate down next to Louisa and drew up a chair.

"It's also lovely baked in bread," Louisa offered. "I've some growing in the herb garden I planted at Moreham Hall."

"Now they've both gone off." Rafe brought his hand down on the table and the crystal jumped. "This is *not* a tea party. We have not gathered to chatter about Shakespeare, the culinary arts, or gardening. We are here to discuss what is to be done about Elizabeth."

"Now that you mention gardening," Louisa ventured, "I

would be willing to take her back to the country, away from this dreadful, noisy city. We could putter around, until this whole dreadful thing has blown over?"

"No, no, no." Madeleine put down her coffee cup and joined the fray. "She should not run away from the scandal. She should face it head-on, chin up. And with a dramatic story." She pursed her lips. "I shall think of something."

"I can only imagine," Rafe murmured.

Madeleine held up a hand for silence. "Elizabeth is ill. Something chronic, incurable . . . she swoons, frequently, often without warning—"

"People will say she is with child," Alix said.

"Too much champagne then . . ."

"They'll say she's a drinker," Louisa responded. She glanced at Rafe, the words, *like her father and her eldest brother*, unspoken but voluble.

"Corsets too tight?"

"She should have excused herself and made her way to a retiring room," Alix said.

Madeleine frowned. "None of you are *helping* . . ."

"Perhaps the ton is not discussing me at all," Elizabeth suggested, over the rim of her coffee cup.

Four pairs of eyes swiveled towards her.

"Of course they are," Rafe said. "Don't be ridiculous."

Louisa nodded, "I'm sorry, my dear, but I must agree."

Alix added, "The only cards that have arrived this morning are from old biddies notorious for their curiosity. Lady Morton's arrived at 8:00 A.M. sharp."

"That creature." Elizabeth's cup rattled in the saucer as she set it down. "What could *she* possibly want? She's never stepped foot across this threshold before."

"She wants to see how you are doing, of course," Louisa said quietly. "She wants to see if you've been crying, if you're remorseful, or defiant. To see if you will add any delicious details to the malicious soup she's stirring. She'll watch how you walk and how you sit, and speculate later whether Rafe has beaten you."

"He *wouldn't*!" Elizabeth sputtered.

"I *ought* to have!"

"There were no other cards . . . ?" Elizabeth toyed with her knife.

"And if I might inquire, whom are you expecting to call?" Rafe's eyes narrowed. "Certainly not James Dinsmore?"

Elizabeth flushed.

"You're more likely to hear from Ashton or Lounsbury than that scounderel."

"You've always thought the worst of him, Rafe." Elizabeth's chin jutted defiantly.

"Events it would seem, have proven me right."

Madeleine cleared her throat, as if trying to clear the air. "Perhaps she should marry him."

"Never," Rafe spat.

"Why not?" Elizabeth dropped her knife and straightened.

Alix put a hand on her husband's arm as she spoke, to keep him in his chair. "I know you don't like him, my love, but it is a reasonable solution . . ."

"It's an appalling solution." Rafe leaned back in his chair, with an air of finality.

"Rafe, did you ever consider, that . . . that James"—Elizabeth stumbled over her words, so much easier to think than to say out loud—"that he might be falling in love with me?"

"No."

"Why? Am I that unattractive, Rafe, that unlovable?"

"James Dinsmore is incapable of love," Rafe replied softly.

Everyone in the room suddenly studied their plate, or their hands. Elizabeth was momentarily stunned into silence. "But he loves Anne—"

"I suppose, in his own twisted way. Certainly she's the

only one to whom I've ever seen him express any tenderness."

"Last night—" Elizabeth started again.

"Don't confuse lust with love. You were young and willing and he took advantage. It probably amused him to dally with my sister; I wouldn't be surprised if he saw seducing you as revenge for my failure to offer for Anne."

"It's always James you fault, never Anne."

"With good reason. Anne has a sense of right and wrong. James has none." His hazel eyes met hers. "But let us say, for the sake of argument, Anne was behind what happened. All the more reason you shouldn't marry him. Would you want a man with so little morals that he'd play whoremaster for his sister?"

Alix gasped. Madeleine stared at Rafe. And Louisa gazed with worn eyes at her daughter. Elizabeth ignored the remark.

"And if he asks you for my hand?"

"Why then,"—Rafe slashed open a roll with his butter knife—"I'll kill him."

Chapter 6

"Only listen to this James!" Anne, stretched out on the faded silk divan wearing her nightdress and robe, sat up and began reading: "The Dinsmore assembly, held Wednesday last, was a glittering affair." She perused the column quickly. "I won't bore you with the list of guests and what was served." She glanced over at her brother who was also in his dressing gown, hair unbound over his broad shoulders, sipping coffee. "I'll skip straight to the delicious part:

> "A certain young lady in her first season, who for the
> sake of her noble family, we shall henceforth refer to
> as Lady E, made a lasting impression on the guests
> assembled at the Dinsmores. According to our
> source, the lady did more than come out—she went
> in, as into the library, alone with a certain notorious
> Lord D. There the two engaged in something far less
> intellectual than reading."

Anne chuckled. "*Less intellectual than reading* . . . , don't you *adore* it, *Lord D*?"

"Always exciting to see one's endeavors in print," James remarked dryly.

"Most satisfying." She smiled. "And you know how I labored over that particular phrase. Now where was I? Ah yes—

> "Scandalized guests discovered the couple. Her
> brother, who, this writer ventures to guess, was pay-
> ing more attention to his young bride than his young
> sister, whisked Lady E home."

Anne lowered the broadsheet. "What I would not give to see His Lordship's face when he reads *that* line."

"I, for one, am grateful I shall not be there when he does."

"No doubt he shall be *extremely* vexed with you. You should probably avoid places you might encounter him for the next few weeks." She set the broadsheet down with a sigh. "Though truly, it is most unfair. Why should you be blamed because Elizabeth hasn't the good sense God gave a goose? I tried to warn Moreham he needed to keep an eye on her. That he should select a wife able to guide his sister through the pitfalls of the ton." Anne tsked. "Women in our society can be dreadfully unforgiving."

"Indeed," James said eyeing his sister.

"Indeed," she agreed, lifting a delicate flowered teacup from the table at her side. "How *lovely* of them to publish my work so promptly."

"For what you paid the scoundrels, I should hope so."

"An investment in Elizabeth Harcrest's future, or what remains of it." She saluted him with her cup. "I must thank you, brother dear, for taking the time out of your busy schedule to deliver it to the printers. *Prior* to the actual event," she said with amusement. She took a sip of tea and closed her pale blue eyes, savoring the taste. "This blend is marvelous, you really should try it."

"I'm quite satisfied with my coffee."

"And of course I owe you even greater thanks. I hope you didn't find seducing Elizabeth too tedious."

"Not at all."

"From what I could see . . . well, from what *everyone* could see, Elizabeth appeared to be enjoying your attentions."

The silver coffeepot in James's hand wavered and a few drops splashed onto his saucer. He tightened his grip. "Naturally. What else should she have expected from the notorious Lord D?"

A peal of delighted laughter escaped from Anne. "What else? But to dally with an awkward little virgin . . . I suspect the experience must have been unsatisfying, to say the least."

"To say the least," he murmured blandly, thinking of how close he had come to making love to Elizabeth Harcrest. His blood pulsed at the memory. He felt himself hardening beneath his nightshirt. He didn't want to think about Elizabeth, how she'd looked, how she'd felt beneath him, the fevered keening that escaped her throat when he'd stroked her. "So Anne, what are your plans for this afternoon?"

She stretched back luxuriously on the worn couch. "It's a lovely day for a ride in the park, don't you think? Make the rounds, see who is about, wonder aloud what poor Moreham will do about his scandalous sister. Shall you come with me?"

"I've an appointment with my tailor."

"Afterwards perhaps?"

"I need to purchase some new handkerchiefs."

Pale blue eyes met deep blue ones. Anne shrugged. "Very well, but you shall miss all the fun."

"I can only imagine."

Anne continued as if she had not caught the acerbic note in her brother's voice. "I shall express my regrets that such a scandalous thing should have occurred in my home." She placed a hand dramatically on her chest. "Our families are so close; I vow I feel responsible for this dreadful situation in which Elizabeth finds herself."

"You missed your calling, Anne," James said with a bored lightness that had nothing to do with the weight that was compressing his heart. "You really should have been an actress."

A chill crept into her eyes. "Do not compare me to that slatternly lot. I am the daughter of the Duke of Dinsmore. I will be spoken of with respect."

"Anne," James studied his sister over his coffee cup, "how long do you intend to carry on this vendetta against Moreham?"

"For as long as it takes for him to experience all the humiliation and rejection I have. To wonder, every time he passes people at a party, clustered together laughing, if he is the subject of their amusement." A brittle smile stretched her lips. "For as long as it takes for him to regret he ever laid eyes on that little French bitch, Alix de La Brou."

"He wouldn't really kill James, do you think?"

Elizabeth and Alix were monogramming table linens in a small sitting room off Elizabeth's bedchamber. The house was quiet. Rafe had told the butler to inform callers—of which there had been few—the family was not at home to visitors. Still, Elizabeth couldn't resist glancing out the long windows of the sitting room to see if anyone was coming down the drive.

"I wouldn't underestimate him Elizabeth. He's angry." Alix pulled her needle through the downward sweep of an elaborate M. An understatement; Rafe was furious. Last night, it had been all she could do to prevent him from storming back to the Dinsmores and calling James out. Towards the early hours of the morning she'd finally convinced him a scene on the Dinsmore's dance floor would only make the scandal worse.

She studied the figure of her sister-in-law. Elizabeth looked remarkably fresh. The rose of her fichu brought a soft glow to her cheeks, her eyes were bright, and her hair was loosely, but artfully arranged in gleaming chestnut waves. As Elizabeth turned her head towards the window for what must have been the hundredth time, Alix couldn't help thinking she resembled one of the rosebuds on her gown. "Elizabeth," she said with a sudden surge of suspicion, "are you watching for James?"

"Certainly not," Elizabeth replied, pulling a stitch so tight the fabric pleated.

Her sister-in-law was a terrible liar. *He's not coming*, Alix wanted to say, but she knew Elizabeth wouldn't listen. In her own way, Elizabeth was as stubborn as Rafe.

Silence stretched as tautly as the linen in their embroidery hoops.

"Elizabeth." Alix stopped stitching. "Marriage to James Dinsmore might resolve this difficult situation." Her finger traced the *M*. "But marriage to a man you barely know . . ."

"I've known James Dinsmore my entire life."

"You know one facet of his character, the charming social James Dinsmore . . . but there are others . . ."

"Are you referring to his fondness for horse racing? For gambling? His debts? His drinking?" Elizabeth paused, then added almost casually. "Or his reputation for seducing women and frequenting houses of ill-repute?"

"Elizabeth." Alix's voice was shocked. "A young lady should not know of such things."

"Shouldn't know, or simply shouldn't speak of such things? Let us not pretend, Alix, only consider how I was raised. You didn't know my father or my brother George, but let me assure you they drank and gambled and whored and made no effort to hide their pleasures from Louisa or from me." She examined her needlework. "Did you know they considered Rafe, with his careful planning, his studies, his interest in economics, an oddity?"

"He has told me some things."

"I will not repeat my mother's errors. The only veil that will be over my eyes when I walk down the marriage aisle will be one made of lace."

"Are you so sure you know James Dinsmore then?"

Elizabeth glanced at the window. "No." She turned to face Alix. "But there is something about him . . . a goodness, a sense of honor, buried deep perhaps, but still there. I can feel it."

Alix said nothing, but her expression clearly conveyed her skepticism.

"Haven't you ever met a person, looked into his eyes and known in that instant that you could trust him?"

Alix thought of the first time she'd seen Rafe. "I have."

"And were you right?"

She thought of the lies he'd told when they'd first met, and the things she'd kept concealed. And the disaster the two of them had nearly made of their lives. "It's not that simple, Elizabeth. And James . . ." Her hands fluttered as if the right words were small birds and she might somehow pluck them out of the air. "He is so much older, and experienced, and he's . . . well he's . . ."

"A Dinsmore?"

Alix nodded.

"That doesn't make him bad. It makes him proud and, I'll admit, rather arrogant. But consider his situation: his father mad, his sister an angry spinster, his title withheld, his fortune entailed. What else is he to do but seek amusements and grow increasingly bored with them? He's like a little boy who has lost his way."

"He's not a little boy, Elizabeth, he's a man."

Elizabeth thought about how his hands and his lips had

explored her body, how he'd looked as he'd held her close and pleasured her. "I am aware of that."

Alix frowned at the flush drifting up her sister-in-law's slim neck. "I'm not talking about what passed between you two last night."

The flush became distinctly crimson and spread to Elizabeth's cheeks.

"Elizabeth listen to me. There is an innocence to what boys do. They are just discovering the boundaries of their world, the damage they cause." She stopped, knowing she must continue, must say her mind, but aware that whatever words she chose would hurt Elizabeth. "The damage they cause is . . . unintentional."

"Are you saying what happened between us was . . . that James planned it?"

"I wasn't there, Elizabeth." Though, she thought bitterly, a good deal of the ton conveniently was. . . . And that footman who appeared at Rafe's elbow to let them know their carriage was ready at the precise moment word had begun to spread through the crush. Rafe had wanted to charge to the library, but she had convinced him it would only make things worse.

"Is that what you are saying Alix?" Elizabeth demanded.

No matter what arguments she presented, Elizabeth would reject them; her sister-in-law was infatuated with James Dinsmore. "What I'm saying is that James knew better than to take you into the library alone. He knew the risks to you and to your reputation."

"And if I tell you that it was my idea to go into the library?"

"I'd say you did a very mad thing, but I would still say that James should not have taken you."

"And if I tell you that he resisted, that it was I who encouraged him?"

Alix, her mouth drawn tight, said nothing, only picked up her needlework and began to work the petals of a flower.

"Last night was not planned. It just . . . happened. But I feel somehow that it was meant to be. He will come for me." *Perhaps not today*, she glanced out the window, *but I know he will.*

They continued to stitch in quiet, if not entirely comfortable, silence.

"*I'm bored and* I'm tired of sitting. I need some fresh air." Elizabeth began putting away her needles and thread. "Do let us go riding."

Alix looked doubtful. "Rafe has put it out that we are not at home to visitors."

"Just a brief ride, a quick turn about the park. We won't stop. We won't speak to a soul. If anyone tries to engage us, we'll simply wave politely."

"Elizabeth, I don't know."

"I suppose we must stay inside then." Elizabeth sighed, peering through her lashes. "After all, Rafe does always know what's best."

Alix's eyes narrowed. "I know what you are up to Elizabeth Harcrest. You are trying to manipulate me."

Elizabeth picked up a needle, but her hands remained motionless in her lap. Her eyes drifted towards the window. *She'll learn*, Alix thought, *soon enough.*

"Such a beautiful day."

Weaving her needle into the corner of her work Alix said, "Very well, a brief ride." She rose, praying that the lesson Elizabeth was about to learn would be brief as well.

"*Do you like* it? It's last year's habit, but I've trimmed it with some new lace and changed the collar. The hat is new."

James studied his sister in her navy blue habit, trimmed with red. The hat was a small tricorne, perched jauntily on her pale blond hair, a rich red feather curling down towards her cheeks. "Very elegant, Anne. Heads will turn."

She smiled. "And ears, too, I've no doubt." She pulled

on a pair of red kidskin gloves. "Are you certain you will not change your mind and come riding with me?"

"Quite certain," he said firmly.

"Very well then," she said, giving her hat a quick pat to make sure it was securely pinned. "I'm off." Halfway across the sitting room she turned, her eyes shining like a child on her way to a birthday party. "I do hope you shall be here for dinner. You wouldn't want to miss hearing what the critics have to say about Elizabeth's performance."

Chapter 7

***

She forced herself to breathe in time with the horse's hooves, to relax the muscles in her face, to smile as if she didn't care that she'd been cut. Not once, not twice, but four times in the last half hour. Elizabeth had been trained to sit straight in the saddle, but this afternoon, it was not the old lessons of her riding master, but the new ones from the ladies of the ton, that kept her spine rigid. Despite the nearly overwhelming desire to whip her horse into a gallop and ride hell for leather for home, she kept her mare at a steady walk.

Four times she'd smiled and lifted her hand to wave at someone, only to have the other woman look through her as if she weren't there. She resolved not to wave again, unless she was certain her greeting would be returned. Finally an old schoolmate, Sarah Harrington, had ridden toward her, hand raised. Elizabeth raised hers in return, then caught the expression on Sarah's face. She was staring past Elizabeth. She was waving at someone else. Elizabeth's arm hung in midair; any movement she made would only make things worse. Even so, she pretended to wave at someone just beyond Sarah.

"Lady Elizabeth thinks I was waving at her." Sarah turned to her companion, a woman who yesterday would have been thrilled to exchange greetings with an earl's daughter. She raised her voice as she passed, to ensure her words would carry. "As if I would greet a woman of such slight character in public."

"Ignore her," Alix said firmly. "Her sort are always waiting for an opportunity to act superior to their betters. You are *Lady* Elizabeth Harcrest, sister and daughter of the Earl of Moreham. So chin up, smile—the face you show makes it clear you know this—see if you can't manage a laugh."

Manage a laugh? She fixed her eyes straight ahead. She smiled. Several young bucks dressed in the latest fashions, lifted their tall hats and smiled in response. Not the polite smiles they offered to Alix, but insinuating smiles. One of them made a quick motion with his tongue. Elizabeth blushed. She dropped her eyes and caught sight of one of the men brushing the tight fabric of his crotch.

The men passed, suggestive laughter trailing behind them like smoke. "Home." Elizabeth exhaled sharply. "I want to go home."

"Another half mile to go," Alix responded, her voice as falsely pleasant as the expression frozen on her face.

"Can't we simply cut across the park?"

"And have these creatures believe they forced us to retreat? I think not."

An open carriage carrying three young ladies, two young men, and an elderly chaperone rolled toward them. One of the young ladies appeared to be relating a story with great animation; the ribbons on her hat fluttered with the intensity of her tale. As the carriage passed, the young people erupted in laughter and the chaperone swiveled her head and glared at Elizabeth.

"I'm ready to admit defeat, only let us go *now*."

"This ride was your choice," Alix said, "You must see it through."

Elizabeth had the distinct feeling her sister-in-law was referring to more than their turn through the park.

"Merde." Alix swore sharply. Her gray eyes cut to a figure in navy and red trotting toward them.

"Are you sure it's not too late to cut through the park?"

"Far too late," Alix hissed through a stiff smile, then returned Anne Dinsmore's merry wave.

"Alix, Elizabeth, delightful to see you," Anne greeted them. "Allow me to introduce my riding companion, Sir Edmond Bogglesworth."

Sir Edmund, a plump bespectacled man who resembled Humpty Dumpty, bowed his head and intoned, "Ladies, an honor."

Alix and Elizabeth returned the greetings and introductions.

"A lovely day for a ride isn't it?" Anne continued cheerfully. "Have you ever seen such a blue, blue sky? It's almost as if the clouds have been forbidden to appear."

"Indeed," Alix said.

Elizabeth found herself suddenly wishing for clouds, great, heavy, gray storm clouds that would mass over Anne Dinsmore's head and douse her. She imagined the plume on Anne's hat, drenched and dripping down her face and smiled—her first real smile since she'd entered the park.

Annoyance skittered across Anne's face. "You're looking well, Elizabeth," she said sharply.

"I'm feeling quite well," she replied, keeping the smile in her voice. "And you?"

Anne feigned a yawn, smothering it with a red-gloved hand, "Last night's party . . . so many details that required my personal attention."

"I can only imagine," Alix replied so pleasantly, it was almost impossible to detect the river of sarcasm flowing beneath her words.

"But I wanted everything to have that perfect Dinsmore touch." She smiled at Elizabeth.

"And it did, Anne, truly it did," Alix said dryly. "You have a gift for making an impression; it seems your hand is in everything." She smiled at Sir Edmund.

"I was saying to Lady Anne." Sir Edmund laughed cheerfully. "Lady Anne you outdid yourself last night. Everywhere at once, seeing to everyone's needs. I told her, 'Lady Anne, you mustn't overdo it; a delicate thing like yourself. Mustn't tire yourself out.' Why I knew a woman once who died of exhaustion."

All three women turned to stare at him.

He blinked and cleared his throat.

"Sir Edmund is a wise man," Alix said, breaking the silence. "It can be dangerous to overdo things." She leaned forward in her saddle. "And you do look a trifle drawn, Anne. I hear that tea-soaked cloths will do wonders for puffiness around the eyes."

Sir Edmund's round head bobbed above his lace stock. "Excellent properties tea has, most excellent. Made my fortune importing the stuff, don't you know? Family used to be sheepherders, can you imagine?"

For a moment, Lady Anne looked as if she could imagine Sir Edmund chopped, dried, and boiled. "Sir Edmund has considerable properties in London and in the country."

"For your flocks?" Elizabeth couldn't resist inquiring.

Sir Edmund chuckled. "No indeed; my family moved out of that business. Decades ago of course, Tudor times. You see first we . . ."

"Such a shame," Anne spoke swiftly to sever a discussion of her companion's involvement in trade, however many centuries removed, "that James couldn't join us this morning."

Elizabeth stiffened.

"But he had so many things to do. An appointment with his tailor, shopping for handkerchiefs." She waved a gloved hand. "Such a busy, busy man, my brother." Her pale blue eyes rested on Elizabeth and she smiled. "If I see him this evening, before he goes out, shall I give him your regards?"

"That woman," Elizabeth exclaimed, striding into the sitting room where they had been sewing earlier, "is *impossible*! I'd like to . . . to . . ." Her eyes caught a glint of silver at the corner of Alix's embroidery hoop. "I'd like to stitch her thin lips *shut*."

"Is that all?" asked Alix, eyeing a pair of silver scissors. "Wouldn't you prefer to cut her tongue out first?"

Elizabeth started to laugh, a laugh she couldn't control, a laugh that rolled, and twisted and turned into a cry. Her back lost its starch, her shoulders slumped, she dropped into a chair and let tears flood her palms.

"*I instructed you* not to let Elizabeth stray from the house today." Rafe's voice was calm, but sparks flared in his eyes. "I *told you* no good could come of it."

"I know you did and I had every intention of obeying . . . but Elizabeth . . ." Alix stopped pacing.

"Convinced you otherwise," he said, frustration threading his voice.

She nodded. "She was so restless, and she kept glancing out the window, checking the front drive."

"For Dinsmore, no doubt."

"I thought perhaps a quick turn in the park might help her see things more clearly."

"I gather it did," he said grimly.

"It was awful, Rafe, you cannot imagine. She was cut directly five times—the last time by some snippy miss from the country."

The muscles around his jaw tensed.

"And the men, if you could have seen how they leered at her. One of them, one had the nerve to gesture . . . with his tongue."

Rafe drew back his chair, and patted his knee. "Come sweetheart." His arm curved around her as she settled in his lap. He wrapped one of her long mahogany curls around his fingers. "And Elizabeth, how did she bear up?"

"With tremendous dignity. You would have been proud, Rafe."

"If only she'd exercised such dignity earlier," he said bitterly. *I'd like to beat those upstart young bucks to a bloody pulp . . .*

"What's done is done, Rafe, you and I know better than most that the past cannot be mended. The question before us now is, how shall we make the best of this disaster?"

"What do you propose?"

"I think Louisa was right. Elizabeth should return to the countryside until this scandal has run its course."

"Scandals in the ton never run their course. If Elizabeth leaves town, speculation might take another, more malicious turn." His hand strayed to his wife's belly. "I will not have the family name damaged any further; I will see an end to it."

Alix covered his hand with hers and looked up at him. "Will you demand that James Dinsmore offer for her then?"

"James Dinsmore," he spat the name as if something foul had crossed his tongue. "Have that foul libertine *profit* from disgracing my sister? He'd squander her dowry on waistcoats, gloves, and baubles for other women. I swear to you Alix, I will do everything in my power to make certain James Dinsmore never lays a hand on my sister again."

James hadn't the slightest intention of dining with Anne. After giving instructions to have his purchases delivered, he headed directly for his private club. The setting wasn't quite as rich as White's or Boodles, but then neither was the play at cards or dice. It was exclusive, and quiet, and the conversation more likely to run to economics and political events abroad than to the latest social scandals at home.

He inhaled sharply as he mounted the steps; he could imagine what Anne would have to say about her ride in the park, a malicious stream of gossip about Elizabeth that would doubtless continue through the soup, meat, sweets, and brandy. He understood her need to savor her revenge, he thought, as he handed his tricorne and cape to a servant. But he was plagued by concerns about Elizabeth's welfare. He'd debated with his internal misgivings—he didn't dare call them conscience—throughout the day.

Elizabeth might be young and inexperienced, but she knew the rules of decorum—*every* young girl entering her first season had such things pounded into her head. Often, he reflected, to the exclusion of all other practical thought. She *knew* his reputation.

James gestured for a servant to bring him a brandy. He was a wastrel, a libertine, a worthless cad. She had no business entering a secluded library with him. He took a swallow of brandy. She had no business kissing him. Foolish chit, she had no business *trusting* him. What had she been thinking? Everyone knew he wasn't worth a damn.

Several young men, clustered around a table scattered with glasses and bottles of wine, waved him over. *They'd be talking about the revolutionary tribunals in France*; he wasn't in the mood. A pinched-looking gentleman glanced up from a heavy tome he was perusing and nodded. *Morton, he'd want to discuss the trial and execution of Louis XVI.* A useless exercise, what was done, was done. A heavyset gentleman, elegantly clad in gray silk, caught his eye and crooked a thick finger. *Lord Grenville*, a politician with a notoriously jaundiced view of the world. James smiled, just the sort of company he required.

"James." Grenville gestured toward an empty chair. "Good of you to join me. Wasn't sure I'd find you here this evening."

"Indeed?" James arched a brow. "And why ever not?"

"You're quite the talk of the town today. Is it true you led Lady Elizabeth Harcrest astray?"

"Grenville, old man, I'd have thought such gossip was beneath you."

"I don't spread the stuff, my boy." Something like a smile curved Grenville's thin lips. "But I do collect it."

"Why should it interest you if I dally with a lady?"

"I understand you did much more than dally . . ." He waved a heavy hand. "But that is not what interests me. I'm curious as to why you did it. Moreham's a powerful man, with powerful friends."

James shrugged. "The lady's charms are powerful too." He took a sip of brandy. "Have you seen her?"

"I have. She's charming. But there's equally lovely and far less dangerous prey to be found . . ."

"Perhaps I enjoyed the challenge."

"Then I've read you wrong, Dinsmore. You've always struck me as a man who does things for a purpose, not one of these fools who dash up the mountain simply because it's there."

James swirled the liquor in his glass, watching candle-light dance on amber. *Why did people suddenly seem determined to find the best in him?* "Damn waste of time, dashing up mountains. And to what end? Simply to beat one's chest about cresting the summit of a rock?"

Grenville took a slice of cheese from a platter in the middle of the table and chewed thoughtfully. "Seems like your sister Anne is doing much of the crowing over this particular accomplishment. Did you seduce Lady Elizabeth out of some notion of revenge?"

"I've no interest in revenge." James sipped his brandy and eyed Grenville over his glass.

Grenville matched his stare. "A sense of loyalty then?"

James's eyes glanced down. "That's a handsome waist-coat, Grenville. Who's your tailor?"

Grenville didn't waste a glance at his lavender and gray waistcoat. "No one nearly fashionable enough for you, Dinsmore." He chuckled, reaching for another slice of cheese. "I thought I had the right of it, you did seduce her for Anne." Grenville didn't wait for confirmation, and went on, "Noble, in a perverse sort of way. But now what, my friend, shall you offer for her?"

"Can you see me as a husband?" James plucked a slice of cheese from the platter. "I doubt Moreham could. He'd never have me."

"He nearly had your sister."

James stiffened. "But he did not, did he?" he said with a casualness he was far from feeling. "And if my sister is not good enough for his lordship, then for certes I am not good enough for his beloved sister."

Grenville dabbed at his lips with a napkin. "No jabs of conscience then, the girl is most likely ruined and you are content?"

"Damned if you aren't as inquisitive as Torquemada tonight." James swiveled in his chair, glass aloft. "The service in here is frightfully slow. A man could perish from thirst." A man in livery materialized from the shadows, decanter in hand and refilled his glass.

"It won't end here you know. Moreham will come after you."

"It is his right," James admitted, raising his glass to drink.

Grenville's thick arm shot out with surprising speed. He caught James by the wrist and held it. "I knew your father James, knew him well. Before his mind . . ."

"Drifted?" James offered, bitterness like dregs at the bottom of his voice.

"We served together in the war department, he had the sharpest mind of any man I ever met. You've a sharp mind yourself, if only you'd use it. If you get tired of playing at games, Dinsmore, you let me know." Grenville's grip tightened. "And if you ever need help, for God's sake, ask. I owe that much to your father."

James's blue eyes widened slightly. "Damned if everyone I meet these days doesn't seem to think I'm in need of saving."

Chapter 8

The members of White's were engaged in the usual: smoking, drinking, playing cards, placing bets. "I should call the bastard out and kill him. *Then* this whole mess would be over," Rafe said, expertly folding a deck of cards. When Rafe Harcrest was truly angry, he didn't drink, he stripped men of their fortunes. Cole cast a glance around the room. "I'm told the betting's running about even as to whether you'll do that, or demand he marry Elizabeth, make an honest woman out of her."

"My sister *is* an honest woman," Rafe snapped, "that's her damn problem. Too honest. Sees no harm in people, no harm in doing what she calls 'experiencing' life—"

"Admit it my friend," Cole interrupted, "Elizabeth has the high spirits of your late father and brother George. She's had them since she was a child. Since she's been under your care these last thirteen years, you've been determined to smother them." Cole raised his hand to silence a protest. "I thought you might have learned your lesson with Alix.

Women are like high-spirited fillies, the more you rein them in, the more they want to run . . ."

"I tried to ease up on Elizabeth, and look where it's gotten me. Did you see that scandalous rag this morning?"

Cole pursed his lips.

"Of course you did, admit it Davenport, the whole town's seen it." He nodded towards a cluster of foppishly dressed men. "Weatherby there had the nerve to praise my sister's *literary interests.* That man can barely read, someone must have read it to him."

"Most likely Anne Dinsmore."

"Damn it, it wasn't *Anne* Dinsmore who had my sister's gown around her elbows!"

"But it *was* Anne who was trumpeting the news about Hyde Park. You should have seen her this afternoon, dressed in a red and blue riding habit. You'd have sworn she was from some regimental band."

"You were in the park this afternoon?"

Cole nodded.

"Then you saw how Elizabeth was greeted?"

Cole nodded again, his face grim.

"I had hoped Alix was exaggerating." Rafe drummed his fingers in an angry tattoo on the table. "I will not let him marry her."

"Has Dinsmore asked?"

"Elizabeth imagines that he will, but he hasn't had the decency to show his face at my door. Which makes him either a conscienceless rake or inexcusable coward."

"James may not be entirely respectable, Moreham, but the Dinsmore family name is. And he is heir to a dukedom."

"Heir to a madman. Heir to an impoverished, entailed, obscure estate."

"One might have said something similar about you thirteen years ago."

"But I didn't go about frittering what was left, and I

didn't ruin innocent young girls to bolster my fortune. I worked to repair it." Rafe's drumming fingers clenched.

Cole leaned forward, his voice very low. "And some might say a peer working in the French textile trade to rebuild his fortune is an even greater scandal than a peer seducing an heiress."

"I will not apologize for engaging in trade."

"But you're not likely to trumpet it about either."

"So you think I should force Dinsmore to come up to scratch." Rafe changed the subject.

"I think you have little choice. A duel might restore your honor, and perhaps, on the surface, Elizabeth's, but it will not stop the talk. You could do worse than James Dinsmore."

Rafe snorted his disbelief.

"At least Elizabeth likes him."

"For his pretty blue eyes and his blond tresses. A schoolgirl's crush." Rafe's long fingers toyed with the stem of his untouched wineglass. "My sister imagines she sees beyond a pretty face, and believes there is goodness in a heart that has none."

"And what if she is right? What if she can find goodness in James Dinsmore?"

Wine splashed redly on Rafe's fingers. "And what if she is wrong?"

"Then she has a marriage no worse than any other arranged marriage in the ton."

"Where to sir?" the coachman asked, as he swung open the carriage door.

James paused, feeling the cool night air sweep over him. He hadn't really considered his destination. It was 11:30, too late for the theater, too early to go home. He hadn't the funds to gamble, and he was in no mood for a brothel. He mentally reviewed the parties whose doors would be open to him that evening.

Dull, duller, dullest.

Particularly without the intriguing prospect of Elizabeth Harcrest's attendance.

Little chance she'd show her face after what had happened. *What he'd done to her* . . . The night air suddenly seemed damp and heavy. James squared his shoulders as if to toss it off. Christ, but he was becoming maudlin about the girl. "Get a grip on yourself man," he muttered.

"Beg pardon, sir?" There was a hint of surprise in the coachman's respectful tone.

"Lady Lambert's." James named the place he was most likely to find Lounsbury and Ashton. Mindless chatter, that's what he required, talk of horseflesh and whores. No more pensive ponderings about the worth of his soul or redeeming his future. He climbed into the carriage and the coachman swung the door shut behind him. James leaned out the window. "Lady Lambert's. Do you know the address?"

The coachman nodded, "Yes, sir."

"Then let's put some speed into it." James rapped the door with a gloved hand for emphasis.

"So I said to Hardy, if you're not going to take the bloody horse back, the least you can do is provide the funds to nurse the damn nag back to health . . ." Lounsbury, as usual, was lamenting his difficulties with a recent purchase.

"Quite right, Lounsbury."

Odd, James reflected, how some people could continue the same conversation night after night. He supposed Lounsbury found it comforting, the mental equivalent of a favorite pair of worn slippers. He focused on the stripes in Lady Lambert's ballroom wallpaper. *Were there thirty-two or thirty-three?*

"I say," Ashton hurried up to them, face flushed with brandy and dancing, "that Neville-Smythe chit is a sprightly dancer."

"Skin seems a bit spotty," Lounsbury, at last dropping the

subject of horses, lifted a lorgnette to examine the girl in question.

"Who says I was looking at her face?" Ashton giggled.

Lounsbury let his eyeglass drift lower. "My *word.*" He nudged James. "Take a look Dinsmore."

"A mere *Miss* Neville-Smythe won't catch Dinsmore's eye," said Ashton. "I hear James has been after nobler sport."

"Indeed, I've heard much the same. Lady Elizabeth Harcrest! Dinsmore, you dog."

It was precisely the type of moment Anne would relish: Elizabeth Harcrest's reputation being dragged through the muck. Only James felt it was himself that was suddenly immersed in filth. He had the urge to leap from his chair and plunge himself into a bath, a very deep one.

"Lady Elizabeth? Isn't she the one whose brother you said would have my arm if I asked her to dance?" Ashton leered. "You seem to have both arms Dinsmore, and from what I hear, you did much more than dance with her."

With expensive soap.

"You've been most closed-lipped on the subject Dinsmore." Lounsbury turned his eyeglass full force on James. "Do tell."

And a scrub brush. A stout one.

"A gentleman must never kiss and tell," he said quietly.

"What a rubbishy cliché!" Lounsbury hooted. "A gentleman doesn't make love to an earl's daughter in the library either!"

Lounsbury was right. No amount of soap and brushes would scrub his honor clean. He might mouth the code of a gentleman, but he'd lost all sense of how to behave as one.

"Come on, spill the juicy details." Lounsbury leaned close.

"Tell, Dinsmore, tell," Ashton encouraged him.

"Lounsbury," James said softly, as he rose gracefully from his chair, "as you so astutely pointed out, my behavior last night was unworthy of a gentleman. Nevertheless, Elizabeth Harcrest is still every inch a lady."

He'd made up his mind.

He would ask for Elizabeth's hand in marriage.

A bit late, true, but it would repair some of the damage he'd done to the girl's reputation. He would tell Anne as soon as she returned from whatever affair she was attending. James settled into the most comfortable armchair he could find in the sitting room outside his sister's bedchamber—damned difficult since most of them were delicate straight-backed things. She'd protest, of course, but she'd gotten more than her pound of flesh. . . . It was time to put the scandal to rest. . . .

"You must be drunk."

James awoke to find his sister leaning over him, inhaling sharply.

"I haven't had a drop since I left Lady Lambert's." He yawned, fumbling for a watch hanging from a fob beneath his green and gold striped waistcoat. "It's four-thirty now, so that was at least"—he yawned again—"four hours ago. I've been waiting for you."

"You might have come with me. The Lindsay's card party would have been far more amusing had you attended. Though we did have ourselves quite a laugh over poor Moreham's predicament."

There was the sound of a door slamming several floors below them, echoing up the corridors like an angry wooden slap. The house should have been quiet; most of the servants had gone to bed ages ago. Apparently a few of the clumsier ones were moving about.

"I find myself increasingly uncomfortable with the things being said about Elizabeth," James began.

"Nothing is being said about her that isn't true, brother."

Somewhere in the house, feet pounded on stairs. Pitiful

really, the performance of the serving class when they weren't paid regularly. James glanced quickly at Anne, who also looked irritated by all the noise. Then he continued, "You know she didn't expect to become a sideshow for gossipy matrons, or a nasty item in the latest London broadsheet."

"But *you* knew, James. Well ahead of time. It's a bit late to be cultivating a conscience—"

"I'm seeking to retrieve my honor." The words sounded hollow even to his own ears.

"I thought you were helping to retrieve *mine*."

"I thought I was too, Anne." Silence settled over the room. *How could he explain?* He spoke again, after several long moments. "This thing has gone too far. Elizabeth didn't cause any harm to you. Moreham's the one who led you to believe he'd offer for you, then scurried off . . ."

Anne held up her hand. "You needn't elaborate, James. I know precisely what he did. I'm the one who has to listen to snide insinuations whenever he appears with that French creature. *I* will be the one who decides when the Harcrests have suffered sufficiently."

As if to emphasize her words, the loud bang of a door being flung open resounded down the hall. He'd have to have a talk with the housekeeper about the servants in the morning . . . unless of course his father was wandering. He pushed the thought from his mind. Now was not the time to wonder whether dementia, like the Dinsmore title, would be passed down.

"Consider this then." James swept a stray lock of hair off his forehead. "Consider how humiliated Rafe will be when I offer for his sister. No one else will. What man would want my leavings? And her dowry, all that Harcrest money, will be in Dinsmore coffers. Isn't that what you wanted from the first, Moreham's money? You'll have achieved all the things you set out to when you first set your cap on the earl."

Anne stiffened. She would *not* have achieved everything.

She would still be unmarried. She'd still be the source of whispers and false pity: poor Anne, another season and still no husband. Still be prey to clumsy attempts at matchmaking; friends seating her at supper parties next to their half-witted cousins and bumbling brothers, men who could barely get a fork to their mouths, much less make intelligent conversation.

"You won't marry that girl," she said, her voice rising. "I won't permit it." If James married her, Elizabeth would find a husband in her first season! No standing in corners, watching others dance, pretending to be disinterested. No waiting to see who would be left to take her in to supper. The whole scandal would fade from people's minds. She could just imagine the gossip then! *Poor Anne, even her rakehell brother has found a wife, such a shame about her . . .*

"Might I remind you Anne"—James drew himself up, his voice as cold as winter—"that I do not require your permission to wed Elizabeth Harcrest?"

And from Anne's open bedchamber door came an even colder voice.

"But you do require mine," Rafe Harcrest said. "And you and the rest of the devil's minions will skate in hell before I grant it."

Chapter 9

"*Moreham! How* dare *you enter my personal apart-*ments uninvited?"

"After the injury you and your brother have done to my sister, Anne, there is little I would not dare to restore her honor."

"Her *honor* Moreham?" Anne's shock faded, and as her color returned, she gave a brittle laugh. "Elizabeth was an unruly child, and now she is an unruly young woman. If it had not been James in the library, mark my words, it would soon have been another."

"But it was James." Rafe strode across the cream and gold Aubusson carpet, until he reached Dinsmore. The two men stood, face-to-face. "And it is James who owes me satisfaction."

"A duel?" Anne asked, voice full of scorn. "Don't be *absurd*, Moreham. How barbaric, how *old-fashioned*. Do you think waving pistols at dawn will stop people from talking?"

"It will give them something different to discuss," Rafe

said, never taking his eyes from James. "Your brother's death."

"You will not kill him," she hissed, "he will never accept such an outrageous challenge."

"Name your second, Moreham," James replied coolly.

"Davenport. And yours?"

"Grenville."

"Lord Grenville?" Rafe arched a brow. "Ashton and Lounsbury will be devastated at being passed over. Grenville is far more respectable a choice than I would have expected from you."

"That's always been your problem, Moreham, so set in your expectations, so certain you see the right of things—"

"I see the right of you, or rather I should say, the wrong of you."

"Naturally, you've always looked for the worst in me. And in Elizabeth," he added softly.

"Don't speak her name Dinsmore."

"She wanted him, Moreham, think on *that*." Anne's voice was vicious. "I saw her. *Everyone* saw her. She—"

"Enough, Anne," James said firmly, never taking his eyes from Rafe's.

"Choose your weapons, Dinsmore."

"I've heard you're an excellent marksman, Moreham."

"You've heard correctly." Rafe smiled, a curve of the lips that was anything but warm. "I take it then that your choice will be swords?"

"Do you take me for a coward?"

"I take you for a dishonorable cur."

James's smile matched Rafe's. "I choose pistols."

"Pity, I should have preferred to slice you with a sword, to leave your flesh as tattered as your honor."

"You're an animal, Moreham, a bloodthirsty animal!" Anne grabbed Rafe's arm. "It's no wonder you're so at home with the French. To imagine I ever considered you for a husband!"

"Even more incredible," Rafe said, removing her hand, "is that I ever considered you for a wife."

"Leave my sister be, Moreham," James demanded. "Whatever has gone before, this quarrel is now between the two of us. If you wish to fight with swords, so be it." He dipped his head, his tone deceptively polite. "Never let it be said that I denied satisfaction to a Harcrest."

Rafe inhaled sharply. "I will send word of the appointed place and time. You'll understand if I do not wish either of you a good night."

"You'll be the laughingstock of the ton, Rafe Harcrest," Anne called after him as he strode towards the door.

"Perhaps." His voice was cold. "But I promise you, Anne. You won't be laughing with them."

The slamming of the door echoed throughout the room.

When it faded away, Anne faced her brother. "I'll find a way to stop to this James, I promise you. I know the right people, I will speak with them."

"You've spoken with enough people, Anne." James's mouth was a tight line. "I've agreed to meet Moreham and I will."

"But you could be killed!"

"It's reassuring to know you have so much faith in me, Anne."

"It's not that I don't have faith in you, it's just that . . ."

"It's just that you don't have sufficient faith," he finished the sentence for her. "Apparently a widely-held opinion of me."

"Not one that I share," she insisted.

"Ah." His tone was mocking. "But I do. I am thinking it might be better for everyone involved if Moreham did kill me. The earl would have his satisfaction, Elizabeth her honor restored."

Anne hugged herself. "And what about us, what would we have?"

"Why Anne, you'd have everyone's sympathy and I . . ."

His customary expression of studied boredom faltered. He looked momentarily perplexed. "Why I suppose I'll be rid of this damnably unfamiliar sense of guilt."

She was excited, dressed for a party. Everything looked perfect, she knew it. She entered a ballroom. People started to laugh. She asked them why but they turned away. Again and again. She searched desperately for someone who would talk to her. And then she saw James! But he was far away, she couldn't reach him. She fought through the crowd to find him . . . there he was! Holding out his arms to her! Then he turned and swept up another woman—

Elizabeth sat bolt upright in bed, clutching at her chest, with a pain as fierce as if her heart had been torn in two. She wouldn't let herself think this way. James Dinsmore would come for her. He would. Something special had happened between them in the library, just as she had always known it would. She knew he wouldn't realize it right away—he was so jaded about love, about life, her James. She wanted to explain it to him, what she felt for him and why she had gone into the library with him. But everything had happened too fast. And then the door had opened.

She could tell by the light in the room that it was late; much later than she usually rose. She'd had such trouble falling asleep. She would dress carefully and she would wait. She'd be more patient today and she wouldn't go out. She had no desire to face more snubs.

When she entered the breakfast room, wincing at the brightness of the sunlight that spilled from the long-paned windows, she found Alix sitting by herself at the table. "Good day, Alix," Elizabeth said, motioning for a maid to bring her some chocolate.

Alix nodded stiffly.

"I see Rafe has gone out already."

She nodded again.

Alix was never particularly talkative in the morning, but she usually could muster a greeting. *Was Alix snubbing her, too?* Elizabeth tried again. "Has he gone riding?"

"He's gone to Monsieur d'Elon's."

"The fencing master? It's been ages since he's practiced with the sword." *Thank God, Alix was talking to her!* Elizabeth took a slice of bread from a silver basket and began buttering it.

"He's not practicing."

Elizabeth looked up from her bread. "Then whatever is he doing there?"

"Preparing for a duel," Alix said harshly.

The butter knife clattered against the plate as it slipped from Elizabeth's fingers. "James Dinsmore?"

Alix nodded again, but this time her eyes focused on Elizabeth. They were full of pain and anger.

"I'll talk to him, Alix." The words tumbled out. "I'll make him stop, I'll make him see it's not necessary . . . I'll tell him it was all my fault, that I'm sorry, so, so sorry. I—"

"It's too late for all that, there's nothing you can say or do now that will change his mind." Her voice was bitter. "I was up half the night trying to convince him not to risk his life for . . ."

"For me."

"He said it was a matter of honor."

"But I am the one who should pay the price. Not Rafe, not you, Alix . . . Alix, I never meant—"

Alix held up a hand. "I understand. You never meant to cause harm. But you did. And it cannot be undone."

"I am the one who should pay the price," Elizabeth repeated.

"You will." Alix's eyes fell, and her hand drifted towards her belly. "We all will."

* * *

Rafe's arm swept up and his blade thrust towards Cole's neck. Cole parried the blade sweeping downward towards Rafe's belly. Rafe parried. The blades met on guard. The two men stepped back, circling each other warily. Both were breathing hard, beneath their fencing vests their shirts clung like second skins to their sweat-drenched bodies. Rafe lunged upward to the right, to the left and then towards the middle. Cole countered all three, and lunged forward, his blade striking Rafe on the hip.

"Enough," Monsieur d'Elon, a tightly compact little man dressed in scarlet, clapped his hands. "Salute and retire gentleman."

"Have you had enough?" Cole asked Rafe.

"Have you?"

"You both have." D'Elon clapped again.

They saluted and sheathed their swords.

Cole clapped Rafe on the back. "Monsieur was trying to save you embarrassment, my friend."

Rafe raised an eyebrow. "Monsieur was trying to spare your pride to ensure you would return and continue to squander your fortune on lessons . . ."

D'Elon himself interrupted, "Monsieur believes you *both* are excellent swordsmen, well-matched, and hopes you both return to demonstrate to the rest of his students how the art of fencing should be practiced." He swept an arm towards a table set with pitchers of ale and glasses. "My lords," he smiled, *"en garde."*

Cole filled two glasses and held one out to Rafe. "To more such bouts," he said smiling, but his eyes were grim.

"Do you doubt it?" Rafe took a deep swallow.

"I do not doubt that you are the better man." Cole lowered his voice so their conversation would not be heard above the din of swords and the occasional coaching shouts of *tierce, quatre, en garde*. "But such encounters at dawn have been known to go amiss."

Rafe pulled a kerchief from his waistcoat pocket and

mopped his brow. "That's why I've asked you to be my second. You'll keep a wary eye on him."

Cole nodded. "And kill him if he kills you."

"No," Rafe said firmly, "not if he fights with honor."

"After the way he's behaved towards Elizabeth, do you imagine the man *has* any honor?" Cole continued without waiting for answer. "It's a shame he didn't choose pistols, then you could have shot him through the heart and have done with it." He smiled ruefully. "But then he's probably heard of your reputation with pistols and hoped you'd prove less skilled with the blade."

Rafe shook his head. "He did choose pistols. I asked him to alter his selection."

"He must have been relieved."

"In truth," Rafe said, curiosity in his voice, "he didn't seem to care."

"I've heard he's a passable swordsman."

Rafe shrugged. "Then it's to be hoped you've found a passable physician to attend us."

"Better than passable, the finest surgeon in London."

"Very good. And there are some papers I'd like you to look over, as well."

"What sort of papers?" Cole asked.

"I've made you executor of my will."

"Haven't you some Harcrest relative who'd be better suited?"

"I can see you're honored," Rafe said dryly.

"I am, Moreham, indeed, I am, but your business dealings are, how shall I put this, rather complex?"

"Afraid to soil your hands with *work*, Davenport?"

"That's not it, and you know it. I respect what you've done, Moreham, respect it a great deal. I'd feel dreadful if I ran it all into the ground. I've not got the sharpest head for business, you know. Haven't got your patience for long-range planning."

"Not to worry, my friend," Rafe replied. "I've made

arrangements for the business. It's my family I'd like you to keep an eye on. Louisa and Elizabeth—"

"*Elizabeth?* Upon further reflection, I might have better luck overseeing the Byzantine workings of your financial empire—"

"Nevertheless," Rafe continued, "if anything happens to me, I'm entrusting you with the guardianship of Elizabeth, Alix, and the babe."

"Elizabeth is *with child*?"

"Davenport." Rafe shook his head. "Don't make me challenge you to a duel as well. My sister's virtue is intact."

"Then what . . . then who?" He stared at Rafe. "You're going to be a father!"

Rafe smiled, his first genuine smile since the night of the Dinsmore's assembly.

"Damn it all man, you should have told me sooner." Cole raised his glass. "To your health and to Alix's." He took a swallow of ale and raised his glass for another toast. And then he paused. "Moreham, if Alix is carrying your child, perhaps it might be better if you reconsidered your challenge to Dinsmore."

"Do you think I will lose?"

"I think if Elizabeth married . . ."

"James Dinsmore?" Rafe made no effort to conceal his disgust.

"It wouldn't be the worst thing that could happen . . ."

"I cannot imagine anything worse."

Chapter 10

James ordered the footmen to collect mirrors and bring them up to the empty room that had once served as the Dinsmore's nursery. The furniture had long ago been sold as a sop to the omnipresent creditors. He now stood before their reflections, critically assessing the position of his hands and his feet. He lunged, over and over, until the movement was as fluid as a dancer's.

There was a time when he'd fenced every day.

In his early twenties, he'd developed a taste for other men's wives, and thought it prudent to keep his sword and his skills sharp. And indeed, there'd been a few discrete duels. James saluted himself in the mirror and lunged. Though he'd found that most men preferred not to risk life, or at least limb, to salvage the already sunken reputations of their wives.

James parried up, over, and then down, frowning at a weakness he perceived in his grip. He adjusted his hand. Rafe Harcrest, Earl of Moreham it appeared, was cut from a different sort of cloth. *Cut . . . from a different cloth.* It was an odd choice of words. But he'd heard the queerest rumor that Moreham had refurbished his fortune by importing textiles from France. Not just investing, as proper gentlemen might, but setting up a business and overseeing it himself. Anne had dismissed the rumors, but then, he mused, she would have had to. His sister would never have considered marrying the earl if he'd truly soiled his aristocratic hands with trade.

James parried low. When he'd first heard the rumors, he'd felt a glimmer of admiration for Moreham. The man hadn't taken the standard course of action, hadn't sought to marry money, or win it at the gaming tables, or set his family heirlooms on the block. He glanced distastefully at the mirrors. In reflections he could see the emptiness of the room from every angle. And in the center of the room, in the center of every mirror, was the reflection of an even emptier man.

Perhaps he should allow Rafe Harcrest to kill him. He'd meant what he'd said to Anne; it might be the best thing for everyone involved. Rafe would have his satisfaction, Elizabeth would have her honor restored, Anne would have the sympathy of the ton, and he'd simply have an end to things. No more worrying about his father's madness or whether it would become his own. No more wondering about when or if he'd inherit the title and what pathetic little of the Dinsmore fortune would remain when the old man died. No more fretting about Anne, nor wondering how to protect her from the petty cruelties of the ton. A bitter smile twisted his handsome face; he had to admit, he wasn't certain that it was his sister who needed protecting.

James studied his appearance in the mirrors. A tall slender man dressed in the height of fashion stared critically back at him. "Popinjay," he muttered.

I am what you made me.

"I didn't have any choice, what else could I have been?"

A man? the arched brows seemed to inquire. *A man like Rafe Harcrest? A soldier, an adventurer, a businessman.*

"He was a second son, he didn't have my responsibilities."

What responsibilities? The eyes swept his silken suit, his Holland linen. *Seducing other men's wives? Drinking till all hours?*

"At least I don't gamble."

Only because you haven't the blunt.

"I should have married for money." He sighed, looking away.

If only he'd settled down with some wealthy heiress, it would have solved so many problems. His face and figure had attracted nearly as many as his future title. Why had he looked past the eager young things to dally with the safely-marrieds? He'd never touched a well-bred virgin. Not until Elizabeth. When they'd been discovered, why hadn't he declared for her, and forced Moreham's hand?

Elizabeth was wealthy. She was titled. She was beautiful. Lord knew she was exciting. Why had he delayed? *Because of Anne. Anne wants Elizabeth destroyed.*

Looking again at his reflection, his eyes mocked him. *You've ignored Anne's wishes often enough when it suited you. What's the real reason?*

He raised his sword, whirled to his left, slashed up to the right, down to the left, across to the right, then lunged for his reflected heart. Steel tip quivered against polished glass. A scratch appeared.

I'd make a wretched husband.

It lengthened.

Moreham wouldn't have me.

Stretched from reflected heart to reflected belly.

Elizabeth deserves better.

At the sound of clapping hands, James withdrew his sword. In the mirror, he could see his sister standing a short distance behind him. She looked like a malevolent angel on his shoulder.

"Congratulations, brother dear," she said, "it appears you've bested a shadow of yourself."

Dear Lord Dinsmore . . .

Too distant. Elizabeth crumpled the paper and pulled another sheet from the box on her desk. *Dear James.* Was that too personal? She crumpled the sheet, pulled out another. Her lessons in deportment had never covered the proper address for a man with whom one had disgraced oneself at a ball. Her fingers tightened on her quill. *My Dearest Lord Dinsmore.* She stared at the neat script. Was he hers? Was he dear? She didn't know what he was to her, or she to him.

All she knew was that she needed to contact him.

Good manners said she should inquire after his health, ask after his family, comment on the weather. How absurd! She could almost imagine words forming on the page. *My Dearest Lord Dinsmore, It was delightful to see you last evening . . .* and to kiss you, and to feel your hands caress my skin. She inhaled deeply. *I enjoyed myself immensely . . .* enjoyment, an understatement; she couldn't begin to describe the sensations that had swept through her body. *I was quite devastated to leave . . .* another understatement. Was there a word stronger than devastation, one that might describe the unutterable humiliation of being discovered half-clad by the matrons of the ton? Of being forced to leave by the servants' stairs and then having to face the justifiable fury of your brother?

I hope this letter finds you well. And that my brother doesn't kill or maim you tomorrow at dawn. *And that you are . . .* What? she wondered. Pining for me? Wishing you could be with me? At least thinking of me? Was he thinking of her at all? Or was she just one night's amusement? Was he laughing at her, perhaps with his friends, or worse, with Anne? Why hadn't he come?

I have been out of sorts lately and my doctor has insisted that I remain at home, abed. I'm desperately unhappy, I've let everyone around me down, and I dare not show my face abroad for fear of being snubbed.

I should welcome a visit from you. How pathetic. She, who'd been courted by so many eligible young men, was pursuing a completely ineligible one who, for all she knew, didn't want to see her.

She tore the blank sheet into strips.

What was the point of writing a letter to James?

She needed to *talk* to him. Not to discuss what had occurred at the ball, she told herself. Certainly not to try and gauge from his expressions if he had any feelings for her. Nothing so shallow or selfish, she reassured herself firmly. She needed to see James Dinsmore on a matter of life and death. She must convince him to refuse to meet her brother.

Rafe was far too stubborn. He wouldn't even discuss the duel with her. Said it was no business of hers. And Alix was no help. Alix had said it was her duty to stand by her husband's decision. Guilt clawed her stomach at the thought of the pain she was causing her sister-in-law. *Of course* she'd known she was taking a chance slipping off with James, but she'd imagined that she'd face any consequences alone. Not that she'd given it a *great deal* of thought. . . . She'd never really believed they'd be discovered.

She crumpled the strips of paper and dropped them to the floor. She checked the clock on her desk. A rosy-cheeked shepherd held the time for a golden-haired shepherdess. Half-past four. She stared out the window at the street beyond the gates. She *could* tell her mother she wished to go shopping, but then Louisa would insist she, or Alix, or a groom, or a footman, or a maid accompany her. And the Dinsmores? How would she get past the butler, the servants, past Anne, and find James? What if he wasn't there?

She glanced at the clock again, feeling unreasonably annoyed by the smiling shepherd and his insipid mistress. Two minutes had passed. She needed an idea. She thought of all the plays she'd seen, the books she'd read. Stories of women who'd disguised themselves as chambermaids, serving girls, gypsies, soldiers, or footmen. Absurd fictions. This was real life, and someone she loved might lose theirs if she didn't figure out a way to reach James Dinsmore—and soon.

"Lord Dinsmore, sir." Despite his years of strict training, the footman standing at the threshold of James's dressing room shifted nervously on his feet.

James's valet frowned. He had reminded the downstairs servants countless times that his master wasn't to be disturbed at his evening toilet—particularly on a night such as this. His master was stopping at White's. He must be perfectly dressed, not a hair out of place. It must be clear from his master's appearance that James Dinsmore took his dressing as seriously as his dueling.

"What is it?" the valet demanded.

"There's a lady at the servant's entrance, sir."

"Ladies do not use the servant's entrance." The valet gestured with his hand. "Send her away."

James turned to look at the footman. "How do you know she is a lady, Hobbes?"

The footman, encouraged that the master knew his name, took a step forward into the room. "Her clothes, sir, and her hands, and the way she carried herself, head up, like she'd never had to answer to no one."

"I see." He arched a brow. "And what does the lady want?"

"To see you, sir."

James nodded. "I see."

The footman glanced at the valet, who was fastening the buttons of James's brown and gold striped waistcoat, and lowered his voice. "She said she was your mistress, sir. And she's carrying a bundle she claims is your babe."

"I think I would know if I'd gotten one of my mistresses with child." James stood holding out his arms so the valet could slip on his amber velvet coat. "I can't imagine who the lady, or the child, might be."

"She was very insistent that she knew you, sir. Said you had to see her. Threatened to leave the babe on the stoop if you didn't."

The valet sniffed.

"On the stoop?" James straightened the cuff of his coat, glancing towards the long windows as he did so. "I suppose the evening is warm enough for a well-swaddled babe." He looked over at the footman. "The babe is well-swaddled?"

"Oh yes, sir, can't even see the little tyke's face, nor its mother's. She's wearing one of them cloaks with the great big framed hoods and a veil."

"The master would never dally with anyone so unfashionable," the valet muttered. "He is a man of principle."

"Thank you for you faith, Crandall."

"Not at all, sir."

James adjusted his other cuff. "Still, I doubt my sister would take kindly to a babe squalling on the doorstep, even if the brat is mine. Although if tonight should prove to be my last, she might appreciate a small piece of myself for the world to remember me by." He smiled wryly. *Rather fitting, that it should be a bastard.*

To the footman he said, "You may show her up."

The footman returned up the back stairs to James's private quarters, escorting a heavily cloaked and veiled woman. As the footman had said, she was clutching a bundle to her chest, a heavily swaddled bundle that squirmed and mewled in her arms.

James stood as the lady entered, waiting until his footman and valet left the room to speak. "Will you unveil, ma'am, so I might know with whom I am speaking?"

The woman shook her head.

"Come, now, my dear, if we have been on intimate enough terms to have produced a child together, you cannot be shy about baring so innocent a portion of your body as your face?"

The woman shook her head again.

"Perhaps this is a game. Your anger is piqued because it has been so long since we last parted that you have carried and borne a child. My child, I am given to understand. I suppose I am to guess, then, the identity of the lady hidden beneath the cloak." He began to circle her. "Let me see if I can recall the names of those lovelies who graced my bed last summer and last fall. He assessed her form, inhaled her perfume. "Too small to be Barbara, too tall to be Jane. Too shy to be Sophie." He heaved a mock sigh. "Lord knows she was inventive between the sheets." The figure twitched and he chuckled softly. "Far too impatient to be Arabella."

He came round to face her. "Alas, I'm afraid I shall need more clues. Shall I inspect the child and see if he, or is it a she, bears the mark of the mother?"

The woman clutched her baby more tightly, and the bundle gave a peculiar howl.

"You are the strangest of callers, my dear. You will not speak, you will not unveil. I doubt you've left a card. I am left with but one recourse." He stepped closer to her.

She stepped back.

"Come, come, you cannot be fearful of me. Of a friendly kiss." He caught her around the waist and drew her close against his chest. He lowered his lips to hers and kissed her through the fine mesh of her veil. "Just as I suspected." He traced the shape of her mouth with the tip of his tongue. "The taste of Elizabeth Harcrest."

She struggled in his arms. The bundle struggled in hers.

It dropped to the floor.

James stepped back, eyes fixed as the folds of swaddling fell in a heap, from which emerged a stout brown pug. The dog assessed the room with large liquid eyes, then sneezed to make his disgust clear.

"Oh my," he said. "I should hope our coupling produces more handsome offspring than that."

"Roland!" Elizabeth dropped to her knees. "Are you all right?" The pug took a step towards her, then sneezed again.

"He looks all right."

Elizabeth glared up at James. "I've no intention of coupling with you!"

He put a hand to his heart. "Then I fear it is I, rather than that dog—that is a dog isn't it?—who has been wounded."

Elizabeth rose to her feet. "Of course he's a dog! He's Madeleine's dog," she said as if that made everything clear. "And you will be wounded for certain if you don't call off this duel."

"I have no intention of calling off the duel."

"But why?"

He looked at her for a long moment. "It's a matter of honor."

"Ridiculous, it's a matter of pride between men. If anyone's honor is at stake it's mine, and I'd rather be disgraced than have either of you harmed."

He smiled, amused. "Most women would be delighted to have two men swinging swords about for the sake of their honor . . ."

"I'm not most women."

"So I'm beginning to understand."

"Then you'll do it," her voice rose expectantly. "You'll call off the duel?"

He folded his arms across his chest. "No."

"But—" she began.

"Elizabeth." His voice demanded that she listen. "Your brother has requested satisfaction, and while you may believe it is a matter of pride, I believe it is a matter of honor that I give it to him. Despite what others, and possibly you, may think, I do have a sense of honor."

"I know that James. I've known you forever. Can't you just apologize?"

He shook his head. "I'm afraid not."

"I think it takes courage for a man to say he's sorry publicly, greater courage than taking the field at dawn."

"The flattery's a nice touch, Elizabeth, but it won't work. You see," he said carefully, "I'm not sorry."

"Rafe was right? You *wanted* to see me disgraced?"

"No. Well, yes, perhaps, initially." He ran a hand through his hair, disarranging his valet's careful work. "Let me explain."

"You've nothing to explain. I understand perfectly; you're nothing more than your sister's puppet!"

"Good Lord woman, you leap from conclusion to conclusion like a child playing skipping games."

She drew back her veil and her enormous hood flopped back over her shoulders. "So now you're likening me to a child?"

"That's not what I meant at all." He paused, distracted by the accordion folds of fabric and ribbon collapsed about her shoulders. "Where did you get that ridiculous cape?"

"You are likening me to a child, and it was my mother's. We keep it about for the occasional masked ball."

"I take it back," he said, amusement and exasperation combining in equal parts in his voice. "You are a child, a wild child. Playing dress up in your mother's old clothes, appearing unchaperoned at the servant's entrance, claiming to be my mistress, claiming that that"——he cast a quick look about for the dog, who had settled into a plush brocade chair and was happily chewing the tassel of an embroidered pillow——"creature is my offspring."

"How else was I to see you?"

"You weren't *supposed* to see me!" He glanced around his dressing room, at his dressing gown draped over a chair, at two crumpled stocks on his dressing table and the discarded choice of ribbons for his braided queue. "At least not *here*. You were supposed to wait for me to call."

"I did. An entire day and a half."

"Such a paragon of patience," he said in a mocking tone. "I declare, Elizabeth, you'd rival a saint."

She placed her hands on her hips, parting her cloak in the process. "You of all people should know I am no saint."

His eyes swept over her breasts, the inviting curve of her lips. "Indeed, you are no saint, Elizabeth Harcrest," he said softly, "but verily you could tempt one."

She flushed, caught off guard. But only for the briefest moment. "And how would you know James Dinsmore? You're the furthest man from sainthood I've ever met."

"Most likely," he agreed.

"And exactly when did you plan to call upon me?" she demanded.

He frowned. "You Harcrests' can be damned persistent!"

"And you Dinsmores are damned evasive!"

"I hadn't decided."

She snorted. "You weren't coming."

"Why did you want me to call Elizabeth? What did you expect we would discuss? The weather, the latest fashions, drama, literature, philosophy, horseflesh, marriage?"

Her bravado seemed to fade with her color. "Do you want to marry me?" she asked in a voice that was nearly a whisper.

"Why do you even ask Elizabeth? What does it matter? Your brother has declared me unfit for it. It's among the reasons he wishes to kill me." He stepped closer to her and curled a finger under her chin. "Do you want to marry me, Elizabeth?"

"If it would put an end to the duel."

"How very noble," he said, caressing the line of her jaw. "Perhaps you could be a saint after all." His breath was warm against her lips. "The patron saint of desire." He kissed her.

It was Elizabeth who broke away first. "You won't fight him then. You'll call the duel off?"

"Don't you know," he said, a trace of regret in his teasing voice, "things never turn out well for saints?"

Chapter 11

She glanced out the window of the hired hack, staring absently at the traffic and pondering her next step. The pug lay contentedly in his swaddling bands, snoring on her lap. It had been a perfectly useless visit. She hadn't been able to persuade James to call off the duel. The only thing that had changed was James's pillow and carpet: Roland had chewed a hole and lifted his leg. Elizabeth scratched him behind his ears. "So glad someone enjoyed the outing."

The afternoon was deceptively light, the day looked as though it was still young, but time was passing quickly. Much too quickly. *Think, Elizabeth*, she exhorted herself. Rafe was always reprimanding her for not thinking things through; she'd show him this time. She'd find a way to make things right. She reviewed her visit with James. At least she had gotten to see him. She'd assured Louisa a visit to a bookseller would be just the thing to cheer her spirits. Louisa had eyed the old-fashioned cloak with curiosity, but believed her explanation: she needed to shield herself from potential snubs. Thank goodness her mother hadn't noticed the dog bundled in her shopping basket!

The corners of her mouth curved at the memory of the scene she'd made on the back stairs. She'd been part imperious, part hysterical, completely dramatic and, thinking back on it, the whole thing had been rather cathartic. Though she'd felt the oddest pang in her chest at how easily the Dinsmore's servants accepted the notion that an irate mistress of James's might appear on the doorstep.

She had a nagging suspicion she wasn't the first.

Her hand stilled on the pug's ears. He nudged her to indicate she should continue scratching. "Men," she muttered, ruffling the fur on the pug's square little head, "you're all the same, only thinking of your own pleasures." He sighed. Elizabeth thought of James kissing her through her veil. She closed her eyes. The pleasure, she knew, hadn't been only his.

She opened her eyes. She needed to *think*, not fantasize. Think about what he'd *said*, not what he'd done. She'd asked him to withdraw from the duel. He'd refused. He'd said he couldn't apologize, that he wasn't sorry. His words, the resolution in his tone, had struck her as odd, but caught up in the moment, she'd let slip the opportunity to question him. *Why* wasn't he sorry?

Had he thought he was avenging Anne's honor?

That would explain why he hadn't asked for her hand.

Though he'd *said* Rafe had called him unfit. Did that mean he'd asked and been refused? It was just the sort of pigheaded thing her brother might do. Reject an offer of marriage out of hand and never even tell her. And what would she have said? James's words whispered across her mind, as his lips had whispered across hers. *Do you want to marry me, Elizabeth?*

If it will put an end to the duel, she'd said. And then he'd kissed her again. Not a light, teasing kiss like the first, when he'd said she tasted of Elizabeth Harcrest.

His second kiss had been hard, demanding, enveloping. The feel of it lingered. Not just on her lips, but across her skin, and deeper still. It surged through her veins, pulsing in places that ached for his touch. Elizabeth shifted in her seat, her clothes suddenly too warm, too tight, too rough across her breasts and thighs. He'd called her the patron saint of temptation, and when he'd released her, he'd reminded her that saints must suffer. If there ever *was* such a saint, Elizabeth had a strong conviction she must have burned for her sins.

Alix sat up in the bed, her mahogany hair tangled loose about her shoulders. Her gray eyes were nearly as dark as the predawn light beyond the bedroom curtains. She watched as Rafe dressed himself. He slid a gray superfine coat over his broad shoulders, and swept his tawny hair free of his collar. He tied it back with a black silk ribbon. He hadn't called for a valet this morning. He hadn't wanted even the briefest moment of this time together disrupted.

"Must you go?" she asked, as he reached for his cravat.

"You know I must," he said glancing up as he tied it.

She swallowed the arguments she'd already exhausted. "Don't die."

He looked at her wrapped in the sheets of his great bed, the tangle of bedclothes around her mute witness to the love they'd made throughout the night. He shook his head. "Always so demanding."

Alix ignored his attempt at lightness. "I couldn't bear to live without you."

"I've no intention of dying." He leaned over and kissed her. "I love you." His eyes slid down to the slight curve of her belly. "And I've a son to raise."

"It might be a girl." Her hand rested on her belly. "You've read women wrong before."

Rafe's hands lingered on his wife's shoulders. "That's

why I know God won't dare give me another female. He knows I've got my hands full on that score."

She leaned into him and he kissed her again—a farewell kiss. He straightened, and his glance fell upon the pug, who, during the course of the night, had made his way into their bedchambers. He was happily snoring atop a pair of half-chewed slippers. He scowled. "The only reason I'm allowing that beast to remain is because he's got a cock and balls."

"I hate Anne Dinsmore." *More than the peasants that killed my father, more than the man who tried to kill me*, her eyes said.

"I know. But," he added in a voice grown suddenly cold, "I promise you, after this morning, all you will feel for her is pity."

She shook her head. "I will never forgive her for putting our happiness at risk."

"So long as you forgive Elizabeth." Alix didn't respond and Rafe wasn't sure she'd heard him. But he didn't repeat himself. He wasn't certain he wanted to hear her answer.

"Have you had much traffic this morning?" Rafe asked the gatekeeper.

"Just you and one other fancy-looking coach." He peered into the carriage. "Not as fancy as your rig, that's for sure. Don't mean to offend my lords, but it's my duty to ask, what brings you out into the park so early this morning?"

"Bird watching," Rafe said dryly.

"Bird watching?" The gatekeeper scratched his greasy gray head, pausing to examine something beneath his nails. "Never heard that one before. What kind of birds would that be?"

"Peacocks."

The gatekeeper shook his head with disgust. "Noisy screechy creatures, disturbing the peace . . ."

"I quite agree." Rafe drew a bag of coins from his waist-coat pocket, dangled it out the window. "The birds startle quite easily. I'd be most appreciative if you kept this entrance closed for the next hour or two so we can observe them undisturbed."

The gatekeeper stuck out a filthy hand. "Yes, sir, no problem there, my lords. You can count on me."

Rafe slid back against the cushions as the coach rolled on, his fingers drumming silently on his knee.

Cole, seated across from him, next to a pinch-faced surgeon, speculated that his friend was playing out the opening moves of the duel ahead. He turned his gaze towards the window. The trees lining the road were wrapped in a mist that rose from the damp grass. The sky was light, but the moon still ruled the sky. Odd to think that most everyone he knew still lay abed, while he rode to a damp clearing in the park to watch two men try to kill each other.

"Can't you stop him?" Phoebe had asked as they'd lain together the night before. But there was no stopping Rafe when he'd set his mind on something. They'd all warned him he was holding the reins too tightly on Elizabeth, that she'd bolt if he didn't loosen up. And she had—straight into Dinsmore's waiting arms. Cole had a suspicion that Rafe was angrier at himself for mishandling Elizabeth than he was with Dinsmore. Dinsmore was just a convenient scapegoat. Rafe held the belief that if a man planned his life carefully, he could control it. A grim smile curved the corners of Cole's mouth; he doubted there was much a man could do to control the course of his life, and he knew for certain there was little a man could do to control the women in it.

Elizabeth had the wildness of her late father and brother George, but she also had the quiet determination of her mother Louisa. Had she truly been "experimenting" with Dinsmore or was there something deeper involved? Lord help them if she'd decided James was like some neglected rosebush in need of a good pruning and a bit of attention. If that were the case, then Moreham had best kill Dinsmore, or Elizabeth would surely find a way back to him.

Dinsmore really wasn't such a bad sort, Cole mused, though he would never voice his opinion to Rafe. Actually, James reminded him of himself fifteen years ago—spoiled, bored, and restless—before he'd met Phoebe, of course. The lines around his eyes softened as he continued to stare out the window. He saw a coach with the Dinsmore family crest drawn up by the side of a clearing, a lovely bit of garden really, bordered by flower beds. James Dinsmore stood, still as a nearby statue of a nymph, hands resting on his sheathed sword.

"He's here," Cole said, as the coach slowed to a stop.

"Are you ready, my lord?" The surgeon spoke for the first time since he'd been introduced earlier that morning.

Rafe eyed his battered leather medical bag. "If you're asking am I prepared for your handiwork, then, my good sir, you're asking the wrong man."

The surgeon's mouth flapped as if he were trying to recapture his words. "My lord, I'm sorry if I've offended you. I didn't mean . . . I mean, I only meant . . ." He was still scrambling to make amends when the carriage door swung open.

The footman holding the door handle was a wiry little man in shockingly ill-fitting livery.

"Jervis," Rafe said, a hint of amusement in his voice. "I was unaware your duties included my stables."

Jervis, his manservant of fifteen years, flashed a wealth of missing teeth. "You didn't think I'd miss this, did you, Captain? No, indeed, I wouldn't." He patted his coat pocket. "I brought along some of my remedies, just in case you might be needing them. Not that I'm expecting you'll be needing him." He nodded dismissively towards the surgeon. "But I figure you'll fight better knowing you've got sure hands standing behind you."

The corners of Rafe's mouth twitched at Jervis's enthusiastically mixed metaphor. "After your last potion—tree fungus, wasn't it?—I've no doubt the knowledge that one of

your home remedies awaits me should I falter will bolster
my fighting arm."

"It worked didn't it?" he protested.

Rafe turned his attention to the company in the coach.
"Gentlemen, shall we proceed?"

Cole slid a leather case out from under his seat and followed Rafe into the damp dawn air. The surgeon scuttled behind.

James nodded as they approached. His second, Lord
Grenville, greeted them. "Good morning, my lords."

"And good morning to you, my lord." Rafe turned toward
James. "Dinsmore, so good of you to show."

"Far too early to visit my tailor," James replied pleasantly.

"No need to hurry." Rafe handed his hat and coat to his
coachman. "Indeed, after this morning, most likely he'll be
measuring you for a different sort of suit."

"Are you so certain?" James asked, removing his own
jacket and hat and handing them to his coachman. He shook
out the ruffles of his sleeves.

"Gentlemen," Lord Grenville cleared his throat. "Shall
we begin? No doubt, it is well understood by both parties
why we are met this morning. Lord Moreham believes he
has been offended by Lord Dinsmore's attentions to his sister."

Rafe stiffened at the use of the word *attentions*, but said
nothing.

"Lord Moreham, I must ask you, is there nothing Lord
Dinsmore might offer that would satisfy your honor and the
honor of your sister?"

"An abject apology to my sister for laying hands upon her
person, an admission to the ton that he is a loathsome
scoundrel, exile to some far-flung corner of the continent
with a promise never to see Elizabeth again."

Lord Grenville cleared his throat.

James paused as if considering Rafe's words, then he

shrugged. "I regret, my Lord Moreham, that I cannot agree to all of your terms." He did not offer to explain and Rafe did not ask him to elaborate.

Lord Grenville cast both men the briefest look of disappointment. "Very well. We shall continue. My Lord Davenport, have you brought the weapons?"

Cole stepped forward, offering the leather case. Lord Grenville opened it. Three finely fashioned Spanish blades lay in a bed of black velvet. He examined each one in turn, testing the sharpness of the blades, the balance, the strength of the grips. Assured the swords were in order, he offered the case first to James and then Rafe.

Each man having chosen a blade, they stood at attention as Grenville explained the rules that would be followed, the distances that must be observed, the conditions under which either man might claim victory or admit defeat.

"It is understood then?" he asked. "Should one man call for mercy, the other shall grant it and claim victory?"

James and Rafe both nodded. Somewhere in the trees beyond the flower beds a bird called and another answered. The mists had begun to thin, diluted by the first rays of the morning sun.

"Very well. You may salute."

James and Rafe faced each other, simultaneously drawing their swords up hilt to chin, then down in a graceful arc to end in position with blades pointed directly at one another. They paused. Blue eyes met hazel. Neither blinked.

Grenville's voice cut through the stillness. "*En garde.*"

The two men circled, assessing the other's position, looking for an opening. Rafe lunged low; James caught the blade and turned it, then lunged at Rafe's hip. He twisted his body away from the blade and thrust upward. James dodged back, parried the blade, circled and thrust.

Steel clattered against steel, the only conversation now possible between them.

• • • •

"*Can we not* stop them now?" Grenville murmured to Cole. "Surely His Lordship's desire for satisfaction has been quenched with so much blood?"

Rafe and James circled each other in the morning sun, their breath as ragged as their blood-spattered clothes. James had a slash to his arm and several cuts on his left hand. Rafe's left hand too bore several cuts and blood stained his hip where James's sword had glanced him. Where blood had not glued their clothes to their bodies, sweat did.

Cole shook his head. "Where Elizabeth is concerned, Rafe is not a reasonable man. Do you think Dinsmore will call cry mercy?"

"I cannot say, but I doubt it."

"He's fought bravely today."

A wry smile creased Grenville's face. "More bravely than you expected, you mean."

"I did not say so."

"Ah, but you thought it." Grenville raised his hand. "It is what everyone thinks of James, that he has no thoughts but for fashion, exerts himself only for a glass of wine or to try on a new waistcoat. But there is more to him that that. . . ."

"I have not seen it," Cole said blandly.

"You have not looked for it."

"Fair enough."

There was a grunt as Rafe's blade bit into James's leg. He staggered back, drew up his sword. Rafe met it, grabbed his wrist, knocked him off balance and threw him to the ground. With a rush he was on James, muddied foot on his chest, bloodied sword at his throat. "I should kill you, you bastard."

"Then do." James's words were strained, but defiant.

"Don't Moreham," Grenville and Cole cried simultaneously.

"Beg, Dinsmore," Rafe said coldly. "Tell me you are not worthy of a woman such as my sister. Tell me you're sorry you ever laid so much as a hand on her."

"I am not worthy of your sister," he said hoarsely.

Rafe's arm did not move, but with his wrist he teased the blade across James's neck. "And—" he prompted.

James swallowed hard.

"Apologize for touching her Dinsmore."

"No," he whispered, "I cannot."

Rafe's eyes narrowed. "Cannot?" He pressed the point of his sword and a bright spot of red appeared at its tip. "Come, come man, you *will* not."

"I cannot say I regret making love to Elizabeth." He lifted his chin and the spot at his neck lengthened into a scrape. "I will not die with a lie on my lips."

Rafe assessed the bloodied figure beneath his blade. An expression that might have been understanding, perhaps laced with pity, flickered across his face. "Do you fancy yourself in love, Dinsmore?" he said softly.

James closed his eyes.

"She is not for you," he added, even more softly.

With a flick of his wrist he brought his blade up, opening James's cheek.

"So she will never again be cozened by your pretty face." The deep gash on James's face ran blood. "So that wherever you go, people will know you for the dishonorable cur that you are!"

Chapter 12

Elizabeth gave up any pretense of trying to sleep. It was very early, but she rang for her maid and dressed. Then tried to keep busy. She read, but after her eyes slid past the same paragraph four times, she put the book aside. She thought she might write a letter, but didn't know to whom. She'd received a note from Arabella Norcroft's mother, requesting that she "cease importuning" her daughter. The cool formality of the words had taken her breath away. She wished Arabella were here now, with her warm brown eyes and her teasing good humor. They'd have found some way to laugh over this whole hideous situation. Though there wasn't anything remotely funny about her brother dueling with the man she . . . Elizabeth paused uncertain exactly how to complete her thought.

Her chest felt suddenly tight.

She couldn't breathe.

She needed to walk somewhere. She needed to talk to someone.

She ventured down the stairs into the parlor. Alix was sitting alone, methodically tearing linen into strips and laying them in a basket at her feet. From the size of the pile, she'd made enough to bandage the entire household twice over. Nevertheless, Elizabeth offered to help.

"It is not necessary," Alix said, her gaze making Elizabeth feel as if she were an ogre, too large and clumsy for the room.

"I am disturbing you?" her statement rose on a questioning note.

"Not at all," Alix replied. She turned her eyes towards the window that overlooked the front steps of Moreham House.

"They haven't returned . . ." Elizabeth ventured.

"Your *brother* is still out," Alix said stiffly.

Elizabeth cursed herself silently. *I said* they *instead of* he. *How can I be so thoughtless?* "I think perhaps I shall return to my room."

Alix nodded, her eyes still fixed on the glass.

They both have to return safe and unharmed, Elizabeth told herself as she mounted the stairs. Each footstep seemed to echo: Rafe, James, Rafe, James. *Where are they now? What are they doing at this precise moment? Are they hurt?* And why, oh why, did she have to feel so hideously helpless?

As she reached the top of the stairs she heard the front door open, footsteps, and men's voices. She heard Alix crying out Rafe's name, the sound hopeful and yet terrified. Elizabeth started down the stairs two at a time. When she reached the final landing she stopped, staring at the sight below. Rafe's bloodied arms were wrapped tightly around Alix. Her hands were on his face. She seemed to be laughing and crying and kissing him all at once.

Immediately footmen and maids surrounded the couple. Everyone was expressing concern and anxious to help.

Louisa was there, with the pug worrying the hem of her gown. Elizabeth didn't know where to look; she didn't know what to say. Her brother was alive, and despite the blood he didn't seem to be seriously hurt. *James. What of James? Was the blood his? Was he hurt? Was he even alive?* She needed to know; she wanted to scream the questions. She pressed her lips together and hurried back up the stairs to her room. She crawled under the bed and pulled her limbs together tightly as if she might somehow vanish completely.

"You are hurt." Alix kissed Rafe again, her lips salty with her tears and his sweat and blood. Not ready to ask how close she might have come to losing him she said between kisses, "I have a bath waiting upstairs, warm water, fresh soap, and bandages." A weak laugh escaped her. "Enough bandages to wrap you from head to toe."

He loosened his embrace. "Did you think me such a poor swordsman, my love?"

"I did not know what else to do . . ."

"You did the right thing." His hazel eyes were warm. "There is nothing I would welcome more than to shed these ragged clothes and step into a warm bath. And while I do not think I need quite so much bandaging as you suggest, there are some rather nasty cuts on my hands and arms which need to be tended to."

Jervis, who had elbowed his way through the clustered servants, held out a handful of gray fluff. "I've got a good bit of lint to pack them gashes with."

"Thank you Jervis, but I think I shall surrender myself to my wife's more tender ministrations."

"If you say so." Jervis's mouth quirked skeptically. "But I've some salve with bear grease. Works wonders, won't hardly leave a scar . . ."

"Sell them to James Dinsmore, his need's the greater."

Jervis made as if to spit, then caught himself, muttering, "Sooner use 'em on a pig."

"He's alive then?" Alix asked. "You didn't kill him?"

Rafe shook his head.

"That's good," she said. "Elizabeth will be relieved to hear it."

He glanced around. "Where is she?"

"I think perhaps she is embarrassed, after all the trouble she's caused."

"Perhaps." He looked as if the last bit of his energy had suddenly drained away. "But I don't want to talk of Elizabeth now. I'm sorely in need of that bath you mentioned." His arm around her waist, he allowed her to guide him up the stairs. But he paused as they reached the first landing and bent his lips to her ear. "And after you've tended to my wounds, I can think of some other parts of my body that would appreciate your attentions."

James's blood splattered the inlaid marble floor of the entrance hall like obscene raindrops. Lord Grenville and the surgeon held him upright. Every item of clothing, every visible part of him, appeared covered in blood. Anne screamed when she saw him.

"Anne," Grenville said sharply, "I know he looks alarming, but you must get hold of yourself. He needs your help."

She nodded. Inhaled sharply. Gestured towards a door to her left. "Take him in to the dining room. Put him on the table." She turned to a footman. "Tell the kitchen we need water, lots of hot water, bowls, and clean linen." She pressed her lips together, a hand motioning him to wait a moment longer. "We'll need a sharp knife, too, to cut his clothes off. And tell his valet to have his bedchamber ready."

The footman stood, waiting to see if her instructions were complete.

Anne scowled at him, "Are you waiting for my brother to bleed out on the floor? Off with you!"

She turned her attention back to James. "Is he conscious? Can he walk?"

"A little," the surgeon said. "I've given him laudanum for the pain."

Together they carried James into the dining room. A maid scurried to remove the silver candelabras from the long mahogany table as they lifted him onto it. More maids appeared carrying bowls of water and linen. Anne worked with the surgeon to remove James's clothes, her face tightening as each sword cut was exposed.

"Lord Moreham," she hissed at Lord Grenville, "tell me he is dead."

"He is not."

"Then tell me he suffers as badly as my poor brother."

Grenville did not answer. He turned towards a footman, motioning the man to remove the pile of rags from the table that had been James's waistcoat and shirt.

"He is *wounded*?" she demanded.

"He is, but not so severely as James. He has had his satisfaction, Anne. The thing is done."

She glanced up at him, her hands deep in a bowl of red-stained water. "Oh no, my lord, the thing is not done. *I* have not had *my* satisfaction."

Grenville frowned. His opened his mouth to respond, but Anne's attention was turned elsewhere.

"You clumsy fool!" she shouted at the surgeon, who had pinched the flesh of James's lacerated cheek together and was preparing to stitch it with heavy black thread. "You will scar him forever!"

The surgeon shot a look at Lord Grenville, an expression that clearly sought His Lordship's assistance with this grief-maddened woman. Finding none, he turned back to Anne, his words respectful, but his tone condescending. "But Your Ladyship, the skin of the face is most delicate, there is no help for it, your brother will be scarred." He pinched James's swollen flesh more tightly together and bent with his needle.

"*Stop!* My brother is the most handsome man in London. I will not have you mar him."

Still not releasing James's cheek, the surgeon tried again. "There is nothing anyone can do, my lady. The wound must be closed or else it will fester. And then I must bleed him to make sure his blood is balanced and clean. Time is of the essence. I beg of you." Here he cast another glance at Lord Grenville. "Let me work."

"*I* will close the wound," Anne said coldly, "*you* will leave." She turned to one of the maids, who was emptying a bowl of dirty water into a bucket on the floor. "Fetch my embroidery silk from my bedchamber and a packet of my sharpest needles."

The surgeon stretched his hand as if to protest, but Anne was no longer looking at him. Nodding towards a footman who had stepped forward to remove the bucket, she said, "You may toss that out. But first, take him."

He stared up at her face, a study in pale concentration. *Which pain was worse? The cuts of the sword or his sister's slow, careful stitching?* He wanted to tell her it was all right, she needn't work so hard; but his lips were numb from the laudanum. He slipped into unconsciousness dreaming of the scar, a blazing red line against the blackness of his eyelids . . .

In the weeks that followed, as he lay feverish in his bed, his hands would drift upward trying to touch the wound, but the linen swathing his face and hands made it impossible.

If he believed his laudanum dreams, half of his face had been ripped apart.

He knew it wasn't true, but in his darker hours the poetry of the notion appealed to him. He pictured one side of his face hideous, one side beautiful, one side his past, the other his future, one side an image of who people thought he was, the other who he knew himself to be.

When at last the bandages were removed, his hands went to it immediately.

His fingers explored the ridge of skin that curved from the middle of his cheek to just below his eyebrow. It felt like less than he'd imagined. Less than he deserved. He would not look at it. He ordered the mirrors removed from his rooms. Anne interpreted this and his reluctance to leave the house, as an act of wounded vanity.

"It's not so bad James," she said one morning as they sat breakfasting in her chambers. "Truly it's not. If you'd just look . . ."

"I'd rather not," he replied, attempting to smile, but finding his mouth only crooked on one side.

She pressed her lips together then tried another approach. "You look rather dashing you know. A bit dangerous . . . the ladies will find you irresistible, I'm sure."

He fingered the scar. "Ironic, when you consider that's what earned me this pretty souvenir."

"Moreham's perfidy caused that scar, don't ever forget that James."

He smiled his crooked smile. "You needn't worry that I will forget my scars or how I came by them."

"Precisely," she said, "and this is why you should take a look. You'll see; it's not all that bad. And then you can begin to go out and about again."

"Take up where I left off, as it were?"

"Exactly."

James had no desire to take up where he'd left off. But he knew if he explained, she'd misinterpret his meaning, launch into another tirade against Moreham and Elizabeth. *Elizabeth.* He resisted the urge to touch the scar. A permanent reminder, Rafe had said, that she wasn't for the likes of him. "Is Elizabeth Harcrest still making the rounds?" The question slipped out, before he realized he'd said it aloud.

"You cannot *imagine* how long I've been waiting for you to ask that question." Anne's lips curved in a satisfied smile. She slid her breakfast plate forward and leaned across the tea table. "Elizabeth *did* venture out a few times after her brother made his ridiculous attempt to restore her honor, a few card parties here and there, the odd small assembly. Out of respect for Moreham, no one cut her directly, but it was clear that no one of any real standing would exchange more than pleasantries with her."

She pointed to the coffeepot and James filled her cup. "Of course, the Davenports rallied around her, and a few other odd people. Louisa even made several appearances with her, stayed the entire evening without pleading a headache, can you imagine? And Moreham's appalling mother-in-law, of course." She made a noise of distaste. "You should have *seen* the woman's gown the other night. Exquisite fabrics. I would love to know where she gets them. But the *colors* . . . tangerine and dark purple! . . . even the memory makes me shudder."

"Elizabeth?" James prompted, offering her a porcelain pitcher of cream.

"Elizabeth," she poured a dollop into her cup and stirred it with a silver spoon. "Well, of course, nothing Moreham can do will erase what people saw at our ball."

"Or stop their talk."

Anne pointedly ignored the sarcasm in his voice. "Elizabeth tried to hold her head up, I'll give her credit for that. But the sparkle from that diamond is clearly gone. I vow, she looked nearly as drab as that wren-friend of hers Arabella . . . I cannot remember her surname."

"Norcroft," he supplied, familiar with the girl who'd spent so much time at Elizabeth's side. "She's not so drab, not her conversation at least, and she's got rather nice eyes."

"If you say so." She waved dismissively. "But her family is certainly nothing to speak of . . ."

"Elizabeth looked pale?"

"All the pink muslin in the world couldn't create the illusion of roses in her cheeks now. And her gowns just hang on her. You'd think with all their money, the Harcrests might have a modiste do something about that, tighten the waist, add a bit of flounce . . . though I suppose that could accentuate how gaunt she's become."

"Has she fallen ill?" James struggled to keep his voice as unconcerned as his sister's.

"How should I know?" Anne leaned back in her chair, and sipped her coffee contentedly.

"Don't be coy Anne, it doesn't become you. You know everything anyone of consequence does in London."

"In London, yes." She smiled over the rim of her cup. "But *she* is no longer in London."

"Where has she gone?" he demanded.

"The countryside." Anne lifted her cup from its flowered saucer. "I do believe Lady Elizabeth Harcrest's season is officially over."

Chapter 13

No one has lain eyes upon him in weeks. Anne has put it about that the wounds he received from your brother have brought him to "the very threshold of death's door" and that he tosses and turns in the agony of fever. For my part, I wonder if his condition is truly that serious—the woman takes far too much delight in describing her brother's sufferings. I swear, Elizabeth, her eyes sparkle and she's more color in her face when speaking of it than a woman about to meet her lover. And she makes herself seem a veritable angel of mercy! More like a demon from the netherworld, if you ask me. And speaking of lovers, at some later point I simply must tell you of Anne's latest suitor, Sir Edmund Bogglesworth. But I will not digress since I know James must be much on your mind.

A rumor has sprung up, this one most definitely not spread by Anne. According to my chamber-maid, whose cousin's friend works in the Dinsmore

*kitchens, James's face is frightfully scarred. So
ashamed is he that he will not venture out and has
ordered all the mirrors removed from the house. I
would not have thought him so vain, but I am little
acquainted with the curious minds of men. It would
be a shame if this story should prove to be true.
Would you still love him if he were not so beautiful?*

Elizabeth tucked the letter from Arabella back into her
stays. Thank goodness for Arabella! If it wasn't for the notes
she kept sending against her mother's wishes, Elizabeth
wasn't certain what she would do. Arabella's letters always
included all the latest London gossip, running commentary
on the most outrageous fashions, and most important of all,
updates on James Dinsmore's health.

She dared not ask anyone else about James's condition,
particularly since Rafe had become feverish from his
wounds. After her brother recovered and began to squire her
about London, she did not want to be caught scanning the
crowds, searching for a glimpse of James's golden head. Far
too many people were watching her, just waiting for another
hideous breach of decorum. Truly, the duel had changed little. Oh, she was no longer cut directly; at parties she was invited to dance, led in to supper with suitable men. But just
below the polite surface, in the retiring rooms and cloak-
rooms, she was met with raised eyebrows, polite rebuffs, and
barely concealed laughter. Rafe finally decided they would
leave London and return to their country estate long before
the season was over. And here at Moreham Hall, it was
deadly dull, and no one spoke of James at all.

Was he seriously ill or had he truly become a recluse?
That had been her worry for weeks. She'd almost convinced
herself this concern was simply because it was her foolish
indiscretion that had caused the duel, caused his wounds.
But the last line of Alice's latest letter haunted her. *Would
you still love him if he were not so beautiful?*

James was handsome to look at, and her bones seemed to

dissolve a bit when she thought of his body. But was she so terribly shallow to be drawn to him *only* for his face and body? It was his *mind* that drew her. When they were leaving London, as she watched the coachmen load all the trunks and valises filled with the gowns that were to make her first season a grand triumph, her most painful realization was how much she would miss his wit and his sharp, teasing humor.

Still. What if his face *was* marred? How awful were the scars? Was he missing an eye? An eye patch might be rather dashing so long as she didn't have to look under it. What if Rafe had cut off his nose? She winced. Could she kiss a man without a nose? The contents of her stomach swirled, and she felt the blood leave her cheeks. *How can I be so petty, so self-absorbed when James might be suffering?* No matter what the state of his outward appearance, it didn't change what lay within. Hadn't that been what she believed all along, even though everyone else saw him merely as a beautiful, golden rake? That deep inside was a sensitive man, a caring man, a man who could comfort his sister with words of magic?

If not for the awkwardness that had developed between them since the duel, and the ban on James Dinsmore's name, she'd have asked her brother and sister-in-law for their views on the nature of love. Did they believe in love at first sight? *The idea you could lock eyes with a man and know you are meant to be together forever. . . .* She considered James's eyes, the brows that came to a slightly wicked point in the center, those brows that rose when he looked at her, as if to say, *I know what you're about, Elizabeth Harcrest . . .*

She shook her head, bringing her thoughts back to reality.

It was pointless to think about James.

And it was the purest torture to contemplate a future that could not—*would* not—be. He was in London and she was exiled to the countryside. Rafe would make certain their paths never crossed again.

• • •

"*So the Harcrest's* are long gone, left London for the remainder of the season," Lord Grenville said casually, though his eyes as they studied James were anything but.

"So Anne told me." James sipped his wine, then held the glass upward, examining its color in the light of the candles that lit the tables of the exclusive private club. His wounds had healed sufficiently, and he had rejoined society, though nothing was the same. "An excellent vintage—seventeen sixty-eight?"

Grenville's nod indicated agreement, not just of the year of the wine, but of James's obvious wish to change the subject. "You always did have a fine palate for wines," he said, then added, "you and Anthony."

"Your son had the finer palate. And the finer heart."

"He was a good man, my son."

"I think of him often, and of our last year of university together."

"He was a serious lad; he didn't make friends easily. It did my heart good to see you together."

"Those were happy times." James traced the fine line his sister had sewn. Since coming out of seclusion, women continued to cast him admiring looks despite his scar, but where once he'd found wicked pleasure, he now found only boredom. He had begun to withdraw from female company, seeking solace in books, brandy, and clubs where only the forthright talk of men could be heard. Which is why he'd accepted Lord Greville's invitation this evening. "It would have been better had the fever taken me."

"The fever took you both," Grenville reminded him. "But Anthony's lungs were never strong. The Lord saw fit that you should survive."

A curious smile, drawn down by the taut scar, flickered across James's face. "You still believe in God?"

"I do," Grenville replied, "I believe he has plans beyond our understanding. We must have faith."

"And is this why you continue to have faith in me?" James glanced about the room; several men who had been staring at him dropped their eyes. He turned his gaze back upon Lord Grenville. "Do you imagine I survived as part of some greater plan, that my life has some larger purpose?"

"It might have, if you wish it to be so."

"Have you some position for me amongst the clergy then?" His voice filled with amusement. "I think I should make a poor priest."

Grenville smiled. "I have in mind to invite you to join a brotherhood of a different sort." He gestured discretely toward the quiet clusters of men seated around the room and lowered his voice. "Are you aware of the nature of this club?"

"It's an oasis, a safe haven, a precious refuge, where for a brief moment in time men can escape the relentless machinations of women."

Grenville pursed his lips like a disappointed schoolmaster.

"Some sort of philosophical society, isn't it? Membership by invitation only?"

Grenville nodded.

James studied the soberly garbed men scattered throughout the room. He flicked a wrist encircled in simple, but crisp white lace at them. "I assume fashion is not an issue here, and that gambling is not part of the appeal."

"Not for money," Grenville said softly, "no."

James cast him an inquisitive glance.

He continued. "You are correct in assuming that this is an exclusive club and that membership is not extended lightly. We have an interest in philosophy, yes, and in affairs of state. We are affiliated, though not directly, with his majesty's government."

James was silent for a full moment. "You are *spies*?" he whispered, incredulous.

Grenville nodded slightly.

James's fingers slid down his scar. "And you think I've fallen far enough to join your . . . *brotherhood*?"

Grenville's eyes blazed within their wrinkled settings, though he kept his voice low. "Though you and others might consider our work ungentlemanly, we do not. Nor do we consider ourselves fallen men. Far from it—"

"Listening at doors, reading other men's correspondence . . . wouldn't you consider that ungentlemanly?"

"Laying about drinking, gambling, spending money on clothes you cannot hope to pay for, seducing women . . ."

James flicked his finger up the scar. "Touché my lord."

Grenville pressed his lips together. "I had not meant to say that, to lose my temper like that, James. I apologize."

"You only spoke the truth." He folded his hands upon the table. "In all this time you have not said a word against me, you have stood by me,"—his voice softened—"like a father might stand by his son." Grenville made as if to speak, but James raised his hand. "It is I who ought to apologize. You have not judged me, I should not presume to judge you."

"It is true we do those things which you have described, but for a purpose, a noble purpose—to guide his majesty with knowledge of his enemies' intentions, to protect our country, to protect our sons."

"But we are not at war—"

"We will be soon enough. Already people are suffering."

"Not in England."

"In France. Like plague, the misery spreads. Unchecked it will spread throughout the continent, cross the channel and spill onto our shores."

"And what is it you would have me do?"

"Go there."

"They are in the midst of a revolution, not exactly the time for a grand tour." James attempted to keep his tone light, to conceal his shock.

"I want you to establish a network so that we might work towards the end of this vicious new government." Grenville sat back in his chair, his dry fingertips pressed together in a gesture oddly reminiscent of prayer. "Tell me James, have you anything *better* to do with your time?"

Did he have anything better to do with his time? "Well, my Lord Grenville . . ." *I could continue to dance attendance upon Anne, listen with half an ear to her gossip, while pretending not to notice how people eye my face and whisper behind their hands.* He'd made a game of it, catching the stares and holding them, gauging the expressions in their eyes. Disdain, pity, revulsion, intrigue, attraction—he'd seen it all. It no longer amused him. Society no longer amused him. "Why me?" he asked, at last. "I've no particular skills."

"Ah, but you do." Grenville tapped his fingertips together. "You've a quick mind. More than that, you've an ability to move easily amongst different sorts of people, to establish a rapport, to lead them . . ."

An image of Elizabeth, leading him into the library flashed in his mind, and James stiffened. "To seduce them, don't you mean to say?"

Grenville pressed his fingertips together. "Not a word I would have chosen, no. Though I suppose one might argue that effective leaders have seductive qualities. . . ." He spread his hands dismissively. "But this is a matter of honor."

He thought then of Anne, and how she'd encouraged him to think of her revenge in terms of honor. "So," he said, allowing bitterness to bleed into his voice, "you believe me honorable enough to spy?"

"I believe you honorable enough to engage in what will be a dangerous and most important mission." Grenville placed his hands flat on the table and leaned forward. "I have seen you fight—with courage, with skill, and with passion."

"Need I remind you that I lost?"

"I was there. I saw what happened. You chose to let Moreham win." Grenville's eyes narrowed their focus to the thin red line on James's cheek. "You gave him his satisfaction, but you would not apologize. You offered your life rather than forswear what you knew to be true."

James began to protest, he didn't know *what* was true, not then and not now. He only knew that when Moreham's steel had pressed against his throat he could not say he was sorry for touching Elizabeth. He knew that as surely as he knew he would never touch her again. He fell silent, and emptiness swept over him.

It was emptiness, he knew, of his own making.

He'd allowed himself to drift through life, purposeless, nudged occasionally in some direction by his sister's anger, or his father's madness. He'd jested with friends that life was short; it should be spent in pleasure, not wasted in struggle. But the truth was darker.

He feared the seeds of his father's madness might lie buried within his own mind.

Even now they could be growing, the tangled vines of delusion.

Anne's obsession with Rafe troubled him deeply. Even more troubling was his own obsession with Elizabeth. For what else could it be? He'd only touched her once, yet no matter how he tried to weed thoughts of her from his mind, or memories of that night, they flourished. He told himself it was society that no longer amused him, but he feared the truth was that *the absence of Elizabeth Harcrest* was what left society wanting.

Wasn't this how madness began?

He should have let Rafe kill him that morning.

"You are very quiet James. I realize I have approached you with a matter that is shocking, overwhelming even. I suppose I should have prepared you in some way, but time is of the essence."

James snapped from his thoughts back to the present. He stared at Lord Grenville, still amazed at the turn their conversation had taken. It was time to make a change in his life.

He needed to stop mooning about things that could not be . . .

"I need an answer now, James. I have waited long enough for you to heal. You can do this job. Come man, what do you say?"

"You'd like me to establish a network . . ." He had been asked in all seriousness to become involved in an adventure as farfetched as any his father, in his dementia, might conceive! His lips curled at the irony. He continued to study Grenville's face across the table, a man who had once been friends with his father, a man so like his father. . . . *Was Grenville deranged, too?*

"That's it precisely, it will be a simple thing, you'll see." Grenville hesitated, then added, as if it were a small thing, hardly worthy of mention, "But more importantly, there is a gentleman we'd like you to assist in leaving France."

"No doubt someone whom the new government in Paris would prefer remained as a guest of their country?" James picked up his wineglass as if fascinated by the contents.

"Someone the French would dearly like to have as a guest of Madame la Guillotine. You have heard of Calonne?"

"Louis XVI's former Finance Minister? Isn't he here in England, organizing the émigrés?"

"Not simply organizing. He has a scheme to buy up masses of the new currency, the assignat, inflating the value and at the same time spreading forged assignats throughout the country."

"Speculation. Isn't that bankers' work?"

"Which is why we have need of the services of a particular banker, a gentleman who is currently hiding from the authorities near Rouen."

"And is that all?" Twirling his glass by the stem, James was fighting an overwhelming urge to laugh, though whether at Grenville's schemes or his own decision to join him, he couldn't decide. "Or do you need me to storm La Force and fight the National Guard singlehanded?"

"Not single-handed, no, indeed." Grenville rubbed his hands together. "But it needs to be done rather quickly—within the next two months. I've handpicked a team of men to go with you, all fluent in French, as you are, all with unique skills . . ."

"I can only imagine," James murmured, wondering who amongst the three of them, he, his father or Grenville was most mad.

". . . skills that I'm sure you'll find most useful. And I shan't need you to do anything quite so dramatic as the things you've just named. As for the network, well, you're in luck. It shouldn't be too much trouble, most of the groundwork has already been laid."

"Has it?"

"Yes, although . . ." Grenville paused. "There is one more thing I should mention."

James looked across the table, noticing how the old man's gray eyes seemed to gleam in the candlelight. "Yes?"

"You'll need to pay a little visit to Rafe Harcrest, the Earl of Moreham."

James nearly snapped the stem of his wineglass.

Chapter 14

They'd chosen a table in the corner of the crowded pub of the inn where they'd spent the previous night when they'd arrived in their coach from London. James surveyed his companions as they gathered around the scarred wooden table. *Handpicked for their unique skills*, Grenville had said. After spending some time in the men's company this past week, James had a fair idea of those skills, and no doubt a number of them were hanging offenses. Not for the first time, he found himself wondering where His Lordship had found this group.

Marcus was slim and as elegant as the quill he seemed always to be twirling in his left hand, his dark eyes inspecting the world from under brows arched in mild amusement. Andre's compact body was so unable to contain his restless energy, even his mop of dark curls and his bright blue eyes seemed to crackle with it. And David, with his dark blond head bent over hands always working at some clever construction of wood or metal, was so quiet and gentle that at times he appeared almost slow-witted. But when he lifted his head, there was a powerful intensity in his brown eyes.

They'd chosen this table rather than having their meal brought upstairs because Marcus had said—and Andre had agreed—people were always more curious about what went on behind closed doors than out in the open, under their noses. And the hubbub of voices, the clatter of plates and tankards, and the scraping of chairs in this pub on the outskirts of the Harcrest family land made it difficult to hear the conversation at one's own table, much less overhear that of one's neighbor.

As they sat down, Andre caught James's eye. "So His Lordship, the earl, has sworn to kill you if you go anywhere near his sister?" He shook his head and whistled softly.

"My business is with His Lordship, the earl, not his sister."

"But how can you resist slipping off to see her . . . ?" Andre smiled. It was the kind of smile that made a man wonder if his sister was sufficiently chaperoned. "I hear tell she's a rare lovely sight. Popular topic of conversation she is round here, the wild and beautiful sister of the Earl of Moreham."

"A man's life hangs in the balance," James replied in a terse voice. *I won't look for her, won't seek her out even if I catch sight of her . . .* He looked slowly around the table. The future he'd chosen was with these men and with a fugitive desperately waiting for rescue. "We've no time for women." This was said in a voice that made clear the subject was closed.

Though apparently not clear enough for Andre. "But you wouldn't need to make the time. The lady is so close! And who could say that it wasn't an accident, or even fate, if your paths should somehow cross today?"

"And if it looked as though your paths might cross, we could hurl Andre under the hooves of her horse," David suggested with a smile, "then I could step forward to the rescue, offer to re-shoe her mount . . ."

"Which of us do you think she'd find more appealing?" Andre inquired.

"No doubt Dinsmore would like to toss you both under a team of horses' hooves," Marcus murmured, lifting his quill from the sheet of paper upon which he'd been writing.

"You wound me, Marcus," Andre said cheerfully. "Can you blame us if our natural curiosity has been aroused? It is all folks around here can speak of, the beauteous Lady Elizabeth and the infamous duel her brother fought to secure her honor." He stroked his smooth cheek innocently. "We just want to get a glimpse of her, see what all the fuss and bother is about."

Marcus tapped his quill into an inkwell. "All your years in this business, you ought to know how people like to spin a simple tale into something far more dramatic. The lady's probably nothing more than passing fair." His eyes strayed speculatively to James. "And the duel, why I'll venture it was nothing more than a misunderstanding between two proud and honorable men."

James knew they were attempting to lead him into a discussion of Elizabeth. They'd been trying since they'd arrived at the inn the previous afternoon and heard the talk of the duel and the abrupt end to Elizabeth's first season. It seemed the locals could speak of little else, unless it was his own scurrilous behavior. He knew, too, that the men at the inn recognized him. His family home was nearby; he'd stopped here before. They made little effort to hide their stares. They dared not approach him, but when he had led the group to their table he overheard, "He's come for revenge," and "He's come to steal her back." He would no more acknowledge their speculation than he would acknowledge the pain that twisted in his gut at the mention of Elizabeth Harcrest's name, and he would not be drawn into a discussion by this banter. He said nothing.

"Dinsmore knows how to keep his mind on the task at hand," Marcus concluded.

"No reason a man can't have a little work *in* hand at the same time . . ."

"In case you hadn't noticed, I *have* my work in hand. Women . . ." Marcus shook his head in mock disgust. "Sometimes I wonder if you've anything else on your mind beyond the fairer sex."

"Can you think of a finer thing for a man to have on his mind . . . or in his bed?" Andre responded, winking at a barmaid. "Besides, they're a puzzle, a challenge, each one different . . . and nothing keeps a man's wits sharper than trying to unravel 'em." He turned his attention to the sheet of paper beneath Marcus's quill. It was a list of names, many of them written numerous times. He ran a blunt finger down them, stopping at one. "You need a little work there. The shape of the *R* doesn't look quite right."

Marcus slid the paper out from under Andre's fingertip, studying the offending *R*. After a moment he began carefully reshaping the letter.

"We need more ale," said David, who'd been examining Marcus's writing box, running his fingers along the sides, opening the compartments and tapping the wooden sides speculatively. He put the box down and raised his mug.

The barmaid Andre had been admiring left the table she'd been serving in mid-order and hurried over. "Mr. David," she said, a trifle breathlessly, "is there something you need?"

He nodded and a lock of dark blond hair slipped loose from his carelessly tied queue.

The barmaid's hand rose as if she'd like to smooth the strand back into place. She caught herself. "Is there anything I can get you?"

"A pitcher of ale would be grand."

"We've freshly baked bread and a lovely bit of Stilton."

"By all means, bring the bread and cheese, too."

She took a step away from the table, then turned back,

twisting chapped hands in her frayed gray apron. "Mr. David . . . I can't thank you enough for them toys you designed for my son. He's never had real toys before. And they're so clever, all them little joints and working parts. I ain't never seen anything like it. And you fixed the kitchen door, it closes so nice and smooth, not even a squeak . . ."

"It's just something I do." He shook his head as if her compliments embarrassed him. "Keeping my hands busy."

"You're a marvel, you are," she insisted.

He looked at her and smiled. "It was my pleasure."

Her eyes followed the fall of his hair, lingering on the broad spread of shoulders beneath his disheveled queue. She moistened her lips. "I'll be getting that pitcher then."

As she hurried off, deftly swinging her hips around chairs full of customers and tables laden with pewter mugs and plates, Andre sighed. "I just hope she remembers the bread and cheese." He glanced over at David. "Making toys for her children," he said admiringly, "I never even noticed she had any."

David chuckled. "Perhaps if you'd looked beyond her bosom . . ."

"It is a very fine bosom, you must admit."

"David." James cleared his throat, loud enough to attract all three men's attention. "I've no doubt your intentions in creating diversions for the serving maid's son spring from the purest and most altruistic of motivations. However, you may be certain I'll be watching closely to make certain that during our *very brief stay here*, no maids are seduced and no silver disappears from the kitchen of this establishment."

David blinked as if bewildered, and James saw Andre stifle a grin. But it was Marcus who spoke. "Not to worry, Dinsmore. If either of them falls into trouble, I've some papers somewhere about which ought to do the trick, orders from the local constable releasing a miscreant into our care."

"Thank you, Marcus, but I'm certain we'll have no need of your handiwork," he replied warningly.

Marcus shrugged.

David pulled a watch from beneath his waistcoat. "Hadn't you better start out, Dinsmore? You wouldn't want to be late for your appointment with His Lordship."

"Wouldn't do to annoy the earl," Andre added, with a knowing flash of teeth.

Annoyance. What the earl felt for him was so far beyond annoyance, James doubted there was a word in the English language to describe it. He wouldn't be surprised if the earl began frothing at the mouth when he was ushered into the room. When he'd protested he wasn't the man to meet with Moreham, Grenville argued he was *precisely* the right man; sending an enemy would convince the earl they were deadly serious about exposing his involvement in trade *if* he didn't agree to let them use his networks in France. And Grenville appeared to have been right: for much to James's surprise, the earl had agreed to see him.

If he'd only known about Moreham's involvement in trade before! If only *Anne* had known. She would have been appalled. She never would have considered marriage with a man who had lowered himself in such a manner. The withdrawal of Moreham's suit would have been a matter of relief, not of revenge. For his part, he felt a growing admiration for the man. He wished it were possible to get to know the earl better—and his sister, too, he admitted. To call him friend, or perhaps something closer. He traced the ridge of his scar. None of that was possible now. Moreham had called him a dishonorable cur for seducing his sister. After today's meeting, he would add blackmailer and spy to his list of epithets.

"Do you wish us to follow after you?" Marcus asked.

James shook his head. He needed to convince the earl to cooperate, and he needed to do it swiftly. This was no longer about what had passed between the Dinsmores and the Harcrests. Every day in hiding brought the danger of discovery closer to their fugitive.

"In case you find yourself in need of some assistance?" David added.

"We'd be most discreet," Andre said.

He had delayed this meeting long enough; surely it couldn't be any more painful than their last encounter. "I need you to make certain that everything is ready for our departure immediately upon my return."

"Already done," Andre said.

"So you'd like us to come along, then . . ." Marcus began gathering up his papers as if the matter had been settled.

"Not if the earl sends out the entire staff of Moreham Hall to beat me to a bloody pulp," James said firmly.

"That's just why we were offering," David said softly.

"James Dinsmore? On his way *here*? As sure as a skunk on a rubbish pile, the fellow's up to no good. You want me to gather up some of the stable lads, lie in wait for him, and finish the job you started?" Jervis Jones leaned across the massive mahogany desk in the Earl of Moreham's study and drew a finger dramatically across his throat.

Rafe noticed that his manservant's stock was soiled. He shook his head. "As pleasing as the thought might be, you aren't to lay a hand or a stick on him."

Jervis frowned.

"I'll have your word on it or I'll have you whipped."

Jones sighed with disappointment and dropped into a chair. Rafe didn't bother to remind him that a properly trained servant would never dream of sitting in the earl's presence unless first given permission. But Jones wasn't a properly trained servant and never would be.

"Would you be wanting me to follow him then?" Jones tried another tack. "See what he's about?"

"That won't be necessary. I know precisely what he's about."

"Is it Elizabeth?" Jones fingered the sleeve where he kept a thin blade.

"He's been sent by the Foreign Ministry, Lord Grenville's orders. He wishes to discuss textiles."

"Textiles?" The word hung in the air like the odor of an onion gone off. "What does Dinsmore have to do with the government? What do you think he knows? Do you think it's some filthy scheme for blackmail?"

"I don't know, which is why I agreed to the appointment." Rafe leaned back in his chair and frowned. His fingers drummed the polished surface of the desk, disturbing the piles of paper that were neatly arranged on its surface. He straightened them. "It's possible that he is seeking financial remuneration in return for not exposing my disreputable involvement in trade to the ton."

"You should have cut the bastard's throat when you had the chance."

Rafe didn't respond. He'd been through a great deal with Jones and was remarkably free with the man. Still, some subjects were not open to discussion. He wasn't entirely sure why he *hadn't* killed James Dinsmore. There were times, looking at the shadowed circles beneath his sister's eyes, when he wished he had.

"His coming here's wrong and you know it. You've done a respectable thing, rebuilding your family's fortune through trade with France. No selling off the land, no cheating folks at cards, like some people of your class been known to do . . . no offense, my lord."

Rafe nodded, a glimmer of amusement in his hazel eyes.

"No gambling on futures . . . just hard, honest, decent work. Ridiculous the ways we got to sneak about like we're doing something disreputable. Middlemen, cover companies, moving money around all those banks . . . so many accounts only you can keep them straight . . . and all for some bolts of cloth and lace."

"The finest silks, brocades, and laces. Very difficult to acquire with the French in the midst of a revolution, which makes them increasingly desirable to the ton and even more profitable."

"It's not as though you need the blunt anymore."

"Indeed, as you so colorfully put it, I no longer need the blunt. But do not forget that many of those factory owners, middlemen, cover companies, shipping clerks, and ship owners are our friends. They've come to depend on us for work. And in these difficult times, I will not contribute to their misfortunes by leaving them to their own devices."

"The whole thing makes my head hurt." Jervis Jones touched his cheek gingerly and winced.

"I believe that would be your rotten teeth. You really ought to see a barber before the only thing they're good for is chewing soup."

"You're trying to put me off the subject, but I know you too well." Jervis tapped his long nose. "Besides, I've got some remedies I want to try first, before I let that fellow go poking and prodding about my mouth."

"Wish you'd some concoction that would cure what ails Elizabeth," Rafe said softly, the humor leaving his eyes. "You have been keeping an eye on her . . . ? And you haven't let her know she's being followed?"

"You know me, Captain, wilier than a fox sneaking towards the coop when I want to be, like an owl winging his way through the night, like a hawk . . ."

Rafe held up his hand. "I believe I have sufficient understanding of your skills. Tell me Jones, is she still . . ." He let the words trail off, as unwilling to voice what he knew his sister had been doing as he was uncertain how he might put a stop to it.

"Aye, Captain, she's still at it."

"I suppose I might order her to remain in the house . . ."

But they both knew he wouldn't; Elizabeth already seemed so much a prisoner of the estate. She didn't ride out. She no longer went to the village. She sent few letters and received fewer still. Perhaps he ought to invite her friend to visit. What was the little brown-haired chit's name—Arabella Norcroft? It would be good for Elizabeth—that is, if the girl's mother allowed her to come.

Damn James Dinsmore!

He should have killed him. He might still. If his family was destined to be completely disgraced, he might as well find some satisfaction in it.

Chapter 15

She stood on the wall feeling the uneven stones beneath the thin leather of her slippers. Inhaling deeply, she steadied herself, spread her arms for balance and began to walk. She slid one foot in front of the other, slowly, carefully, so that she didn't slip and fall to the rocks that littered the bed of the stream below. Loose mortar skittered beneath her feet. She couldn't see the pebbled bits striking the surface of the water because of the blindfold, but she imagined them disappearing into circlets of foam. *Try not to think of them*, she told herself. *Just walk to the end of the wall.*

It was a game Elizabeth played at the beginning of each week. A game she'd begun when she'd realized that she was well and truly disgraced, when even the daughter of the local squire looked through her after church as if she weren't there.

Perhaps, she'd begun to think, she shouldn't be.

And so, each Monday, she'd walk through the meadow to the bridge, climb the wall, don the blindfold, and walk. She slid a foot forward, her arms wavering like a bird attempting to take flight. *I'd like to fly away, from all of this, from the memory of the snubs and whispers, the duel and the scandal. Most of all*, she thought, *I'd like to fly away from the memory of James Dinsmore and the kiss that never should have happened.* If she allowed herself, she could recall every detail of how his lips felt against hers, the soft sure slide of his tongue, the warm rasp of his cheek under her hand. *If* she allowed herself.

A bitter laugh escaped and her balance wavered.

Fragments of memory, lips touching lips, tongues exploring, and the hands that followed. Hers, tracing the lines of his face, the broad planes of his shoulders, the muscles of his back beneath the silk of his coat. Sparkling threads of excitement, weaving through her body and tightening. He'd whispered her name against her throat. "Elizabeth," he'd murmured against the curve of her breasts, his mouth seeking her aching flesh.

The sole of her slipper scraped against uneven stone.

How deeply enmeshed had James been in his sister's schemes? Like a miser fingering a precious hoard of gold, she worried over details of that night. Had there been a note of doubt when he'd drawn her down on the couch? Had there been a hint of pain as he'd fumbled with her stays? She couldn't recall. And yet other details remained so crisp, so sharp. Anne's dress, cream over a red petticoat, red ribbons at the sleeves, the neck, crisscrossing the bodice. There'd been a scrolled pattern in the weave of the ribbons. Gold stitching. A much bolder dress than Anne usually wore. She'd stood out from the onlookers in the library like a scarlet banner of outrage.

Relentlessly, Elizabeth continued to replay her memories. The sound of Anne's voice when she'd discovered them. "Lady Elizabeth Harcrest." The tone shocked, but the words pitched loudly enough for everyone to hear. To know. To push forward and see the scandal firsthand. How quickly James had released her. How easily he had let her go.

A chill breeze whipped at her cheek, tugged at the curls held bound by the blindfold.

Perhaps he hadn't been involved in Anne's machinations? After all, she'd been the one who'd pursued him, encouraged him to take liberties. And afterwards, he hadn't called on her. *I had to seek him out.* . . . Her foot bumped against a jutting stone, and she wavered on the uneven surface, her arms bobbling for balance. He hadn't apologized for what he'd done. He hadn't asked her to marry him. It didn't matter, he'd said, because Rafe had declared him unsuitable. He'd had the courage to face her brother across swords, but not to ask him for her hand. And she hadn't been able to bring him round.

A depressing weight swept over her.

A slight lean to her right and she would fall as neatly as a ballast stone.

So simple, so easy, no more memories, no more doubts, no more disappointment to be found in the eyes of the people she loved, no more questions. The wind caught her skirts and whipped them tight around her ankles. She lifted her left foot. She let herself tilt to the left and felt her weight begin to shift.

Instinctively she scrabbled for balance.

Fought to regain her footing. Found it.

She couldn't do it. She couldn't jump or make herself fall. It would be cheating. She stood inhaling deeply of the damp spring air. She wanted answers. She slid a foot forward and then another. A few more cautious steps and her toe struck the raised edge of a large stone. She was at the end of her walk.

She lowered her arms and allowed her concentration to fade. She became aware of the sounds around her. Wind ruffling the leaves, water rippling over the rocks in the stream, birds chirping, a horse cropping grass some distance away.

Which was odd, since she hadn't ridden to the bridge, she'd walked.

The sound of someone breathing, deep inhalations held long and softly exhaled, as if they didn't want to be heard. She knew exactly who it was. Fumbling with the knots of her blindfold, Elizabeth swore. "Blast it all, Jones, you've no business following me about like some buckskin-clad nanny. I'm a grown woman!"

She must be mad! Didn't she realize she might tumble to her death? He'd seen her from a distance and recognized her immediately, the wind wrapping the skirts of her pale green gown around her slim figure, teasing loose ribbons in her chestnut hair. Only as he rode closer did he notice the sash tied around her eyes. When she raised her arms and began to walk, he'd reigned his horse in, shocked. Her head was tilted slightly back, her arms were flung wide as if she was offering herself up to the sky.

A wave of anger swept over him. *Did she still think everything was some sort of game? Had she learned nothing over the past weeks?* Sliding from the saddle, he looped the mare's reins over the branch of a nearby tree and slipped off his boots. He wanted to shout at her to stop, but he was afraid he might startle her. Walking softly but swiftly he headed for the bridge, eyes locked on the figure of Elizabeth Harcrest. She was nearly halfway across.

The thought whispered that the earl would be furious with him for being late. His stocking feet slid across the damp grass, and mud began to cling to his silk stockings. *Late and unpresentable.* This visit to Moreham Hall was turning out a disaster. He cursed himself for a fool; how could he have thought it would be anything else? He'd promised himself he would not look for Elizabeth, would turn away if he saw her. . . . But he'd never expected this. His breath caught as her footing wavered; his lungs paralyzed until she righted herself and resumed walking. *How could Moreham let her wander about like this? Good Lord,*

*didn't the man know what trouble the girl got into when she
was left unattended?*

He broke into a run. He'd be damned if he'd let her slip
again.

"*Sneaking about, intruding* on my privacy, I don't care
what my brother says, Jones, you're a bloody spy and you
ought to be ashamed of yourself. Haven't you got better
things to do with your time?" Elizabeth yelled, the sash still
wrapped around her eyes.

"To be perfectly honest, I do," James Dinsmore snapped.
"Though the unknown Mr. Jones and your brother have my
sympathies. What the *devil* do you think you're *doing* up
there?"

"James?" The blindfold fell away in her hand and she
stared at him, her eyes seeking proof of what her ears had already recognized. Just saying his name seemed to require all
the breath in her lungs. Her eyes raced over him, trying to
see all of him at once, but she kept getting caught on details:
the sun separating strands of his hair into shades of gold, the
weave of his dark blue jacket, the lion design on his pewter
buttons, the narrow stripes of his waistcoat, his left hand
resting at his side, encased in a smooth-fitting yellow glove.
She was avoiding looking at what she desired to see most:
his face.

"Elizabeth," he ordered. "Come down this instant." He
extended his right hand.

Could she bear it if he bore the visage of a monster?
Slowly, slowly, slowly, she lifted her eyes, seeing first his
chin with a hint of golden bristle, his mouth pressed in a dangerous line, the hollow of his cheek. Then an angry purple
line, like the imprint of a whip, curling towards his eye, cut-
ting through the outer edge of his eyebrow and ending just
below the crease of his brow.

It was shocking, like looking at a vandalized painting of
a renaissance angel.

"Elizabeth," he repeated, his outstretched hand so close he was nearly touching her.

She stared dumbly, as if a gentleman had never offered her his arm. She wanted to reach out to him, to caress his face. *He is still so beautiful. How he must have suffered.*

"For God's sake, Elizabeth, what are you doing up there?" Fear made his voice sharper than intended. He knew he mustn't startle her, frighten her into stumbling. Though by the way she'd been staring, he imagined his face had already done that well enough.

Elizabeth was shaken from her reverie. Did he sound angry with her?

She'd played this scene over and over again in her dreams. Though she'd told herself it would never happen, still she'd allowed herself to imagine a moment when their paths crossed. She'd imagined him regretful, begging her forgiveness. She'd imagined him forceful, sweeping her in to his arms. She'd imagined him courtly, promising his undying love. But she'd never imagined him angry.

What right did *he* have to be angry with *her*?

For that matter, what was he doing *here*, on Harcrest lands? After so much time had passed? Arabella had written several weeks ago that he'd been recovered enough from his wounds to leave his bed. "I beg your pardon, Mr. Dinsmore," she said stiffly, "but I believe it is *I* who should be asking *you*, what it is *you* are doing *down there*."

"Trying to save your damned neck. Now take my hand and come off that wall."

"My neck, as you can plainly see, is fine." She lifted her chin to demonstrate the veracity of her words. "I thank you for your concern, Mr. Dinsmore, but I assure you, I am perfectly fine without your assistance."

Lord but she was a stubborn chit! And Lord knew how late he was going to be for his meeting with her brother. He resisted the urge to check his watch and glance down at his stockings, which from the feel of them were sodden at least to his calves. Keeping his eyes level on Elizabeth, he forced his voice to do the same. "You are being foolish. Now take my hand."

"The last time I took your hand I was being foolish. I've learned my lesson."

"Ah yes, I can see." He couldn't restrain the sarcasm that crept into his words. "Walking on the wall of a bridge blindfolded, where the slightest misstep will send you to death is so very sensible."

"At least the pain will be brief."

He deserved that he supposed, but still her words hurt. "Perhaps," he said, more calmly than he felt, "but then again, you might simply be dreadfully injured. Shatter a limb. Be forced to live on, crippled and in constant pain."

"I hadn't thought of that," she said, glancing over her shoulder at the rocks that thrust up sharply through rushing water.

"Let me help you down, Elizabeth."

She was perfectly able to get down on her own. Usually she'd sit and sort of scoot off. But she didn't want James to see her in such an undignified position. And she didn't want to take his hand. She didn't know why. After all, he had touched her in far more intimate places than her fingertips. She shivered at the memory. Perhaps that was it—she thought they'd shared something special, and here he was, calm as you please, speaking to her as if she were a recalcitrant child. "I do believe you've helped me *down* quite enough," she said sharply.

James caught her emphasis on the word down. So she blamed him for her come down, did she? And even though he held himself responsible, or perhaps because she did, his temper began to flare. "You went willingly into the library, Elizabeth. I didn't force you. If you'll recall, I didn't force anything that night . . ."

He was right, of course, about that night and even about the way she was behaving now. It was humiliating. She'd been humiliated so often of late, she ought to be immune, she thought. But she wasn't, especially in front of him. She closed her eyes, and took the only course left open to her. She jumped.

"Elizabeth . . . *no!*" James dove forward, arms out-stretched, but he'd been taken unawares, and she was be-yond his reach.

The soles of her slippers skidded across the damp grass and she fell with a resounding thump upon her bum roll. *Devil take it all, she couldn't seem to do anything right these days!* She peered up through her lashes at James. While he hadn't laughed, the corner of his mouth was definitely twitching.

She retrieved the sash that she'd used as a blindfold. "Don't you dare attempt to draw some moralistic parallel be-tween slipping and paying the price. I've heard more than enough of that . . ."

"The thought never crossed my mind." Without asking her permission this time, he reached down, grasped her hand, and pulled her to her feet. They stood for a moment, close enough to kiss. His head bent down towards hers. "Morals seldom do."

Elizabeth closed her eyes. She felt James release her hand.

"Like you," he said softly, "I have learned a great many things since that night in the library. In different ways, we both have paid dearly."

Her eyes were open now, and they were drawn to his scar. "Your face . . ." She reached out as if to touch him, but he moved back. "I'm so sorry," she said. "If only I could have set things right . . ."

He shook his head. "Moreham was right to challenge me as he did. If things had been reversed, and he had dishonored Anne . . ." His words trailed off. Things *had* been reversed, and he hadn't challenged Rafe to a duel. Instead he'd lent himself to Anne's schemes for revenge. He was despicable. "This scar is no more than I deserve."

"No—"

"For what it's worth, Elizabeth,"—he raised his hand to prevent her from saying anything more—"I'm sorry for everything that has happened to you." *But not for touching you. I will never regret that single sweet moment.*

She didn't know what she wanted him to say, but she knew it was something more than this . . . weak apology. She began to wrap her sash around her waist; tying it so tightly it felt uncomfortable. "Is that all you have to say?"

"Would words set things right?"

It wasn't the question she'd been expecting. "You're quite right," she snapped. "Mere words would never suffice."

Pain glimmered like a lost coin in the depths of his blue eyes.

"You really should be on your way," she added, plucking a straw hat from where she'd left it hanging on the branch of a tree. "Surely you must realize that if my brother were to discover you here with me he would shoot you like a pheasant and with considerably less regret."

She turned, gathered up her skirts, and, as if she were retiring from a ballroom floor, made her way slowly and regally across the meadow towards the manicured lawns of Moreham Hall.

Chapter 16

As she marched up the hill, her back ramrod straight, Elizabeth cursed herself for a fool. She'd done it *again*. Acted without thinking! *After everything that's happened you'd think I could plan ahead, even the slightest bit.* . . . But she'd been so shocked to open her eyes and see him standing at the foot of the bridge. It was one thing to dream about a man, to imagine what you'd say to him, but to have him show up like that . . . just suddenly *there*. All the speeches, so carefully scripted during long nights she hadn't been able to sleep, had completely run out of her head. Of course, she'd imagined James on bended knee, not scolding her as if she were a half-witted child. *He must think I belong in Bedlam, walking on the bridge like that!* She resisted the urge to look back over her shoulder. Alix's mother Madeleine once told her only a girl just out of the schoolroom would give a man the satisfaction of glancing over her shoulder. Madeleine had lived at Versailles, attended the Queen. She was experienced in handling men.

Elizabeth kicked at a clump of grass, scattering tiny

crickets in all directions. She'd sworn that if she ever crossed paths with James Dinsmore again, she'd be as composed and elegant as Madeleine de La Brou. Instead, she'd ranted at him about how he'd ruined her! When she knew perfectly well she was equally at fault! She'd known the risk when she'd slipped off with him. She simply hadn't expected to be caught—at least not so publicly. Of course it would have helped if James had offered to marry her. A familiar heaviness settled over her, the weight that had nearly pulled her off the bridge. *What was he doing here, on Harcrest lands?* She hadn't even asked.

He had to be meeting with her brother. There was no one else on the estate that might give him leave to call, no one else with whom he might have business. Rafe had made no mention of such an appointment; then again, her brother refused to speak James Dinsmore's name aloud. What ever could they have to discuss—unless it was she? Doubtless that was the answer. How infuriating that he'd keep her in the dark about issues that concerned her future. *How typical.* Elizabeth lengthened her stride as she neared the house. How fortunate she'd found a way round her brother's infernal passion for secrecy ages ago.

James was ushered into Rafe Harcrest's study, a massive room with an elaborately patterned red carpet spread on the floor and towering bookcases reaching from floor to gilt-trimmed ceiling. The Earl of Moreham sat at a heavy mahogany desk; books piled high around him, poring over columns of figures. Carefully marking his place with a silver letter opener, he closed his account books, sat back in his leather armchair, and studied James, his eyes lingering on the scar. The expression in their hazel depths was difficult to read. Was it satisfaction? James wondered.

"You are late, Dinsmore," he said coldly. "I will presume your lack of punctuality is not intended as a discourtesy to me, but rather to some accident on the road." He stared pointedly at James's muddied Hessians, but made no effort to inquire as to the nature of the accident, or whether James had suffered any injuries. Rafe motioned with an elegant hand to a straight-backed chair that had been drawn up in front of the desk. "Sit."

James would have liked to refuse the command, or better yet, to pull up one of the upholstered wing chairs that were scattered about the room. Instead, he nodded and thanked Moreham. He arranged his long limbs in the chair with languid ease. "I apologize for my tardiness. It was unavoidable. It is good of Your Lordship to see me."

"Let us not play at words, Dinsmore, we both know perfectly well that goodness has nothing to do with this meeting. Indeed, I should be surprised if you had a passing acquaintance with that sentiment."

"Forgive me, my lord," James said, looking down at his gloved hands and flexing one, slowly, like a leopard considering his claws, "but I have not come here to discuss my character."

"Ah yes," Rafe smiled grimly. "You've come to destroy mine."

"Despite how it may seem, the purpose of my visit is on Lord Grenville's behalf. And I do not seek your destruction, but rather your cooperation."

"My cooperation?" Rafe's brows arched skeptically. "If Grenville wishes to gain my *cooperation*, he has chosen a most peculiar messenger."

"He thought by sending me to speak for him, he might gain your attention." James knew he must choose his words carefully. "It was essential to convince you of the urgency of his request."

"Request? Don't play me for a fool. I served in his majesty's army. I know the difference between a request and a requisition." Rafe's fingers drummed impatiently on the desktop. "You and Grenville have gained my complete attention. Now tell me *precisely* what it is you want."

"It has come to the attention of certain circles within Whitehall that over the past several years you have built up a network of trade relationships throughout France. Extensive relationships that you have taken great pains to conceal with cover companies, false fronts, holding companies, and middlemen." James paused, to let his words sink in. "You even have a number of ships, chartered in other men's names."

"You've forgotten to add that these are very lucrative networks." Rafe's fingers stilled. "Isn't that really what this meeting is about, Dinsmore—extortion?"

"It is not." James forced his voice to remain cool. "We have no interest in your money, only in access to your networks. Your connections in France are most impressive, my lord, and even more impressively concealed."

"You wish to use my connections for spying." Rafe spat the words as if they fouled his tongue. "Gentlemen do not poke about in each other's business, listening at doors, and reading one another's mail."

The very words he had said to Grenville! "And gentlemen do not soil their hands with trade," James countered quietly.

Rafe's mouth tightened. "This estate was mortgaged to the hilt when I inherited it. I would not stand idly by and see my stepmother and half sister deprived of home and security. I did what I had to do to protect them." Light from the tall windows that lined his study caught the gold signet ring he wore on his left hand and the jeweled Moreham crest blazed. "Family, honor—these things may mean little to a man like you, Dinsmore. But they are everything to me."

James would not discuss Anne, he would not betray her confidence, nor dishonor himself by attempting to defend what he had done on her behalf. His eyes locked with Moreham's. "Your honor is secure, Moreham. It would serve His Majesty's government far more to have your networks continue to operate as they have in the past . . . discreetly. Indeed, immediate access to your networks would be invaluable in a matter of critical importance to His Majesty's government."

"So you've gone from panderer to patriot? Fascinating." Rafe's words were sharp, but his tone betrayed curiosity. "And you need my voucher to make introductions, do you not?"

"It would smooth the way." James nodded. "I understand your people are rather fiercely loyal to you."

"As I am to them. And I should appreciate more detail before I put so much as a single life at risk."

"The factories you deal with make textiles, not just pretty cloth for ladies' gowns and gentlemen's waistcoats, but common stuff as well, woolens, osnabrigs. Large sums of money pass through these institutions, with few questions asked."

"And is it fabrics or funds which have caught the attention of Lord Grenville?" Rafe didn't wait for an answer. "I shall hazard a guess . . . the funds. But the sums are hardly worth blackmailing an earl to acquire." He sat back in his chair. "And you wish my shipping and banking contacts as well? Tell me, Dinsmore, speculation is involved, no doubt, but what else is at stake here, and why is it of such urgency?"

"A man's life."

"One man?" Rafe prompted. "He must be important," he added when James was not forthcoming with additional details.

"He is."

"And will you be representing Lord Grenville at that appointment as well?"

"I will."

Rafe eyed Dinsmore curiously. "These are dangerous times in France. A man may lose his life for saying the wrong thing, wearing the wrong color, looking askance at his neighbor—"

"Are you concerned for my welfare, Moreham?" James asked, amused.

"My wife is French, in case you have forgotten."

"I doubt I ever could," James said dryly, thinking Anne rarely referred to Alix without appending some epithet against the French.

"She barely escaped the assault of a bloodthirsty mob on her family's chateau; her father, the Comte de La Brou, was not so fortunate."

Elizabeth, sitting atop a ladder in the library next to Rafe's study, her ear pressed against the back wall of the bookcase, lost her grip on the leather-bound volumes of erotic poetry piled in her lap. *James Dinsmore is planning to go to France and he chastised me for walking blindfolded on a wall?* Everyone knew what was happening in France; the terror sweeping the country as centuries of peasant wrath boiled over. They'd executed their *king* in January! Now the revolutionaries seemed to have gone mad, slaughtering people left and right—they'd even built a machine, the guillotine, to do the work more efficiently. Making a grab for the sliding books, she very nearly bumped her head against the shelf above it.

She'd discovered this listening post when she was fourteen.

Eager to impress her Latin tutor—who had the loveliest blue eyes—she'd climbed up prepared to do a bit of extracurricular reading. She'd been shocked and then utterly engrossed by what she found, until she'd been disturbed by voices. Certain she'd be caught with the scandalous volumes in her hand, she was trying to stuff them back in the shelves, when she realized the voices were coming from the *back* of the bookcase. Leaning her head in amongst the books, she found that if she stayed very still, she could make out nearly every word that was said in her brother's study. It was a fascinating discovery.

Catching the falling books at the last possible moment before they hit the floor, Elizabeth gathered them back into her lap, anxious that she was missing something important being said in the study. Not about Rafe's business dealings. She'd heard all about *that* ages ago. He'd been at it for years, and as far as she knew, there hadn't been a breath of it amongst the ton. But now James Dinsmore knew. Would he tell Anne? If he did, the scandal would spread through polite society like a burning ember on a carpet. And coupled with what she'd done. . . . She flattened her ear against the wall.

"You have my cooperation Dinsmore. Not because you threaten me, or because I fear exposure. I would give aid to anyone brave enough or mad enough to risk his life to save victims of the revolutionaries. Along with the list of contacts, I shall include letters of introduction . . ."

Of course, he has little choice, Elizabeth mused. *The family reputation, or what is left of it, is at stake . . .*

". . . trust is a rare commodity in France these days, there is far more at stake than reputations. Do not abuse their trust or mine, Dinsmore."

Even through wood and plaster, she could hear the warning in her brother's voice. *Rafe will have to trust James Dinsmore, just as I did.*

"You are staying nearby?"

"At the Hart and Hounds."

"It will take some time to draw up the list and write the letters—"

"Forgive me if I put undue pressure on you, Moreham, but every day the situation becomes less secure. The revolutionaries are turning upon each other, seeking not only aristocrats, like our fugitive, but counterrevolutionaries and spies. We hope to leave for the coast by week's end."

Undue pressure? As if blackmail were not enough! Elizabeth wished she could brain James with the books she was clutching. Her brother's response was far more polite.

"I understand your need for haste. I shall endeavor to have the papers for you by tomorrow, Wednesday afternoon at the latest."

"You have my deepest gratitude."

"I have no desire for your gratitude," Rafe interjected sharply.

For several moments she heard only silence. Then he spoke again, the harsh tone of his voice giving way. "Tell me Dinsmore why are you risking your life in this way, for a man you don't even know? You've never expressed much interest in politics. Indeed, if I recall, you once described men who debate politics as being all mouths and having no ears. Have you suddenly found a cause? Are you now driven by some newfound sense of honor?"

"I have no sense of honor. You've said so yourself. Surely if you've forgotten, my face should remind you. Marked for the world to see as a dishonorable cur? I believe those were your words."

"Close enough. Though I also recall you refused to apologize for touching my sister."

"An apology you will never have."

"Just as you will never have her."

"You've made that abundantly clear, Moreham."

"So is it a heroic gesture you think to make, some form of redemption that you seek in France?"

Elizabeth pressed her ear so tightly against the wall it began to throb.

"Redemption?" James laughed, a bitter sound. "Do you think redemption is possible for a man such as I? It would be enough for me if I might find . . ."

"Elizabeth?"

Whatever it was James hoped to find in France, Elizabeth was unable to hear. The lilting voice of her sister-in-law interrupted her eavesdropping. "Are you in here?"

A string of curses she'd heard from a groom after a carthorse stepped on his foot sprang to mind. Quickly she shoved the pile of erotic poetry into the space where her head had been and hastily snatched up a copy of *Caesar's Gallic Wars* from a lower shelf. Opening it on her lap to a random page, she called, "I'm here. Just searching for something amusing to read."

Alix peered anxiously around the shelves. "Have you seen Roland? Apparently he has escaped from the kitchen. I thought I might find him here. He seems to have a penchant for the library."

"That pug has a *penchant* for anything he can chew," Elizabeth said, descending the ladder. "I do not understand why you didn't leave him in London with your mother."

Alix laughed. "Madeleine cannot tolerate dogs, but Roland, he was a gift from Lord Rothwell."

Elizabeth wrinkled her nose. "The widower with all the children?"

She nodded. "My maman believes that if she returns the dog, Lord Rothwell will think she is not maternal enough to marry."

"But your mother . . ." Elizabeth paused, not wishing to damage the relationship so carefully mended since the duel, yet finding it difficult to picture Alix's flamboyant mother surrounded by children. "She isn't exactly what one thinks of as maternal."

"No, she is not. But then she has not had much practice, living apart from my father and me for so many years. She has a good heart, my mother, and she is very fond of Lord Rothwell." Alix's gray eyes grew thoughtful. "Our impressions of people, so often they are based on how they look or how they dress . . . on façade."

"But most people, at least those among the ton, spend a tremendous amount of time and money creating just the right appearance. Isn't it appropriate, then, that we should judge them on it?"

"Ahhh," said Alix. "Always remember that façades, like sleights of hand, are not merely about what a person wishes you to see, but also about what they hope to conceal." She smiled brightly. "Now then, shall we go and see if we can't find that rascal Roland?"

Chapter 17

Alix's search for the pug was leading them farther and farther away from Rafe's study. Elizabeth's eyes narrowed as she watched her sister-in-law peering under the chaise in the music room; she felt fairly certain Roland wasn't anywhere near the salmon and gold brocade sofa. "No sign of him here," Alix said, straightening slowly, hand on her growing belly. "Perhaps he's gone upstairs." Elizabeth had seen the pug try to climb stairs; it was a major effort for his little brown legs, and he usually settled on the fourth or fifth step, waiting to be carried the rest of the way.

Her sister-in-law must have been instructed to keep her away from the study.

So Rafe and Alix were making an effort to prevent her from discovering James's visit. Did they think she would be devastated by the sight of him? Or did they imagine she would make a fool of herself by flinging herself into his arms? How would they react if they were to discover she and James had already met? She hadn't been devastated and she certainly hadn't thrown herself into his arms. Though she had to admit she'd made something of a fool of herself, plummeting to the ground like that. She bit her lower lip, remembering how he'd smiled at her and pulled her to her feet. All that she'd heard had set her thoughts and emotions spinning. James Dinsmore was staying at the Hart and Hounds for the next three days, but by week's end he'd be on his way to France.

She had less than two days to decide what she should do.

The well-fed figure of Sir Edmund Bogglesworth was spilling over the edges of her Louis XIV armchair. From the sheen of his superfine wool jacket, Anne guessed the garment must have cost a pretty penny. Though rumor had it, Sir Edmund, an obscure country squire only recently come to town, had plenty to spare. She smoothed the skirt of the dress she'd reconfigured yet again, folding her hands in her lap, forcing herself to follow his conversation.

"You may not believe this to look at me," he said nodding his several chins, "but I was a sickly child. Yes, a sickly child. It's a wonder I made it out of infancy. It was the milk you see, couldn't bear the milk. Must have gone through every available breast in the village near my country estate, Hamcroft. That's up north." He nodded as if she should know and she nodded back in response. Thus encouraged, he continued.

She admired the stitching on his waistcoat and the fine silver buttons. It would have looked handsome on James. Her eyes drifted to a chair by the tea table. Her brother should have occupied it, but instead her cousin Agatha Leech sat there, her new chaperone. Half deaf and three-quarters blind, Agatha leaned towards Sir Edmund as if he were recounting the most fascinating of adventures.

"I had faded away to nothing, no bigger than a rabbit, I'm told. My own mother had given me up for dead when this old midwife from the village near Hamcroft says she can save me. Fed me scotch and sugar from her little finger, drop by drop, can you imagine?" He shook his chins at the wonder, and as if she understood, Agatha nodded her own chin, the one with the two gray hairs that Anne longed to reach over and pluck.

"More tea, Sir Edmund?" She lifted the china pot, hoping the offer of beverages would stem the tide of his talk.

Edmund waved the pot away, the massive gold rings on his plump fingers glittering with the gesture. But Agatha held out a shaking cup. Anne filled it praying that she wouldn't spill the expensive oolong tea on the carpet. The cup found its way safely to Agatha's lips and she gave a contented slurp.

Anne shot a surreptitious glance at Sir Edmund to see if he had noticed this appalling lapse of manners, but he had resumed his story.

"Ever since that day, I have started my morning with a bit of scotch sugar, and so you see me now, as hale and hearty as a horse, with never a day's illness since those tremulous early years." He sat back in his chair, folding his hands over the spread of his waistcoat.

Almost as if he were expecting applause, she thought.

If James were here, he'd have ready some subtle innuendo about horses or village breasts that Edmund wouldn't understand. Afterwards, they'd laugh at his ignorance in the privacy of her boudoir. But James was gone, leaving only a brief note, reassuring her that he loved her. She hadn't the faintest idea of where he was, or how long he'd be away. But she knew very well why he'd left. He'd been humiliated by that beast Rafe Harcrest, marked forever by that frog-loving brother of a slut. She smiled at Sir Edmund, "Your childhood experiences are truly harrowing, sir. How fortuitous it is that you have survived to provide us with such charming company."

"It is you, Lady Anne, who are the charming company."

She lowered her eyes with practiced modesty. "You flatter me, Sir Edmund."

"I only tell the truth"—he patted his stomach for emphasis—"as you'll realize when you come to know me better. Why in Hamcroft, I'm known far and wide for my honesty, my fairness in dealing with my tenants."

She'd heard his estates brought in a considerable sum a year. "Do tell us more about Hamcroft."

"It would be my pleasure. Though it would be an even greater pleasure if I could show them to you." He narrowed his pale blue eyes suggestively and waggled his brows.

Agatha spied the look and misinterpreted it completely. "Oh sir," she cried with alarm, "you've caught a cinder in your eye! Let me get you a cloth with a bit of cool water."

Sir Edmund flushed. "No, no, really, Miss Leech, it's entirely unnecessary."

"No, no, don't try and be polite about it, sir. I can see you flinching. It's this inferior wood, it is, full of sparks and cinder. And the chimneys haven't been cleaned proper in ages."

"My eyes are fine, Miss Leech," Sir Edmund said in a voice that made Agatha sit back. "Do not trouble yourself any further on my account. As for the fire on the hearth, I had not noticed it, so taken am I by the light of Lady Anne's eyes." He smiled at her. "But as I look at it now, the draw seems perfectly fine."

Anne's eyes met his, reconsidering. Perhaps there were greater depths to the pale puddles than she'd suspected. "Hamcroft," she prompted. "You were about to tell us about the estates and your family . . . how long have they occupied the land?"

His smiled broadened. "My baronetcy is but a humble title in comparison with the great name of Dinsmore. But it is as old as the name of Dinsmore. Indeed, much older in its claims than many of those popinjays who strut about the ton wearing titles fresher than their linen."

Anne's eyes widened at his indelicate choice of words, though she agreed with him, and was amused by his metaphor.

Sir Edmund waved a hand. "I am indiscreet in speaking so frankly to a lady of such gentle breeding, I apologize."

"No apology is necessary. You have said you are an honest man. Frankness of speech is honesty's hallmark."

"Well said, lady." He reached for a gooseberry tart. Between bites that left sprinkles of crust in the folds of his starched holland stock, he continued, "London is littered with upstarts. Last year's merchant is this year's lord."

She nodded, offering him another tart.

"And if that were not bad enough, there are those of noble birth and breeding, who welcome this lot, even stooping to join them in their sordid business affairs. I'm sure you know to whom I refer."

Anne put down the plate of tarts and poured herself a cup of tea, having long ago learned that an air of indifference was the greatest accelerant to gossip.

"I understand he even challenged your brother to a duel."

"Moreham?" It was with tremendous effort that she hid her excitement, affecting a tone that hinted at boredom. "That tediously self-righteous man, whatever has he done now?"

"Not now, but for the past several years, under society's very nose." Sir Edmund leaned conspiratorially over his girth. "I took a trip to France before the troubles began. Something of a grand tour, see a bit of the world . . . though I don't believe the French have anything but corruption to offer English gentlefolk. While I was there, I met a fellow who told me the most interesting tale about the Earl of Moreham and the textile trade."

"The earl involved in trade? Sir Edmund, surely you jest?"

He shook his head. "No, indeed, I swear, the story I shall tell you is the God's honest truth."

Oh, James, Anne thought with delight, *if only you were here*. And she offered Sir Edmund her first genuine smile of the day.

• • •

They found the pug curled under Rafe and Alix's bed.
Roland stretched and yawned and wriggled out from under
the tester, eager to play. The two women tossed him a ball of
rags, commenting on his antics and avoiding meaningful
conversation. Which was fine with Elizabeth. She doubted
she could have managed to string two sentences together co-
herently. She was absorbed with thoughts of James. If only
Alix hadn't interrupted her eavesdropping in the library, if
only she could have heard the rest of the conversation in
Rafe's study. Of all the men in England James could have
approached for help with his venture in France, why her
brother? Surely there were other men with networks that
could be used to transfer money to France? It didn't make
sense.

Unless James had other reasons for coming to Harcrest
Hall.

Over and over she considered the last words she'd overheard him say, *Redemption? Do you think redemption is
possible for a man such as I? It would be enough for me if I
might find . . .*

Find what?

She wrested the rag ball from Roland and tossed it,
watching the pug race after it in eager pursuit. *Blast it all,
how had he answered Rafe's question?* She'd known him
forever, since she'd been a child, but understand him? It was
rather like trying to see clearly through a multi-faceted gem.
Had he responded to Rafe like a jaded libertine? *Redemption? It would be enough for me if I might find a fine bottle
of wine and a couple of ripe wenches.* Or perhaps he'd assumed the pose of a carefree adventurer. *Redemption? It
would be enough for me to shed the stale air of the ton, to
feel the wind of the channel at my back, and the promise of
a good horse between my knees.* The pug pounced on the rag
ball, tumbling over it, and falling against Alix.

She laughed, bending over slowly and tickling his round,

brown belly. Then plucking the ball from between his paws, she tapped him with it on his wet, black nose, and tossed it towards Elizabeth.

Roland scrambled up and after it.

When she met James at the bridge he said they both paid dearly. Could his response have been regretful? *Redemption? It would be enough for me if I might find a way to redeem myself in your eyes. If through my actions, I might somehow atone for the wrongs that I have committed against you and your sister.*

The rag ball landed several feet from Elizabeth and rolled. Roland stalked it, paws forward, haunches up, dark eyes intense.

They both had *paid dearly*, she reflected. Though she hated to think of herself as ruined—as if she were a torn gown that could never be mended, or a letter stained with ink that could never be cleaned—she knew her life was changed forever. There were times, such as this morning, when the weight of despair was almost more than she could bear. Had suffering brought his spirit equally low? *Redemption?* She imagined him shaking his golden head sorrowfully. *It would be enough if I might find an end to unhappy life in the welcoming arms of death.*

Roland pounced again, attacking the bundle of rags with his sharp teeth and shaking it fiercely.

She'd been waiting for a sign, certain in her heart that they were meant to be together and that someday he would come for her. True, after so many weeks her confidence had begun to wane, but today both had happened. She'd opened her eyes on the bridge to find him standing with his arms outstretched. And while he hadn't kissed her, she'd had the strongest notion that he wanted to. It was why he'd leaned close and why she'd closed her eyes. *Magnetism.* It was possible that the response James had given Rafe had been romantic. *Redemption? It would be enough if I might win back your respect and with it, the hand of your sister, Elizabeth.*

In his enthusiasm, Roland lost his grip on the ball of rags and it shot across the room landing with a soft thump close to the bedchamber door. Surprised, he swung his wrinkled face from side to side, searching for his elusive prey. He might not have found it, had not the door swung open. Cocking his head in the direction of the noise, he spied the ball and shot toward it. But just as he was about to leap upon it, he was scooped up in the firm grip of Rafe Harcrest.

"I thought I had given orders banning this fellow from these premises," he said casting a mock frown at the squirming pup against his chest. Roland licked his chin.

"It appears, my love,"—Alix smiled up at him—"he finds you are irresistible."

"The little mongrel is completely indiscriminate," he said, reaching out a hand to help Alix to her feet, "lavishing attention on anyone who might scratch his belly or pass him a scrap of food from the table."

"You judge him too harshly," she said, lifting the pug from out of his arms. "If you paid him better mind, you'd notice he's fonder of you than anyone else in the household. And loyal. Why the other day, I found him defending your stockings from the upstairs maid. Wouldn't let her pick them up and put them in the wash."

Rafe rumpled the pug's velvety ears, and Roland enthusiastically licked his hands. "The misguided things men do for love . . ."

Elizabeth changed the subject abruptly. "Have you finished attending to business for the day?"

"Why do you ask?"

From the worried glance he shot Alix, Elizabeth could tell he was making an effort to keep both his voice and expression bland. "You've spent such a long time closeted in your study this afternoon," she smiled innocently. "On such a lovely day as this, I thought we might all go for a walk in the garden. Or a ride?"

Rafe cleared his throat. "I think a ride would be too vigorous for Alix in her delicate condition." Alix crossed her hands over the slight swell of her belly and nodded. "Perhaps a walk, a short walk. Then I'm afraid I must return to my study. Some important correspondence I must take care of . . . and speaking of correspondence,"—he reached into his waistcoat—"I've a letter here for you, Elizabeth."

"A letter? For me?" Excitement rippled through her. *Could it be from James?* Something he'd hadn't had the chance to give her when they'd encountered each other so unexpectedly? "I didn't know the post had come today," she said.

"About an hour ago."

Was it something James felt compelled to dash off to her before he left? Something her brother had been brought round enough to agree to deliver? "Do you know from whom?" she asked, far more casually than she felt.

"A devoted friend." He smiled.

Elizabeth held out an eager hand. Perhaps it was a promise to return when he'd completed his mission in France, a vow to win her hand. Rafe placed the folded missive in it. She turned it over, scarcely daring to breath.

It was from Arabella Norcroft.

Chapter 18

Elizabeth left the bedchamber, explaining that she wanted to enjoy the contents of her letter in private. Alix waited until the door clicked shut behind her sister-in-law, before turning expectant eyes upon her husband. "Well," she asked, "What did he want?"

"No 'my darling husband, how I've missed you since we parted this morning'?" he teased her, "No, 'the hours seemed like years'?"

"Was it blackmail then?"

"But a few months married, and already the light of romance has vanished from your eyes." Rafe heaved a mock sigh.

"You shall see the light of murder in them, if you do not tell me everything that went on in your study this very moment."

His eyebrows rose. "And some people say the French are a bloodthirsty race."

She scowled at him.

"Very well." Rafe dropped into a chair by the bed. "James Dinsmore wishes my assistance in traveling to France."

"Cease teasing me," she said impatiently. "What did he really want from you?"

"I am quite serious." The tone of his voice made it clear that he was. "Dinsmore intends to go to France."

"Has he lost his mind?"

"He seemed quite sane."

Alix, who had been standing, slipped into a chair next to Rafe. "Why on earth would a sane man go to France now? Some misplaced sense of adventure?" She frowned. "Or perhaps he is driven by some sort of death wish?"

"I cannot tell you his purpose." Rafe's fingers drummed on the arm of the chair.

Alix's frown deepened. "When I agreed to marry you, you swore not to keep any secrets from me."

"This is different . . . it has to do with politics. Lives are at stake."

"And to whom do you believe I might pass this sensitive information? The downstairs maid, the gardener's assistant?" She paused, searching for an even more incredible candidate. "Anne Dinsmore?"

"Indeed, I know how well you can keep secrets, my love." He sighed. "I will tell you everything. It is a fool's errand, an attempt to smuggle out of France a man of great importance to the British government, Gerard de Joley."

"Joley?" Her expression was incredulous.

He nodded. "Do you know him?"

"I know *of* him. Who in France does not? I have never met him, though I believe Madeleine has . . ." Her voice trailed off, then took another path. "But I do not understand. How does James Dinsmore come to be involved in such a plot?"

"Connections. Connections to certain people in White-hall, whose knowledge of our connections in France bring him round again to us. It appears, try as we might, we cannot be shed of the Dinsmores."

"You do not think James would tell his sister about your connections in France?"

Rafe shook his head. "However tempting it might be to expose our involvement in trade, such gossip would put his own life at risk."

Alix reached out her hand, touching his. He looked down at it and then at her, and for a long moment her gray eyes searched the depths of his hazel ones. "Would you . . ." She paused searching for the appropriate verb. "Would you be *disturbed* if he should die in France?"

"If you had asked me that question before this afternoon, I would have said my only regret upon hearing of James Dinsmore's death would be that it had not been at my hand. But now, after speaking with him, hearing what he plans and why, I find myself feeling differently about the matter . . ."

"Elizabeth would be glad to hear you say so," she said, adding softly, "thank heavens she does not know that he was here."

"But she does. They met this morning by the bridge."

"But how do you know? I have been with her for over an hour. She said nothing to me."

"Apparently, my love, you are not the only woman in this house who knows how to keep secrets." Rafe grimaced. "I set Jervis to follow her. He didn't have a chance to tell me until after James had left that he'd seen them together."

"Was it arranged, do you think?"

"I asked Jervis that same question. He said from what he observed, they both seemed surprised . . . and that their parting looked rather final."

"A small favor."

"A very small one," he said dryly.

Alix's hand, still resting on Rafe's, caressed his reassuringly. "With so sensitive a purpose, James could never have revealed to her the reason for his visit."

"No," Rafe agreed. "He would not."

"So Elizabeth cannot possibly know." Alix smiled encouragingly. "And *that* you must admit, is a considerably larger one."

Sitting at her dressing table, Elizabeth stared at the familiar handwriting of Arabella Norcroft, the letters of each word neatly formed, all except for the last, which finished with an odd curl or dash, as if her mind had become impatient with the slow pace of her hand. She loved Arabella's letters, always filled with descriptions that revealed the quick wit carefully hidden beneath the sober exterior her mother forced her to assume. Arabella's correspondence was her only link to the outside world. And yet, as she turned the letter over, breaking the wax seal, she couldn't shake her disappointment that the letter hadn't been from James.

> *Mother insists we must leave London for Hartsdale by the end of the week—I'm certain by the time you receive this letter, dear Elizabeth, we shall already be there. My sister, Annabella, is expecting her first child any day now, and Mother is convinced it will be a boy. Nothing must suit her, but that the family should be gathered 'round Annabella's bed, as if prepared to welcome the arrival of a long-awaited prince. As for the season, Mother says it shall make no difference if I should miss a few parties since, as she is increasingly fond of pointing out, despite her best efforts I have failed to attract the attentions of a suitable gentleman.*
>
> *I might have I suppose, had I met one. What about My Beloved, Mr. Thomas Stirling, you are no doubt wondering, the dashing gentleman with whom I was so desperate to dance at the Dinsmore's ball? Alas, upon further acquaintance, Mr. Stirling's handsome face turned out to be nothing more than a charming cover for a book filled with empty pages. When I think of the fuss I made over him to you, my cheeks flush crimson with embarrass-*

*ment. When next I cast my eyes upon a man, I vow I shall
read well beyond both cover and title.*

Elizabeth smiled at her friend's turn of phrase, her smile
broadening as she continued to read:

> *How I wish I could see you, dearest Elizabeth. I must
> confess that London and the season are not half so en-
> tertaining without you. Hartsdale is so near to Moreham
> Hall. I believe no more than three day's ride even in the
> worst of weathers. I have asked my mother if you might
> visit with us.*

Her heart leapt. She finished the page and turned it over.
Her heart sank. Arabella's mother had stated such a visit
would be *not merely out of the question, but beyond speculation*, in view of Elizabeth's *scandalous cavorting with that
disreputable libertine, James Dinsmore.* She had attempted
to reason with her *most unreasonable parent whose mind is
surely cast more solidly than the iron of any cannon on His
Majesty's ships!* But her mother stood firm, her position *appallingly old-fashioned even as we stand, less than a decade
shy of a new century!*

The last page contained a single paragraph, repeating
Arabella's assurances that the scandal meant nothing to her,
less than the feathers on Lady Ellsworth's turban! She
missed Elizabeth, she wrote, *even a day apart from your
dear companionship seems much too long.* And she concluded, *I pray dearest Elizabeth that I shall soon see you
again.*

Elizabeth swept the pages from her desk in a sudden rush
of anger.

She'd made a mistake. Even worse—she'd been caught.
She *understood* that she'd been wrong, was ready to repent,
to beg society's forgiveness but society had no interest. She
couldn't turn the clock back to the night of the Dinsmore's
ball. All she could do was wait. Wait until society decided to

forgive or forget—which might take until she was in her dotage. She must hang her head in shame and do nothing, *nothing* while James Dinsmore could do anything he damn well pleased. She was ruined, but he was simply notorious—a label, she had no doubt, that only made him seem more dashing. She leaned down to pick up the scattered pages of the letter, determined to rip them to shreds. She tore one into satisfying bits. She reached for another. Then she stopped, staring at the two pages lying nearest her skirts. *Hartsdale is so near to Moreham Hall, I believe no more than three days' ride even in the worst of weathers. I have asked my mother if you might visit with us.*

She reread the brief lines on the other page; *even a day apart from your dear companionship seems much too long. I pray dearest Elizabeth that I shall soon see you again.* With the hateful page that separated them gone, these lines now read like an invitation. . . . Her anger flared anew.

It was appallingly, unrelentingly unfair! James Dinsmore could move on with his life. He could go to *France* and she couldn't even go to Hartsdale! She picked up the papers and set them side by side on her dressing table. She wished she'd heard his answer to Rafe's question. She couldn't imagine that he'd answered he wished for death. Why involve her brother, and spy networks, and fugitives in France? Why not just put a pistol to his head, fall on his sword, or leap from a bridge?

James Dinsmore didn't want to die, any more than she did. She'd been walking the bridge, tempting death to take her, because she didn't know what else to do with her life. They'd been unfairly parted by her brother's impulsive behavior. *A duel, in this day and age!* But now . . . now . . . She'd bet James was doing the same by going to France. He would most likely deny it. He was accustomed to denying—his desire for responsibility, his ducal title, the estates that went with it, his desire for her. She drummed her fingers on the dressing table in a gesture reminiscent of her brother's.

She'd always believed the world of rakes was divided into two sorts. There were men like her late father and her brother George, who became bored with life because they'd tasted too much of its pleasures, and then there were men like James, who had become resigned to the notion that they would never truly taste those pleasures. *James Dinsmore was blindfolded on a bridge of his own making and it was time,* Elizabeth decided, *that someone brought him down-to-earth.*

She pushed aside bottles of perfume, brushes, and pots of powder, clearing a space. Reaching into a drawer she pulled out several sheets of pink stationery, a sharp quill, and a bottle of nearly fresh ink. She dipped her quill, and then sat for several moments more, tapping it against the rim of the bottle. And then she began to write.

"*And so you* see," Elizabeth said the following morning as she sat at the breakfast table with Rafe, Alix, and Louisa, "you simply must allow me to pay a visit to Arabella at Hartsdale. Read the letter." She gestured with a bit of toast.

"Elizabeth," Louisa tsked. "One really shouldn't point with food."

"I'm sorry, Mother." She put the bread down. "I just want Rafe to see how anxious I am to go. You all have been terrific really. And I'm sorry, truly I am. I should have listened when each of you tried to warn me about the consequences of my behavior." She glanced earnestly about the table, her eyes meeting Rafe's last. "I've learned so many lessons since London."

He raised an eyebrow. "Such as?"

She caught her breath. In the speech she'd practiced last night, she'd expected her brother to be moved, not skeptical. "So many lessons," she began, stalling for time. "I hardly know where to begin."

It was Alix, surprisingly, who came to her rescue. "Rafe," she said gently, "we all know how Elizabeth has suffered and what she has undoubtedly learned from the experience. I hardly think it necessary to grill her over breakfast. And you were saying just the other day you thought a visit with Arabella might do her good."

"I had in mind for Miss Norcroft to come here . . ."

Elizabeth leapt at this opening. "And I should have preferred her to visit at Moreham Hall as well. But as you can read in the letter, her sister is lying in and her mother wishes the family to be at her side . . ."

"Yes, well, I suppose that's understandable," he muttered, eyes sliding over Alix's expanding shape.

"Arabella will be so bored and I . . ."

"Have been bored buried here in the countryside as well," he finished.

"That wasn't what I meant to say." Elizabeth flushed, swept by a wave of guilt for what she intended to do. *But if it works*, she told herself, *if things turn out to plan, or even if they turn out very wrong, at least the family will be relieved of the burden my behavior has placed upon them.* "It's been quiet here and I've had a great deal of time to think. But it would be nice to spend some time with someone my own age."

"Alix is not so much older than you," Rafe reminded her.

It was Louisa, this time, who came to her aid. "Their ages are close, but you must admit," she said, eyes shifting ever so slightly towards Alix's hand with its jeweled wedding band, resting on her belly, "their interests have diverged."

"I suppose," he said reluctantly.

"Oh do say yes, Rafe." Elizabeth reached into her lap and pulled out the letter she'd written and sealed the night before. "I have penned a response in the hopes you might agree. Only say the word, and let me send a footman to catch the mail coach as it passes through town." She dropped her head slightly and peered up at him with wide eyes. "Please Rafe?"

His lips twitched.

"Only think of how quiet it will be here without me, Alix by your side, Louisa puttering about the garden. The weather turning warm, the flowers coming into bloom." She resisted the urge to add, *Jervis no longer tasked with following me about.*

His lips twitched again. "I know you, Elizabeth Harcrest. You've not only written the letter, but prepared the speech, and I wouldn't be surprised to discover, ordered the maids to begin packing your bags."

"You know me too well," she confessed, thinking it unwise to tell him her bags were, in fact, already packed. She didn't expect to need very many things where she was going.

"Indeed, I do," he said firmly. "Which is why I shall expect regular correspondence from you while you are away."

"You're the best brother in the world." Elizabeth cast a brilliant smile at him, as she raised her right hand as if swearing an oath. "And if it's regular correspondence you require, regular correspondence you shall have." *And a challenge it will be. The first of many,* she reminded herself, offering a silent prayer that they'd all be so easily resolved.

She'd need to add a postscript before she sent her letter off to Arabella.

Chapter 19

The four men sat playing a desultory game of cards at the table they'd dragged into the center of the upstairs room of the Hart and Hounds. The afternoon sun struggled to make its way through a single diamond-paned window on the far wall. Its rays highlighted the dust that swirled in delicate patterns everywhere, over the two rope beds that were set at angles beneath the window, the nightstand with the chipped pitcher and basin, and the battered desk pushed into a corner of the room. A trunk, several valises, and a medical chest were piled near the door.

David sneezed, breaking the silence. "It's been three days since you met with the earl. What do you think, Dinsmore, has he had a change of heart?"

"Not Moreham." James fingered the scar on his cheek. "When Harcrests set themselves to do something, they see it through. He'll deliver."

"And if he doesn't?" David persisted.

"Moreham said Wednesday at the latest; the information will be here today," he replied with more confidence than he felt. "And if it isn't, well then, we'll make do without it. It will be a bit more of a challenge, but we'll pull it off." He smiled. "Consider what we've accomplished thus far."

Andre chuckled. "David's tumbled the kitchen maid, I've won a respectable sum off the crowd downstairs and Marcus,"—his eyes settled briefly on the figure across the table—"Marcus has somehow managed to keep his linen immaculate and his hair unruffled."

"Good hygiene." Marcus cast a critical glance at Andre's rumpled stock and unbuttoned waistcoat. "I'd offer you some lessons, but I abhor expending my energies on hopeless causes."

"Marcus, Marcus, Marcus." Andre shook his head, loosening several strands of dark hair from his loosely clubbed queue. "What you fail to comprehend is that the ladies can't resist my style. They take one look at me and are overcome with the urge to clasp me to a nurturing bosom."

"Which is why, no doubt, after all the time you've spent in the tap room, the kitchen maid has been overcome with the urge to sweep our friend David to her nurturing, and, I might add, most generous bosom."

Andre put down a card. "That is because I did not turn the full force of my attentions upon her."

"I see." Marcus studied the card, considering. "Then do tell, my friend, if the object of your attentions has not been the maid, and you emptied the meager pockets of the locals our first evening here, what has kept you so very busy below stairs?"

"Andre has been spinning tales," David offered, putting down two cards.

Andre smiled as if accepting a prize. "You would be astonished how many of my new friends have relatives who work in the homes of the quality. Not just locally, mind you, but in London as well. Quite a source of bragging rights it is. Why John—the craggy-faced gent with the three fingers, the one who always sits at the table nearest the fire—he has a sister whose youngest daughter is a downstairs maid in the London home of Lady Bessborough."

"Simply riveting," Marcus said in a voice that suggested the opposite.

"Oh but it is. It was Dinsmore's idea." He nodded approvingly at James. "He suggested so long as his presence is to be a source of gossip, it might as well be useful gossip. He's had me putting it about that he's waiting here, pining with love for the Lady Elizabeth."

"A tad heavy on the treacle," James said without looking up from his hand. "But the sort of sugary stuff the gentle folk below stairs enjoy."

"I had 'em licking their bowls clean and begging for more," Andre agreed. "I told them Dinsmore here had sworn to put aside his rakish ways forever if the lady would have him. He called upon the earl that day to beg forgiveness for his grievous impertinence to the lady and implore His Lordship to grant him the unimagined honor of the lady's hand in marriage."

"Did you invent these fascinating details yourself?" Marcus's question was directed at Andre, but he cast a curious look at James.

James wondered if Marcus knew how often he'd found himself wishing the tale were true.

"Dinsmore helped me with a few bits here and there," Andre acknowledged, spreading his winning hand upon the table. "I told them Moreham's said he'll think upon it and Dinsmore here has sworn to remain until he has got word from His Lordship."

"Well done." Marcus folded his cards. "That should neatly explain the presence of the earl's messenger when he arrives."

"*If* he arrives," David interjected, bringing the conversation full circle, back to its beginning.

James shot him a look of mock disapproval. "Oh ye of little faith. The earl's messenger will bring word of the rejection of my suit. I will, of course, be distraught. And while you, my faithful servants, pack, I shall be forced to drown my sorrows in countless bottles of this establishment's fine stock of wines."

"And shall you be needing any help with these bottles, a bit of shared comfort in your time of need?" Andre asked hopefully.

"Unfortunately for you my suffering will be a private affair. Though expressed loudly enough to whet the eager appetite of your new friends below." He pushed the pile of winnings in Andre's direction. "By the time we set out tomorrow, everyone hereabouts should know that I am a desperate, bitter man. That life holds nothing for me here in stubborn, stifling, hopelessly outmoded Olde England. And, like every truly mindless romantic in this day and age, I'm off to a land where I can breathe free, a land of *liberté*, *egalité*, and *fraternité*. France." James nodded at David. "With Andre's assistance, I expect news of my lovelorn state will travel faster than your carefully modified coach."

David grinned at the mention of his favorite project.

"If everything goes as planned, my passage through the country will be followed with amusement, with pity, with scorn. With every range of emotion." James smiled his twisted smile at the men gathered around the table. "Except suspicion."

The messenger from the earl arrived just before tea, bearing a thickly wrapped package of names, addresses, and letters of introduction. Marcus immediately sat at the desk in the corner and began transcribing the names and addresses with vanishing ink on sheets of stiff ivory wallpaper decorated with a delicate gold pattern. As soon as he finished a sheet and the ink was dry and no longer visible, he would motion to David, who was sitting at the table where the men had been playing cards. David would take the sheet, brush it with paste from a pot, and then carefully press it into the inside of a small wooden trunk.

The trunk belonged to James. Having examined James's luggage earlier in the day, David had seized upon it as being the perfect size and shape for his project. Without asking, he'd unceremoniously dumped the contents on the larger of the two rope beds.

"I do hope you intend to repack those when you've finished," James had remarked, eyeing the untidy heap that had been several neatly folded shirts, stocks, a nightshirt, and several pairs of stockings.

David had grinned. "Not to worry, everything will be as good as new when I've finished with it. Maybe even better." He patted the trunk confidently.

Watching him working now, James had to admit the handiwork was that of a master craftsman.

"It does look handsome." David nodded, as if acknowledging the unspoken compliment. "Marcus picked out the paper, and he's got tastes nearly as fancy as yours."

James stepped closer to the table and picked up one of the sheets David hadn't yet brushed with paste. "The writing disappears quite neatly. How will you retrieve it?"

"I've mixed up a special solution. Swab the writing with it, and so long as it stays wet, you can read it. Soon as it dries, poof it's gone again." His smiled broadened. "But here's the best part . . ."

"I can only imagine."

David waved a brush full of paste as if to wave away James's concerns. "I've mixed the solution with your cologne. Those Frenchies will never suspect."

"I don't wear cologne."

From the desk, he heard a dry chuckle, followed by a slosh. "You do now." James turned and saw Marcus holding an elegant glass bottle with a cork stopper.

"At least tell me you picked the cologne with as much care as the paper."

"Alas no, though I did suggest he mix in sandalwood rather than musk. If it will make you feel less violated," Marcus said, taking out the stopper, "later I'll show you how that philistine has desecrated my writing desk." A pungent, and not entirely pleasant odor wafted across the room. "You'll be grateful when the gendarmes are looking for those incriminating letters of introduction . . ."

"Gad that's vile." James fanned a hand beneath his nose. "I believe now would be a good time for me to begin calling for drink. Andre?"

The dark-haired man, who'd been silent through this exchange, leaning against the single window tapping his foot restlessly, turned immediately. In another moment, he was across the room, flinging the door open, and calling loudly down the stairs, "Wine, my master needs BOTTLES OF WINE, DAMN YOUR EYES, not tepid pots of tea!"

He'd always prided himself on being a quiet, well-bred drinker, never noisy in his cups. However, while much of the wine was poured out of the window, a good portion made it down James's throat. At first, he felt distinctly uncomfortable striding about the room, loudly bemoaning the perfidy of women. But soon he discovered it felt rather satisfying to voice some of the injustice he felt at being manipulated by his sister, caught up in Elizabeth's wiles, rejected by Rafe Moreham.

And the wines of the Hart and Hounds weren't half bad.

The more he drank, the less troubled he was by the voice in his head defending both Anne and Elizabeth. Anne, the voice argued, had been injured. She'd struck out the only way she had known how and turned to the only person she believed could defend her. Elizabeth was headstrong and young; she couldn't begin to understand the temptation she posed.

"Gentlemen," he said, loudly enough for his true voice to silence the smaller one and carry through the thin layers of plaster and horsehair that made up the walls of the Hart and Hounds, "I was raised to believe that women are weaker vessels in need of man's protection. *Vessels* . . . The first time I heard that expression, I didn't think of glassware or porcelain. Oh no, I thought of ships. And then someone, a woman most like, corrected me." He took a swallow from the glass he held in his hand. "But now that I think on it, I believe my first impression was correct. Women are like those sleek little barks that coastal smugglers use, slipping about men, gone before you know it. And we poor sods are like warships lumbering after 'em, but weighted down with all those masts, and cannons, and whatnot."

Marcus looked up from his work. "The analogy's a bit muddled Dinsmore, but I believe I follow you."

"Nothing weaker-vesseled about women at all." James snorted. "It's a ruse, that's what it is, to make us believe they need protecting." He waved his glass, warming to the topic. "It's all for show, like hoops, and wigs, and bum rolls. Man never really knows what he's in for when he's with a woman. Not really."

A shadow passed over Marcus's face. "I quite agree."

"You know, I used to find all that amusing, a bit like unwrapping a present, peeling back all that linen and lace . . ." He thought of Elizabeth, lying back on the chaise, her gown slipping from her shoulders, and poured more wine into his glass.

Marcus put down his quill. "If you don't mind, I think I'll join you in a glass."

"Don't mind at all." James picked up the bottle, glancing about the table with a bemused expression. "Sorry old man, but it appears I've only the one glass."

"Not to worry, I'll take the bottle."

"Nearly empty," he apologized as he passed it.

"It's enough. *To women*," Marcus said, raising his bottle and clinking it lightly against James's glass. "*May they forever remain another man's problem.*"

● ● ●

Standing near the window later that evening, a line of bottles at his feet, James considered whether it might be amusing to drop them out the window: the first fallen soldiers in their mission for the king. He picked one up and held it out the window, swinging it gently by the neck. But as he was about to release it, a coach drew up in the darkened courtyard. He was sober enough to realize it would be unwise, as well as most impolite, to strike an unsuspecting guest on the head.

He glanced down, curious to see what manner of person was arriving so late. A caped figure alighted from the carriage with the aid of a livened coachman; it was too dark to make out the colors of the livery. But as the figure passed briefly through the circle of light cast by a torch near the door to the inn, James drew back. Perhaps he wasn't as sober as he thought because his eyes most definitely were playing tricks on him.

He could have sworn he'd seen the face of Elizabeth Harcrest.

It was, of course, impossible. There was no plausible reason why she would be traveling alone, at night, much less making a stop at the Hart and Hounds. He set the bottle in his hand back down upon the floor; it rattled against its companions. All his ranting for the common rooms must have gone to his head. He'd spent too much time thinking and talking about her today, that was all. *Elizabeth*, he reminded himself of Marcus's toast earlier that evening, *is another man's problem.* "Moreham's problem," he muttered.

"Did you say something?" David looked up from the table. He'd completed the work of papering the interior of the trunk and was repacking James's clothes, though not nearly as tidily as his valet had done.

James shook his head. "Simply wondering when we might be off."

"I'm ready," Marcus said, tucking the last of his quills into his writing desk.

"Is all the other luggage stowed on the coach?"

"This is the last bit," David said, closing the trunk.

"At last." James swept his cloak over his shoulders and picked up his hat. Striding across the room to the door, he swung it with a gesture as grand as if he were liberating a cell full of prisoners. "Gentleman, let us be off."

"What," said a voice from the hall, "without me?"

Now his ears were playing tricks with him. Otherwise, he might have sworn the teasing tones belonged to Elizabeth Harcrest. But she was safely stowed at Moreham Hall with her blessedly overprotective brother. James stood with his hand on the door, steadfastly fixing his eyes on his travel companions. He saw Marcus pause, hat in hand and bow his head. David, he noticed, was doing the same. It was with a deep sense of foreboding that he turned. The caped figure from the courtyard stood on the threshold.

"You are, of course, going to invite me in," she said.

"Would it make a difference if I did not?"

"Not a bit."

He took off his hat and gestured towards the room. "That's a far more fetching mantle than you were wearing upon your last visit," he remarked as she swept into the room. "Though your fashion sense appears to improving, lamentably, your common sense remains lacking."

"Coming from a man who is about to set off on a foolhardy mission to France, I'm not entirely certain how worthy a judge you are of common sense." She slid her hood back with a blue-gloved hand. "Though you are correct about the mantle."

"There is nothing foolhardy about a man, having seen the error of his ways, seeking to begin life anew in the free air of democratic France."

"Seeking to free someone from France, more like."

James heard, rather than saw, David and Marcus drop

into their chairs. He swung the door shut quickly. "Elizabeth, what *is it* that you *want*?"

She sat down at the table, arranging her skirts neatly about her ankles. Then glancing up with a smile bright as a schoolgirl's on her first day of class, she said, "To go with you, of course."

"No," he replied without hesitation.

"I'm all packed," she continued as if she hadn't heard. "And I've instructed my coachman to load my things onto your coach."

"You are *not* going with us to France." Trying hard not to shout, he put as much emphasis as he could on the word *not*.

"Why not?"

A million reasons sprang to mind. He voiced the first to reach his lips. "You don't speak French."

"Oh, but I do," she replied fluently in that language. "I had a governess when I was younger who said that any young woman who learned a foreign language was setting her feet on the road to perdition. So, of course, I applied my-self quite vigorously to their study."

"Of course," he repeated dryly.

"I'm best in French, but my Italian and German are quite passable, too."

"Your reputation . . ."

"Is thoroughly ruined."

"Your brother . . ."

"Has already tried to kill you." She looked pointedly at his scar. "He doesn't know where I've gone. He believes I'm off to visit my friend, Arabella Norcroft."

"The wren."

"Don't call her that," she said with a hint of anger. "There's far more to her than meets the eye. Just as there's far more to me." She glanced around the room. "Why should men have all the adventure?"

"This isn't an adventure, the kind you read shut up in your comfortable chambers at Moreham Hall. This is real and it's important. A man's life is at stake, Elizabeth, and your traveling with us will only put him further at risk."

"You know this for certain," she said, toying with the buttons on her gloves. "That the French would be less suspicious of a group of Englishmen traveling aimlessly about the countryside simply because they yearn to breathe the air of freedom, than a man who was, say, eloping with the sister of an irate earl?"

"Oh, no, Elizabeth Harcrest. We are *not* getting *married*."

Elizabeth took a deep breath. She'd expected him to be resistant but she never imagined he'd be so *adamant*. Mortification mixed with anger gave force to her words. "Did I say *anything* about getting married, James Dinsmore? Why would you think I would want such a thing after the shabby way you've treated me? We're eloping is what we'll *say* when we've reached France. Besides, it makes more sense if you're traveling to all the centers of textile production because you're being dragged by a young wife eager for new silks and laces, instead of being there just for simple curiosity."

"She has a point," David muttered.

"They always do," Marcus warned. "The trick is not to listen."

James shook his head, abandoning all pretense of calm. "You want to travel with us because it's *an adventure?* You want to pretend to elope, but you don't wish to be married? This is madness, utter madness, far worse than your foolishness of WALKING BLINDFOLDED ON A BRIDGE!"

"Indeed." She straightened in her chair, her eyes holding his as firmly as his arms had held her when she'd fallen. "It is madness, but not the sort of madness you suggest. Not insanity, James. It's anger. When I discovered why you had come to Moreham Hall, I was livid. And not just because you hadn't come to set things right, but because you alone— not I—had that power. Why should men have the power to change their lives, to change the lives of others, and women have none?"

"Because that's the way things *are*. That's the way they have always been—"

"Things change," she cut him off. "You of all people should know that. I'm just trying to take control of the changes in my life."

As am I, James thought. "You've chosen an odd way to go about it, Elizabeth."

"I might say the same about you."

The girl was as pigheaded as her brother! He was getting nowhere with this approach, and so he tried another tack. "And what if someone you or I know should see us together in France, what then?"

"It won't happen," she said firmly. "Not with the places we're going. Amiens, Rouen, they are backwaters. Paris is where the fashionable set brave enough to venture to France gather."

"And how do you know all this? Rafe can't possibly have confided in you."

"Oh, he didn't." She laughed at the outrage in his voice. "He would never do such a thing. I heard it all through the library wall."

He narrowed his eyes at her. "If your brother doesn't know, what's to keep us from delivering you back to him this instant?"

"You might," she acknowledged, "but then I might tell him that you lured me here with false promises."

"You wouldn't!" he exclaimed.

"Oh I suspect she would," Marcus murmured.

"It would be your word against mine. And he *might* believe you. But then,"—she added, her fingers tracing circles on the tabletop—"you *might* risk him demanding back his letters of introduction, or worse, telling his contacts not to help you at all."

"She's good," David whistled through his teeth.

"This is outrageous, it's . . . it's bloody *blackmail!*"

She raised her eyebrows. "After what I overheard in the library I don't think you're the one to be making a fuss about a little blackmail . . ."

"This is different. We're trying to save a man's life."

"So you've said. And I'd like to help." She glanced around at the men, all still wearing their cloaks and holding their hats in their hands. "From the looks of it, you were about to set off. You're wasting valuable time sitting here arguing with me."

"I could just kill you," he said, in what he hoped was a sufficiently menacing tone. The thought of wringing her neck *did* seem frightfully appealing at the moment.

"I suppose you could," she agreed, standing up and drawing her hood over her chestnut hair. "But then you'd have to waste even more time finding a place to dump my body."

Chapter 20

"*Is this* all *your luggage?*" *James stared aghast at the pile* of hatboxes higher than a man's head and the trunks piled haphazardly atop the men's belongings on the back of his coach. "Or is there more I can't see in the dark?" He peered at the sections of the vehicle that lay beyond the circle of light cast by the courtyard torches.

"That is all of it. I packed as lightly as I could; I didn't know how long we'd be gone." She paused as James held open the door to the carriage, one foot on the step. "How long will we be gone?"

"I don't know," he sighed, "but I'm quite certain it will feel like an eternity."

"An eternity?" she said, climbing into the coach. "Perhaps I should have packed more hats."

The seats, she found, as she settled her skirts, were uncomfortably high. She supposed it was to accommodate James's longs legs. The upholstery smelled strangely of sawdust and fresh varnish. It wasn't nearly as comfortable as the carriage she'd arrived in; the carriage she'd sent on to Arabella's, with its trunks and valises stuffed full of novels, fabric scraps, piles of ladies magazines, and the letters she'd written describing the wonderful time she was having at Hartsdale. She hoped she'd written enough. Lord knew how long an eternity might actually turn out to be.

The coach rocked as James and Marcus Tyndale, the man whom he'd introduced as his secretary, settled in around her. She leaned back and closed her eyes. She was fairly certain that no one in the poorly lit courtyard of the Hart and Hounds had noticed her carriage had been empty of passengers. She had the coachman's word he'd tell Rafe he'd delivered her safely. It made her uncomfortable to think of how she'd secured that promise—by telling the coachman she'd seen his sister, a downstairs maid at Moreham Hall, pocketing silver spoons. She'd suggested that if such behavior were exposed, then both brother and sister might lose their jobs. She winced, recalling the look of panic on the man's face. She'd almost abandoned her plans at that moment, wanting to reassure him she'd never tell, wanting to slip him some coins. But if Rafe were to discover what she'd done, he'd be more sympathetic to the coachman's dilemma if he knew she had not bribed but blackmailed him.

She allowed her eyelids to flutter open a fraction, sliding a glance at James. Him, she hadn't felt badly about blackmailing, not a bit. In fact, it was his meeting with her brother that had given her the idea. One could even say he was the one *responsible* for setting this whole plan in motion. . . . She closed her eyes again, resisting the urge to let slip a smile of satisfaction. She almost wished her brother could see her now, though she knew he'd have an apoplexy. He was always excoriating her for not planning ahead. Well, she'd done it this time, and she had to admit, things had worked out awfully well. All the time she'd spent thinking through and rehearsing her arguments as to why James should take her to France. She frowned, remembering the only part of her speech that hadn't been rehearsed, the part that had taken her unawares, spilling from her lips with un-expected passion—the part about not wanting to marry him.

Oh no, he'd protested. *We are NOT getting MARRIED.*

He'd been so vehement; the memory made her cringe. Until that moment she'd thought she *did* want to marry him. Well, not anymore, not if every English man and woman in France saw them together, formed a choir, and sang the news at Almack's. She resisted the urge to slide her foot over and kick him in the shins with her pointed shoes. *The miserable cad.* He was every bit as bad as Rafe and Alix and Phoebe and Cole had said. If there had been a stack of bibles in the coach, she'd have put her hand on them and sworn right there and then not to waste another moment thinking about James Dinsmore and how he was throwing away his life.

She was only eighteen. She had her whole life ahead of her—and this adventure offered her a chance to change everything, forever. *For the better,* she amended quickly. And who knew? Perhaps she might even change someone else's life—not James Dinsmore's, of course—but some poor unfortunate Frenchman. She imagined herself, arm around the waist of a wounded young nobleman, supporting him as they ran through the fields, a company of gendarmes hot on their heels. She pictured the looks of surprise on James's and his companions' faces—they'd be sitting at dinner or cards, or even better, carousing with loose women—when she'd stagger in with their fugitive. As the rocking of the darkened coach lulled her into exhausted sleep, she found herself wondering about the fugitive. *What did he look like? And where was he now?*

Gerard de Joley, Comte Verignac, former financial adviser to His late Majesty, Louis XVI of France, stared warily at a sleeping hen. The roof of the henhouse was low. Crouching, he quietly stepped closer to the bird. Then, with lightening speed that had made him an admired fencer in the court of

Versailles, he snatched at the speckled egg he knew was hidden in the nest. It felt warm and heavy in his hand. God willing, it would feel even more so in his stomach; he hadn't eaten in days. If he weren't afraid the peasants would notice the missing bird, or that someone might see his campfire, he'd have taken the chicken as well. Saliva flooded his mouth at the thought of crisp, brown, roasted chicken sprinkled with herbs.

Swallowing, he slipped the egg into the pocket of his coat—the coat he'd stolen from the back of a wagon parked in the yard of another farmhouse. This was what he'd been reduced to, stealing eggs and the filthy vestments of peasants. He was glad he hadn't listened to the pleas of his youngest daughter to take her with him. She was safer far from him, staying with friends in Paris, certainly better off than hiding in the countryside, living in a hole that used to be part of an ancient Roman plumbing system. When the Englishmen came to get him and he reached England at last, he'd have access to the money he'd transferred there. He'd send for her. Gerard fingered the eggs in his pocket, wondering if he dared take another. He didn't want the old woman who owned the coop becoming suspicious, though in truth, she appeared half-blind. Which was why he'd chosen her coop in the first place. He hefted each of the three eggs in his pocket, savoring their weight. They would have to be enough. He couldn't take a chance, not now, not knowing that the Englishmen were on their way. With a reluctant glance back at the rows of nests, he slipped out of the henhouse and vanished into the darkness of the French countryside.

James turned to look at Elizabeth, what he could make of her in the darkened interior of the coach. Now that she was asleep, he felt free to examine his unwelcome travel companion. There was the outline of her profile, the high forehead, the little tilt at the tip of her nose, the faint curve of her lips—was he imaging things or was she smiling? Probably she felt fairly pleased with herself after her outrageous performance at the inn; she probably thought she'd won a victory. A *skirmish*. He wanted to wake her up and tell her the *battle* was far from over. She might force him to take her to France, but he'd be damned if he'd let her have any "adventures."

Adventures. The power to change her life. What was she thinking?

His eyes rested on her hair, her curls nothing more than a dark mass falling down over her shoulders, down the back of her cloak, the cloak that covered her body down to her ankles. His gaze traveled to her ankle, a gleaming curve in pale silk. He stared at it, forcing his breathing to remain slow and calm, which was unfortunate. Each deep breath brought the scent of her to his nose, a scent of soap, warm skin, clean hair, and wool. Elizabeth Harcrest. The woman he'd enthusiastically toasted out of his life not more than an hour ago. How could he have imagined he'd be so easily shed of her? He grimaced. He supposed keeping her trussed in the carriage, or locked in whatever chambers they could find would attract too much attention in France. But he'd keep a close watch on her. *Of that, my lady, you may rest assured.*

She mumbled in her sleep, pulled her cloak closer, and turning, her hip settled comfortably against his. He moved over, re-creating the space between them. It was his eyes he planned to keep on her, he vowed, nothing more. She sighed, turned again and slumped against his shoulder, her hand coming to rest on his thigh. He felt the blood rush to his groin. *Absurd*, he remonstrated with himself. *It was just a hand.* He stared at the slim fingers, curled inches above his knee. It wasn't as if the hand was moving, or she was moving. As if she were naked, creeping slowly up his thighs, toward his aching flesh. He forced himself to recall her scornful reaction to his refusal to marry her. *Why would you*

*think I would want such a thing after the shabby way you've
treated me?*

He had treated her shabbily. Repeatedly. Intentionally. It
was good that she understood that he was completely unsuitable and that marriage between them was out of the
question. So why did the tightness between his legs now
seem to be traveling to his chest? He looked up and caught
Marcus's eyes on him. In the dark, it was impossible to read
their expression, but when he spoke, he could have sworn
there was an undercurrent of sympathy in his voice.

"I don't suppose we could leave the earl's sister at the inn
in Bristol?"

"And risk Moreham's wrath?" James shook his head.
"And what if she came to harm, left alone at a public inn?"

"There's an even better chance she'll come to harm in
France."

He glanced down at Elizabeth's sleeping form, resisting
the urge to put his arm around her. He knew Marcus was
right.

"We could leave Andre or David with her, to arrange for
her return home. A suitably slow return," Marcus added.

"We need them both. And while a slow return might buy
us time with Moreham, what of our friend in France? He
doesn't have the luxury of time."

Marcus sighed. "Has she got a passport, do you think?"

"I suspect so. She seems to have thought everything
through rather thoroughly."

"Yes, I must admit, I found her arguments convincing.
But then I've been cozened by women before."

James heard bitterness in the man's voice. He wondered
at it, but didn't know Marcus well enough to ask about its
source, and Marcus wasn't the sort to invite confidences.

"Still," Marcus continued, "I suppose such skills may
come in handy considering our purpose in France."

Oh no, he wanted to say, Elizabeth wouldn't have the opportunity to practice her so-called skills on anyone. Lord

knew the chit was far too dangerous already. He mumbled noncommittally.

Marcus laughed softly. "I nearly forgot, Dinsmore, congratulations on your forthcoming nuptials."

"We're *not* getting married," James muttered to no one in particular.

"Something about it just doesn't feel right," Rafe said to Alix as they lay together against the pillows of their great four-poster bed several hours after Elizabeth's carriage left the hall.

She ran a finger down his chest. "It feels good to me. . . ." Her hand disappeared beneath the covers. "Very good indeed."

"Insatiable wench." He caught her hand before she reached her objective. "I was talking about Elizabeth."

"She will be fine." She wiggled up against him and nipped his neck. "She's on her way to Hartsdale where she will undoubtedly enjoy a pleasant visit." She ran her tongue up his neck to his ear. "She's a lovely girl, Arabella. Quite nice. And on the subject of nice,"—she sucked the lobe of his ear—"this is quite nice, too."

He turned and kissed her, a kiss that started out slow and warm, his tongue tracing the familiar shape of her lips, sliding into her mouth. Her arms wrapped around his neck; his hand slid down the soft curves of her body, softer and fuller now that she was carrying their child, pulling her down underneath him. She could feel him rising against her belly. She lay back against the down-filled mattress, closing her eyes and letting her legs slide languorously apart. She felt his fingers rest on her hip, felt him lift himself, just enough for a hand to wander . . . or a mouth. She shivered, wondering where and how he would touch her next. He had amazing hands and an even more amazing tongue.

"Something doesn't feel right."

"You . . . stopping," she moaned.

"She packed so lightly, left so quickly, didn't even take a maid."

Reluctantly, Alix opened her eyes. "She said her maid was suffering from a fever and that it would be a poor thing to bring illness to the Norcrofts. She said Arabella would provide a maid. And she didn't know how long she might be staying, so she'd send word if she needed more things. You can always question the coachman when he returns."

"I suppose." He didn't sound convinced.

Alix raised herself up on her elbows and looked into his eyes. "You worry too much about her. You held the reins too tight and look what happened . . ."

"I didn't hold them tight enough . . ."

"We've had this argument far too often of late. We will not bring it to bed, not tonight. Regardless of whether you watched her too little or too much, you know Elizabeth has learned a bitter lesson. You should be glad she's been invited to Hartsdale. I should never have expected Arabella's harpy of a mother to extend such an invitation. Perhaps it's a sign that society is prepared to forgive her. She won't act so impulsively again, you'll see. She'll think things through, just like you, my love." She kissed him reassuringly on the nose.

"She didn't tell us about seeing James Dinsmore."

"Jervis told you it appeared to be an unpleasant encounter, no doubt she was too embarrassed or upset."

She reached over and smoothed the crease that had appeared between his eyes. "If you are so concerned, you could ride over to Hartsdale in a day or two."

"If she's there, she'll know I've come because I don't trust her, and the Norcrofts will know it, too. . . . And if she's not there, well then . . ."

"You'll create a scandal far worse than the one in London."

He nodded; Alix slid her hand behind his neck, pulling him down against her.

"You'll just have to trust her," she whispered into his tawny hair.

"I know," he whispered back, "and that's what worries me most."

Chapter 21

They were angry with her. Elizabeth could understand that, but they'd been traveling in the coach for hours, and neither James nor his man Marcus had uttered a single word. They'd ridden through the night, and that was understandable. Clearly, the men were in a hurry. But after the sun had risen, and they'd stopped for a brief breakfast and then continued on, it was inexcusable.

"It's a lovely day today, isn't it?" she said.

The interior of the coach remained resolutely silent.

"Not a cloud in the sky. Delightful traveling weather."

Still no answer.

"It bodes well for the crossing, I should think. I'm sure you've heard the tale of the poor Duchess of Northumberland. It was many years ago, of course, but my mother loves to tell the story. A storm blew up, so with wind and waves so violent, the duchess was nearly swept into the sea, chaise and all. She insisted the captain turn back. I don't think I should have done anything so foolish; I'd at least have gotten out of the chaise." She paused. "Though do you suppose a chaise might float?"

The only sound in the coach was of horses' hooves, jangling traces, and wheels grinding over gravel.

"Shall we stop this evening or ride straight through? Not that I'm complaining," she added hastily, at the same time thinking longingly of her toothbrush, and her hairbrush, and her lemon soap. "I was just wondering how I shall enter the inn without attracting too much attention. I could pretend to be the maid . . ."

James turned to her. "I don't think so," he said dryly.

"Oh, but I could, I've got a terrific ear for accents."

"Yes," he said, "but can you start a fire in the chamber hearth?"

She pursed her lips.

"How are you at making beds?"

Her lower lip twitched.

"Ironing shirts?"

Her lip twitched again. "I can make a pudding," she offered.

"Well, that changes everything," he said clearly unimpressed.

Marcus made an odd sound in his throat and purposefully bent his head to a book on travel he had been holding open on his lap.

"Well then, what's your bright idea James Arthur Evan Dinsmore?"

"You'll pull up your hood and enter on my arm."

"But people will think . . ."

"Precisely what they think whenever I enter an inn with a hooded lady. That you're my mistress."

Elizabeth blushed. "But when you call for separate rooms, what will they think then?"

"I won't."

"But you must," she said, trying to sound firm, rather than scandalized.

"That would arouse suspicion, which as you will agree, is the last thing we want. And besides,"—he patted his pocket—"I haven't the funds for more than one room. We aren't traveling with the Harcrest largesse, my dear. Regretfully, the accommodations on this trip will not be up to the standards to which you are accustomed."

Her eyes narrowed. He didn't sound regretful at all. Indeed, she thought she caught a glimmer of amusement in his voice. But at least he was speaking to her, and at least she'd discovered they'd be stopping. "You'll be sleeping on the floor, of course."

"No," he said firmly, "I will not. I'm paying for the room, I'm paying for the bed, and I fully intend to enjoy the accommodations such as they are." When she opened her mouth to protest, he added, "Might I remind you that you, Elizabeth Anne Louisa Grace Harcrest, are the uninvited member of this excursion?"

She closed her mouth, though only for the briefest moment. "Very well. We shall share a room. I expect that you will behave as a gentleman. There will be nothing improper between us."

He stared at her. The corners of his eyes crinkled. The edges of his mouth turned up. A smile spread across his face. And then he laughed, a rich, wholehearted sound that bore no resemblance at all to the polite affectations of amusement he uttered in society. "Nothing improper," he sputtered, when finally he managed to catch his breath. "Beyond blackmail and the occasional death threat, I swear to you, Elizabeth, nothing of the slightest impropriety will pass between us."

He was right, Elizabeth thought. No one paid her the slightest notice when she entered the seedy inn with James. Or at least they pretended not to notice her, addressing their conversations to him, or to Marcus, or one of the other servants, the slight, dark-haired Andre, and the large blond

David. There was something odd about those three, she thought. They didn't seem the usual sort to be servants. There was a hint of the aristocrat about Marcus; she could more easily imagine him giving orders than taking them. She supposed he might be a gentleman fallen on hard times, forced to hire himself out. Andre seemed far too cocky to be a serving man, and David . . . she hadn't figured him out yet, but he struck her as too . . . distracted.

The men didn't make her uncomfortable. She silently amended that thought; Marcus made her uncomfortable. She had the distinct feeling he'd have sent her packing if only he could have convinced James. Andre and David had accepted her presence with amused curiosity. Andre had actually winked at her when James wasn't looking. Of course, she hadn't acknowledged him, but she suspected she could win the two men over easily enough. It never hurt to have the servants on one's side.

Thinking of sides made Elizabeth increasingly aware of how stiff one side of her body was, stretched out on the hardwood floor as she was. She pulled closer the musty blanket James had tossed her, and rolled over. As she did so, she became aware of the horrifying layer of dust beneath the bed. James really ought to speak to the maid. If they even had maids at such an establishment. She wriggled away from the bed and tried to find a comfortable position. She put down her arm, the one between her body and the floor. She stretched it out. She tried pillowing her head on it. She found herself wishing that arms, like wigs, could be removed at night.

She rolled over onto her back.

She heard James sigh contentedly. Despicable toad.

"This mattress is surprisingly comfortable." His voice floated down from the bed. "Not the usual scratchy straw affair you usually find in such places. Generous, too. Good heavens, at least three, perhaps four grown men could make their rest here without even touching."

She found herself thinking that he had, indeed, spoken the truth when he'd claimed he was not a gentleman. "I'm perfectly fine down here. Thank you very much. I understand hard surfaces are most beneficial to posture and circulation."

"I shall bear that in mind."

She heard him plumping the pillows. She ought to have taken one when he'd offered earlier. But she'd been so distracted when he'd hung up his coat over the chair, slung his waistcoat after it, then sat down, and began pulling off his shoes and stockings. She tried not to stare at the fine layer of gold hair that covered the muscles of his calves. And then he'd stood up and begun unfastening his britches as if she weren't even there. She should have looked at him as casually as if he were an old piece of furniture, that's what she should have done. But instead she told him she was going to sleep on the floor now and would he please hand her a blanket from the bed.

She turned again. No matter which way she turned it didn't make her any more comfortable. The floor was still hard and cold, and she was beginning to accumulate bits of grit in her blanket.

"Elizabeth." James's voice was soft. "You might as well come to bed." When she remained silent, he continued. "I really won't lay a hand on you." His voice lightened. "No matter how tempting a target your neck presents."

She heard him patting the mattress; the muffled *plumph, plumph* was more tempting than a pot of steaming chocolate on a cold morning.

"You can sleep under the covers, and I'll sleep on the top of them."

She thought of him, long-limbed and naked under his nightshirt. "You can sleep under the covers," she said quickly. "I don't need them."

"Ah, yes," he said, "I'd almost forgotten that you were still wearing all those layers of traveling clothes."

As if she'd strip with him in the room—not if her clothes were armor, which, after two days of traveling, they did seem to resemble. "You didn't say what time we were leaving in the morning," she protested, "and since I haven't a maid, I didn't want to slow you down if you were in a hurry to set off."

"Thoughtless of me, thoughtful of you. We'll be off in a few hours, as soon as it's light." He *plumphed* the mattress again. "Come on up with you then."

"Hands to yourself, James Dinsmore," she muttered, as she climbed in beside him.

"Safe behind my head," he chuckled. She glanced at him. *Just to make certain*, she told herself. In the pale shaft of light from the window, she could see that his arms were, indeed, folded under his head; the position made full play of the muscles of his chest. Elizabeth caught a glimpse of golden hair tangled in the vee of his nightshirt. She lay down on her back, staring at the ceiling and holding herself so stiffly that she almost considered returning to the floor.

"So," he said after several very long, very uncomfortable moments had passed, "you're a right-sider."

"I beg your pardon?" The sound of his voice and the question took her by surprise. She hadn't the vaguest notion what he meant.

"You sleep on the right side of the bed."

"Oh." She paused, considering. "I haven't ever thought about it. I've never shared a bed before. Except when I was little and it was stormy and I'd crawl into my nanny's bed. Then it didn't really matter what side I was on, so long as she held me close."

"Nanny Bell. I haven't thought about her in years. She did have a way of making you feel that so long as she was around, everything would be all right."

They lay together, lost for a moment in their separate memories of the old woman, who'd passed away when Elizabeth was twelve. Rafe had replaced her with a string of tutors and stiff-faced governesses.

"So are you a left-sider?" she asked, cursing herself almost as soon as the question left her lips. She really didn't want to know. Right, left, however he responded, her brain would forever be branded with the image of him lying on that side of the bed, a faceless, naked woman curled against him on the other. He was accustomed to sharing his bed. Why else would he have asked her which side she preferred? She'd always known he was a libertine. Still, knowing was different than picturing . . .

His response was not what she'd expected. "We didn't have anyone like Nanny Bell to run to when we were frightened. After my mother died, if I was home and it started to storm, I'd scrunch against the wall to leave room for Anne. I knew if the thunder got very loud, she'd come running. To make sure I was all right, she'd always say . . ." His voice trailed off. "The wall was on the left side of the bed, so I suppose that makes me a left-sider."

The image of the two of them, young Anne and James, huddling together while the lightning flashed outside the windows and rain pelted the glass was strangely reassuring. Her tensed limbs began to relax, and she allowed her shoulders and spine to appreciate the plush comfort of the mattress. *He hadn't lied about that*, she mused, as her eyelids began to take on weight. That was the problem, James Dinsmore didn't lie. *Oh no, Elizabeth Harcrest. We are not getting married.* The words seemed to follow her as she rolled over on to her right side, away from them, away from James, and into a fitful sleep.

The men were up at dawn, making sure that the luggage they'd stowed on the coach hadn't been stolen during the night, that the horses were fresh and ready to go. Elizabeth had asked for a few moments to freshen up and James had sent a maid up to the chamber to help her. He wanted time to talk to the men about her.

"She's even prettier than the locals described." Andre nodded appreciatively over a chunk of bread and some cheese.

"Clever too," David added. "Might even turn out useful to have her on this little excursion."

"She's a nuisance," Marcus said firmly. He reached for the loaf of bread that was set between the men on a table and tore off a hunk.

"The question, gentlemen, is not what she is, but what we do with her." James glanced around the table. "I don't think we should tell her everything about our mission in France."

"I don't think we should tell her anything," Marcus said. "She knows far too much already."

James motioned for the bread, and Marcus passed it to him. He took out a knife and carefully cut a slice, then beckoned for the cheese. "There's the rub. She knows far too much already, and if I know Elizabeth, which after all these years, I sometimes begin to believe I do, a little information will make her curious for more . . ."

"Too much information would put her in danger." Andre waved his chunk of bread warningly. "If she were captured and the French set their minds to finding out everything she knows . . . we'd all be in trouble."

"Women aren't designed to stand up to torture." David nodded, chewing.

"Only to inflict it," Marcus murmured so softly that the other men didn't catch what he'd said.

"What we need to do is tell her enough to make her believe we've taken her into our confidence, to prevent her from prying any further into our business . . ."

"So how much would that be?" Andre asked.

"She has a rough idea about our route, so we could take out the map and discuss that with her." James chewed, considering. "But I don't want her to know about the trunk, or the panels in the coach, or Marcus's writing box."

The men nodded.

"And the fugitive?" Marcus asked. "She seems to know about him."

"We'll give her a rough outline of what we plan to do, find some role for her to play that keeps her out of our way and out of danger."

Marcus raised a brow. "I suspect that'll be a challenge nearly as great as getting Joley out of France."

"We could lock her in the carriage," David suggested.

"I'd be willing to distract her," Andre volunteered

"Neither of those options will be necessary; Elizabeth is supposed to be my fiancée, which makes her my responsibility. A responsibility, I doubtless have no need to add, that I take as seriously as our mission in France. At this point, she doesn't appear to know the identity of our fugitive, and I'd prefer to keep it that way."

"If she's so curious, how do you suggest we keep it from her?" Andre asked.

"From here on in, none of you know who he is. If she asks, or tries to pry in any way, you tell her it's as much of a mystery to you as it is to her."

"And if she doesn't believe us?"

"Make her."

Andre and the other men around the table nodded.

"I may not be able to wrap Elizabeth Harcrest around my finger,"—James smiled without a trace of humor—"but I intend to do my best to keep her under my thumb."

Chapter 22

They'd been riding in the carriage for nearly an hour when Marcus broke the silence. Writing desk balanced on his knees, quill in hand, he looked from James to Elizabeth, and then back to James. "Your wedding license—shall I draw up a simple license or a special one?"

"Sorry?" James said.

Elizabeth stared at the man as if he'd lost his mind.

"I've always wanted to try my hand at an archbishop's signature, but I suppose a special license might raise some questions as to how you managed to acquire it so quickly and without anyone hearing of it. Unless you've some special connections of which I'm unaware Dinsmore?"

"No."

"It's unfortunate we're not closer to Scotland. The paperwork for Gretna Green would be quite simple."

"Heading in the opposite direction I'm afraid."

"A small wedding it is then, with the fewest possible witnesses. Easier that way, less signatures to create." Marcus lifted his quill, but stopped short of writing. "It just occurred to me you might be married on shipboard; even less paper-work there. Of course,"—he tapped the tip of the quill feather on his lip—"you might marry in France."

Elizabeth couldn't decide which was most bizarre, the man's references to marriage licenses, forging, or the fact that this was the longest speech she'd heard from him since they'd met three days ago. "Since we are only pretending to elope, I fail to see why Lord Dinsmore and I should need any sort of documents, forged or otherwise."

"Paperwork, licenses, contracts, certificates, they are the key to our modern society. You'd be surprised how many doors open to a few flourished signatures and an official looking stamp or two."

"It wouldn't be binding, would it?" She slid a glance at James. "I shouldn't want to find myself unintentionally bound to Lord Dinsmore."

"So young and innocent," Marcus said dryly, "to think that a document, particularly one such as a marriage license, could ever be binding. People are bound only if they wish it so, not simply because some fancy bit of scrollwork says they are."

What a peculiar secretary James has chosen, Elizabeth thought. "Is that why you became a forger, because you've such contempt for legal institutions?"

Marcus shrugged, his expression making it clear he had no intention of answering her question. "A marriage license will make it easier for you to travel with Dinsmore, raise less questions—not to mention eyebrows. A married woman traveling with her husband is subject to far less . . . how shall I put this? Discourtesies."

Discourtesies. She wondered if James's secretary was aware of the many cuts she'd suffered in London, the slights that had followed her to the countryside, driving her to this moment. "Still, if people suppose us to be eloping and not yet married, it will be easier for Lord Dinsmore and me to explain our need for separate lodgings."

"That matter has been settled," James cut in sharply. "I have no interest in paying the cost of extra rooms, even if they should be available, which is unlikely considering where we are headed. And I have enough on my mind without wondering every moment what trouble you might have gotten yourself into left unattended in a public inn."

Elizabeth ignored the latter part of his answer. "I've been thinking I should send word to my brother asking him to send me some additional funds. I'll tell him that the Norcrofts have the cleverest seamstress visiting and that I'd like to have some dresses made."

James arched an inquisitive brow. "And where will you have this money sent, and how do you propose it might reach us once we begin traveling in France?"

She frowned.

"Of course, if your sensibilities have been distressed after only one night together," he volunteered, "it's not too late to have you delivered safely home."

"That will not be necessary," she snapped.

"It was worth a try." He smiled, a curve that was thrown off center by the scar. "So what shall it be, shall we tell anyone who might be curious that we were married in a quiet country church, sheep grazing in the cemetery outside, while we pledged our troth at an old wooden altar? Shall we say that you wore fluttering ribbons and I sober silks?"

She looked at him as if she were considering his suggestion. "You know, I'm not certain which part of your story people will have the most difficulty believing, that you have gotten married or that you were actually in a church."

Marcus smothered a cough that sounded suspiciously like laughter.

She continued, aping his casual tone. "If we must pretend to have married, let us tell people it was on shipboard, crossing the channel. I wore a sensible navy traveling gown; you were in brown serge and puce.

"Puce? I never wear puce."

"The ceremony was unremarkable, the words spoken hurriedly so that the captain could get back to the business of sailing."

"What an appallingly grim imagination you have." He gave a mock shudder. "And to think, I once imagined you a romantic."

"I gave up on romantic illusions," she said, her voice deceptively light, "about the time I began to wonder how your sister could have known precisely when to open the door to the library and when to have my brother's coach brought round."

"Arabella." Her mother's voice, drawing out the last syllables of her name, echoed up the staircase. "Ara-bell-ahhh." It was a command not a question. Marking her place with a bit of grosgrain ribbon, Arabella Norcroft closed her book.

Her mother entered the room just as she was setting it down on a side table. "Reading," she said disapprovingly. "Nearly as bad as leaving the windows open at night. Invites in all manner of corruption."

"You were calling for me, Mama?" she asked in an attempt to distract her mother from a discussion of her "unnatural" propensity for books.

"It's most peculiar, my dear, most upsetting."

"What is?"

"The carriage downstairs." Her mother drew her chin up disapprovingly. "It has the Moreham coat of arms on the doors."

"Is it Lady Elizabeth come to call?" She tried hard to keep the excitement from her voice. It would be just like Elizabeth to show up unannounced on her doorstep.

"It doesn't appear so, though considering that one's wild behavior, the impertinence wouldn't surprise me at all." She motioned for her daughter to follow her. "The coachman said he has some packages for you." The starched lace of her cap shaking with disapproval, she started down the stairs.

Arabella trailed after her. Though her mother had forbidden her to see Elizabeth when they'd both still been in London, she'd stopped short of refusing to let the girls correspond. There was always a possibility, her mother said, that society might forgive Elizabeth Harcrest. Or that some gentleman might be willing to overlook her indiscretions, marry her for her title and fortune, and restore at least some of the luster to her tarnished reputation. If such a thing was to occur, it might be well if Lady Elizabeth remembered Arabella with affection. By affection, she knew her mother really meant something more akin to patronage; her mother considered every relationship outside the family in terms of how it might advance Arabella's marital prospects.

A girl with limited endowments, her mother was fond of saying, should be careful not to squander them. Arabella had only to look in the mirror to know that by "limited endowments" her mother was referring to more than her modest dowry. Her figure was little better than that of a boy's, her hair was an uninteresting shade of brown and had less waves than a pane of glass. Her bookishness, her mother frequently pointed out, only made things worse.

They reached the bottom of the stairs and turned, approaching the open door to the parlor. Arabella could see her sister Annabella propped up on the chaise, a great pile of embroidered pillows behind her head, her eyes closed as she listened to their youngest sister, Annelise, practicing the pianoforte. It might have been her imagination, but Arabella could have sworn that some of the stiffness in her mother's bearing eased. Doubtless it was the soothing sight of pretty, pregnant, successfully married Annabella. Her husband, Rupert Fenwinkle, as Annabella liked to tell anyone she thought might not be aware, was cousin to Sir Edmund Bogglesworth, a baron, no less, with considerable estates to the north. *Hamcroft*. Whenever Arabella thought of the name, she couldn't help envisioning the stout Sir Edmund with an apple in his mouth.

Annabella lifted her head from the nest of pillows as Arabella and her mother passed by the door. "Is it someone come to call, Mama?" She loved visitors, could talk for hours about who was wearing what, who was courting whom, and who had won or lost at the gaming tables. Now that she was pregnant, she also enjoyed lengthy discussions on the proper clothes and furnishings for a child. Arabella wondered if the baby would appreciate the hours that had been spent on choosing just the right pattern of French wallpaper for the sitting room next to the nursery.

"No one of any consequence, my pet. Do not bestir yourself." Arabella's mother paused for a moment, her finger in the air as if testing the wind. "Annelise, that should have been an E, not a D. You must read the music more carefully or you'll give your poor sister a megrim."

"Yes, Mama." There was a rustle of sheets of music being turned back. Annelise began playing the piece from the beginning.

As they reached the front steps of the house, Arabella caught sight of the coach with the familiar Harcrest coat of arms and felt her heart skip with excitement. Maybe, just maybe, it *was* Elizabeth come to call. It would be extraordinary for her to appear without sending word first, but then Elizabeth was extraordinary. She had a fearlessness about her that Arabella envied, as if she didn't care a whit what people said or thought about her. Arabella would wager a year's pin money that Elizabeth Harcrest didn't leave a party distraught with worry that she'd said or done the wrong thing. She knew her mother would say Elizabeth was bold because she had the protection of wealth and privilege, but she knew it was something deeper, something Elizabeth had been born with, something, she thought with a deep internal sigh, she'd never have.

A coachman in Harcrest livery stepped forward. "You are Mrs. Frederick Norcroft?"

"I am."

"And this would be your daughter, Miss Arabella Norcroft?" he inquired.

"She is." Her mother answered for her.

"My mistress, Lady Elizabeth Harcrest, wished me to deliver the following message. Knowing that Miss Norcroft and her sister, Mrs. Rupert Fenwinkle, would be visiting for the duration of Mrs. Fenwinkle 's lying in, she has sent several packages of ladies' magazines and novels to help pass the time. Moreover, she has enclosed in these cases several yards of fabric, which she hopes you will be able to use to make clothing for the child."

"As if we were charity cases," her mother muttered under her breath. "Do tell Lady Elizabeth that we find ourselves astonished by her gifts," she added more loudly for the benefit of the coachman.

"And do express to her how much we appreciate her generosity," Arabella appended quickly.

Her mother's mouth twitched with ill-concealed displeasure as the coachman began to unload the carriage. "You may put the case with the ladies' magazines and fabric in the parlor. As for the others,"—she waved dismissively—"ask Miss Norcroft." She turned on her heel and marched up the steps into the house.

Arabella stepped forward, embarrassed by her mother's brusque response to Elizabeth's gifts and anxious to have the cases upstairs in her room where she could savor their contents at leisure. Sharing books was nearly as entertaining as sharing witticisms. And it gave her a glimpse into her friend's mind; a glimpse, she secretly hoped, that might show her how Elizabeth had learned to dare so much and fear so little.

"If you'll follow me,"—she beckoned to the coachman—"I'll show you where to put the cases."

The coachman nodded, but then he hesitated. His eyes flickered uncertainly towards the front door of the Norcroft's home.

"Is there something more?" she prompted.

He glanced at Arabella, then once more towards the front door. Apparently satisfied that her mother would not be returning, he reached into his pocket and withdrew a packet of letters. "Lady Elizabeth asked me to give these to you when I was certain there was no one else about. Said to tell you they was of the utmost importance. And that you should make sure to read the one on top,"—he pointed at it—"the one addressed to you, *in private*." He placed particular emphasis on the last two words.

"I see," she said. But she didn't, not at all. Only the top letter was addressed to her, the rest were addressed to Lord and Lady Moreham and to the Dowager Marchioness, Lady Louisa Moreham of Moreham Hall. It was with difficulty that she restrained the urge to rip the letter open right there and then. "Oh my dear Elizabeth," she murmured softly to herself, "what have you got up to now?"

Two days later, when the coachman had returned from Hartsdale, Alix burst into Rafe's study jubilantly waving an opened letter. "There, you see, I told you everything would turn out just fine."

"I presume that is a letter from my sister."

"It is. There is a letter for us, and one for Louisa as well. Elizabeth is having a wonderful time, though she misses us all dreadfully, and she begs us to kiss the pug for her."

"You'll forgive me if I refrain from passing on that bit of affection. It's bad enough that the beast has taken to sleeping on my pillow."

"He likes you."

"He drools."

"He does not," she protested.

"This epistle." He beckoned with long elegant fingers. "Have you checked to make certain it came from Hartsdale?"

Alix stopped, planting her fists on her hips.

While he knew his wife meant it as a defiant gesture, Rafe couldn't help thinking that her rounded belly undermined the pose. She looked adorable. He schooled his features to remain attentive to the tirade he knew was coming.

"Of course I did not check the return address," she stormed, slipping into French. "I refuse to be suspicious of her."

"Only because you have not known Elizabeth for as long as I have," he replied in the same language.

She handed him the letter. He immediately turned it over.

"Well?" she demanded.

"It appears to have been sent from Hartsdale."

"Which proves my point." She lifted her chin triumphantly.

"Which proves the letter was sent from Hartsdale, not that my sister sent it from there."

"It is in her hand, is it not?"

He unfolded the letter; his eyes sliding carefully down the page. "So it appears to be."

"And there is a postscript from Arabella Norcroft, is there not? Thanking us in a most polite manner for sending Elizabeth to stay with them." She cocked her head. "Or perhaps you think that part is a forgery?"

He shook his head. "My sister could never manage a hand so neat."

"Concede, then, my love." She came round his desk. "Your sister is precisely where she ought to be."

Rafe pulled her onto his lap. "I will concede," he said kissing the soft curve of her neck. "Only that you are precisely where you should be."

Chapter 23

Sitting atop a pile of trunks in the miserable drizzle of Calais, Elizabeth reminded herself that she no longer cared what James Dinsmore thought or felt. She had no intention of apologizing for suggesting James had been involved with his sister in planning her disgrace. He hadn't answered, of course, certainly not with his servant, Marcus, sitting across from them, but the temperature in the coach seemed to drop several degrees. James had proceeded to bury his nose in a volume of poetry while Marcus had concentrated his energies on forging their marriage certificate.

He deserved the barb for mocking her loss of romantic illusions—when he'd been the one responsible. And he'd been infuriatingly smug, dismissing her idea of financing separate quarters, and suggesting that she was in need of supervision, as if she were a harebrained child. She'd been clever enough to convince him to include her on this trip, hadn't she? She toyed with the beads of moisture on her gloves; she was well-accustomed to James Dinsmore's arrogance. Usually it amused her. It was a pose, really, to make people believe he didn't take anything seriously, not even himself.

"Citeness Dinsmore." The French customs official cleared his throat loudly, seeking to attract attention. "If you would be so kind as to stand so that we may inspect your luggage." Elizabeth shot a surprised look at the man, uncertain what had startled her most, that she hadn't noticed that the little Frenchman with the greasy hair was standing so close, that he'd addressed her by the egalitarian title, *citizeness*, or that he'd called her by her newly borrowed name, Dinsmore.

"But of course," she said in French, rising from her seat, the smallest of James's trunks. She smoothed her skirts which had become increasingly sodden since they'd come ashore and taken their place in this interminably long customs line.

"The case belongs to your husband, yes?"

Husband. The word was unsettling. "Yes."

The man unsnapped the straps holding the trunk closed and began rifling through the contents: shirts, stocks, nightshirts. Elizabeth turned away. They hadn't touched, not since he'd helped her up from the grass at Moreham Hall, and they hadn't kissed, not since before the duel. If they kissed, she wondered, would she run her hand down the angry ridge of his scar? She could almost feel the skin smooth beneath her fingers, and the even softer touch of his lips against hers . . . *stop, stop, stop!*

And there it was.

The real reason she'd said what she had about James's plotting with Anne. She needed to remind herself that no matter how drawn she was to the man, her instincts were probably wrong. And the question had done the trick, dividing them as fiercely as an axe through wood.

"Citeness." The greasy customs official was holding up a bottle and uncorked it, sniffing. "What is this?"

The pungent odor of James's cologne, the one he'd begun

wearing shortly before they'd disembarked the packet boat that had brought them to France earlier that day, assaulted her nostrils. She wrinkled her nose. "It is my husband's; everything in that case is his."

The official recorked the bottle, and waved a grime-lined hand over it. "It is strong, no?"

"It is strong, yes," she agreed, wondering vaguely if the cologne was some peculiar form of retribution. James's new scent was nearly as off-putting as her question had been.

The official put the bottle back and closed the trunk, turning his attention to the remainder of the luggage. He began opening hatboxes. "You have a great deal of hats, citizeness."

She nodded absently.

"Aristocrats in our country have no need of such things."

Something in his tone caught her attention; Elizabeth glanced over at the man.

He smiled broadly and seizing a straw bonnet decorated with ribbons and flowers, he waved it about announcing loudly, "Aristocrats in France have no need of such hats since most of them no longer have heads."

There was a ripple of laughter from his fellow customs officials and the national guardsmen loitering about the line.

Despite the revulsion rippling through her, Elizabeth forced her expression to remain calm. She knew they were looking for a reaction. She was trying to come up with a flippant response, when she felt James's arm settle around her waist. He spoke in fluent French. "My wife, it is true, is devoted to her hats. But she is even more devoted to the cause of Revolution. It is why she refused to marry me until I renounced my title and why she insisted that we begin our new life, as husband and wife, in the new France. Long live the Revolution," he shouted. Those in and around the line echoed his cry. Elizabeth, her lips dry, mouthed the words.

James quickly removed his arm, but he remained reassuringly close as the officials rifled through the remainder of their luggage. The amusement they found in delaying their English visitors waned as the drizzle turned into rain. Just as the last paper was signed and stamped, and the last piece of luggage reloaded onto the coach, it turned into a downpour. James held open the door of the carriage and motioned for Elizabeth to hurry. He leapt in after her.

"What about Marcus?" she asked, raising her voice to be heard over the sound of rain pelting windows and the roof.

"He and Andre are riding on ahead to make certain everything is set for our arrival."

"How long will it take to get there?"

"We should reach the outskirts of Amiens by tomorrow afternoon. Of course it all depends on what time we reach the inn tonight. The roads here are awful and with the rain . . ." He shrugged.

Elizabeth fell silent thinking of the inn and the room—and the bed—they would share. Her mind turned to the ploy she'd used to create a distance between them, her question about his involvement in Anne's schemes, and then, unexpectedly she found herself wondering how Anne was faring without James. "Does your sister know where you are?"

His blue eyes appraised her carefully. "Why do you ask?"

"You've always seemed so inseparable. I remember when we were children, you were always watching out for her, always the first one there if she needed help."

"She knows I've left England. I told her I needed some time alone, to think." Unconsciously he touched his scar.

"But you haven't told her you've gone to France?"

"I didn't want to worry her." He paused. "Does that surprise you?"

"No, not at all. I was just wondering, What if she should hear rumors?"

"There is no reason to expect that rumors of my—or our—sojourn here, should make their way back across the channel." His eyes narrowed. "Tell me, Elizabeth, this unexpected show of concern for my sister. Are you suddenly afraid she will catch wind of what you've done now and tell the ton?"

"Don't presume to read my mind James Dinsmore."

"Presume to read your mind?" He raised his hands in mock surrender. "I'd sooner presume to read those indecipherable scratchings on ancient temples in the Far East."

She scowled at him. "I simply found myself thinking about her and wondering how she was faring alone."

"Of course," he said in a voice that made it clear that he didn't believe her. "To set your mind at ease, my sister knows better than to give credence to a piffle of gossip that might reach her ears . . ."

Elizabeth bit back the retort that sprang to her lips: that Anne knew better than to believe the truth of the gossip that circulated through the ton, since she'd spawned so much of it herself.

"If Anne suspects some strange rumor she hears is true, she will take pains to seek out proof before putting faith in the story. And in the case of our little sojourn, it is unlikely anyone will discover we have been together. You have taken pains to make everyone believe you are at Hartsdale, while I have spread rumors that I am wandering abroad, disconsolate over the loss of you and,"—his fingers glanced his scar—"and of course, my disfigurement."

Elizabeth heard it again; the airily dismissive tone he'd used in the coach when he'd discussed their supposed wedding. She wouldn't pursue his feelings for her, but she wondered how he truly felt about the scar. "You aren't disfigured, you know."

He shrugged. "I haven't given it much thought."

"You aren't." She persisted.

He glanced at her curiously. "Are you one of those women who finds my scar wickedly attractive? A dangerous angel, as one particularly amorous lady described me?"

"If you're trying to impress me with your adventures since our infamous encounter several months ago, you needn't bother." Elizabeth didn't add that it wasn't his face or figure that had drawn her to him, and that no matter what he looked like she'd always . . . She refused to allow herself to continue along this line of thought. "A dangerous angel, how amusing. Certainly not the term I would use."

"And what term would you use to describe me, Elizabeth?" His voice was subtly less certain.

"To tell you the truth," she deliberately echoed his earlier words, "I haven't given it much thought."

"Liar," he munnured softly.

"No more than you," she murmured back.

"As for Anne being alone," he said, abruptly steering the conversation back to its original course, "let me set your mind at ease. Our cousin Agatha is staying with her and she has a suitor who has been dancing vigorous attendance upon her, Sir Edmund Bogglesworth."

Anne glanced about the fussily appointed parlor of Lady Morton's London town house to see if any of the other couples engaged in cards, backgammon or checkers might be paying attention to her conversation with Sir Edmund. "Tell me," she asked in her most casual tone, "how you came to hear this story about Moreham's involvement in trade."

"Oh, I didn't simply hear it, my dear." He chuckled, moving his checker. "I saw the fellow in the silk quarter of Lyon. Haggling like a fishwife over bolts of silk."

She studied the board. With one move she could easily take two of his men, but that would shorten the game and possibly Sir Edmund's temper. She wanted to keep him talking. Haggling and fishwife were not words Anne had ever thought she'd hear in association with the character of Rafe Harcrest, Earl of Moreham. She moved her checker into an exposed position.

"You should be more careful, Lady Anne." He waggled a plump finger at her. "Now I fear I must be most ungentlemanly and take your piece."

"How could I not see that?" She flipped open her fan and fluttered it, as if covering her embarrassment. "But I was so distracted by the notion of the earl haggling. Are you certain he was not purchasing silks for his wife?"

"This was long before he married."

"His stepmother Louisa, perhaps?"

"Haven't seen the woman, I admit, but I think I'd have heard if she were the size of ten or eleven women."

"He was buying that many bolts of silk? Mightn't they have been for decorating purposes?" Anne thought of the renovations Rafe had done to his London home, Moreham Hall, last winter, the renovations she'd thought had been in preparation for his marriage to her. With difficulty she stifled her sudden urge to topple the checkerboard. She slid a checker into a safe position.

"Clever girl." Sir Edmund smiled across the board at her. "It was the wrong sort of material for upholstery or drapes."

"You seem to know a great deal about fabrics."

As she hoped, he took her words as a compliment and continued talking. "I have been doing some renovations at Hamcroft, of the private rooms. He paused, a sly smile coming into his pale blue eyes. "I'm thinking that a wife would want a less masculine, less Spartan décor."

Anne fluttered her fan; she was having trouble imagining that any aspect of Sir Edmund's life might be Spartan. "Indeed."

"Indeed," he repeated with emphasis.

"And what has brought on your sudden desire for matrimony, Sir Edmund? I had heard you were a confirmed bachelor."

He leaned back in his chair, folding his heavy hands over his stomach. "Up until a year ago, I, too, believed myself a confirmed bachelor, content in my solitary ways. But then I attended the wedding of my favorite nephew Rupert Fenwinkle. He asked me to stand up with him, his father having passed away of a winter vomiting sickness. I found myself strangely moved when I saw his bride, Annabella Norcroft, coming down the aisle towards him. And it seemed to me when the minister spoke the words of the ceremony, binding those two young people together, that I was hearing them for the first time. I resolved there and then that I should be married, too." He unfolded his hands and leaned forward. "It would be selfish of me not to share all that I have to offer with the right woman."

"Such a romantic tale." Anne snapped open the fan that hung at her wrist. "I believe it is your move, Sir Edmund."

His eyes shifted from her to the board. "Yes, it is." He moved his piece. "She is with child."

"Your nephew's wife?"

"Yes."

"Congratulations."

"She is lying in at her mother's. A bit peculiar if you ask me, but then I imagine most women like to be with their mothers at such a delicate and emotional time."

She nodded absently. Anne rarely allowed herself to think about what daughters did with their mothers. She didn't need a mother, she didn't need a father; they managed quite well by themselves, she and James.

"Hartsdale," he continued, "it's near your estates in the country, I believe."

"A ride of a day or two, depending on whether you go by carriage or by horseback, and the weather, of course."

"Mrs. Norcroft has invited most of the family to visit, keep the young lady company, await the big event. First grandchild, you know. She's certain it will be a boy."

Anne smiled politely, wondering how she could steer the conversation back to Moreham and his doings in France. She found it difficult to imagine Moreham involved in trade, and yet his fortune had taken an extraordinary turn for the better since he'd inherited what little had remained of it from his sot of a brother, George.

"With the season coming to an end, you and your father

and your cousin will, no doubt, be planning to return to the country soon. And since my family will all be gathered so nearby, I was wondering, Lady Anne, if you and Miss Agatha might honor us with a visit. Of course, your father, His Grace, is welcome, too, if his health and interests permit."

What had he been rambling on about? While the man had glimmers of intelligent conversation, most of the time he was interminably long-winded. She glanced up at him, smiling prettily. "I'm so very sorry, Sir Edmund, but my mind was on the checkers game. Would you be so kind as to repeat yourself?"

"I was wondering, Lady Anne, if you would honor me, honor my family, by paying a call upon the home of my cousin, your neighbor, Mrs. Frederick Norcroft."

Chapter 24

Elizabeth was no longer worried about how she'd manage to spend a night in a bed with James Dinsmore. She'd have happily stripped off her clothes and slept with a cow if only they'd stop traveling. She was exhausted. She felt as if every bone had been rattled loose and her skirts were as sodden as if she'd been sitting atop the carriage instead of inside it.

It was all the checkpoints. There seemed to be one in every town: Ardes, St. Omer, Aires. She'd lost count after Lilliers. National guards, local officials, grubby gangs with woolen caps, all of them armed, all of them demanding that they get out of the coach and show their papers. She'd been terrified at first, standing in the pouring rain, watching as the men searched the coach. She'd been frightened at the second stop. By the third, she was nearly as calm as James appeared to be. And by the fourth, the inspections began to blur into a miserable ritual.

And there had been the stream they'd crossed. Swollen by the rain, it was more like a river. Halfway across, water had begun to trickle through the cracks of the carriage door. The trickle had quickly become a flood and Elizabeth, kneeling on the seat, with her skirts gathered up in her arms, found herself immensely grateful James's coach had been built with its unusually raised seats. When she'd commented on them, James said she should thank David; the seats were among the modifications he'd designed. She'd meant to ask him if he'd taken David on because of his design talents and his fluency in French, because otherwise the man seemed less than skilled as a coachman. But the coach had lurched, and she'd had to grab at the door to keep her balance, and then she'd forgotten.

The coach slowed. "Please Lord, I promise to repent every last sin if only that's the inn and not another checkpoint."

"Every last sin? I'm afraid we haven't got that much time. We'll need to be off early in the morning."

Elizabeth hadn't thought she'd spoken loudly enough for him to hear, but she found she didn't care. "James, is this it? Is this the inn?"

He smiled at the excitement in her voice. "Yes, indeed, Citizeness Dinsmore, this is where we shall be stopping for the night."

She arranged her sodden hat on her head and smoothed her skirts. They were stopping. Finally stopping. And there would be a warm fire, and warm food, and warm sheets. Perhaps even warm water with which to wash. She leaned forward expectantly. The carriage door swung open. She saw Marcus holding a lantern. Beyond him, across a muddy yard, she could see a low building with plaster-daubed walls and a tiled roof. It looked like heaven.

The problem with living in a tunnel that was once part of an underground plumbing system is that while it keeps the rain off one's head, it doesn't keep it from running in a steady stream beneath one's feet. Gerard de Joley braced his back against one side of the tunnel and stretched his legs across to the other. It was uncomfortable, but it kept his shoes dry. He wondered where the Englishmen were. They were to meet him in two weeks' time; that was what the note in the tree stump had said. Gerard didn't know the identities of the Englishmen, any more than he knew the identity of the individual who was helping him hide in the tunnel, or the individual who left rocks on the stump to let him know there was a letter or a bit of food hidden inside. It was better this way. There'd be no one to betray if he was discovered and tortured. But it made him feel oddly abandoned. *Ecœurant* mawkishness, he chided himself. It was simply that he was unaccustomed to being alone. He'd been a courtier. Most of his life he'd been attended by servants or surrounded by companions. Even his private moments had been shared, with his wife, or his mistresses, or his daughter, Marguerite.

Marguerite, with her dark eyes and dark curls, so like her mother's, and the funny little overbite that made her plump mouth look like she was pouting. But she didn't pout, his daughter; she far preferred to laugh. He'd no doubt she'd have found a way to laugh, even here, in this muddy hole. He imagined her sitting by a cozy fire in some well-appointed salon in Paris, engaged in witty banter, or more likely, passionately arguing politics. Many times he'd argued them with her, debating the future of the nobility late into the night, until the candles guttered down into pools of wax and the food grew cold on their plates.

At the memory of food, his stomach gurgled nearly as loudly as the water running beneath his outstretched legs. It had been two days since there was food in the stump, three since his last visit to the old woman's chicken coop. As soon as the rain stopped and the ground dried enough so it wouldn't leave a record of his tracks, he'd risk another trip. Gerard thought of the rows of hens on their nests, imagining them roasted with potatoes on rows of plates. . . .

* * *

James Dinsmore looked down upon the sleeping form of Elizabeth Harcrest. He hadn't had to coax her to share the bed this evening, he thought wryly. While he'd been downstairs talking with Marcus, David, and Andre, she'd cleaned up and climbed in. Made herself comfortable. She was lying on her stomach, face buried in the pillows, hands fisted in the sheets, which were drawn tightly around her chin. A light spluttering sound issued from her, a sound, which had he not been a gentleman, he might have considered a snore. She'd taken most of the pillows, he noticed, and more than her share of the covers. And while she might claim to favor the right side of the bed, tonight she was sleeping dead center.

He ought to wake her. He was damn tired, too. And yet, he found himself oddly reluctant to do so. It had been rough traveling today, and there'd be more of the same tomorrow. She'd foisted herself on their company, he reminded himself; she should be grateful she wasn't sleeping on the floor or on the tables in the common room, with the rest of the company. He reached out to shake her, but his hand stayed. She'd stood the traveling well. She hadn't complained about the roads, or the rain, or the food. She hadn't swooned, or wept, or made a goose of herself at the sight of the rough gendarmes and their weapons.

In fact, her presence at their frequent stops had actually been rather helpful—not that he'd ever tell her. Quite a number of the guards had spent more time inspecting her face and figure than their coach and papers. James didn't think there was much chance the false panels in the sides of the coach where they'd hidden their cache of counterfeit assignats, or the panels behind the seats where they'd stored old clothes, wigs, jars of hair dye, and pots of face paint would be discovered. Still, it didn't hurt to have her as a distraction.

"Elizabeth," he said softly, hoping the insistence in his voice would encourage her to move.

The spluttering stopped.

He waited.

She mumbled something incomprehensible, pulled the covers tighter, and burrowed her face more deeply into the pillows.

He glanced about the room. None of the furniture looked as inviting as the bed. And besides, every available piece seemed to be draped with an article of Elizabeth's damp clothing. A particularly charming bit of lace nonsense was draped over the arm of a straight-backed chair. He'd just have to pick her up and move her over. Pushing back the lace sleeves of his nightshirt, he leaned over the bed, drew back the covers, swept back the tangles of chestnut curls and slipped his hands around her rib cage just under her arms. It wasn't a good enough grip, he slid his hands farther underneath her and encountered breasts. Soft warm breasts that filled his hands, the nipples pebbling ever so slightly against his palm. His groin tightened in response. He cursed under his breath. He was supposed to be looking out for Elizabeth Harcrest, not molesting the girl in her sleep.

Reluctantly he slid his hands out from under the tantalizing weight that filled them. He drew the covers farther down. She was wearing a voluminous nightshirt. Not at all what he expected, particularly in view of the expensive examples of unmentionables that adorned the room. Well, he'd always secretly believed a man never really knew a woman until he'd slept with her. In Elizabeth's case, he wasn't sure he'd ever really know her. Which might be for the best. He studied her draped form, trying to make out the indentations of her waist. Nothing too dangerous there, he told himself, as he reached for her. He lifted. Her bottom came up against his stomach. He could feel her thighs against his belly. The urge to pull her closer and down was nearly overwhelming. He released her.

James pulled the covers back up over Elizabeth, and she mumbled something about the hour being too early and besides she'd already practiced. He didn't have the foggiest notion what she was talking about, but he thought Moreham shouldn't allow her to practice anything. She was far too dangerous as it was.

He raked a hand through his loosened hair. Come hell, high water, or Elizabeth Harcrest, he was going to sleep in a bed tonight. He climbed in beside her, his back turned resolutely to her curves and nudged. She didn't budge. James Dinsmore, heir to a duchy, lay on the edge of the mattress, without a pillow, one arm and half a leg dangling over the side of the bed, four toes exposed to the cold. He nudged her again. She settled her back against his and sighed.

"Elizabeth," he said firmly, "move over."

"Just some hot chocolate please," she mumbled.

"Move *over*."

Startled, half-awake, she scrambled over, taking the remainder of the covers with her.

"And give me back some of the damn covers."

"You don't have to be so cross about it!" She thrust the covers at him, her voice sounding to his ear unreasonably offended.

He moved away from the edge of the mattress and took a portion of the bundle of sheets and blankets she held bunched in her arms. "Thank you," he said as politely as if she'd agreed to allow him to promenade her around a dance floor. He made a great show of spreading them down over his long legs and tucking in his toes. "Now a pillow, if you please."

She tossed one at him. "If I'd known you were so possessive about your bedclothes, I'd have wrapped myself in a shawl."

As he caught the pillow, he allowed his eyes to wander slowly over her. He started with the rumpled chestnut curls that fell below her shoulders, moving to the laced vee of her oversized nightshirt, down to her hands covered by cuffs edged in lace. He recognized the lace. Anne had stitched it. "And this shawl, would it be yours? Or something you pilfered from my trunk?"

She flipped a curl over her shoulder in what was meant to be a gesture of defiance, but only served to offer him a glimpse of breast between the vee. Catching the direction of his glance, she snatched the nightshirt closed. James felt the same sense of heavy regret as when the curtain fell on the last scene of a brilliantly sung opera.

"Since it is your nightshirt, I can understand why you would be interested in an explanation of how I came to be in it."

He nodded.

"But it is your fault, really."

James turned towards her, leaning on one elbow. "Sorry? My fault?"

"If your men had not been so consumed with keeping that little trunk of yours dry, perhaps they might have noticed that the lids of *my* trunks were left gaping in the rain."

He made a silent promise to himself to warn David to take better care to conceal his concern over the welfare of the little trunk. "I see. You have my deepest apologies. I shall speak to my men in the morning. In the meantime, while your things are drying, you are welcome to my nightshirt."

"It's not as if I enjoy wearing your things," she sniffed. "Frankly James, since we find ourselves sharing such intimate quarters, I feel compelled to tell you . . . well . . . your cologne . . . it's . . . less refined than your usual choices."

"You don't like it?" He pretended to take offense, though he agreed with her; the stuff David had concocted to make the invisible ink on the interior of the trunk reappear smelled so noxious it made his head spin. "It's all the rage in London, but then you've been out of circulation these past months, and styles do change so quickly amongst the haute ton . . ."

Her sharp intake of breath told him his attempt to change the subject had been successful.

It was a cruel thing to say. He knew it. But she was noticing far too many details about his belongings. And with her sitting so close and wearing so little, he was noticing far too many details about her. "I'm sorry, Elizabeth. It's been a long day and I'm tired. I shouldn't have spoken as I did."

"No, you shouldn't have. I may be in your bed, James Dinsmore, but I'm not your wife or your mistress. So you may keep your hands, your opinions, and your blasted apologies to yourself." She pulled her pillow to the far side of the bed and turned her back to him, dragging the bed-clothes with her.

James felt chill air on his toes, but he didn't ask for the covers back.

The old woman stood uncertainly before the desk of the officer in charge of security for the department of Rouen. She was unaccustomed to dealing with the authorities. She'd spent most of her life trying not to be noticed by such people. She'd long ago learned that if a peasant such as she lifted her head up, most likely she'd get her ears boxed. Still, she'd walked all morning through the mud left by last night's rain and the information she had was important.

The officer looked up from his work, his black eyes taking in her ragged skirt, her soiled apron, and the strings of gray hair hanging loose from her cotton cap. "You have business with me, citizeness?" he inquired, his voice skeptical.

She licked her thin dry lips and managed a low, stuttering sound.

"Yes?" he prompted.

"Someone," she said softly, then cleared her voice and started again. "Someone has been stealing my eggs."

"I see." The officer pushed his tricorne hat with its bold revolutionary cockade back on his head and scratched at an elusive flea.

"Not just one egg, but three." She held up three wrinkled fingers to emphasize her point.

"And these eggs, is it possible they might have been stolen by a rat? Or perhaps a fox?"

"A rat would not have taken so many, and a fox, why he'd have taken my chickens, not their eggs." She shook her head. "No, it was a person; of this I am sure."

"So," he repeated, examining a speck between his thumb and forefinger, "someone has been stealing your eggs."

"And my neighbor Jacques's coat, right off the back of his wagon. A good coat it was, too, not more than two or three years old."

He flicked the speck away. "And why do you think this is a matter for the Rouen Committee of Public Safety? Most likely it is the prank of some neighbor's boy."

"No, no, citizen. The neighbor's boys have all joined the army." She leaned forward. "I think, citizen, that there is a fugitive hiding in the area. I think you should send some soldiers to watch my coop."

"We have arrested all of the fugitives in this area."

"Perhaps it is some other enemy of the republic who is stealing my eggs," she insisted.

The officer reached for a sheet of paper and picked up a pen. Dipping the nib in a bottle of ink, he asked, "Your name?" The old woman supplied him with her name and address, watching as the pen moved swiftly across the page, leaving marks she couldn't read. When the pen stopped, the officer looked at her. "This is very interesting information, citizeness. You can be certain we will give it all the attention it deserves."

She smiled, revealing several missing teeth and thanked him.

The officer watched as she turned and walked away. As the heavy wooden door closed behind her, he picked up the paper and added it to the pile on the corner of his desk.

Chapter 25

When would he get it through his thick skull Elizabeth Harcrest was not for him? Her brother had made it *clear* she was beyond his reach, and now so had she. Why, *why*, had he ever insisted they share a bed? Was it simply because she was—

"*There* Dinsmore, see how neatly it comes through," David whispered pointing at the list of names and addresses appearing on the interior of the trunk with each swipe of the solution from the cologne bottle.

"Very good." With an effort, James forced himself to focus on the business at hand and not Elizabeth, sitting on the other side of the paneled dressing screen. "These two here." He pointed at several darkening lines. "Tell Marcus and Andre to ride ahead again today and arrange for me to meet with them tomorrow in the merchants quarter in Amiens. Make sure you take the appropriate letters of introduction from Moreham and conceal them in Marcus's writing desk. Tell them to deliver the letters, but to say nothing. If they're caught, they should say they are merely servants;

they have no knowledge of what's in the letters or why I want to meet with these men. All negotiations are to be left to me." *That's what Grenville sent me to do. That and only that. No point wondering if what I feel for Elizabeth might be . . .*

". . . stronger. I thought about making the solution stronger, but this seems to work just fine. What about her?" David shot a thumb over his shoulder, in the direction of the screen. Elizabeth was supposedly making ready to leave, though James heard precious few sounds of movement from that quarter. Good God, what had he been thinking? *Of how warm she is, and just how good she smells . . .*

"*Stinks*, this mess does." David recorked the bottle, then handed it and the rag he'd used to swipe the trunk's interior to James. "Better slap a bit of this on your face, Dinsmore, just as a precaution, in case anybody asks about the smell."

James pressed the rag to his cheeks and neck, hoping the odiferous solution would be better at keeping Elizabeth at arm's length than he had.

If you tell a man never to touch you again, Elizabeth reflected sourly, *first make certain all the laces on your gown have been fastened.* James made it clear at the outset that he would not hire a lady's maid for her; he couldn't afford a maid's gossip any more than he could afford the additional expense. And furthermore, the lack of a maid would lend credence to the parts they were to play—aristocrats intent on setting aside their traditional privileges. When she'd pointed out he had *three* servants, he said *that* was a different thing altogether.

She'd set about dressing this morning as if she had always done so. She arranged her hair simply in a twist at the neck. She tied her stays and petticoats as best she could. But when she'd stepped into her gown, she knew she was in trouble. There were two buttons in the middle of her back that, however much she twisted and turned, she simply couldn't reach. So she sat, behind a screen, dress drooping off her shoulders, waiting for James to finish his toilette.

The notion that she'd have to ask him for help was galling.

He had David helping him to dress. The more she thought about it, the more annoyed she felt. Clearly, James's decision not to allow her a maid was a form of torture. He and David were probably whispering about her, laughing about her predicament, plotting new ways to humiliate her. She quietly inched her chair closer to the screen and peeked between the panels. Surprisingly, James was fully dressed. He even had his jacket on! If he was finished with his toilette, what was the delay? James and David seemed to be discussing something about the small trunk.

So they had been taking special care of that trunk!

There *must* be something hidden in it. Not weapons. She would have seen them when she searched for a nightshirt. . . . Some kind of secret papers, perhaps? Or counterfeit currency? She recalled overhearing her brother discussing a plan he'd heard from French emigrés, a plan to flood the New Republic with false assignats and undermine the economy. . . . She pushed Rafe from her mind with some effort and focused on the situation at hand. What was James hiding from the French? And what, she wondered, her mouth tightening, was he hiding from her? She lifted her chair to move it back so they wouldn't know she'd been spying. The hem of her gown snagged, and her unfastened bodice was pulled to her waist. She was just grabbing for it when James and David appeared, suddenly in front of her.

David glanced appreciatively, then dropped his eyes. "Sorry, my lord, must check the team we've hired for the coach. I'll be back for your and the lady's things as soon as everything's set."

Not until the door closed behind David, did James speak. "Do you intend to ask for help?" His blue eyes drifted coolly over her exposed breasts and shoulders. "Or would you rather wrestle with your gown for the remainder of the morning?"

She tugged the gown back up. She'd ride to Amiens stark naked before asking *him* for help. She twisted around once more in a desperate attempt to reach the elusive buttons.

"You are a stubborn one, Elizabeth Harcrest," he said as his fingers met hers over the mother of pearl discs. She looked at him; his face was close enough to kiss. Her breath caught as she felt him fasten up the remaining buttons.

"You can breathe now," he said.

For a moment she wasn't sure she could. But, determined to appear as unaffected as he was by the contact, she exhaled. "I had every intention of doing so. It's something I do quite naturally."

She looked lovely, he thought, with her hair pulled back simply. It emphasized the delicate shape of her face and her large hazel eyes. The rose traveling gown brought out the color in her cheeks and in her lips. He traced them with his eyes.

"You, however, seem to have forgotten the trick." She smiled as she'd learned to do in the early, happier days of her season and brushed past him. "Shall we make Amiens today do you think?"

"Weather and roadblocks permitting."

"And you will show me the maps with our route, just as you promised?"

"I shall," he said, reflecting that a lengthy discussion of maps, roads, and local history would be a suitably safe topic between them.

"And will you finally tell me the name of the man whom we seek?"

"I've told you I have no intention of discussing the matter with you. It's safer if you don't know. We've been through this before."

"I thought you might have had a change of heart." She

shrugged, then added, "but of course, first you'd have to have one."

"Quite true," he agreed, echoing her tone with a lightness he didn't really feel.

"I suppose that means you won't tell me what you've got hidden in your trunk."

His eyes narrowed. Was she teasing him or had she discovered something she shouldn't have? He had to stop underestimating this girl, *this woman*, posing as his wife.

"Nothing. Nothing you haven't seen and worn." James held out his hand, resolving never to leave her alone with his luggage again. "And now, Lady Dinsmore, I believe it's time to go down to breakfast."

Anne Dinsmore wasn't sure which was the worst part of returning to the country after the season, traveling for hours on end with her father and Agatha or having to oversee the reopening of the house. Striding through the rooms as the maids flipped back the dust covers from the furniture, she was acutely aware that each year there was less furniture and fewer maids. Passing through the portrait gallery, she made a mental note to have the paintings rearranged so that the spaces left by those that had been sold would not be so obvious.

She gracefully arranged her muslin skirts in the chair behind the delicate pearwood desk, picked up an ivory-handled letter opener, and began slicing open the envelopes that had been arranged in neat piles on her blotter. Calling cards, invitations—country entertaining was a bore compared with London. She flipped over Sir Edmund's invitation to visit his sister, Mrs. Frederick Norcroft, at Hartsdale. How tedious. Not a decent family for miles, unless one counted the Harcrests. Not likely there'd be an invitation from them.

If James had been here with her, he'd have kept her amused. She smiled. He'd have contrived some clever reason for her to call upon Moreham Hall and see how Elizabeth was faring in social exile. A neighborly concern for Alix's welfare, perhaps. The French cow was breeding, and despite their differences, it *was* the polite thing to do. Anne knew just the outfit she'd have chosen for the visit, a lovely vertical stripe that showed her long narrow waist to its best advantage.

But James wasn't here. She'd heard some rumor he was in France. Absurd. She didn't know where he was, but she knew he had better sense than that. She jabbed the sharp blade of her letter opener into the soft surface of the blotter and twisted. A jagged tear appeared, just like the tear Moreham had made on her handsome brother's face, like the rip he'd made in their lives.

He oughtn't to get off so lightly, Moreham. Enjoying his summer in the country with his French wife and his child on the way—a boy, no doubt. He ought to suffer, as she did. Trapped in an empty house, surrounded by babbling idiots, like Agatha, and her father, and Bogglesworth. Thinking of Sir Edmund reminded her of the story he told about seeing Moreham in Lyon. Most likely a lie invented to impress her. A man of Moreham's standing would never soil his hands with trade. Nevertheless, it might be amusing to repeat. Prefaced with the appropriate expressions of disbelief, of course.

Anne smoothed the tear on the blotter with the tip of her blade until it was nothing more than a jagged line. Perhaps she would pay a call on Hartsdale. Amusing stories, like soup, were always the better for a few juicy morsels to flavor them up.

Chapter 26

"This is the route we are on now," James said unfurling a map across Elizabeth's knees. "Rouen is here. Not much farther as you can see." He tried not to smile as she stifled a yawn. If she had thought their time in Amiens would be a grand adventure, she'd been sadly mistaken. Each morning he'd dragged her out of bed early to meet the textile merchants whose names were listed in David's invisible ink on the inside of his trunk. He'd leave her to sit with the wives while he spent the day negotiating with the men over endless cups of coffee and glasses of wine.

At first he'd brought her along because, as he'd told her at the onset of the trip, he didn't trust her alone in the inn. But gradually he realized he *needed* her. The merchants were suspicious. Times were tense in France. The political ground was constantly shifting, and today's friend could easily become tomorrow's enemy of the people. And though the government was encouraging the continuation of trade with England, everyone knew the two countries were on the verge of war.

The merchants met with him because of the letters of introduction he carried from Rafe Harcrest, an English merchant they knew and had learned to trust over the course of many years of transactions. It was a trust they did not automatically extend to James. But when they met his wife, their suspicions eased. What English spy would travel with his wife? And when they learned James's wife was sister to the man Harcrest, they listened with care to what he had to say. He realized Grenville had been right; the skills he'd developed enchanting and seducing his way through the ton were well suited to the task of recruiting volunteers. He could tell from their eyes, from the expressions of their mouths, or the movements of their hands, who would be willing to provide assistance for his network and who would not.

And when he was uncertain, he found himself soliciting Elizabeth's opinion. She studied people nearly as carefully as he did. Indeed, comparing observations had once been the source of much of their banter in the ballrooms and house parties of London. She had a gift for seeing beyond the social pose. Though not because she was looking for a weakness she might exploit. Even so, he had no doubt her skill at seeing through people had been sharpened by her encounters with Anne and her circle of harpies. *And with me.* He glanced at her, sitting beside him in the coach, and wondered what she saw when she looked at him. Highly unlikely it was anything good. He turned his head to look out the window.

"Christ," he said, as he caught sight of the men standing in the road ahead of them. "Get out your papers. It's another bloody roadblock."

The Norcrofts' house party was dreadfully dull. Still, Anne reflected, as she gazed at the women gathered about the parlor sewing baby clothes and talking softly, it did have a certain appeal. She pulled her needle through the cambric of a tiny shirt; first there was the lovely way in which everyone in the house fussed over her. She smiled. Her family might have less money, but the Dinsmores had been peers when the Norcroft babies were still wrapped in rags, their fathers chasing sheep. And then there were the comforts of the house. Not as large as her father's country home, but not as drafty, either. Plenty of fuel in every fireplace, plenty of food on the tables, not a threadbare carpet or curtain about the place. Of course, the stuff wasn't of the quality of her father's things; it was all *new*.

"What a charming gown you are making for the baby, Mrs. Fenwinkle," Anne said conversationally. "The fabric is as fine as anything you'd find in London."

Annabella Fenwinkle shook out the little gown, the better for her noble guest to admire it. "The fabric is a bit extravagant for an infant, but it was a gift. From a family that lives far above our simple country ways." She paused to make certain she had Anne's attention. "The Earl of Moreham and his lady," she said, emphasizing Rafe's title.

Anne's wasn't aware her hands had tightened on the little shirt she was holding until she heard the cambric start to tear. "The Morehams," she said, with none of the emotion she was feeling.

"I believe they are your neighbors?" Annabella persisted.

Anne nodded.

"I was not at the earl's wedding," Annabella continued, patting her stomach as if the pregnancy and not her common status had been the only thing that prevented her from receiving an invitation. "I understand they are a handsome couple and that Lady Moreham is most elegant."

"Her style is very . . ." Anne paused, as if searching for just the right, polite word. "French. I'm afraid I've always preferred our simpler, English fashions."

There was a murmur of agreement around the circle of women.

Annabella, clearly put out that Anne's status as the daughter of a duke was upstaging hers as the mother-to-be, made another attempt to flog her connection to the Morehams.

"My sister Arabella, you know, was bosom friend to the earl's sister. Before the . . ." Her mouth froze on the *S* of scandal, as it suddenly occurred to her where and with whom the scandal had taken place.

Anne smiled, her eyes gliding over the drab figure of Elizabeth's friend, Arabella. Of course she'd recognized the little wren the moment she'd laid eyes on her. "Such a painful episode, so disappointing when a young lady from such a good family, a young lady who is supposed to set the example for us all . . . falters." Her hand fluttered to her breast, but her eyes remained steady on Arabella. "We are all wounded by it, are we not? Still I cannot help feeling sorry for her, buried in the countryside."

Arabella tried to hold Anne's gaze, but in the end, she dropped her eyes. If she were bolder, more quick-witted, like Elizabeth, she'd have delivered some witty retort to Anne's barb. *Lady Elizabeth Harcrest? She's far from buried, far from the countryside, indeed she's far from the country. And she's traveling with your brother.* Wouldn't Anne's jaw have dropped? Not to mention the rest of the sewing circle. Arabella slid a glance through her lashes at the women, imagining them erupting in scandalized chaos. Like a coop full of headless chickens, they'd be, desperate to run off and spread the story. She dropped her eyes to her sewing; her hands were shaking as she imagined the trouble Elizabeth would be in then. And for the first time in her life, Arabella Norcroft felt infinitely grateful she hadn't an adventurous, impulsive bone in her body.

The gendarmes at the checkpoint on the road to Rouen were in a particularly surly mood. They scrutinized the papers James gave them, demanding over and over that he explain *what* he was doing in the area, and *why* he'd chosen to travel at this time.

"Tell me again, Citizen Dinsmore, why are you visiting Amiens and Rouen?"

"Who are you meeting with?" A guardsman shoved James with the butt of his rifle.

"Textile merchants in Amiens and Rouen," he responded, resisting the urge to grab the musket and hit the man over his heavily jowled head with it.

"Then where are your goods?"

"We're having them shipped back, we've purchased far too many things for our carriage to accommodate them all."

"As if an Englishman would tell you the truth," a guardsman with crooked teeth snapped. "Let's search them." The gendarme with the musket turned the muzzle towards James. "You others,"—he jerked his head towards Elizabeth, Marcus, Andre, and David—"over here."

"I don't know why we should bother to search them, we should take them in—or better yet, cut out their hearts." A young guardsman brandished the bayonet attached to his musket.

The gendarmes untied the luggage from the coach and tossed it down onto the road. Rifling the contents, they amused themselves by trying on Elizabeth's hats, mocking Marcus's severe waistcoats, and pocketing Andre's shoe buckles. The young guardsman pulled the bottle of cologne from James's trunk, shook it, unstopped the bottle and inhaled. "*Merde*," he jerked the bottle back, splashing the trunk and its contents with the liquid. "This must be the scent of decaying aristocracy."

The others, with the exception of the jowled gendarme with the gun pointed at James's head, gathered round, sniffing and snorting.

"*L'eau de* rotting regent."

"*Cologne de la corpse de Citizen Capet.*"

Elizabeth, who was not standing far from the trunk couldn't help but agree. She waved a hand, fanning away the odor.

"Look! Even his wife can't stand the stink." The young gendarme moved away from the trunk, pointing the bottle at her.

She turned to look at him, noticing as she did that there was something peculiar about the lid of the open trunk. Where the cologne had splashed, brown specks were beginning to appear. She knew she needed to get a better look. Taking a step towards the soldiers, she continued to fan the air beneath her nose.

"It is noxious, is it not?" she agreed in the fluent French Rafe had hounded her to learn. She'd have to thank him someday. "I have begged my husband to dispense with it, but he swears . . ." She glanced at James and then back at the soldiers and the trunk—and realized that the brown specks were *letters*. Where the cologne had splashed, writing was emerging—more of it with each passing moment. *So that was what James and his men have been trying to conceal!*

"He swears," she repeated, trying to keep the sudden jangle of her nerves out of her voice, "that it enhances his manly vigor." She took another step closer to the trunk. "I don't suppose any of you citizens might care to keep it? Or accidentally spill it out? As a favor to a lady?"

The soldier with the cologne replaced the cork with a flourish and held the bottle over the little trunk. All trace of humor vanished. He glared at Elizabeth. "This is a Republic, citizeness. In case you haven't heard, we don't grant favors to ladies anymore." He dropped the bottle into the trunk and kicked the lid shut.

When they were finally back on the road, James turned towards her, fuming. "I thought I'd told you to stay silent, do nothing, and let me do all the talk—"

"So you would have preferred that I let those men discover the writing on the inside of the lid?"

"I would have handled it." A muscle in his jaw tensed. "You unnecessarily put yourself at risk . . ."

"I put *myself* at risk?" She stared at him in disbelief. "If the soldiers had been paying attention to the trunk rather than your cologne, we *all* would have been at risk. We might have been dragged off to prison, or more likely shot."

"And they might well have shot you on the spot it they had taken your . . ." Desperately he searched for a word to describe her outrageous behavior. "Your *flirtation* amiss."

"Flirtation?" She was nearly speechless. "Flirtation! I should have let them shoot *you*! You've been hiding things from me throughout this venture. Tell me what else might miraculously appear in your luggage, or fall out of the panels of the coach, or . . ." She glared at him. "Unexpectedly walk through a library door."

"I didn't ask you to come along on this venture," he flushed. "I don't owe you any explanations."

"You're right." She inhaled sharply. "You don't."

"She'll drive me to madness," James muttered to Marcus later that evening after they'd stopped for the night at an inn on the outskirts of Rouen. "Did you see how she approached those soldiers?"

"Quite the timely distraction," Marcus observed, taking an olive from an earthenware bowl on the table.

"After I expressly told her not to say anything—to anyone."

"Clever how she provoked them into closing the lid of the trunk."

"Provoking. Everything about Elizabeth Harcrest is provoking. She never does what she's told, never does what's expected of her. I swear, if I didn't know better, I'd think she didn't slip away unnoticed, but that Moreham packed her off with his blessing. It's his revenge, that's what it is. I ruined his sister's reputation, and now he's ruining my life."

"One might say she *saved* all of ours today." Marcus popped an olive into his mouth.

"Are you saying I should thank her?"

Marcus shrugged.

"Next you'll be proposing I should bring her into our confidence, explain what we are about." *I don't owe you an explanation*, he'd said. And he didn't. So why the bloody hell did he feel that he did? "I'm traveling with a party full of lunatics. Wouldn't be surprised if Grenville recruited you all straight out of bedlam."

"Put you in charge, too." Marcus consumed another olive.

"Are you suggesting,"—James's eyes narrowed—"I'm as mad as the rest of you?"

"Rather obsessed with madness aren't you, Dinsmore?

"Damned hard not to be when you're surrounded by it," James said flatly.

Marcus continued as if he hadn't heard. "I'm suggesting that like the rest of us, you were looking to make a change in your life, to do something different . . . save some lives, rather than wasting your own."

"Tell me, Marcus, is that why you're here?"

Marcus evaded the question. "You did well in Amiens. I wasn't at all certain that last merchant was going to agree to help us. You played him most skillfully. Grenville will be pleased."

"It wasn't easy. There's talk that the Girondins may be losing power in Paris. There's a number of aristocrats among them, expatriates, too, and they're the ones who've been encouraging maintaining relations with England. If the Jacobins tighten their grip, I suspect there'll be a crackdown on anyone in France suspected of having foreign contacts."

"All the more reason to finish up our work in Rouen, find Gerard de Joley and carry him safely back to England."

"Elizabeth Harcrest as well," James added without thinking.

"I see that all my talk of business has done little to distract your thoughts from the lady." The concern in Marcus's eyes was at odds with the lightness of his tone. "Do you think you shall have trouble returning her to Moreham Hall?"

James ran his hand through his hair, resisting the urge to retort, *No more trouble than I already have.*

Chapter 27

They'd been in Rouen two days when James told Eliz-
abeth they were going on a picnic. "A picnic?" she said, her
voice rising in question. "Have you lost your mind? Haven't
we got work to do? Aren't we supposed to be paying a call
on the merchant Brisant?"

"Briyard. And Marcus is handling the appointment. Don't
forget a good straw hat; the sun is rather fierce today." He
gestured toward the pile of hatboxes in the corner of the
sunny little room they were sharing. "The one with the flowers and ribbons is quite fetching."

"You know I would never dream of venturing out without
a hat. What is all this about?" Her eyes narrowed. "What are
you up to James Dinsmore?"

"A man tries to take his wife for a luncheon al fresco on
a lovely day in a lovely city . . ." He swept an arm towards
the window where just beyond the pointed rooftops, the
river could be seen, flowing blue and serene. "And he is
greeted with rank suspicion. I vow, I am wounded."

"You're no more wounded than I am your wife. Tell me James . . ."

"When we get there. Now be quick about it, before the Brie melts."

"If you are planning a seduction," Elizabeth said a short time later, when they'd arranged themselves in a field outside the city, "I should tell you it will come to naught."

A smile as glancing as the breeze played across his lips and was gone. "Alas, a brief taste of married life, and already she has grown bored with my charms. It is what I have always feared. It is why I have never been married . . . before this."

"You have never married, James Dinsmore, because you find it far too amusing to remain a bachelor. Though I doubt even the most amorous lady would have you on this blanket." Elizabeth wrinkled her nose. "It reeks of horse sweat and hay. If you haven't another in the carriage, let us put it away and sit on the grass."

"Ah, so you're not averse to my charms. I am so encouraged I would almost grant your wish and roll up the blanket, but I cannot."

"Why ever not?"

"It's the red and white weave," he said. "Red for the blood of the martyrs, white for the lost Bourbon."

"It's a code, a signal?"

He nodded.

"Are we waiting for a signal back then? From the fugitive?"

"We're waiting for the fugitive."

"We just wait? We don't do anything? It doesn't seem very dramatic."

"If our luck holds it *won't* be dramatic." He poured her a glass of pale golden wine and handed it to her. Then he poured one for himself and lifted his glass. "To a smooth, uneventful, and entirely boring rescue."

She didn't raise her glass, only sipped at the wine.

"I would have thought you'd had more than enough excitement this year," he said, all trace of flirtation gone from his voice.

Color washed her cheeks. "I have had enough . . . and despite what you and Rafe may think, I *have* learned from my mistakes. It's just that . . . that this seems so . . . *easy.*"

"Easy?" He took another sip of wine. "You were hoping for a trial by fire? Something that would burn away your sins?"

She pressed her lips together. "I expect that seems ridiculous."

He shook his head, sunlight playing across the gold of his hair. "You are so young, Elizabeth, so unfailingly optimistic. Despite everything, you still seem to think you can just move forward, start fresh." His fingers played with the stem of his glass. "You may change where you are, but you can't change who you are. The past follows after you like that pile of hatboxes."

She didn't feel like arguing, so instead changed the subject. "If I hadn't come on this trip, you'd have looked rather foolish on a picnic alone."

"I'd have brought charcoal, sketched the view."

"I didn't know you liked to draw."

He tore a piece of bread from the loaf that sat between them and handed it to her, with a slice of cheese. "There's a lot you don't know about me."

They ate in silence for several moments.

"For example," he said, eyes fixed on the horizon as if he were studying it for a composition, "I intended to betray you that night at the ball."

"I know," she said, her eyes also fixed on the horizon. "You did it for Anne, didn't you? She was angry that Rafe didn't marry her."

He nodded.

"But you had doubts, didn't you? That's why you kept asking if it was really what I wanted?"

"I tried to warn you," he said, swirling the wine in his glass. "But I didn't stop you. Nor did I stop myself."

"Nor did I." She turned her eyes from the horizon and looked at him.

He didn't meet her gaze. "You were playing that night, looking for excitement. I was not."

She wanted to ask if that was why his touch felt so serious that night, if that was why things had happened so fast, why he'd come so close to making love to her. Why no matter what she said or did she couldn't seem to keep her distance from him. She looked away, suddenly embarrassed and ashamed. How could it be that she could *think* these things, could *feel* them, and yet could not *speak* of them? "Is that why you did not come for me?"

"I wanted to." He fingered his cheek. "I was going to, when your brother called me out. Rafe made it clear he'd never accept me, that I wasn't good enough for you. And he was right."

"Why didn't you apologize?" she asked, turning her eyes once again to him, to the scar that marred the perfect beauty of his face.

It was only then that he turned to look at her, his eyes hollow and dark. "Because I wasn't sorry."

It hurt to ask the question, but she did. "You weren't sorry you ruined me?"

"Oh, no." His laugh was bitter and broken. "I deeply regret that. But for as long as I live, Elizabeth Harcrest, I'll never regret touching you."

Gerard de Joley watched the couple seated on the blanket, trying to decide if these were his rescuers. The blanket was correct, red and white, but he'd been expecting men, massive, soldierly men, men who looked like Swiss guards or Grenadiers. Not this tall languid-looking courtier and a pretty woman. He swept his hand through his hair, painfully conscious of how dirty it was, how dirty *he* was.

He wanted them to be his rescuers. He wanted them to take him away from his filthy hole in the ground in their well-appointed carriage. He wanted it so much he could almost taste the food laid out in colorful abandon on the blanket. The pale yellow cheese, the crisp brown bread, the rosy grapes, the golden wine. Gerard licked his chapped lips.

He couldn't let desperation overcome his caution. If he approached and was mistaken about who they were, they would report him. They might not think he was a fugitive, but considering how he must look, they'd almost certainly believe he was a criminal or a deranged lunatic. To have successfully hidden from the authorities all these weeks and lose his chance at escape because he hadn't been cautious enough? If they were his rescuers he knew they would come again.

It was painful to wait. But he would.

"Gourneau." The captain of the Rouen National Guard in charge of overseeing the security of the area rapped his knuckles on his lieutenant's desk. "Are you eating your lunch here?" He gave the pile of eggshells a disgusted flick of his fingers.

"No, sir." Lieutenant Goumeau, who'd been signing papers, put down his quill and straightened in his chair. "Those shells are not from my lunch, sir. They are evidence."

"Evidence of what? A chicken?" The captain's voice sounded dubious.

Gourneau shook his head. "They're from an old woman on the outskirts of town. It's the second time she's been here. Claims someone has been stealing eggs from her. Wants us to do something about it."

"I hope you told her we've more important things to do here than chase local sneak thieves."

"I did, sir." The lieutenant batted the shells with his quill.

"But she's insistent it isn't anyone local. Says she saw the culprit and didn't recognize him. Says he was wearing a coat stolen from a neighbor."

The captain, a burly bald man who'd been a miller before the revolution, scratched his nose. "Anything else suspicious reported in the area? Any fugitive aristocrats thought to be hiding there?"

"No, sir. The family that lived there was rounded up and sent to Paris weeks ago."

"So what did you tell the good citizeness with the shells?"

"I thanked her for her dedication. Told her we were spread a bit thin here, and that the Republic was dependent on the sharp eyes of her citizens. Told her if she saw anything peculiar, besides egg thefts, such as strangers hanging about, she should file another report with us."

The captain eyed the tower of papers on the corner of the lieutenant's desk. It looked as if another sheet would send it toppling to the floor. He nodded approvingly. "*Vive la Revolution.*"

For as long as I live, Elizabeth Harcrest, I'll never regret touching you. The words hung heavy. The weight of them seemed to press the air out of Elizabeth's lungs and flatten her heart. *So you love me?* She wanted to ask. But that wasn't what he'd said. *So you want me?* He'd wanted many women over the years. He'd had most of them. *Am I different?* She wanted to know. And if he said she wasn't?

"Thank you for telling me." Even as she said it, it sounded absurdly polite.

"You're welcome." He responded in kind. "It's the least I could do."

She looked at him, at this beautiful scarred man sitting so close she could wrap her arms around his neck and kiss him without having to do more than lean. The Elizabeth who walked into the library with him those many months ago would have reached for him. *The old Elizabeth*, she thought. She'd learned. The new Elizabeth was more cautious—at least with her heart. *You could have me,* she wanted to say, *so easily. But you have to reach out to me. Tell my brother to go to hell, James. You were worthy of me then. You're more than worthy of me now. Especially now.*

After several moments of strained silence passed, she asked, "If you haven't come to France to make a change, as I have, to experience a trial by fire, why have you come?"

"I decided that a man who hits bottom and knows he's going to stay there ought to find something to do with his time. A spy is as good—or as bad—as anything else I might have chosen. When Lord Grenville presented me with the opportunity, I took it."

"You are down to be sure, but you're a man. You're not so disgraced as I, and certainly not as permanently. I've put myself so far beyond the pale. . . . How can you be so . . . so . . ."

"Cynical?" he offered.

"Complacent. *Accepting.*" Her pain burned down, igniting a white flare of anger.

"What can I change Elizabeth? Can I bring my mother back from the dead? Can I bring my father back to his sanity? I could marry some upstart merchant's daughter, bring my family back to fortune. Sell my name and, of course,"—he gestured towards his lap—"my noble seed. Now that would be the honorable thing to do, wouldn't it?" His tone was still polite, but the eyes he turned on her were fierce.

"It's what other men in the ton have done," she began.

He didn't want to hear what other men had done. Other men hadn't had parents like his, hadn't seen how love could fill a home. And how the absence of that love could destroy it. He cut her off. "Do you want to hear something peculiar, Elizabeth?" He didn't wait for her answer. "I know all about what your brother did to replenish the fortune your father and brother squandered. I know how he 'soiled' his hands with trade. And I respect him for it. Hell, I envy him. He's earned enough to live as he pleases. Marry as he pleases. Perhaps I should have done the same. But it would have killed Anne."

James raked a hand through his hair. "Isn't it ironic? Anne never would have wanted to marry your brother if she'd known where he'd gotten his money. She wouldn't have given a second thought to revenge. And *none* of this would have happened. *Complacent? Accepting?*" He repeated her words, spitting them out as if they left a bitter taste in his mouth. "Rather say I am a realist. I've learned not to reach for the things I know I cannot have."

"And how do you know you cannot have those things unless you reach for them?" she persisted.

He stroked his damaged cheek. "People have a way of letting you know."

She shook her head. "Is there anything you'd fight for?"

The finger that had been following the curve of his scar slid to his mouth. He tapped his lips like a child confessing a secret. "I did."

The words were said so softly, Elizabeth wasn't certain she heard them.

But the weight on her heart and lungs seemed to lift. She exhaled for what seemed like the first time in a very long time. Her body seemed to follow the course of her breath, leaning ever so slightly towards James.

He closed the distance.

Chapter 28

He'd lingered at the picnic with Elizabeth for as long as he'd thought they'd be safe from the curious eyes of passing strangers, but the fugitive had not come. James rolled over in the bed, unable to fall asleep. It wasn't just prying strangers who posed a threat. Elizabeth's kiss had enflamed his senses far more than the sun or wine or even danger could ever have done. He'd wanted to make love to her. And they might have, if they stayed. He turned again, his mind filled with thoughts of the fugitive and his promise to Grenville and Elizabeth and Moreham and Anne. *This*, he mused just before he fell into an exhausted sleep, *must be how it feels to experience madness.*

In the predawn hour, the room was soothingly dark, the bed was satisfyingly warm, and his body, including his eyelids, refused to rise. James's brain sent a halfhearted command to his limbs. But the only part responding was the part of him that was nestled against the curve of Elizabeth Harcrest's bottom.

He was accustomed to waking with an erection. He was also accustomed to waking with a desirable woman in his bed. So it was natural that his hips began to follow the direction of his desires. Slowly, almost unthinkingly, he began to rock his hips against hers, his hardness bumping between her thighs. His arms had been draped around her, his hands resting against the folds of her nightshirt. He began to draw it up, his fingers sliding against fabric until they found flesh.

And then they continued to move.

Like silken spiders, his fingertips traced the skin above her knees. They followed the swell of muscle up and then descended, ever so lightly, to touch the soft curls between her legs. She parted her legs, and James moved closer.

With her hand, Elizabeth touched her breast. In her dream she was experiencing the most exquisite pleasure. When her finger closed over her nipple, she felt an arcing connection between her legs and realized she was awake. And that James's finger was sliding with the utmost precision, up and down the cleft between her legs. She opened her lips to protest, but only the faintest whimper of pleasure escaped. It felt so good. He felt so good. She supposed she might pretend to be asleep, pretend her submission was unconscious . . .

She rocked her head back against his chest and moaned. And when his hand came up and caressed her breast, she clutched it. The insistent rubbing between her thighs was not a hand. As she slid against his hardness she thought he would not penetrate her, not now, not this way, with both of them half-asleep and too many things unsaid. She slipped her hand down between them and felt him thrust against her palm. This time it was he who moaned. Elizabeth felt a sense of power and held her hand flat against him, pushing as he thrust again and again, each time harder.

The balance of power shifted, as his hips pumped insistently, his hardness slid faster and faster against her. Ragged breathing sounded in her ears, but Elizabeth didn't know if it was his or hers, or theirs. She clamped her thighs together, not knowing whether she was trying to stop him from entering her or lock him against her forever.

He pulled away from her with a strangled cry.

They lay in silence then, on either side of the bed, night-clothes and nightshirts as tortured as their breathing. For several moments, Elizabeth's heart pounded so loudly the sound drowned out the voice in her head, the one that wondered how it was possible to feel exhilarated and ashamed at the same time. The way he touched her, the way he made her feel . . . Was it because he wanted her? or simply because she was in his bed? And if he wanted her, why didn't he want her enough to marry her?

When at last she found the strength to speak, she turned to face him.

He turned towards her, too, one hand reaching out to brush back a damp curl that fell across her forehead. His touch, so gentle, made her want to reach for him. Instead, she hardened her voice and her heart. "This should not have happened. We are not man and wife, James Dinsmore."

His hand fell away from her face.

"Good God, she's back again." Lieutenant Gourneau nodded in the direction of the old woman who had just come through the door and was headed straight for his desk.

"Who is she?" his captain asked.

"The damned egg lady."

The captain chuckled. "What do you think she's brought this time? Nests?"

The lieutenant didn't have a chance to answer, because the woman had reached the edge of his desk. She stood, twisting the ends of her frayed apron in her leathery hands.

"Citizeness," he said, allowing only the slightest note of irritation in his voice, "you have more egg thefts to report?"

"No, sir. No, citizen." She shook her head. "I've already shown you that evidence. I wouldn't bring you more. No, you told me to come back if I noticed anything else peculiar, anyone suspicious hanging about."

The lieutenant reminded himself he was there to serve the people. The people were the eyes and ears of the Republic. It was his duty to listen, even if some of the people were lonely, crazy old women. "Yes?" he prompted.

"I've got *pique-niquers*, citizen."

The lieutenant schooled his features to appear interested. "*Pique-niquers*?"

"Three days in a row they've taken their lunch in the field near my farm. Three days," she repeated for emphasis. "A man and a woman."

Lovers, the lieutenant thought.

"And they're English," she added triumphantly. "I know because they bought hard-boiled eggs for their picnic at my farm."

The lieutenant straightened in his chair. And this time, he had no need to feign interest.

James finished the egg Elizabeth had refused, and an unusual movement at the edge of the field caught his eye. "Elizabeth," he hissed, nodding in the direction of the bushes. "Don't make any abrupt movements, just slide your eyes over there and tell me what you see."

"There's something moving in the bushes."

He reached for his jacket, pulling it close enough so that he could reach the pistol he'd stashed in the front pocket. When he felt the solid weight of the stock against his hand, he turned.

"Do you think that's our man?" Elizabeth whispered, as a tall blond man in a ragged brown workman's jacket emerged from the foliage and began walking towards them.

The man's steps slowed as he neared the blanket. He stopped, close enough for them to hear him speak, but still far away enough to give himself a head start if he needed to turn and run. His eyes kept shifting from their faces, to the carriage waiting on the road, to the food spread on the blanket, and then back again.

Elizabeth forced herself to smile encouragingly at him, noticing as she did so that the man was keeping one hand in his coat pocket. The pocket bulged, the fabric strained downward as something far heavier than his hand was concealed within. Was it a rock? Was he a mad beggar preparing to strike them and steal their food?

"May I help you, citizen?" James said.

The man cleared his throat, staring hard at them, almost as if he were trying to peer beneath their skin. Elizabeth saw the hand in his pocket move and the outline of his knuckles appeared against the fabric; she realized whatever was in there, he was gripping it tightly.

"Red and white." When at last the man spoke, his voice rasped as if it hadn't been used in a very long time. "Good colors for a blanket."

"Red for the blood of the martyrs, white for the Bourbons," James said.

The man's features twisted, and for a long moment he seemed to be fighting to control them. "Thank God," he breathed before drawing himself up and offering them a courtier's bow. "Gerard de Joley, at your service."

James rose, grasping Elizabeth's hand as he did so and pulling her to her feet. "I am Lord Dinsmore and this,"—his pause was briefer than a blink—"is my lady wife." He inclined his head, and Elizabeth swept into a curtsey. "And it is we, monsieur, who are at your service."

"I wondered why the seats of this coach were so high," Elizabeth remarked as James lifted out a panel. Behind the seat was a space, cramped, but large enough to conceal a man. James motioned for Joley to climb inside. Clutching a hunk of bread and cheese, France's former deputy minister of finance crawled under the seat.

"I apologize for the accommodation, monsieur," James

said, "but it is just until we get you back to the inn where we are staying. I promise, this is not how we intend to take you into England."

"Even if it were," Joley replied, "I would travel without complaint. I am well aware you are risking your lives to save mine."

James, uncomfortable with the minister's thanks, nodded. "I'm going to put the panel back now. Is there anything you need before I seal you in?"

"Have you any more of that chicken you brought with you the other day?"

"Alas no, but I have some very nice pâté."

When Joley was safely concealed and the carriage started off, Elizabeth leaned towards James and whispered in his ear, "How long do you think he was watching us?"

"Based on the request for chicken, I'd say at least two days."

An embarrassed flush prickled her cheeks. James chuckled, which only made things worse. "How can you *laugh?* Who knows what he might have seen?"

"He wouldn't have seen anything improper or unnatural between a man and his wife."

She was aware of the flush moving towards her hairline and decided it would be best if she changed the subject. "If we're not smuggling him out of the country behind the panel, how are we going to get him out of France?"

There was a glint in James eye as he answered. "Papers by Marcus and valet service by Andre."

They reached the inn as day was beginning to turn to dusk. James had the carriage put away and ordered a bath to be brought up in two hours. As soon as it was dark, David smuggled Gerard de Joley up to the room. He was nearly as delighted to see the bath warming by the fire as he had been to see the food. "I am ashamed, my Lord Dinsmore, to be seen in such disarray by your lady wife."

"You have nothing to be ashamed of, monsieur," Elizabeth interjected. "I see nothing but the face and figure of a man who has been unjustly persecuted."

Joley smiled. "You are a lucky man, Dinsmore. Your wife's character is as lovely as she."

James's eyes lingered on Elizabeth for a moment before he thanked the Frenchman.

"And brave," Joley continued, "to venture into France at such a difficult time."

Elizabeth noticed how his eyes slid longingly toward the bath and realized her presence had become a complication. Joley doubtlessly was wondering how he might attend to his toilette with her in the room. And she found herself wondering where the Frenchman would sleep. His presence would be noticed and would surely have to be explained, if he were sent to sleep with David, Marcus, and Andre downstairs.

She turned towards James. "After spending the afternoon sifting in the sun, I find myself in desperate need of a walk. Otherwise, I fear I might fall asleep before your very eyes." She patted her lips as if smothering the delicate beginnings of a yawn. "Dinsmore, will you ask Marcus to accompany me?"

Once again, Joley's eyes shifted toward the steaming bath. "It is cold and dark outside Lady Dinsmore . . ."

"Just the refreshment I require." She smiled, acknowledging his concern. "And I shall be as safe with Marcus as if I were with . . . " She hesitated. She'd been about to say, *as if I were with my husband.* Which was absurd. She was far *safer* with Marcus than with James; he'd never flirt with her, never kiss her, never trail his fingers seductively across her skin. Marcus seemed to worship at the altar of misogyny. "As if I were with a troop of armed guards," she finished.

She saw Joley glance at James, obviously awaiting his decision on whether she would be allowed to walk outside. She forced herself to smile, to appear the picture of wifely patience. *Once again waiting on the decisions of a man*, she thought, resisting the urge to drum her fingers against the folds of her skirt. *The confines of marriage are not that different from the confines of my brother.* "I'll get my wrap," she said a split second before her pseudo-husband gave his approval.

Joley looked mildly surprised.

When she returned from her walk, Joley was dressed in a suit of James's clothes and they were sipping brandy, seated by the fire. They rose as she entered, inquired politely if she'd enjoyed her walk, and James invited her to join them. She sat and listened, as they discussed sites of historical interest in England and what the weather most likely would be like when they arrived. They might have been meeting in a drawing room, instead of engaged in a rescue that might cost them all their lives.

Gradually, as most polite discussions do, the talk turned to family. "Do you have children?" Joley asked.

"Not yet," James answered. "We are newlyweds."

"Congratulations." Joley lifted his glass. "To many long and happy years together, filled with fine and healthy children."

Elizabeth flushed at the toast, uncomfortably reminded of the morning and how close she'd come to behaving as if they were man and wife. Anxious to change the subject, she asked Joley if he had any children.

"Two," he said, staring for a long moment at the fire through his brandy glass before adding, "living. My son passed away four years ago. I have two daughters."

James offered his condolences. "And where are your daughters now?"

"As soon as the troubles began my oldest fled to Austria with her husband and children. My youngest is still in Paris." He turned his glass slowly, as if mesmerized by the flames in the glass. "My Marguerite. She begged me to take her with me, but I did not think it safe. And I knew she did not really want to leave. She was just concerned about my welfare." He made a game attempt at a laugh. "Always fussing at me like a mother hen. Girl thinks I'm in my dotage."

"Is she with family in Paris?" Elizabeth inquired.

Joley shook his head. "Friends. Her late husband, Armand, believed France should be a constitutional monarchy. He was a representative to the National Assembly; the only fortunate aspect to his death from influenza last year is that he wasn't party to the vote for regicide." Joley took a long sip of his brandy. "Armand introduced Marguerite to those radical salons. Girondins, those are the people she's staying with."

"Do you think she'll be safe?"

"That's a question I asked myself over and over in that damned hole." Joley took another swallow of brandy. "One I thought about a great deal before I came here, to Rouen. All I know is that right now, she's safer in Paris than here with me. But as soon as I reach England and have access to my estate, I will send the funds to get her out. Armand gave most of his money to the radicals." He shook his head. "I misjudged when I married her to that one. A mistake I won't make again. As soon as she's safe in England, I swear I'll see her settled with the least adventurous, most conservative-minded man I can find."

"You did the right thing, monsieur." Elizabeth reached out and touched the man's hand lightly, aware of the impropriety, but moved by the pain in his voice. "You are in good hands now." She glanced at James, then turned back towards Joley. "I'm certain that you and your daughter will be safely reunited in England."

Chapter 29

The following morning, Elizabeth awakened abruptly to loud knocking. *We've been discovered!* Scrambling out of bed clutching sheets, her blood was pounding. *I must wake the others quickly and quietly.* "We've been dis—" She stopped in mid-hiss. Joley was sitting in a chair across the room, dressed in clothes from the night before. James was also fully dressed, and he was answering the door.

"We weren't certain you'd be up," Andre said, entering. David and Marcus followed behind.

"I set the time," James pointed out.

"True," Andre winked, "but we all know how hard it is for society gents to wake up before noon." Arms full of packages, he nodded over his shoulder. "Why we practically have to fire a gun next to Marcus's ear to get him to lift his head from the pillow."

"It's a miracle I sleep at all considering how you snore." Marcus, carrying a tray full of covered dishes, scowled at Andre's back.

"And speaking of sleep . . ." David shifted the box in his

arms and pointed an elbow in Elizabeth's direction. "Looks like we woke *someone* up."

"It appears,"—Elizabeth pulled the sheets up around her neck—"*someone* neglected to tell me early morning visitors were planning to call." She pressed her lips into a grim smile. "I would very much appreciate it if one of you *gentlemen*,"—she looked past James as if he was not in the room—"would move that screen." She pointed with a sheet draped arm, "near to the washbasin and my trunk."

The three men hastened to unburden themselves while Joley quickly rose from his chair and moved the screen where Elizabeth had directed. "A thousand pardons, Lady Dinsmore."

"Look on the bright side, Lady Dinsmore," Andre said. "At least Marcus here has brought breakfast. Poached eggs, bread fresh from the oven, raspberry preserves, and hot coffee."

"Coffee?" Joley's face lit up. "I haven't had a good cup in weeks . . . "

Andre made a sweeping gesture with his hand. "If you'll sit down at the table, monsieur, I promise that by the time you've finished, you'll be an entirely new man."

"Well, monsieur, what do you think of your new look?"

Nearly two hours and two pots of coffee later, Joley brought the mirror Andre handed him close to his face, turning his head this way and that. His skin looked spotted; Andre had touched up his features with theater cosmetics. He ran his fingers through his freshly dyed brown hair, then smiled, studying his teeth, which Andre had stained. "I certainly don't look like myself," he said in a slightly amazed tone.

"I'll take that as a compliment. You're not supposed to look like yourself; you're to look like Lord Dinsmore's new coachman, Bernard . . ." He snapped his fingers at Marcus. "What's his name again?"

Marcus pulled a packet of papers from his pocket and held them out to Joley. "Bernard Duval."

Joley unfolded the papers and examined them. "Identity papers, residence papers, travel papers. However did you get these?"

Marcus only smiled.

"There's something missing." Andre was circling Joley, his brows drawn together in a critical frown. "Hair is good, face is good, hands could be a bit dirtier, but we'll remedy that in the stables. . . ." His mouth twitched, then suddenly swept into a smile. "I have it! I know exactly what will complete the picture of Bernard Duval." He rifled through a cloth bag thrown carelessly on a chair near the door. Finding what he was looking for, he tossed a scrap of leather with string to Joley.

Joley caught it. "What is it?"

"An eyepatch."

"An eyepatch?" James, who'd been idly stirring a plate of runny eggs with his bread looked up. "Isn't that a bit too theatrical?"

"Trust me." Andre grinned. "It'll be perfect."

She'd been rattling around the great empty house for days, having tea with her father in the afternoons, sipping oolong, and pretending to be one of his generals. She truly hadn't wanted to be present when Annabella gave birth, so after a week with the dull Norcrofts, Anne had made her excuses and returned home.

Today, for a change of pace, she had her father's manservant tell him she was reviewing the troops; then she'd escaped into the little town that bordered the Dinsmore and Harcrest lands to buy needlepoint thread. As she perused the trays of bright silk spools, she thought about the source of her father's madness. James liked to say it had been brought on by their mother's death, that it was true love's response to grief. She shook her head and the shopkeeper, thinking she was indicating disapproval with his wares, brought out another tray. Anne barely noticed. James might not realize it, but he was a romantic. She suspected her father had *always* carried the seeds of madness within his mind.

The shopkeeper slid a tray of spools closer to her. "These are lovely, just arrived from France." He shook his gray-wigged head solemnly. "If things keep up the way they've been going, it may be some time before we see their like again."

Anne nodded absently. Which was more the dangerous act, to marry for love and risk madness if death parts you too soon, or to marry for money and risk madness from boredom at the company of one's spouse? "I'll take that blue and this green." She tapped the spools decisively with her finger. Sir Edmund Bogglesworth wanted to meet with her father to request her hand in marriage. She didn't know what to tell him, any more than she knew how to circumvent the meeting.

"Excellent choices, Your Ladyship, you've got quite the eye for quality and color. I've got a nice shade of pink . . ."

"No," Anne said more sharply than she intended. She hadn't used pinks since that night they'd brought James home. The night she'd held the flesh of his face in her hands and stitched. The shop felt suddenly close. She needed air. "My man will see to the package," she mumbled as she turned.

"Your Ladyship, are you quite all right?" she heard her groom say.

"I think I shall step outside a moment," she gestured towards the door, and he moved quickly forward and held it open.

Anne stepped out of the shop and stood for a moment, eyes closed, feeling the coolness of the air against her cheeks. *James where are you now? Now, when I need you most?* She followed the thought with a silent curse on the Harcrests, each and every one. Her eyes were still closed when she felt a bump against her skirts, and the roll of something small across her feet. She opened her eyes and found herself entangled in a smart red leather leash, at the end of which was a desperately straining brown pug.

"Well, gentleman, I believe we're ready to be off." James surveyed the room, now empty of all signs they had been there. All except the bed, with its tumbled sheets and dented pillows. But he wouldn't allow himself to dwell on *that*. He swept an arm towards the door. "Shall we descend? Marcus, will you escort Lady Elizabeth?"

As the former financial advisor to the late king of France reached the door, he paused, turning back towards James who was the only one left in the room. "A moment of your time, monsieur?"

"But of course."

Joley closed the door. "I want you to know, whatever happens, I am grateful for everything you have done—for me and for my country."

"The risks we take are but small things, when compared to the value of what you have done for our two countries." James paused. "And what you will do once you are safely in England."

"But you have chosen to venture into these dangerous circumstances . . . and to bring your wife . . ."

"She would not be left behind."

"And you would not leave her." Joley nodded knowingly. "You must be very much in love."

"Indeed, I must," James repeated softly after the Frenchman had gone.

"Oh, mon dieu, I'm sorry." The woman with the pug was chattering nonstop while kneeling and trying to disentangle loops of leash and straining dog. "My dog simply *detests* cats. I believe he must have seen one sneaking about—I was so preoccupied admiring the hats in that window—they re-

ally are charming, aren't they? Such a surprise to find a clever milliner in the provinces. Anyway, I must have been holding the leash too loosely, for one moment he was with me, docile as you please, and the next, off he is running and now he is in your skirt." The woman paused, apparently to catch her breath. "Sort of like men, when you think about it."

"I assure you, I'm fine, really it's not necessary." Anne tried to discourage the woman from her disentangling efforts, but was prevented from catching her eye by the woman's hat, an enormous straw creation festooned with sunflowers and yellow ribbons.

"Not at all, not at all, just one moment. You see, it is done! Now you are free." The woman rose, and Anne Dinsmore found herself face-to-face with Rafe Moreham's mother-in-law, Madeleine de Rabec, Comtesse de La Brou.

"Madame," Anne said.

"Lady Anne." The pug, now held on an extremely short leash, whined.

"I had no idea you were in the area, madame."

"I would not expect you to be aware of all the comings and goings at Moreham Hall." Madeleine smiled, her previous good humor replaced by a mask of practiced politeness. "I am visiting my son-in-law and my daughter. Alix is with child. But I'm sure you have already heard."

"You must *so* be looking forward to being a *grand*-mother."

"Yes, though I am much too young to ever be taken for one." Madeleine laughed. "Indeed, I am thinking of becoming a mother again."

"You are expecting?" Anne let her eyes slip to Madeleine's trim, beribboned waist.

"Of course not." She laughed again, the sound clearly forced. "Lord Rothwell has asked me to marry him. You know His Lordship, do you not? I've heard rumors you two were quite friendly at one time."

"Yes, we were," Anne said, reminding herself she was the

one who'd turned him away. Older, attractive, but all those children . . . besides she'd had Moreham on her hook. Or so she'd thought. "So we may expect a gala wedding next season?" She didn't wait for an answer, but went straight for the jugular. "And speaking of seasons, how is *poor* Elizabeth?"

Madeleine's dark eyes hardened, but her voice remained light. "Elizabeth? How kind of you to ask after *dear* Elizabeth. She is doing well, having a lovely summer, quite the social butterfly."

"Moreham has been entertaining? With Lady Alix in her delicate condition, isn't it rather a strain?"

"His Lordship hasn't been entertaining. Elizabeth has been visiting. She's been away for over two weeks, staying with her friend Arabella Norcroft. Such a fine, upstanding family." Madeleine waved her hand, the one with the leash wrapped round it, inadvertently pulling the pug up short. He yipped and she turned, completely missing the puzzled expression on Anne's face.

"The Norcrofts you say? The Norcrofts of Hartsdale?"

"Do you know them?"

"A passing acquaintance," Anne replied smoothly. "Elizabeth has been visiting with them for the past two weeks?"

"Yes, and she sends back the most entertaining letters. Such a clever girl."

"Clever," Anne echoed, thinking Elizabeth Harcrest must be extremely clever if she'd deceived her family into believing she was staying with the Norcrofts. Was it possible Madeleine was lying to make it seem the girl had been accepted back into some circles of society?

"Well, Lady Anne, I really must be going. You must pay a call on me at the hall sometime," Madeleine said in a vague way that indicated *sometime* meant *never.*

"Oh I will," Anne waved after her. *I will indeed.*

Chapter 30

Elizabeth leaned towards James as the carriage door swung closed. "It doesn't seem right to have Joley riding as our coachman. He was a confidant of the king, a minister, a nobleman of the highest rank. Shouldn't he be riding in here, with us?"

"It feels peculiar, but it's for the best. Think about it, no one looks at a coachman. If we're stopped, the gendarmes will glance at him, at his papers, and then focus their attention on us. The villainous Englishmen."

"I suppose."

"Thanks to everyone's skillful handiwork, no one will connect Gerard de Joley with our new coachman, Bernard Duval. No one even knows Joley's been in the area."

"Thinking about him sitting up there after everything he's been through, living in a hole, stealing to survive—"

"If he's discovered, you must deny you knew he was a member of our company," James interrupted gently, covering her hand with his.

"I will not." She drew her hand back, horrified.

"You will."

"I won't. We've come to save him, not to throw him to the wolves."

"Elizabeth." He gripped her hand again. "If Joley is discovered, there will be little we or anyone can do to save him. And if he's found riding with us, clearly a member of our company, the revolutionaries will add *spy* and *collaborator with the English* to his crimes."

"They'll add that to his list of crimes whether he's riding as our guest or our coachman. You're afraid for yourself."

His grip tightened. "Look at me, Elizabeth. Look at the scar on my face."

Her eyes were drawn to it, the thin red line like a lash of anger.

"You may call me many things, but you may not call me coward. I promised Lord Grenville I would bring Joley safely out of France, and that is what I intend to do. I made that promise knowing full well the cost might be my life or the lives of the men who travel with me. The only thing I did not know—and the only thing I fear—is that it might cost you yours. You, Elizabeth, were not part of the original bargain."

"Bargain?"

"Our lives for his. That man sitting out there beside David has the potential to change the course of history, to help bring down the Revolution and restore the monarchy. His life has purpose."

"So does yours."

"My life is empty, meaningless," he scoffed.

"It means something to me, and to Anne, and to your father."

"My *father*? My father hasn't recognized me in three years. Half the time he thinks I'm a Roman centurion."

"I'm sorry . . ."

"It's not important." He brushed aside her sympathy. "What is important is that you are here and you are my responsibility. And that is why, if Joley is captured, I will swear you had no knowledge of his presence. And if you try and deny me, I will say you are mad, mad with love for me, trying to protect me."

His grip on her hands might well have been around her heart.

"I will do anything, anything, you understand, to make certain you return safely home to your brother."

They spent the morning searching an old woman's field for foreigners. After beating the bushes for two hours in the rising heat, they'd received word that they should march, double-quick, down the road, set up a roadblock and stop every carriage that passed. Tempers were short.

The stout national guardsman, with his tunic unbuttoned and his hat askew, squinted down the dusty, tree-lined road that led out of Rouen. "This is ridiculous, Henri. We're wasting our time standing out here in this accursed heat."

"It is never a waste of time to serve the people, Jean," Henri responded, puffing his thin chest out so that the buttons of his new uniform sparkled like polished gems in the sunlight. "This road leads east to Paris and west to the coast. Who knows what enemies of the Republic might be traveling upon it? The captain said we must be on our guard for foreign spies and fugitives. He said . . ." Henri added with an air of a man revealing sensitive information hitherto withheld, "that there have been reports."

"Reports of what?"

"Unusual activity."

Jean gave a dissatisfied grunt. Henri had volunteered for this job, as had the four other soldiers attempting to find some relief beneath a dusty tree beside the road. He, on the other hand, had been ordered by the captain to join this useless effort. He couldn't help wondering if the "reports" had to do with his attempt to pass some time with the captain's mistress. "Unusual activity," he muttered, shifting his musket on his shoulder. "We've stopped an old man and his son hauling firewood, a cart full of chickens, and a merchant with a wagon full of wool. The most unusual thing we've seen today was the disgusting boil on that old man's face."

"It wasn't that bad."

"How would you know? You weren't the one who had to stand up close to it."

"*I* was checking their *papers*," Henri said smugly, resisting the urge to point out, as he frequently did, that he was the only one in the patrol who could read. "And besides, it's important to examine such things very carefully. That boil could have been some sort of clever disguise."

"Clever disguise my *derriere,* the thing was plain *disgusting.*"

The coach rumbled out of Rouen, the ironclad wheels rattling over stones and kicking up dust that drifted like smoke through the open windows. Marcus wiped his brow with a delicate linen handkerchief.

"I'd close the windows," James offered by way of apology, "but then it would be stifling in here."

"I almost envy the poor bas . . ." Marcus glanced at Elizabeth sitting across from him. "The poor gentlemen sitting outside."

All three of them cast their eyes toward the roof as if they might see through it.

"I wonder how Joley is faring." Marcus voiced their common concern.

"Better than he was huddling in that hole."

Their heads nodded in agreement and in response to the jolting from the poor conditions of the road.

"Still," Marcus added, "it's a shame we aren't able to continue on. We could do some good work together in Paris and Lyon."

"Too dangerous now."

"But if his disguise works, we might continue, using the same cover—that we are simply interested in the fabric trade."

"Paris is too dangerous," James repeated.

Elizabeth realized he was looking at her and leaned forward. "We could go on."

"We cannot."

"I am not afraid James," she insisted.

"But I am."

"Truly," she began, the muscles in her jaw beginning to tense. He wasn't afraid for himself or for the other men. His fear was he might not fulfill his commitment to return her to her brother . . .

"Truly, Elizabeth" he finished for her. "This is *one* thing about which we are not negotiating."

"Andre and I could continue on," Marcus offered.

"No." James was still looking at Elizabeth. "No more changes to our original plan. We have set up a good portion of the networks we need. More importantly, we have Joley." Unconsciously his fingers stole towards the scar on his cheek. "I swore on my honor I would deliver the man safely to England, and I will."

Elizabeth settled back against the cushions, her jaw knotted with the effort not to argue. If Joley's disguise held up to scrutiny, and she couldn't believe it wouldn't (after all who really looked that closely at servants), why wouldn't James agree to continue on to Paris? *Paris is too dangerous.* As if that explained everything. Dangerous for whom, she wanted to ask? She knew for a fact there were still members of English society residing there. They hadn't come to any harm. "Listen James." She spread her hands in appeal. "You can send me back to England with Joley. He can travel as my servant. And someone else can accompany me . . . David, perhaps?"

"No. I will not divide our party."

"I won't be the reason you don't accomplish everything you set out to do here."

He looked at her, his mouth drawn tightly. "Has that just now occurred to you Elizabeth?"

How could he ask that of her, after everything she'd done? She hadn't exposed them. She'd helped! She saved his bloody trunk! And she'd provided him with a reason to keep returning to where they'd rescued Joley. She opened her mouth to defend herself.

And then abruptly shut it.

He was right.

From the very beginning, since that foolish, reckless night, she'd been thinking only about herself, about freedom and adventure. She forced herself to look at the scar on James's cheek. She told herself—and anyone who would listen—she'd *learned* from her mistakes, learned to think things through, learned to take responsibility for her actions. Now she realized she'd still only been thinking of herself. God, she was like a carriage with a wild team, crashing through everything in her path. "James." The pain in her jaw swept down her neck and settled near her heart. "I'm sorry."

He looked at her curiously, but his response was drowned by the sound of David's fist pounding, three sharp raps against the side of the coach. It was the signal they'd agreed upon, the signal that there were soldiers ahead in the road. James's mouth tightened and his eyes slid from hers to Marcus's.

Elizabeth knew what he was thinking; this was it, the first test of the papers they'd forged and the disguise they'd conceived for Joley.

And if they failed, it would be the last.

"Out, out and be quick about it." The coach door swung open and a thin young man in a tightly buttoned uniform peered in at them. He continued to hold the door as they descended, as if they might try and wrest it from him. "This is an official checkpoint for the district of Rouen. Have your papers ready, citizens." He nodded curtly. "Citizeness."

In addition to the thin man who seemed to be in charge, Elizabeth spied five other soldiers. Two of them grabbed the traces of the horses, ordering Joley, Andre, and David to come down from atop the coach. The thin soldier was studying their papers carefully, turning them this way and that, holding them up against the sunlight, as if he might detect secret writing between the lines of text. Elizabeth suspected he was deriving considerable pleasure from having them stand in the blazing sun.

"You are English," the soldier said accusingly. "Why are you in France?"

Out of the corner of her eye Elizabeth saw Marcus stiffen at the insult in the man's tone. James appeared relaxed, his face deceptively open. When he spoke, his voice was calm. He repeated the story they'd been using since they'd arrived in the country.

"Is that so?" The soldier paused and Elizabeth felt certain it was for effect. He smiled slowly. "Then why have you and the citizeness spent so much time eating and rolling about in the fields of Rouen?"

Someone had seen them. Trickles of sweat began to sear slowly down her ribs, but Elizabeth felt ice cold. Who? Spies of the Republic or chance passersby? What had they seen? Had they seen Joley? She fought the impulse to glance in his direction. *He is just a servant,* she forced the reminder into her brain. *No one looks at servants.*

"I am an admirer of your revolution and I come here to learn," she heard James explaining. "But I am also a man. A man newly married and very much in love with his wife." His voice was low and warm, and she looked up at him. What she saw in the blue depths of his eyes mesmerized her. "A revolutionary notion, is it not?" he asked.

Elizabeth didn't know if James was addressing her or the soldier. But it was the soldier who responded first, with a derisive laugh. "Search the luggage," he barked to his companions, "and search the coach, too."

The soldiers tossed down the trunks, flinging them open and rifling their contents with purposeful abandon. Linens were dropped in the dust, powder boxes were emptied, hems and cuffs of dresses and shirts and jackets were fingered and sometimes split. All of Elizabeth's hatboxes were opened and their contents examined, ribbons and flowers and feathers torn away to see if anything had been concealed beneath them. They climbed up into the coach pounding their fists against the panels and slashing with their bayonets at the seats.

One of the soldiers leaned out of the door of the carriage and dumped the papers and quills from Marcus's traveling desk. "Nothing here," he said as he let the elegantly carved wood box fall.

"If you are spies," the thin soldier said leaning up into James's face, "you will not slip through my fingers. Search the citizen and his servants," he commanded over his shoulder.

"The woman, too?" a stout soldier in a rumpled uniform asked.

"Yes," he snapped. "There's no telling what she might be hiding under her skirts."

James and the stout soldier stepped towards her at the same time.

"Is there a problem, citizen?" the thin soldier inquired with mock politeness.

"No." Elizabeth caught James's eyes, willing him to step back, to understand that she could endure this, for him, for Joley, for penance.

He shook his head.

She lifted her skirts. Her eyes remained locked with James's. She saw anger flash hot and raw, and something else, something just as fierce, but far warmer and as comforting as a protective embrace. She held on to that as fiercely as if she had been in his arms as the soldier's hands poked and probed and lingered too long.

The soldiers failed to find anything to support their suspicions; they circled the English party, shifting like a pack of feral dogs. The thin soldier, in particular, seemed reluctant to let them go. He held on to their papers, examining and reexamining the signatures and seals, glancing over to match the descriptions in the identity papers with the people standing before him.

"Which one of you is the coachman, Duval?" he demanded abruptly.

Joley shuffled forward, tugging at his brown-dyed forelock with a dirty hand. "I am, monsieur."

"We are all equals here," the soldier reprimanded him. "You must address me as citizen."

"Citizen," Joley repeated.

"Have you searched this man?" the soldier demanded of his companions.

"I have citizen," one of the soldiers volunteered. "I found nothing suspicious."

"Nothing suspicious. A free Frenchman enslaves himself to English aristocrats and you see nothing suspicious in that?"

"Well, no, citizen," the soldier offered somewhat defensively. "It's not that uncommon for the locals to hire themselves out as guides to foreigners."

The thin soldier squinted at Joley. "Lived here long have you, Duval?"

Joley tugged his forelock again. "Yes, citizen."

"How'd you lose your eye?"

Joley's hand fluttered instinctively to the leather patch. "It's not gone, citizen. But a splinter of rock flew into it a while back, tore my eye up a bit and the wound won't seem to heal."

"You wear the patch to protect your eye then?"

"Mine and other folks." Joley inclined his head towards

Elizabeth and James, lowering his voice as if sharing a confidence. "It's none too pretty. Frightens the gentry."

"Indeed." The thin soldier turned away from Joley with a smile of satisfaction. "Jean," he called to the stout soldier who'd searched Elizabeth. "Come lift this man's patch."

Chapter 31

"*Your dog has entangled me with Lady Anne Dinsmore!*" Madeleine exclaimed dramatically, thrusting the squirming pug at a startled Alix. Taking the dog, who licked her face enthusiastically, Alix demanded, "What on *earth* are you talking about?"

Madeleine settled with a flourish into a large blue damask armchair across from Alix. "I decided to go out walking today in the village. There's a surprisingly talented milliner there, were you aware of that?" Without waiting for an answer she continued, "I was admiring the hats when Roland"—she glanced at the pug with an arched brow; he licked his nose and stared back—"took off without warning. The next thing I know he's completely twisted around Anne Dinsmore's skirts."

"She has that effect on the male species." Alix couldn't resist.

"This is not amusing, *ce n'est pas de tout*," Madeleine said tightly.

Alix schooled her features to attend to her mother's distress. "What did she say to offend you?"

Madeleine inhaled sharply and placed a hand against her tightly corseted waist, "She suggested I could be a grandmother."

"You *are* going to be a grandmother." Alix smoothed the mound of her belly.

"That's beside the point."

Alix waited for her mother to continue.

"And then she had the nerve to ask after Elizabeth. Can you imagine? After everything she has said and done to that poor girl?" Madeleine sniffed indignantly. "And the way she proceeded to bring up the story at nearly every function she attended."

"Her retribution for my having stolen Rafe from her."

"Absurd. Anyone who saw him last winter knows that Moreham was mad for you. Why the first time he laid eyes upon you in London he behaved as if you belonged to him—"

"She did."

At these words, Alix and Madeleine both turned their heads towards the door to the library, where Rafe stood. "How long have you been standing there?" Madeleine asked.

"Long enough to feel compelled to remind you that Roland is your dog, my dear mother-in-law, and to wonder how you responded to Lady Anne." He strode over to his wife's chair and kissed her. He received a lick from Roland as well.

"I know how to deal with spiteful women. I let her know, most casually, that far from being disgraced, Elizabeth is still in demand amongst members of our society."

Rafe glanced sharply at Madeleine, drawing his brows together in a tight frown.

"Do not make that face at me, Moreham, I spent many years at the court of Versailles. I know how to be diplomatic." Madeleine smoothed her plum-colored skirts. "And besides, I said nothing that was untrue. Elizabeth *is* at Hartsdale. I imagine she must be quite a favorite of the Norcrofts, considering how much of the summer she has spent with them."

A muscle in Rafe's jaw twitched. His hand curved around the arm of Alix's chair so tightly that if the roses in the brocade pattern had been real, they would have been pressed into perfume. Alix covered his hand and looked up at him.

"You two are keeping secrets from me." Madeleine eyed them sharply. "I can tell from the way you are regarding one another. I do not like secrets, so confess!"

Alix cocked her head questioningly at Rafe. "It is Elizabeth . . ." she began slowly.

"Yes?" Madeleine prodded.

"Her letters arrive regularly, but . . . something seems amiss. For example, in the one that arrived this past week, she describes a delightful outing to the ruins of an old Norman castle. Yet she says the outing was last Tuesday, and she raves about the lovely weather—"

"*Last* Tuesday?" Madeleine pursed her lips. "The day of the dreadful downpour?"

Alix nodded. "And there have been other errors, little ones, but taken all together, well it is enough now to raise concern . . ."

"So why do you not ride over to Hartsdale and see if she is there?" Madeleine looked pointedly at Rafe.

"And if she is not?" he inquired dryly.

"Disaster?"

"Precisely." Rafe looked as if he might tear the chair arm loose from the frame.

"There is always the chance that she is *not* with Dinsmore . . ." Alix offered.

"Very true." Madeleine folded her hands in her lap. "Most likely the errors in the letters were honest ones; I mistake the date all the time." She smiled. "I am sure that is it.

Indeed, I am certain there is a bright side to Roland's encounter with Lady Anne this morning."

"And what is that?" Rafe's tone was skeptical.

Madeleine smiled. "Wherever Elizabeth may be, thanks to me, Lady Anne believes she is mending her ways at Hartsdale."

The soldier called Jean stared distastefully at Joley's battered eye patch. Then he called over his shoulder to the soldier who'd given him the order to inspect the eye. "I'm standing guard on these two,"—he gestured with his musket at David and Andre—"you flip up the patch."

The thin soldier, Henri, waved the identification papers he had taken from James. "My hands are filled."

"Give 'em back then, citizen."

"Not until we know whether these people are spies, *citizen.*"

"Regard," James whispered to Marcus, "the discipline of the new order."

"You." Jean turned towards James. "What were you saying? I won't have prisoners speaking in code."

"I'm sorry," James said in a tone less than apologetic. "I was unaware we were prisoners. What I said to my companion here was that I hoped your stomach was in good order."

"And why should you be concerned with the workings of my stomach?"

James put a hand to his gorge. "Because I have seen Duval without his patch. Indeed, when I hired the man I insisted he wear it. Believe me, citizen, when the man says his eye is not pretty, he is generously understating the case."

The thin soldier glared at Jean. "Step to it, citizen," he snapped, "and let us find the truth of this matter."

"Why am *I* the one always having to see to the nasty work?" Jean muttered, walking toward Duval as though he had heavy stones in his boots. "The farmer with the boil, the baby with the spots, the old woman with the vomiting sickness . . ."

"These are desperate times!" Henri looked triumphant. "The enemies of the people will take on any guise to escape the retribution of the republic." He waved with his handful of identity papers towards Duval's patch. "Inspect it."

Jean's expression was grim, and his fingers shook as he reached for stained scrap of leather.

"Is this really necessary?" Elizabeth tried to step forward, but was prevented by the rifle of one of the guardsmen. "Look at the man." She gestured over the bar of the gun. "Look at his clothes, his hair, his teeth. You can't honestly believe—"

"Do not tell us what to believe, citizeness." Henri glared at her. "Your kind has done that in this country for far too long." He turned back to Jean. "Lift the damn thing!"

As if he were flipping a spider from a plate, Jean flipped up the patch, covered his mouth and staggered back.

"What did you see?" Henri demanded.

"Yellow ooze, clots of blood." Jean gagged through his fingers. "And the devil knows what *else*." He whispered, "Bits of eyeball."

"Are you certain?"

"Feel free to look for yourself!"

Henri unconsciously took a step backward. "Your word is sufficient." He nodded towards Joley. "Cover that up."

Joley smiled revealing his stained teeth. "As you wish, citizen."

As Henri was redistributing the men's papers, James spoke. "Citizen." He lowered his voice so the others wouldn't overhear. "I don't wish to challenge your authority, but was that necessary? Exposing the man's wound like that . . . and in front of a lady?"

"But of course it was necessary!" Henri bristled. "You may find this hard to understand, Citizen Dinsmore, but the citizens of this country are fighting for their lives against the insidious forces of the ancient regime. Our enemies are clever. They try to disguise themselves as friends, neighbors, sympathetic foreigners. No one is above suspicion and no one is above the law." He narrowed his eyes. "Why do you ask?"

James glanced meaningfully at Elizabeth. "The lady's nerves are delicate. I was wondering whether I should prepare her for similar such . . . incidents."

"Revolution is not for those of delicate humor, citizen. You should have left her at home."

"If only I could have prevailed upon her." James shrugged his shoulders. "But you know how women are when they want something from a man? We are only human, are we not?"

Henri, flattered that the striking-looking Englishman should assume they shared a similar level of experience, nodded as if he were familiar with the problem. "Indeed."

"About Duval's eye, citizen," James continued. "Do you think it will cause us more delays of this nature . . . perhaps we should dismiss him at the next carriage stop?"

"These are difficult times and likely to get worse." Henri lowered his voice to match James's. "Yesterday we received word that Citizen Marat stormed the National Assembly and expelled twenty-two members—Girondins."

"But why?" James made no effort to hide his shock. "They were among the first aristocrats to renounce their titles. And all of them voted for the execution of the king . . ."

"Do not call him the king, he died as Citizen Capet, nothing more," Henri corrected him sharply. "What you say about the Girondins is true, but it appears they were deceiving the people. Fortunately Citizen Marat uncovered their perfidy. Most have been imprisoned. Some reportedly have fled to Caen."

"Isn't that in the opposite direction of where we are headed?"

"One cannot be too careful. I have been instructed that we

should keep our eyes open for anyone of a suspicious nature traveling towards the coast." He glanced over at Joley, "I cannot speak for others and whether they will be as thorough in their inspections as I have been, but if I were you, citizen, I would rid myself of the man. Find a different guide."

"Thank you for your honest counsel, citizen. I shall have a devil of a time explaining why we must let the fellow go, though. Citizen Duval filled my wife's ears with the wretched story of his eight motherless children. It was she, inspired by the spirit of Liberty, Fraternity, and Equality, who insisted we take him on."

Henri smoothed the hairless skin above his thin lips. "Perhaps there is something I could do."

"Oh no, citizen, I couldn't impose on your authority."

"I insist." Henri waved him away.

Elizabeth waited until the circle of soldiers were no longer visible from the rear window of the carriage to ask the question that had been dancing on her tongue since she'd seen Joley's eye. "What was that mess? If I hadn't seen Andre at work this morning I would have sworn on a stack of bibles the poor man's eye had gone to rot."

"A talented man, Andre." James laughed. "That wasn't rot, it was breakfast."

Several hours after they had passed through the Rouen checkpoint, the carriage stopped and the company disembarked to stretch their legs and refresh their dry palates and empty stomachs. David spread the red and white blanket they had used to signal their arrival to Joley, and Andre unpacked a large hamper filled with carefully wrapped parcels of food and several bottles of wine. James sat down on the blanket next to Joley, removed a folded paper from his waistcoat, and handed it to the minister.

"Thanks to these papers, my friend, you may not have to spend your last days in France with quite so much egg upon your face."

Joley, who had flipped up the patch, squinted through egg- and jam-caked-lashes, smiled ruefully, and asked, "What is it?"

"A letter from Henri Forneau of the Rouen National Guard stating that your eye has been inspected and that you have been found to have a most revolting open sore. He recommends to his comrades that they not lift your patch upon the risk of revulsion and contamination. Revulsion and contamination, I like that very much."

"Well, I don't," Elizabeth said handing them both wineglasses and settling down next to James. "It is not at all my idea of fitting luncheon conversation. Though I am curious what made you think to ask for such a favor and why that pinch-faced little man should have been gracious enough to have granted it."

James reached for an open bottle of wine and splashed some into each of their glasses. "I told him Monsier de Joley's eye was too much for your delicate nerves and I wondered aloud how many more times you should have to endure the spectacle. From what he said, we may expect more than the usual number of inspections ahead."

"Why?" Elizabeth halted mid-sip. "Has something happened?"

"It appears Marat has moved against the Girondins—"

"The Girondins?" Joley's glass tumbled from his hand.

"His daughter is amongst them." Elizabeth reminded James.

"Have they all been arrested?" Joley demanded, seemingly unaware of the wine staining his stockings.

"Some have managed to flee."

Joley rose. "I must go."

"Go where monsieur?" James asked gently.

"I must go to Paris. I must find my daughter, Marguerite. I must discover if she has been taken. And if she has, then I will make an offer to those monsters. My life in exchange for hers."

Chapter 32

"*News travels slowly to these parts and none too accurately,*" James said quickly, jumping to his feet. "It is possible the soldier was mistaken about the Girondins. And even if it *were* true, yours is an exchange they would never accept, monsieur. They would keep you both and kill you both." James raked his hand through his hair. "Ousting twenty-two members of the National Assembly and imprisoning them? There must be laws forbidding such a thing," he continued, knowing how weak his argument was.

"Laws," the former minister said scornfully, "you speak of *laws* in the same breath as you speak of these *scoundrels?* There were laws against murdering the king—"

"Perhaps they have only moved against the politicians?" Elizabeth suggested.

"They will begin with the politicians, just as they began with the king and his loyal servants, such as I. But the lust for revenge, for blood, inflames them, and then they'll begin to move against the innocent . . . old men, children, women." He shook his head and whispered, "I have seen it happen before." Then he turned to James, in anguish. "I should never have left her," he said. "I should have known—"

"You could not have foreseen this—" James interjected.

"I was a *fool!* I allowed myself to hope that she would be safe. And now." He turned, his hands tightened into fists. "And now I must go back." He bowed towards the company on the blanket as if he were exiting a drawing room. "Gentlemen, I am sorry to have put your lives at risk on my behalf, but I must do this."

James put out a hand to stop him. "If your daughter is in danger, may I ask how you intend to save her, monsieur? Paris is a long way from here, and there are many checkpoints. Are you certain your disguise will suffice? A coachman from Rouen without a coach walking to Paris will certainly raise questions."

Joley's knuckles whitened.

"And if you are discovered attempting to reach your daughter," James was painfully rational, "what then, monsieur? You will obliterate everything you have done to convince the world that you have turned your back on her—to convince the Revolutionaries that she has nothing to do with the crimes with which you have been charged. Can you not see that she will be tarred with a brush far blacker than association with the Girondins?"

Joley's unclenched hands grasped James. "What else can I do?" he begged.

"Continue on with us to England. Once you have arrived, send for Marguerite, just as you planned. *Think* monsieur. It's only a matter of a few more days. By the time we arrive, we may know better what has occurred in Paris. We may even have word of your daughter's whereabouts." James's voice was reassuring. "You will be safe, monsieur. You will have access to the resources and to the people who can help bring your daughter safely out of France."

"But aren't you those people?" Joley queried James. His eyes swept past to the circle of men seated around the ham-

per. "Aren't you the men who can get my Marguerite out?"
The minister's dignity struggled with his desperation. His
voice broke. "I know you are rescuing me for the sake of
your government and I know her life means nothing to
Whitehall. But I can pay. I can make any one of you—all
of you—wealthy men. I have a fortune in England."

James stiffened at the offer. "Might I remind you, monsieur, that you will only have access to the fortune you offer
so freely *if* you reach England."

"A written promise then." Joley looked wildly around the
circle of men. "You there." He pointed to Marcus. "You are
never without paper or pen. Write it down that I, the Comte de
Joley, swear upon my honor that I will reward the man who
saves my daughter with a fortune."

Marcus sat still, his hands unmoving on a crust of bread.

"A fortune," Joley repeated, his eyes bright. "Surely there
is one amongst you who has need of a fortune?"

James, Elizabeth nearly said aloud. A fortune would lift
the Dinsmores out of decades of debt, restore the Duke's estates to their former glory. There would no longer be any
need for James or Anne to marry for money. Would the
thought even cross his mind?

"And I have sworn upon my honor to see you in England," James said coldly. "Come Monsier de Joley, do not
demean yourself or my men with bribes."

"Demean myself, Dinsmore?" Joley's laugh was bitter. "I
have been hiding in a hole like an animal. I am turning my
back on the daughter I love. Could anything debase a man's
honor more?"

"Enough," James barked.

Marcus dropped his crust of bread, rose, and said, "I'll
go."

"It's Elizabeth, isn't it?" Jervis Jones said as soon as he entered the library.

Rafe leaned forward across his desk. "Have you heard gossip below stairs?"

Jervis shook his head. "Not the slightest whisper." Then he tapped the side of his long nose. "I've been with you long enough to know when your eyes cloud up like somebody's stirred the muck at the bottom of the pond, there's trouble. And the source of trouble's usually Lady Elizabeth."

Rafe ran a tired hand through his tawny hair. "I can't seem to rid myself of this sense of unease. . . . These letters, they keep coming, but something about them is just not right." He shook his head, slowly. "Maybe she really is there, visiting. I was hoping . . . I am still hoping . . . But now I must know for certain that she's not gone off with Dinsmore. She's been following after him since she was a child. Part of me has always known she'd find a way to be with him."

"A suspicious mind's a useful tool when you're dealing with that one." Jervis stroked his chin.

"Dinsmore or Elizabeth?"

Jervis shook his graying head. "He's a clever one, Dinsmore, but I was talking about Elizabeth. The man who marries her will have to keep his wits about him. Or be so old as to have no wits at all."

"Jones, endeavor to remember that you are talking about my sister," Rafe said, his words lacking the sting of a convincing reprimand. "And that if she is with Dinsmore, then she's in France."

"France." Jervis whistled through a space between his teeth. "Christ Almighty. You should have killed the man when you had the chance."

"If he's still alive, I will. If not . . ." He stopped, unwilling to finish the sentence he had begun. *If not, then Elizabeth is probably dead, too.*

"So you'll be wanting me to make for Hartsdale as soon as possible," Jervis added quickly. "Do a bit of reconnoitering, then report back to you . . ."

Rafe nodded.

"And I'm guessing you'd prefer I didn't mention any of this to Lady Alix?"

"While that would be preferable, I've long ago learned the folly of keeping secrets from my wife. She's not been sleeping well, what with the babe's constant movement and her concerns for Elizabeth."

Jervis's hand went instinctively to the deerskin pouch he wore tucked in his britches. "If she's not sleeping well, I've got some herbs that would fix her up right. I could brew them up in two slaps of a beaver's tail . . ."

"Most kind of you, Jones, but it won't be necessary."

"I can fix her a dose before I leave," he persisted, "no trouble at all."

"Not for you, perhaps," Rafe arched a brow. "but Alix would never forgive me."

James turned to look at Marcus. The silence stretched so tautly between the two men that for a moment Elizabeth was not sure whether it was the bees nearby or the very air that thrummed. "Forgive me," James said in a voice dripping with contempt, "but did you just say *you* would go?"

"I did."

"How strange. I could have sworn you were a gentleman. But it seems I was mistaken. Honor means nothing to you, sir; lucre it seems is your true master."

Elizabeth stared at Marcus, wondering how he'd respond to the harshness of this insult. He drew himself up stiffly and she realized the slender scribe was gone; in his place stood a lithe, muscular athlete. "I care nothing for the money. Monsier de Joley may keep his fortune."

"So you say now."

"And so I will say when I return with the girl."

"Thank God," exclaimed Joley, who had been watching the two men as closely as Elizabeth.

"*If* you return with the girl," James challenged him. "If

Marat and his people are seeking to bring down the Girondins, Paris will be more dangerous than usual. Think, Marcus, there will be checkpoints everywhere, searches will be more intensive, ruffians will be roaming the streets, spoiling for an excuse to shed blood. Rushing after Marguerite without a plan, without any idea of what you may be getting yourself into. It's—"

"A death sentence," Andre supplied from his place on the blanket.

"Yes," Marcus said, "and it's a death sentence for Monsier de Joley if he refuses to leave with us now, and most likely a death sentence for his daughter if we leave her behind."

"You are right," James agreed, frustration leaking into his voice. "But dashing off on some ill-planned adventure that is unlikely to succeed puts us *all* at risk!"

"It is my life, Dinsmore; it is my choice."

"Let me remind you Tyndale that Lord Grenville placed me in charge of this company and this mission. Your life and the lives of everyone here are my responsibilities—responsibilities I take quite seriously. I agree that we cannot in good conscience turn our back on Monsier de Joley's daughter, but if *anyone* goes back for her, *I* should be the one."

"No—" Elizabeth cried.

"But I have already volunteered my services," Marcus insisted.

"And I am in charge!"

"Is it the money, Dinsmore?" Marcus countered. "I have heard it said your family's rather strapped."

"Don't." James's eyes glittered, sharp and cold. "Don't think you can provoke me into sending you off. I'm quite willing to sign anything you or Monsier de Joley might require relinquishing any claim to his fortune."

Elizabeth stood, her skirts sweeping the debris of the picnic. "If you are going, then I am going with you."

"If the lady is going, then I am going, too." Andre

recorked the bottle of wine in his hand and stood up beside her.

David dusted off crumbs from the brioche he'd been eating and rose. "The rest of you are helpless without my inventions. So I suppose I shall have to go along, too, just to keep you out of trouble."

"Christ!" James exclaimed, running a furious hand through his hair. "You are all behaving as if this were a garden party! You are not vying to be the blind man in a round of blind man's bluff! This is not a game! Monsier de Joley stands the best chance of getting out of the country if you all stay together."

"We agree with you, Dinsmore, that's why we've volunteered to go with you," Andre pointed out.

"I said out of the country, not into Paris."

"He did say that, Andre." Marcus nodded. "And he is in charge."

"He is at that, but is he the best qualified? He's brave, he's intelligent, and he has a rather amazing gift for talking people into doing what they'd really oughtn't do . . . " Andre flashed a smile at Elizabeth. "But is that enough? I mean, think of it. . . . You can forge your way into any prison, I can pick the lock on any jail cell, and David, well . . . he could probably build himself some contraption and fly himself through the windows."

"As a matter of fact, I've been thinking about something just like that . . . a balloon perhaps."

"So what I'm thinking here," Andre continued, "is that we draw straws."

"This is absurd! We are wasting time!" James looked livid. "There will be no straws!"

"Enough Andre," Marcus said firmly. "Dinsmore is right. We cannot all go back, and we shall not draw straws. If you will allow me to stem the tide of your verbal flow, I'd like to say something in all seriousness." He turned towards James.

"I respect you, Dinsmore. And I respect your right as our leader to go back for Monsier de Joley's daughter."

"Thank you."

"But . . ."

"I should have known there'd be a *but* . . ."

"Andre, David, and I, are members of this company," Marcus continued, as though he hadn't heard the sarcasm in James's voice, "not simply because we have odd and admittedly illegal talents, but also because we have nothing to lose. When I first met you, I believed you were the same." His eyes shifted from James to Elizabeth and then back again. "But I have seen you with her, and I know you have something precious—irreplaceable to lose."

"She is not mine," James said stiffly.

"But she is. As surely as you are hers."

"We are not married. She belongs to her brother."

Marcus smiled. It was a smile that seemed far too melancholy and wise for the youth of his features. "More than any man, I can assure you that it is not the ties of paper or blood that bind a man and a woman, but what is in their hearts. Both of their hearts." His dark brown eyes settled back on James. "Can you deny it, my friend?"

"No," James said softly. Then he added, full voice, "But it is *still* my responsibility to go back—"

"And it is a responsibility I am asking you, as one gentleman to another, to grant me." Marcus stepped closer to James and he lowered his voice. "Dinsmore, I am not a man to beg, but if that is what is required to gain your permission to go, that is what I shall do."

"Tyndale why?"

"I need to do this." Marcus's eyes strayed over James's shoulder to the ragged figure of France's former minister of finance. "I know what it is to be forced to leave someone . . . to leave a child behind."

"Your child?"

His lips tightened. "I had no choice."

"And you think by going after Joley's child you can redeem yourself?"

"If there is such a thing as redemption. And if there is not, then you understand that death is not the worst a man can suffer." He inclined his head towards Elizabeth. "And I shall not be mourned."

"By us you will, and by your child."

"My child does not know I exist. He believes himself the son of another man."

James moved as if to lay a hand upon Marcus's shoulder, but Marcus stepped out of reach. "So now you know my darkest secret, Dinsmore. A man should receive something for such a confession, should he not? You cannot grant me absolution, but you can grant me this."

"A penance?"

"Call it whatever you like." His laugh was sharp. "Only grant me leave to go."

Chapter 33

Jervis Jones swept off his hat. He was covered in dust, and his mud-spattered boots were planted squarely on the library's finely patterned Oriental carpet. The earl's expression held more resignation than hope. "I don't suppose you've ridden hell for leather from Hartsdale bearing good news?"

Jervis shook his head. "You want me to give you the bad news, Captain? Or the *worse* news?"

Rafe winced. "I think I should prefer the bad news first."

"Lady Elizabeth isn't at Hartsdale."

"I see." Rafe steepled his hands on the polished mahogany desk. "Was she ever?"

Again, Jervis shook his head.

"And that would be the bad news, would it?" He closed his eyes. "And now you are going to tell me that my sister has run off with James Dinsmore."

"No."

Rafe's eyes flew open, then narrowed suspiciously. "If

that is not the worse news, might I prevail upon you to tell me what is?"

"You see, I know a fellow, who knows a fellow, whose brother's sister's cousin works in the kitchens at Hartsdale—"

"Jones, I am in no mood for long-winded explanations."

"Long-winded?" Jervis clapped a hand to his chest, clearly offended. "I am the soul of brevity."

"And I am the soul of patience," Rafe said sharply.

Jervis cleared his throat. "To cut a long story short . . ."

Rafe nodded approvingly.

"According to a kitchen maid at Hartsdale, the Norcrofts have been entertaining a lady from hereabouts. But the lady in question was most definitely not your sister."

"Who was the lady in question?"

"Lady Anne Dinsmore."

Rafe closed his eyes again. "Damn." After a moment he opened his eyes, piercing Jones with his gaze. "Do you know *where* she is?"

"Regretfully, I don't . . . but perhaps it's not so bad as all that." Jervis's blunt fingers twisted the corner of his tricorne. "After all, it's only the people *here* who know she ought to be *there*. The people *there*, why they think she's *here*."

"It is a sad reflection on the years we have spent together and the over-familiarity I have allowed to flourish between us that I comprehend completely what you are trying to say. Unfortunately Jones, you are wrong. I can name several people who know that Elizabeth is neither here, nor at Hartsdale."

Jervis tugged the tip of his nose. "For sure, now that I think on it, Captain, there's the coachman. The one who was supposed to deliver Lady Elizabeth to Hartsdale."

"And who has been delivering *letters* from my sister," Rafe prompted.

"Do you think somebody at Hartsdale has been writing them?"

"They are in Elizabeth's hand, but a number of them have postscripts from Arabella Norcroft."

"So Arabella Norcroft's in on it, too?" Jervis looked thoughtful. "Still, that's not so bad. Ten-to-one Elizabeth paid off the coachman."

"Or blackmailed him," Rafe muttered, flattening his hands on the desk.

"Either way he won't let the badger out of the bag. And neither will Arabella, I suspect. Lady Elizabeth is her friend."

"But Lady Anne Dinsmore is not."

"What's she got to do with this? She hasn't been sniffing around here since you sliced up her brother."

"Not sniffing here." Rafe's fingers beat an ominous tattoo upon the desktop. "But in the village, where just this week my charming mother-in-law encountered her."

"I don't suppose,"—Jervis pinched his nose—"Lady Elizabeth's name came up in conversation?"

"Indeed, it did."

"Oh," he said grimly, "that's not good at all."

"No," the earl agreed, "it is not."

As the coach rolled away from the inn where they had stopped to change horses, things felt very wrong to Elizabeth. They were again traveling to the coast with Joley, and she knew she should feel hopeful, but she could not keep her eyes from the traveling desk on the seat across from her. The seat Marcus had occupied for most of their journey. He was gone, leaving his paper and quills behind. He'd have no need for them in Paris, he'd said.

Her gaze shifted from the traveling desk to James, sitting beside her, lost in thought, the unscarred side of his beautiful face turned towards the window. Most likely he was thinking of Marcus, too, of how he'd looked as he mounted his horse in the courtyard, lifting his hand in farewell before turning north and riding off. She knew Marcus was carrying false papers for himself and for Marguerite, but she had no idea what identity he'd chosen for them, or what plans he'd conceived to save Joley's daughter.

She couldn't help wondering if he even had a plan.

James's mind must be filled with the same concerns, she thought as she continued to study his profile. She found herself desperately wanting to tell him that he'd done the right thing, that he'd made the right choice, indeed he'd had no other choice but to let Marcus go. She wanted to reassure him that Marcus would come through this adventure whole and that Marguerite would be rescued. But she knew if she said these words they would be empty. She didn't know these things any more than he did. And if anything *should* happen to Marcus, James would forever hold himself culpable. He would always feel as he did now, that he should have gone in Marcus's place . . .

If she hadn't been here with them, would things have turned out differently? *Would James have gone?* Elizabeth worried her bottom lip with her teeth, unaware of how hard she was biting until she tasted blood. *No*, she told herself. James's first responsibility still would have been to lead Joley and the rest of the company out of France. She reached for his hand, which lay draped loosely across his lap. At her touch, his fingers tightened around hers. A wave of relief that he was beside her and not riding for Paris swept over her, followed by a wave of guilt at the selfishness of her love. She closed her eyes and offered up a silent prayer for Marcus. *Please let him be safe . . .*

"He'll be fine," James said, as if reading her mind.

"Will we wait for him . . . for them?"

"I wish we could, but we cannot. I have no way of knowing how long it will take to find Marguerite, or even if Marcus will find her. Nor have I any way of knowing how long it will take them to reach the coast."

Or if they will *reach the coast,* Elizabeth couldn't help thinking.

"I cannot put Joley or anyone else's life at risk by waiting. Lord Grenville already knows we are coming. He has a ship waiting for us, just offshore. We will signal for it when we reach the coast tonight."

"So soon?" The words slipped out of her mouth before she could stop them. She pressed her lips together to bar the escape of those that would have followed, *and then what will happen to us?*

"So soon?" he repeated her question with a curious smile. "For my part, the sight of you safely aboard that ship cannot come soon enough."

What do you mean by that? she wanted to ask. *Do you wish to see me safe, or do you wish to see me gone?* All the times he'd said he meant to send her back to her brother came back to her in a rush. Was that what he intended to do with her when they returned to England? Send her back? After everything they'd done together, after the way they'd touched? After the way he'd responded when Marcus had said, *It is not the ties of paper or blood that bind a man and a woman, but what is in their hearts. Both of their hearts. Can you deny it my friend?* James hadn't denied it, he'd agreed.

James Dinsmore *loved* her.

She knew it as surely as she knew she loved him.

The cream and yellow sitting room had always been Anne Dinsmore's favorite room in the house. She loved the way the light from the long windows illuminated the delicate gilt plasterwork that edged the ceiling. It made her think of a jewelry box and normally when she did her needlework in the room she felt like a jewel. A rare yellow diamond perhaps.

But not today. Today she felt more like a fly trapped in amber.

It was Elizabeth Harcrest, of course. Since she'd run into Madeleine de La Brou, or rather since the woman's ridiculous little dog had run into her, she hadn't been able to stop thinking about the comtesse's claim that Elizabeth was visiting with the Norcrofts. It *was* possible Elizabeth had arrived at Hartsdale after her departure. And it *was* possible that the Norcrofts hadn't mentioned the visit to her, knowing that relations between the Dinsmores and the Harcrests were strained.

But it was *also* possible Madeleine was seeking to play some sort of trick.

Anne picked up a needle and thrust it sharply through the linen stretched tautly across her embroidery frame. As if Elizabeth would ever be welcome in polite society again— the girl was soiled goods! No proper mama, especially one as particular as Mrs. Norcroft, would ever permit such an unsuitable influence near her marriageable daughter. No respectable man would ever consider marrying her.

Indeed, the more she considered the matter, the more convinced she was that Madeleine de La Brou was lying; it was always unwise to trust the French. How delicious it would be to pay a call upon Moreham Hall. For if she found Elizabeth there, she would expose the lie. And if she did not, she might still raise questions as to the girl's whereabouts. . . . She drew her needle through the linen, thinking. The only problem was how to inveigle an invitation to call at Moreham Hall . . . ?

Her eyes fell upon the form of her cousin, Agatha, crouched in a chair near the window, knitting. Her chaperone. *A poor substitute for her brother's company*, she thought sourly, and not for the first time. The woman had done little since she'd arrived but read her bible and knit stockings for the sick. As she was doing now, knitting tiny baby stockings in the round.

Sensing Anne's eyes upon her, Agatha looked up and smiled.

Anne smiled politely back, wondering what village urchin would be getting knit stockings this time. "Who is the lucky mother?" she inquired in a voice she hoped was loud enough for her cousin to hear.

"Of course I'm knitting another!" Agatha shook her head, with amusement. "Babies have two feet you know."

"*MOTHER,*" Anne said more loudly, "I said *MOTHER,* Agatha, not *ANOTHER.*"

Agatha nodded. "Mother, yes, yes, the baby has a mother."

"*WHO IS THE MOTHER?*"

"Why Lady Moreham." She resumed knitting, eyes focused on her stitches.

Anne drew her cream and yellow armchair up next to her cousin's straight-backed Sheraton. She had never gone into the details of why James was traveling wherever it was he was traveling, or the true nature of her falling out with the Harcrests. She felt it wasn't any of Agatha's concern. However, perhaps it was time to say something. She leaned close to Agatha's wrinkled ear, "Agatha," she said, "I don't really think we should impose . . ."

"Repose? Of course her ladyship is in repose, what else would a woman so far along be doing? Everyone knows it's unhealthy for a woman to strain herself when she is in a delicate condition."

"Impose, *IMPOSE,* Agatha. We have not been invited to call on the Harcrests and with the earl's sister in disgrace . . ." She let the words trail off.

"His Grace," Agatha was saying, "do you think we ought to ask His Grace if we might call?"

Anne had a brief, mortifying vision of both her father and Agatha accompanying her on a visit to Moreham Hall. The old man wandering, mistaking his hosts for Carthaginians, her cousin only able to hear every fourth word of the conversation. If the Harcrests didn't laugh behind her back, they'd most certainly speak pityingly of her, the old maid left on the shelf with the other relics. Would it be worth it to bring them if she knew the last laugh, the last pitying glance would be hers?

"*NO,*" she shouted back, "I don't think we should disturb my father. You know how strange environments unsettle him."

"Strange," Agatha agreed. "It is most strange that Moreham and his wife haven't at least invited us for tea. I have lived a sheltered life and it is possible that my notions of manners are outdated. Nevertheless, when I finish these stockings I shall send them along with a note asking after Lady Moreham's health and sending my best wishes upon the safe delivery of the babe." She clucked and nodded her head. "Most likely we shall receive an invitation then."

Anne considered it highly unlikely, but if her cousin wished to make the embarrassing gesture, who was she to stop her? "When you are finished with the stockings, I shall have one of the grooms deliver them—though I cannot allow you to include my name on the card."

"Why ever not?"

"I would not dream of taking credit for your thoughtful gesture."

Agatha waved her needles in protest. "You are too good, Lady Anne. Far too good."

Anne smiled modestly and snipped a thread from the wings of a little hummingbird she had been embroidering.

Chapter 34

It was dusk when the coach stopped along a lonely stretch of road. *If it could be called a road,* James reflected, glancing out the window. It was really more of a rutted track, one that hadn't been used recently, from the look of the grass growing up and around it. He hadn't been paying much attention to their surroundings; his mind was too filled with thoughts of Marcus. *Where was he now? Would his forged papers hold up to the scrutiny of the checkpoints, especially with the French on heightened alert? Would he find Marguerite? And if so, how would he get her out?*

He looked at Elizabeth, stirring out of a half sleep as the coach stopped, her chestnut curls tickling his cheek. He knew he'd had no other choice but to let the man go. As a gentleman, he would never have turned his back on a woman in danger. But in doing so, he'd put Marcus in danger. The decision to leave the man just didn't sit right. Grenville had charged him with getting the team safely out of France—the whole team.

The door of the carriage swung open, and Andre stood by the folding stairs.

James took Elizabeth's hand and helped her down. A relentless wind swept forward to meet them, whistling up from the face of a cliff a short distance away. It flattened the sparse sea grass and bent the few trees like wizened women in the wake of a king. As they began walking towards the edge of the cliff to meet David, who stood waving a lantern, James felt as desolate as the landscape. Not that he would allow himself to dwell on his true expectations regarding Joley's rescue, now that it had been accomplished . . . . Indeed, when Moreham had asked him that day in the library if it was redemption he sought in France, he'd brushed the question aside . . .

His fingers tightened around Elizabeth's.

It was what he always did—brush aside the expectations of others and fail to set his own. Though he had denied it, deep down he *had* hoped that by saving the Frenchman he might somehow save himself. Yet here he was, the same man he was weeks ago, was he not? He realized it wasn't just the end of this rescue that left him feeling as empty as when he'd decided to go to France, it was the prospect of losing Elizabeth . . . *again*. He had to stop drifting through life, leaving his course up to chance or the machinations of others. If he didn't, he'd feel the way he did now forever. . . .

Elizabeth tugged at his hand, gesturing towards where Gerard de Joley stood a short distance from David, looking out to the sea. "He looks like he's standing on the edge of the world."

"In a sense he is," James said, trying to escape his own melancholy. "He's standing at the edge of his world."

"I'm sorry, James."

He turned to look at her, confused by her tone, which was steeped in regret. The long strands of chestnut hair flying loose about her face made her look like some wild sea creature. He asked, "Sorry for what?"

"For all the thoughtless things I've done." She swept a hand back through her hair, but the wind only loosened more strands. "When I made love with you in the library, it was as if I'd crossed an invisible line. Not by breaking society's rules, but how I felt when you touched me. After . . . I tried to pretend that nothing had changed, that I could go on as before. But I couldn't, no matter how hard I tried. And then, for a time, a very brief, black time, I thought there was no use in trying. That's why you found me walking on the wall. It seems ridiculous now, but I thought I was putting my life in fate's hands. And then you appeared, and I overheard you talking in the library. Do you know, I was jealous of you then?"

"Jealous of me?" he asked, remembering the despair that had driven him there.

"Jealous of you," she repeated. "It seemed as though you'd found a way to change everything about your life. You were leaving England, going somewhere new, becoming part of something new . . ."

"A grand adventure . . ."

"That's what *I* thought it was. I imagined you, us, sweeping in and rescuing Monsieur de Joley." She nodded towards the cliff. "I thought if only we could get him to England, then he'll be saved and his life will be all right. But it won't be." She felt tears in her eyes. "He doesn't want to go, but he has no other choice, and he's leaving his daughter behind, perhaps to die. If I hadn't been here, you wouldn't have had to send Marcus back alone. You'd have delivered Monsieur de Joley to Grenville's yacht, and then all of you could have gone back for his daughter."

"You've abandoned your romantic illusions about France and Joley, yet you still hold on to the ones about me?" James rubbed his temple. "Why? How do you *know* I would have gone back for Marguerite?"

"Because I know you, James Dinsmore." Her voice was as insistent as the wind. "I'm right aren't I?"

"What difference does it make now?" He evaded her question. "I'm taking you back to England."

"There you see—" she began.

"See what Elizabeth?" He did not let her finish; she was probing too closely at the truth. "See that my best efforts are never good enough? That I couldn't sweep in and save Joley, as you imagined, that I had to put more lives at risk?"

"*I* put their lives at risk." She touched his scarred cheek. "*I* forced you to take me with you, *I* was thinking only of what I wanted. I wanted my life to be different and I thought that if I changed *where* I was, then *who* I was would change as well. I was a fool to think it could be that simple."

"Nor more than I. Strange isn't it, the power borders have over us? Social borders, geographical borders?" *Emotional borders*, he added silently. "We so rarely look beyond them or dare to cross them. And when we do." He stopped struck by the realization. "When we do, often we've drawn our borders so tightly around ourselves that we carry them with us."

They both looked again towards the cliffs edge, transfixed by the solitary figure of the Frenchman. A short distance away from him, David was pointing his hand towards a light nearly lost amongst the tossing waves of the sea.

It was the yacht. It was time for them to go.

James looked again at the edge before them; it was really nothing more than the end of a spit of land. It wasn't the end of what he could do, or what any of them could have—unless he made it so. And he would not.

"It would be a waste of the fading light to make David and Andre walk down there only to send them back after Marcus with wet shoes." The thought emerged so suddenly in his head, he wasn't aware he'd said it aloud.

"Wet shoes?" Elizabeth turned to stare at him, "Whatever are you talking about?"

"I'm talking about sending David and Andre after Marcus."

"What about Monsieur de Joley, what about your promise to Grenville?"

He smiled at her, a dangerous smile she recognized from a dozen London drawing rooms. "Technically, this cliff represents the end of France. I've kept my word. I've brought them here. But Grenville said *nothing* about sending them back." He nodded his head decisively. "I shall send them off, see Joley delivered into Grenville's hands, dispatch you to Moreham Hall, and then I shall return to France and join them." He stretched out a hand to her. "Elizabeth, my love, you are positively inspiring."

"Inspiring?" she snorted, releasing his hand and stepping away from him. "If I am so inspiring, how can you speak of dispatching me, as if I were nothing more than tattered baggage?"

"*Tattered* baggage?" He caught a strand of hair the wind was teasing about her face and smoothed it back. "I prefer to think of you as windblown."

She thrust his hand away but he caught her by the shoulders. "Elizabeth, don't be thick."

"Don't be *thick?* Of all the—"

"If I do not return with you to Moreham Hall, how shall I request your hand in marriage? You must agree, considering the circumstances, a letter would be grossly inadequate."

She stopped mid-tirade, her mouth a perfect O.

James laughed. "I was going to seal my declaration of love with a kiss, but with your mouth agape . . ."

"You said you would *never* marry me—"

"I was mistaken." His hand slid from her shoulders down her back, and the wind conspired with them to draw her into his embrace. "As I am discovering, I have been mistaken about many things . . ." He bent his head to kiss her, but she pressed a hand against his chest to stop him.

"What if Rafe refuses you?"

"I will not be refused. You are mine, Elizabeth Harcrest.

You always will be." And this time, when his lips took hers, she did not pull away for a very, very long time.

The sound of David clearing his throat finally drew them apart. "Sorry to disturb you, sir, but I was wondering what you'd have me do with the luggage? It's going to be a tricky thing carrying it down that steep path and I was thinking we might need to leave some of it behind."

"Leave all of it behind," James said firmly.

"All of it?" David turned to stare at the coach, heavily laden with trunks, portmanteaus and hatboxes. "What will the lady do without her clothes?" he muttered.

"The lady," James said so softly that only Elizabeth, still standing close, could hear him, "will be amply covered."

"And the trunk, the little one . . ." He pointed.

"You'll have need of it, as well as all the rest of the baggage."

"I?" He turned back to face James, clearly confused.

"You and Andre. And, of course, Marcus and Marguerite."

"You're sending us back?" The light of understanding dawned on his face. "I'll be damned."

"We may all be." James's words were light, but his tone was sober. "You three have been together for some time now."

David glanced over to where Andre was standing by the carriage horses, examining the straps of the traces. "I've worked with Andre for about five years." He looked back at James. "We met Marcus three years ago. He's a queer sort, keeps his own company, but then you already know that, riding with him in the coach and all. But he's a good man. He'd have come tearing back after any of us, that I know . . ."

"Go tearing back after him," James said.

David nodded.

"Monsieur de Joley gave Marcus Marguerite's address in Paris. But they may already be gone once you get there. Have you any idea how you will find them?"

"Paris has always been a tricky place to operate, all those twisting streets and tight-knit districts. If Marcus finds the lady and gets her out of the city safely, I know where he'll go." He gestured towards the coach. "Andre's got a friend he likes to visit. She lives in a quiet little village, not too far outside the city. But she didn't always live so quiet, if you catch my meaning. Doesn't look askance at the unexpected visitor or two, and she doesn't ask questions. We'll wait for him there."

"And if he doesn't turn up . . ."

"We'll give him a week, like we always do, and then we'll start combing the Paris prisons." David nodded his head back towards Andre. "That one's usually got some connections there."

"I've no doubt. Just as I've no doubt you'll find Marcus and Marguerite and that I'll be back for you all."

The two men's eyes met. There was nothing more to be said, except farewells. David held out his hand, and they shook. "You're a fine man, Dinsmore." His eyes slid towards Elizabeth. "And you've a fine lady, too." He pursed his lips, as if debating his next words. "Pardon my impertinence, but if I was you, my lord, I'd keep a tight hold on her."

Keep a tight hold on her. The words echoed in James's head as he watched David striding back to where Andre stood waiting for him. He turned and reached for Elizabeth's hand. *As if he would ever let her go.*

Anne glanced over the fan of her cards at Agatha, annoyed her hand wasn't better. Her cousin took a card from the center of the little round table in the green room and smiled. It was a good thing the woman didn't gamble, Anne thought disagreeably; *anyone* could read the state of Agatha's hand from her face. She rubbed her temple. "Agatha dear," she said loudly, "I'm afraid we must discontinue play; my head is simply pounding."

Agatha's smile melted into disappointment. "Are you certain, Anne?"

"Quite positive," she said, folding her hand into the deck.

Agatha watched as Anne slid the deck into an ivory box. "I had thought we might compare hands," she sighed, "just to get a sense of how the game might have turned out."

Anne assumed a practiced expression of pain, one she'd long ago perfected in front of her looking glass. She reached for Agatha's hand. "You are right, of course, sweet cousin, but I couldn't bear it, not with the way my head feels. The numbers and the symbols seem to be performing a most uncivilized ballet."

"You poor thing," Agatha was instantly apologetic. "Suffering in silence while I'm rattling on about a silly game. You must lie down. I will ring for something cold. Or would you prefer something hot?"

"I'll be fine." Anne pressed two fingers to her forehead and rose from her chair as if it hurt to do so. Walking stiffly towards a yellow and green brocade armchair near the window, she closed her eyes as if the light hurt them. "I'm sure it's all the worrisome thoughts in my head that are causing this pain."

Agatha drew up an embroidered footstool and settled at Anne's side. "If you'd like, I'll rub your hands, and you can tell me all about what's bothering you."

Anne stretched out one long, pale hand, watching as Agatha's wrinkled fingers moved deftly over it. Her head really *did* seem over-laden with worries. Should she expose Rafe Moreham's involvement in trade now, or wait until next season? And why had the Comtesse de La Brou said that Elizabeth was at Hartsdale? Had she gone there at some point in the summer, or was she missing from Moreham Hall? And then there was the letter Anne had intercepted yesterday, from Sir Edmund Bogglesworth, addressed to her father. The memory of the letter truly made her head throb.

She *needed* to talk to James. She'd have to make do with Agatha.

"Sir Edmund Bogglesworth would like to apply for my hand in marriage."

Agatha nodded.

Despite their proximity to each other, Anne suspected her cousin couldn't hear, but appreciated that she had mastered the art of listening. She continued to muse out loud. "I'm thinking it would not be such a terrible thing to be his wife." She paused, "He can be frightfully dull, but he isn't stupid. Indeed, he is great deal more sensitive to what is going on in the world than one might think." Now she sighed. "Another man might not have given a second thought to Moreham's peculiar activities in France, but Sir Edmund, he filed it away." She tapped her temple with her free hand. "He *remembered*."

Agatha smiled at the gesture. "Extraordinary, isn't it, how rubbing the hands helps ease the head? My mother used to do this for me when I was a child. Now give me your other hand."

Anne obeyed. "Not that he made use of what he knows; he maneuvers rather clumsily around the ton. And I should be marrying beneath my station and my style should I agree to his proposal. . . . But I do believe that if one cannot make a silk purse out of a sow's ear, one can artfully conceal it, if one has the wherewithal. And Sir Edmund has so very much money." She smiled. "Just *think,* Agatha, how nice it would be to buy pretty things without worrying. Never again to decide between a new pair of gloves or butter with tea."

"As soon as I'm done with your hands, I'll ring for some tea," Agatha agreed.

"But I worry about my father." Anne frowned. "About leaving him alone, especially now that James is gone. It was fine when he was just puttering about upstairs, planning his forays, but . . ." She trailed off. "He could be frightening to someone who doesn't understand what a sweet gentleman he is. I would never dream of sending him away. Not merely because of the scandal it would create, all the talk of madness in the Dinsmore blood, but because I should never forgive myself if he were to come to harm because I was not there to oversee his care."

Agatha patted Anne's hand; then there was a discrete knock at the door. Anne withdrew her hand and straightened. "Come," she called, clearly enough to be heard by the doorman she knew to be standing in the hall.

He entered, crossing the green and gold diamond pattern of the carpet, a silver salver balanced in one hand. "A letter, my lady." When he reached the arm of her chair he lowered the tray.

Anne picked up the cream-colored envelope, turning it over, and frowning at the address. "That will be all." She dismissed the footman.

"It's for you," she said to Agatha as soon as she heard the door click closed behind him.

"Whoever could be writing to me?" Agatha inquired, reaching for the envelope.

Anne placed it in her hand. "Someone at Moreham Hall."

Agatha withdrew a note from the envelope and unfolded it. "It is from Lady Alix. She writes with a lovely hand." Her eyes scanned the page. "She thanks me very graciously for the gift of the stockings. Asks after my health, if I am enjoying my stay, and if I would like to come for tea, Wednesday next."

"That is in three days." Anne raised her voice for Agatha's benefit, her mind working furiously. Clearly the invitation was an empty formality, tossed off without any expectation Agatha would accept.

"I hear the hall is quite lovely. And the gardens, well, I've heard it said the dowager countess works miracles with plants."

"Louisa devotes a great deal of time and attention to her gardens. They are justifiably famous. An opportunity to see them should not be missed." *Or rather, this opportunity to call upon the Harcrests should not be missed,* Anne thought.

"I should, indeed, enjoy it." Agatha clasped her wrinkled hands together. "Cousin, you will accompany me?"

"I haven't been invited; the note was addressed to you. . . ." Anne feigned uncertainty.

"An oversight, I'm sure. Naturally Lady Alix assumes you shall be with me. Do say yes. It will be ever so amusing . . ."

Amusing was not the word Anne Dinsmore would have chosen. She made up her mind on the spot. She was going to expose them. Spreading absurd stories that Elizabeth Harcrest was visiting respectable families! And she would expose Rafe's tawdry involvement in trade as well. That would put an end to all the worries that were burdening her mind. Finally Rafe Moreham would receive proper payment for the day he turned his back on her for that French whore.

She put her hand to her chin as if considering Agatha's suggestion. "I do believe you're right, Agatha dear. We should assume her failure to include me in your invitation is an oversight—and one that I shall overlook. After all, she is not an *English*woman. Who knows what dreadful gaps there may be in her social education?"

"Shall I write to inform her you shall be accompanying me?"

"Oh no, let us not embarrass her by calling the error to attention. Moreham and I have known each other since we were children. I will make this visit a very special surprise."

"Lady Anne, you think of everything."

"I try, Agatha." Anne smiled. "Truly I do."

Chapter 35

The path down to the sea was narrow and rocky and the light was fading fast. James, Elizabeth, and Joley picked their way slowly down, leaning close to the face of the cliff and stopping frequently when the wind blew them back, or the rocks and shells skittered from beneath their feet and clattered over the edge.

"To think," Elizabeth murmured as she clutched James's hand over a particularly difficult stretch, "I once did something very close to this wearing a blindfold."

"I'd rather not think about it, the sight of it nearly killed me. Promise me you'll never take such a risk again."

"I'm marrying you, isn't that risk enough?" She let go of his hand so she could gather her skirts to maneuver around a particularly narrow turn. "Although," she added when they reached a wider stretch of path, "I should point out that you haven't formally asked me."

"I intend to. When the moment is right. And there's nothing the least bit risky about marrying me."

She tossed him a mischievous glance over her shoulder. "How dull."

"I said it wouldn't be risky." He smiled at her from the deepening shadows. "I never said it would be dull."

When they reached the beach, they found several sailors from Grenville's crew were waiting. They'd drawn a dory up upon the rocky shore and scrambled forward to help Elizabeth, Joley, and James into it. "Is this your entire company, my lord?" a burly sailor, who'd identified himself as the first mate, inquired.

"It is."

"Did them Frenchies give you any trouble, sir?" The first mate cast a curious glance towards the cliff and the path that was rapidly disappearing in the darkness.

"Nothing we couldn't handle. Shall we be off?"

"Yes, my lord." The first mate issued a rapid series of orders and the sailors remaining on shore, heaved the dory off the rocks. Splashing through the surf after it, they scrambled over the sides. Grappling with the oars, they fought against the waves that seemed determined to sweep them back to France.

Spray washed over the bow where Joley sat unflinching, eyes fixed on the lights of Lord Grenville's yacht.

"Why doesn't he look back?" Elizabeth whispered to James.

As if he heard her question, Joley spoke, his voice carrying above the sounds of the sea. "I will keep forever in my heart the memory of the France that was. I have no wish to see the France that is, the France that would murder a king. I will devote myself to the downfall of the accursed traitors. But I shall never return. And when my Marguerite is safe with me, I swear I shall see her married to a man who will keep her as safe as I should have. No more adventurers like Armand." He shook his fist as if affirming a vow. "Never again."

He did not speak again, nor turn his head, not even when

they reached the yacht, a sleek vessel that seemed almost to dance with impatience to be off across the channel.

Grenville's captain greeted them as they climbed aboard the rope ladder. He had sailors standing by with warm blankets and mugs of brandy. "We've a fair wind," he said. "We should be in England by dawn. And if the Frenchies try to stop us, no offense, Monsieur le Comte, they'll be no match for us. You're welcome to stay on deck, but I've had the stateroom prepared for you, my lord, and my cabin for monsieur."

Joley immediately accepted the captain's offer but James stood with Elizabeth, staring at the coast of France until it disappeared in the darkness. His heart felt like the sea, he thought, rising up with love for Elizabeth, then falling back, drawn down by the weight of responsibility for the lives of the three men he'd left behind.

But unlike the Frenchman who'd sworn never to return, James Dinsmore vowed that he would.

When the door of Lord Grenville's stateroom closed behind them, James knew that it was not food, or drink, or sleep that he needed, but to bury himself in the sweet promise that was Elizabeth. He gathered her in his arms, his mouth and hands desperate to make up for all the time he'd sat beside her in the carriage, or lain beside her in a bed, wanting to touch her, needing to touch her.

"I love you," he murmured against her closed eyes. "More than I can ever say." He felt her lashes flutter against his lips. When she spoke, her breath seemed to flutter as well. "Then show me."

The room was small, but elegant, the walls lined with shelves and drawers and a surprisingly fine writing desk. It boasted the luxury of a small red and gold Persian carpet tacked upon the floor. And tucked into the angle formed by the bow of the ship, flanked by two gently swaying lanterns, was a bed, a red and gold striped coverlet tucked into its polished wood frame.

With the persuasive pressure of his hips, James backed Elizabeth towards the bed leaving a trail of his shoes, his coat, his stock, and his waistcoat upon the fine carpet as he did so. When the bedframe barred their backward progress, his hands took over, his deft fingers unlacing tapes and ties and strings and stays. And when he'd unfastened the last bit of her clothing, he pulled her forward and slid the tangle of linen and cotton and lace down around her ankles. She stepped towards him; one arm across her breasts, the other covering the tangle of curls between her slender legs.

Though his hands had touched the most intimate parts of her body, his eyes had never had such complete liberty. "Botticelli's Venus," he murmured, his eyes caressing the length of her. "Except for one thing." He drew the pins and ribbons from her hair and wind-tangled curls fell about her shoulders and down to her waist.

The intensity of his gaze made her nervous. She spread her fingers wide as if to cover more of herself. "No," he shook his head.

"Then you." She nodded towards his shirt and britches.

He pulled his shirt over his head, feeling her eyes travel with it, up along the flat of his belly, following the trail of fine gold hair that fanned out over his chest. And then he felt them travel down with his hands to the buttons of his britches, following the slide of fabric from his hips, to his thighs, to his ankles. He stepped out of them and as he straightened up, he could feel her eyes as they were drawn to that part of him that showed just how very much he wanted her—now.

He reached for her, unfolding her arms and placing them around his neck. He didn't want her to fear his body, he wanted her to feel it, and he wanted no bar to the passage of his hands or his lips. Gently he began to kiss her, his tongue tracing the shape of her mouth, the sweetness of its contours.

He felt her lips close around his tongue and tug. He toyed with her mouth and when her hands began to wander down from his shoulders, he took advantage of the loosening of her embrace. He kissed her neck and shoulder, trailed his tongue down the valley between her breasts. He felt the muscles in her body begin to loosen, and he tumbled her back onto the bed.

Her eyes flew open in surprise, then closed as he covered her, the hair of his chest sliding up her thighs. His tongue circled the base of her breasts, suckling at the soft flesh, teasing towards the taut nipple. He captured it, sucking gently at first and then harder, drawing the top half of her body up, off the bed, pressing the lower half down with his hips. He felt her legs part, felt the rough curls between her thighs against his flesh and, for a moment, the urge to push them farther apart and plunge into her was nearly blinding. Her hands gripping and smoothing the skin of his back, told him she would have allowed it, but it would have been wrong. She was a virgin, and it was too soon.

He eased his hips down and satisfied himself with the taste of her belly. His tongue dipped and swirled in her navel, a portent of intimacies to come. And then he kissed his way farther down, to the place he wished most to be. She'd be wet, he knew, but he'd make her wetter still. He stroked her and his finger slid into slickness. Her hips rose and he pushed her legs farther apart, stroked and slid, and parted the delicate folds of her body. He blew softly against her, and she shuddered. He lowered his head, his tongue poised to taste the sweet saltiness of her, and suddenly he felt her hands upon his shoulders.

Elizabeth was sitting up. Her hands were locked like a chastity belt across her thighs and her eyes were wide.

James raised himself up on his elbows. "Elizabeth?"

Her lips were tight and her face was flushed.

"Sweetheart? What is it?"

"What you were doing . . ." Her voice quavered.

"Didn't it feel good?"

She nodded. "But . . ."

He cocked his head. "But what?"

Her flush deepened. "I'm not . . . it's not . . ."

"Right?" he offered.

"Clean," she squeaked.

"Clean?" He started to laugh, and then caught himself when he saw how deeply mortified she was. "You're natural, my love," he sat up and ran his hands reassuringly down her shoulders. "Everything about you, about me, about what we are going to do, is as natural as . . ." He gestured towards the planked wall of the ship. "As natural as the sea. Indeed, you taste of the sea."

"That's because I haven't had a wash. I'm sticky, I smell, I'm repulsive."

James heard the quaver of tears in her throat. "Elizabeth, I love you. You are the most desirable woman I have ever known. I want you, I want to make love to you, to touch and taste every part of you."

"I know." She ducked her head. "And I know I must seem absurd to you. But . . ." She looked up. "Do you remember the first time you kissed me?"

"Of course." An image of her, a goddess in amber, spread across the library chaise flashed across his mind.

"Do you remember how the room looked, the candles, the champagne, the firelight and you . . . like a fairy-tale prince in sapphire silk."

"A bit worse for the wear now, I'm afraid." He brushed a curved finger over his scar.

"Not to me, not ever, not when you're one hundred years old with white hair and wrinkles."

"Then what is it?"

"I know that we cannot have that night or that setting again. And though I know that we will have a wedding ceremony, this is our wedding night. I wish . . . " She shook her head, struggling to make him understand.

"You wish it to be special," he said, wondering how he could make it so. He wanted her so much. He'd waited so long; he'd have tumbled her on the deck if the captain hadn't offered them the stateroom. But he knew that she was right, that her first time should be special. And as he thought about it, he realized he wanted it to be special, too, for her and for them. He glanced around the room, searching for something, flowers, candles, rose petals, a pirate's string of pearls. His eyes fell upon a basin of water, a sliver of soap and a hand towel the cabin boy had left for them. He smiled and climbed off the bed.

The soap had been made with olive oil and to Elizabeth it seemed to smell of the fruit ripening in the sun. As James bent over her, swirling the soapy water across her skin in ever widening circles and smoothing her dry with the towel, she felt herself easing back into his hands. He washed her as clean as she imagined any babe had ever been. He didn't stop. Pouring fresh water into the basin, he began to dribble it across her skin, tongue chasing the droplets, his lips sipping the water where it pooled in the hollows of her body. She felt like the ocean beneath the ship, restless and rocking, and she arched her hips.

He dribbled water across them and it trickled between her thighs, his tongue darting after it. Not a drop escaped him to dampen the sheets. She spread her legs to allow him greater access, and he dribbled more water. He parted her folds and let the water drip in a most exquisite form of torture. Elizabeth couldn't help herself; she began to moan low in her throat. And when he bent to sip and suck, her hands sought his body. She clutched at him, gripping and stroking, desperate to communicate the way he made her feel, the way he made her ache and want.

He drew himself up and kissed her and she realized he was right, she did taste of the sea, salty and sweet, and everywhere the spicy scent of olives. She felt him thick and heavy against her thigh, rubbing the wetness where his hands and mouth had been and she wasn't afraid and it wasn't too fast—it was right.

"Elizabeth?" It was a question.

She pressed her mouth against his throat, feeling his pulse hard and fast against her lips and murmured, "Yes."

"I love you." He pressed against her.

"I love you, too." She reached down and touched him, surprised at how much more of him there was. Together, slowly, they began to guide him in.

As he filled her, there was pain, a tight and tearing pain. She bit her lip and braced her back to prevent him from knowing, from stopping. He kissed the sweat that beaded her brow and his fingers teased her sensitive nub, creating a pleasure that drew her up, again and again. And there was a deeper well of pleasure. She could feel James coming closer and closer with each thrust. And it was more important than the pain. It was everything. She gripped him with her hands, pushed against him with her hips, reaching for it. Like a diver reaching for a pearl buried at the bottom of the sea and running out of air, she threw herself against him, her lungs bursting, heart pounding. She drew herself up around him, clasping him tight within her body, and found the pleasure wasn't a pearl at all, nothing so luminous and cool; it was a ruby, fiery and intense, driving through her body and exploding red behind her tightly closed eyes.

Elizabeth and James were still wrapped tightly in each other's arms when the boat reached the shores of England. When they disembarked, they discovered that Lord Grenville had sent a coach for Joley and James, along with fresh clothes and funds for the trip to London.

The Frenchman expressed surprise when James explained they would not be traveling with him.

"I do not understand Lord Dinsmore . . ." he began. "Lord Grenville . . ."

"Convey my regrets to His Lordship," James said. "Tell

him . . ." His eyes slid to Elizabeth. "Tell him I have some unfinished business with the Earl of Moreham." He smiled. "And reassure Lord Grenville that when my business is complete, the networks he desired me to establish will be knit far closer than he ever could have imagined."

Chapter 36

"*I cannot believe you invited that woman to call*," Madeleine hissed as she, Alix, and Louisa sat in the red drawing room waiting for a footman to bring in the guests who had just been announced.

"As I told you before, *Maman*," Alix hissed back, "when I sent the thank-you note for the baby stockings to Miss Leech, I added the invitation *as a courtesy*. I never imagined she would come, not after everything that has passed between our families. But I was so *surprised* by the gift of the *booties,* the stitching is exquisite . . ."

"Peasant women in Alsace knit booties. One thanks them Alix, but one does not invite them into one's home."

Louisa, who was sitting on a red and gold brocade sofa across from mother and daughter, whispered, "It is *possible* that Miss Leech is unaware of the troubles. I doubt Lady Anne would be inclined to discuss her brother's behavior with a companion, even if she is a relative."

Madeleine traced the swirling red pattern of a plume on the arm of her chair with a carefully manicured finger. "She may be disinclined to discuss the scandal in her own home, but I'll wager my new hat she'll have no qualms about bringing the subject up in ours."

If Livingston, Moreham Hall's long-suffering butler, was surprised to see Elizabeth Harcrest and James Dinsmore arrive together shortly after tea, decades of training prevented him from expressing it. "His Lordship will see you in the library," was all he said.

Elizabeth replied, "And where are the ladies?" in an equally bland voice, as if she'd just come down the stairs from her room, rather than having reappeared after several weeks of absence with a man her brother detested on her arm. "My mother and Lady Alix?"

"In the red drawing room." As they mounted the marble staircase, he added, "Madame la Comtesse de La Brou is with them. They are entertaining guests for tea."

The footman, standing by the entrance to the earl's library, straightened imperceptibly when Livingston glared warningly, then gave two discrete knocks with his white-gloved knuckles on the polished paneled door. At the order, "Come," he swung the door open, standing at attention, eyes steadfastly fixed on the twisting flowers and vines that adorned the molding across the hall.

"Lady Alix, you are positively glowing," Anne Dinsmore cooed, one hand casually draped across the narrow waist of her yellow and blue striped gown. Her eyes drifted across the elegantly set tea table and lingered on the mound of Alix's belly. "The very picture of . . ."—she paused as if searching for the correct word—*"robust* good health. I do hope you are feeling well."

Alix's gray eyes met Anne's. "When one's life is so full of happiness, one cannot complain."

"Sugar in your tea, Lady Anne?" Louisa gestured with a pair of silver sugar tongs in an attempt to ease the tension.

"With a disposition such as hers," Madeleine murmured in French behind her teacup, "she probably takes only lemon."

Anne shot Madeleine a suspicious glance before turning to answer Louisa. "Just milk, if you please, Lady Moreham."

"It is so kind of you to invite us to call," Agatha said enthusiastically when her teacup had been filled. "I have heard so much about Lady Moreham's famous gardens. I confess, I have spent much of the summer hoping I might have the opportunity to see them for myself."

"Agatha," Anne said loudly and patted her cousin's hand, "you must not embarrass our hosts. While the countryside does not present the same social demands as the London season on a family as important as the Morehams, still there are expectations. Invitations to call upon all the respectable houses. Despite Lady Alix's delicate condition, I am certain the ladies have been very busy this summer . . ."

"But, of course, the ladies have been busy," Agatha amended quickly, her face coloring like a pink raisin at the reprimand. "We, ourselves, have been most occupied paying social calls. Why just last week we returned from a lengthy stay with the Norcrofts of Hartsdale."

Anne resisted the urge to thank her cousin for so effortlessly introducing the subject into the conversation. Instead, she smiled across the table at her hostesses. "Such a lovely family. Do you know them?"

"We know many people," Louisa answered noncommittally.

"They have a daughter." Anne tapped a finger to her lips as if trying to draw forth a memory. "Arabella . . . I could have *sworn* she and Elizabeth were close as sisters last season.

"The season," Madeleine shrugged, "is such a crush. One may appear to be old friends with a complete stranger, simply because one cannot move away." Her dark eyes narrowed on Anne. "And one does so hate to be thought rude."

"True," Anne persisted, "and yet when I met you in town the other day, you told me Lady Elizabeth was visiting Arabella Norcroft at Hartsdale."

"Lady Elizabeth Harcrest and Lord Dinsmore, my lord," Livingston intoned as if they were entering a ballroom instead of her brother's library. But unlike a formal ball, he did not remain standing by the door.

He exited swiftly as soon as Elizabeth and James stepped into the room.

Elizabeth kept her eyes fixed on the figure of her brother, sitting stiff and straight behind his massive mahogany desk. The sun shining in from the windows behind him framed the broad outline of his shoulders and set strands of gold in his tawny hair alight. When she'd been a child, she'd often imagined God on his throne in heaven must look like her brother behind his desk.

Rafe didn't speak until the door had closed behind Livingston. "I won't say that I'm pleased to see you, because it is not in my nature to lie."

Elizabeth resisted the urge to look at James or touch his hand for strength. He had wanted to address Rafe first, to visit him alone, and to protect her from his anger. But she needed to face her brother. "Rafe, I am truly sorry."

"For which aspect of your appalling behavior? Rolling about on the floor of the Dinsmore's library with this man? Asking us if you might visit Arabella Norcroft while planning to run off? Lying to us? Blackmailing my coachman?" His voice remained cool, but he'd begun to punctuate each sentence with a sharp tap of his finger on the desk. "Or driving this household to distraction with worry?"

"I regret all the things you have mentioned and more." She struggled to keep her voice steady. "You, Arabella, Alix, Louisa, your coachman, they were not the only ones to whom I lied, not the only ones whom I blackmailed."

"How very tawdry Elizabeth. You must be exceedingly proud of yourself."

His voice reminded her of ice upon a windowpane. In the past she would have attempted to melt it with tears. "I am not proud of everything I've done. So many things were wrong, hurtful. I was foolish and impulsive. But I've learned . . ."

Rafe wasn't listening. His gaze had shifted from his sister to James. "I see you are still dancing to tunes played by others, Dinsmore. Your sister . . ." He tapped a finger sharply against the desk. "My sister . . ." another tap. "Indeed, I should call you out again, but I fear I should find a woman come to fight me in your stead."

"Rafe!" Elizabeth was appalled at the cruelty of her brother's words. "James had no part in my plans. I blackmailed him into taking me with him to France."

He continued to ignore her, his eyes fixed on James. "Still hiding behind a woman's skirt?"

"No," James said sharply. "I should have fought back, stood up for what I wanted, instead of letting you mete out what I thought was a just punishment."

"Just punishment? You think that petty scar is punishment enough for seducing my sister before an audience provided by *your* sister? Elizabeth," Rafe demanded, "did your lover tell you that as he lay at my feet in the mud he refused to apologize for touching you?"

"He gave me all the explanations I needed in France . . ." Elizabeth began.

"France. You took my sister to *France,* Dinsmore. She might have been killed. I should have cut your lying throat when I had the chance."

James stepped closer to the desk. "The only lie I perpetrated was in allowing you to believe you could best me. I was not hiding behind a woman's skirt then, and I am not now."

"You hid behind Anne's skirts when you ruined my sister," Rafe said, his voice oozing contempt. "And now you hide behind Elizabeth's to seek my forgiveness."

"Elizabeth knows how deeply I regret my part in her disgrace, but I don't give a damn for your forgiveness, Moreham. You paid my sister very public advances. You led her and most of the ton to believe you intended to marry her. And then you threw her over for another woman. You humiliated her."

Rafe gripped the desk's inlaid edge. "Before I announced my engagement to Alix, I went to see Anne, to explain as much to her as I could. But the circumstances were complicated. I offered her my apologies. I offered to make them public. I never meant to hurt her."

"Complicated circumstances." James's smile was cold. "Admit it, Moreham, you didn't want to let her know you'd soiled your hands with commerce. You destroyed my sister's prospects to save your reputation."

"My marriage to Alix had nothing to do with protecting my business interests. I married her to get her out of France, to save her life. And then I fell in love with her. While I deeply regret the embarrassment the situation caused Anne, she and I were never formally betrothed." The men stared at each other for a long moment.

"James." Rafe broke the silence. "You and I both know your sister was far more enamored of my fortune than she ever was of me."

"Now who is hiding behind a woman's skirts?" James scoffed. "Though it is rather ironic when you stop and think on it. My sister would never have married you had she known the source of your wealth."

Rafe uncurled his fingers, flattening them on the polished desk. "If it isn't my forgiveness you are seeking, then why have you come here?"

"Elizabeth seeks your forgiveness. She desires to make amends so that she can remain close to you. I desire to remain close to her. In fact, I wish to marry her."

"Marry her?" For a moment Rafe looked as if he might vault over his desk and hurl himself at James's throat. "You've dragged my sister halfway across England *and France*, and you haven't married her?"

"Not yet. Though for the sake of propriety, we have been traveling with false marriage papers."

"You must be as mad as your father," he growled. "I could kill you."

"I've no doubt skewering me would render you enormous satisfaction. Let me assure you, however, it would be fleeting. I love Elizabeth and she loves me."

Rafe shot a glance at Elizabeth, who had been standing next to James throughout this exchange. "Is this true?" he demanded.

She reached for James's hand. His fingers closed around hers. "It is. If you intend to kill James, you might as well kill me. For that is what you will be doing, murdering any chance I might have for marriage and happiness."

"How very dramatic," Rafe said, but doubt was beginning to commingle with the anger in his voice.

James heard it and continued. "If you will not listen to Elizabeth, then listen to me. A moment ago, you spoke of madness, you compared me to my father. And he is mad, mad with grief. God knows my sister is becoming nearly as mad with anger at the hand life has dealt her. I had begun to believe I bore the seeds of madness, and that I might pass them along to my children. But now I see it is not madness, but bitterness we have all been carrying. It is destroying us. I will carry it no longer. I warn you, Moreham, do not pick it up—it will destroy your family's happiness as well."

"And so I should be happy at the prospect of seeing my sister wed to the likes of you?"

"In truth, it is not your happiness that concerns me, Moreham." James drew Elizabeth closer to his side. "It is hers."

"If you are so concerned with her happiness, Dinsmore, why haven't you married her?"

"Oddly enough, Elizabeth desires your approval. Family is important to her—and she is important to me. I love her. So I am here to ask for her hand in marriage."

"And if I say no?"

"I came here as a courtesy to Elizabeth. If you say no, I will still marry her. And you can go to hell."

"Did I say Elizabeth was visiting the Norcrofts of Hartsdale?" Madeleine sipped her tea, affecting an air of indifference. "I may have. Or I may have said the Harts of Nordale. English names, English faces, it is so difficult to keep them straight."

"Perhaps." Anne ran a finger around the red and gold rim of her teacup. "But then again, perhaps it is your stories you find so difficult to keep straight."

"Lady Anne." Alix stood up. "I believe it is time for you to leave."

Louisa stood as well. "An excellent idea. A footman will see you to the door."

Agatha looked up from her tea, bewildered. The conversation had passed too swiftly and too softly for her to understand. "Is it time for the tour of the gardens then?"

Anne made no move to rise. "I believe the Harcrests have taken society on quite enough pretty tours. Why between the lot of you, you've created a maze of lies large enough to rival the gardens at Hampton Court and I promise you, by next season everyone will see their way through them. Rafe and his astute investments, heroically restoring the fortune that Louisa's husband and his eldest son drank and squandered. *Astute investments,*" she scoffed. "His Lordship has become nothing more than a merchant." She looked at Alix. "I wondered if he'd met you *before* you appeared in London. Tell me, Lady Moreham, were you *part* of one of his trades?"

"How dare you!" Alix's hand clenched around a butter knife.

"Are you going to challenge me to a duel with the tea things? Slash me up as your beast of a husband did my brother?"

"I should. You deserve it. You, even more than James, are responsible for ruining Elizabeth."

"I?" Anne's voice was incredulous. "Elizabeth should have been taught about the risks a woman faces when she leaves a ballroom with a man. She should have been better chaperoned. And she *would have been* if Rafe had married me." She rose, facing Alix across the tea table. "At any rate, I suspect if it hadn't been James it would have been some other man. Elizabeth is a fool!"

In the tension no one heard the drawing room door click open.

"It would not have been another man." Elizabeth's words carried clearly from the threshold of the drawing room. The women at the table turned. Even Agatha, who realized something far more dramatic than a garden tour was being discussed, swiveled her head. For a moment, the exchange of insults was forgotten, lost in the shock of seeing Elizabeth.

"Elizabeth!" they exclaimed in varying tones of disbelief. Their mouths and arms opened and closed like the beaks and wings of a flock of startled birds. Louisa and Alix started towards her and then froze, as they realized that to ask where she had been would reveal to Anne that she had been missing. So it was Anne who finally broke the stunned silence. "Elizabeth," she demanded, "how long have you been standing there?"

"Long enough to hear you call me a fool, which I have been. A fool in love with your brother."

"So you say now." Anne waved a slender hand dismissively. "But it doesn't really matter. No one cares what you have to say anymore *Lady* Elizabeth Harcrest. You are nothing now, nothing but my brother's soiled leavings."

"Actually." James appeared behind Elizabeth, a hand

upon her shoulder. "She is someone quite special. She is to be my wife and the future Duchess of Dinsmore."

"Rafe would never allow this." Anne nearly choked.

"I had thought to oppose it." Rafe, who had been several steps behind the couple, entered the room. "But after some discussion I found myself swayed by their arguments."

"Elizabeth is with child. That must be it." Anne reached a hand towards James. "You don't have to marry her. In all likelihood, it is not even yours. I have reason to believe the whole family has been lying about Elizabeth's whereabouts this summer." Her voice rose. "Who knows where she's been or with whom?"

"She's been with me," James said firmly. "And there is no child." He slid his arm around Elizabeth's slender waist and pulled her close. "But now that you mention it, I think I should like to have a child with her. Several, in fact." He bent his lips to her ear. "What do you say, my love?"

"I say I'd like to wait," she murmured, "at least until the signatures on our wedding certificate belong to someone besides Marcus."

"After I return from France we shall discuss it further." His words tickled her ear, but his tone had grown serious at the mention of one of the men they had left behind.

"After you return from France?" she repeated, frowning. "Oh no, James Dinsmore, after *we* . . ." But whatever she had intended to say was interrupted by an agonized cry from Anne.

"James, how can you do this to me?" Tears were streaming down her face.

James turned to his sister. "Anne," he shook his head gently, "this isn't about you. It's about what I want. I want Elizabeth. I love her. I want to build a life with her."

"Love? *Love?*" She wiped a hand furiously across her eyes. "Where's the security in that? You think you love this girl? You think it will last forever?"

"Yes," he said, "I do."

"And if it doesn't? If she leaves you . . . if she dies . . ." Her eyes looked wild. "You're bored! *That's* why you want to marry her!"

"I *was* bored, bored with the empty dalliances and the emptier parlor room gossip. And I was bitter. How else could I believe it would be amusing to seduce a young girl in her first season?"

"It was honorable," Anne protested. "You did it for me."

"For you, Anne, I almost convinced myself that by seducing Elizabeth I was saving your honor. But it was a lie, Anne. It didn't make you happier; it only brought more bitterness . . . and it nearly destroyed Elizabeth. I brought disgrace upon us all."

"You dare speak to me of disgrace? Have you any idea what sort of disreputable people you are aligning yourself with by marrying Elizabeth?" Anne flung out a hand towards Rafe. "Are you aware that your brother-in-law is engaged *in trade?*"

"I know all about Rafe's activities." He caught the eye of the tawny-haired man standing by the door, adding softly, "and I daresay mine would be accounted far more disreputable." He turned back to face his sister. "Do you honestly believe what Moreham has done to restore the Harcrest fortune is worse than what we have tried to do to restore ours? And tell me, Anne, which offends your sensibilities more—that he has put his hands to work or that he has succeeded?"

"The ton will hear of this."

"The ton will not." He corrected her sharply. "Elizabeth is family now. If you sully her, or the Harcrest name, you sully the Dinsmore name as well."

Anne's face tightened. "*AGATHA,*" she said loudly, "*WE ARE LEAVING.*"

"But the gardens," Agatha's voice quavered, "we haven't seen the gardens."

"I have seen enough." Her shoulders tight, Anne Dinsmore swept stiffly from the red drawing room, her skirts clutched tightly in one hand, as though the hem might be soiled if it touched Elizabeth or one of the two men standing near the door. Nodding swift apologies, Agatha hurried after her.

Elizabeth clutched James's sleeve. "Shouldn't you go after her?"

James shook his head slowly. "It would serve no purpose. I cannot save her from herself." He drew her into his arms as if they were alone. "And besides, my place is here, with you."

"As mine is with you." She cocked her head and a chestnut curl slipped over one bright hazel eye. "And *our* place is in France."

He smoothed the curl back. "Your place is *here,* at least until I marry you."

"And *then* we'll go to France?"

"Alas, I can see . . ."—he sighed as he bent his head to kiss her—"that while the seeds of madness may not lie within me, they will forever lie by my side."

He would offer her everything a woman
could want—except his heart...

The Souvenir
Countess

by
Joanna Novins

Alix de la Brou is on the run from French Revolutionaries,
and only one man can help her—Rafe Harcrest. When
Rafe's solution is to get married, Alix realizes that she can't
bear the thought of Rafe not loving her as a true bride.

"NOVINS BRINGS A RICH,
NEW VOICE TO ROMANTIC FICTION."
—JULIA LONDON

0-425-19387-X

BERKLEY SENSATION
COMING IN MARCH 2004

Miss Wonderful
by Loretta Chase
A bluestocking and a rafe clash over a matter of business only to find themselves facing an entirely different sort of tension...

0-425-19483-3

Paradise Falls
by Ruth Ryan Langan
In 1890 Massachusetts, Fiona Downey is about to give up the life she knows and begin a journey of love.

0-425-19484-1

Undead and Unwed
by MaryJanice Davidson
Betsy Taylor can't seem to stay dead. To make matters worse, her friends think she is the prophesied vampire queen. And all she wanted was a normal afterlife!

0-425-19485-X

The Seduction
by Julia Ross
Alden Granville has lost a bet, and now he has made an agreement that will make or break his future. The wager: he must bed the mysterious Mistress Juliet Selton.

0-425-19486-8